Yolande knew that she should leave. Hastily. She did not know that her lips were slightly parted, her eyes dreamy, but she saw the emptiness in Craig's eyes change to an expression of tender worship that took her breath away. The seconds slipped away, and not one word was spoken. But two hearts met and the message they exchanged was as clear as though it had been shouted from the battlements.

And then, somewhere close by, they heard Devenish whistling.

Craig started. Dismayed by his shameful weakness, he said brusquely, "You had best wait outside."

She turned from him and, without a word, walked across the Great Hall and onto the steps. The sky had become white. Yolande lifted a shielding hand against the sudden glare. Her head was a whirl of confusion, impressions chasing one another at such a rate she could scarce comprehend them. . . .

FAWCETT CREST BOOKS
by Patricia Veryan:

FEATHER CASTLES

MARRIED PAST REDEMPTION

SOME BRIEF FOLLY

THE
NOBLEST
FRAILTY

PATRICIA VERYAN

FAWCETT CREST • NEW YORK

for Abbie

A Fawcett Crest Book
Published by Ballantine Books
Copyright © 1983 by Patricia Veryan

Library of Congress Catalog Card Number: 83-9609

ISBN 0-449-20625-4

This edition published by arrangement with St. Martin's Press

Manufactured in the United States of America

First Ballantine Books Edition: March 1985

"And love's the noblest frailty
of the mind . . ."

JOHN DRYDEN
"The Indian Emperor," II, ii.

Chapter One

Miss Yolande Drummond was almost two and twenty. She was a remarkably pretty girl, with abundant hair of that rich shade known as chestnut, wide green eyes, and a very fair complexion that, so long as she guarded it from the destructive rays of the sun, seldom threw out a freckle. Her features were dainty, her voice had a husky quality the gentlemen found enchanting, her figure was slender but nicely curved, and she was blessed with a gentle and conformable disposition. She was widely held to be a Fair, and might well have been an accredited Toast save for the fact that before she was out of leading strings it had been decided she should wed her distant cousin, Alain Devenish. Mr. Devenish being possessed of a singularly jealous nature, a fiery temperament, and breath-taking good looks, the gentlemen were given pause by the two former qualities, plunged into despair by the latter, and reluctantly decided that anything more serious than a mild flirtation with the delectable Yolande was a waste of time.

That Miss Drummond had reached so perilous an age without having married surprised a few people who were not well acquainted with her prospective bridegroom. Close friends shrugged off this circumstance, however. Alain Devenish was, they pointed out, a bit of a rascal. Although barely three years Yolande's senior, he had racked up the dubious distinction of having been expelled from Harrow, sent down from Cambridge, asked to resign his regiment and, more recently, been involved in some kind of very unsavoury affair concerning the powerful Monsieur Claude Sanguinet, as a result of which he had barely escaped France with his life. Only the fact that his birth was impeccable, his charm infectious, and his kindness legendary had saved him from social ostracism, but however popular he might be, few blamed Miss Drummond for waiting until her tempestuous beau settled down a trifle.

On a bright morning in early May, Miss Drummond presented a picture to gladden the heart of any man as she stood on the rear terrace of Park Parapine, gazing out over the pleasure gardens and park of her ancestral home. She was clad in a pearl-grey riding habit that fitted her slim shapeliness to perfection. White lace foamed at her throat, and white velvet ribbons were tied in a large bow at the back of her saucy little grey hat. The prospect she viewed was also fair: Beyond the sweep of lawns and flower gardens, the Home Wood presented a verdant border ranging from the tender yellow tints of new leaves to the dark stateliness of evergreens. The air was sweet with the fragrance of blossoms; here and there chestnut trees flaunted their colourful gowns to mingle with the shyer blooms of apple and plums, and lilacs rose richly against a cloudless sky.

Yet, despite all this beauty, Miss Drummond's smooth brow was marred by the suggestion of a pucker, and her lovely eyes were troubled. The sense that she was no longer alone caused her to turn enquiringly, and she discovered that her mother stood watching her.

"Good morning, my love." Lady Louisa smiled, offering a smooth cheek for her daughter's kiss. "Had you a nice ride? A foolish question, no? On such a glorious morning, how could it have been otherwise?"

Yolande loved her mother deeply, but that charming lady's ability to read her thoughts was sometimes alarming, and now she said evasively, "Glorious indeed, especially after so much rain. How pretty you look, Mama. A new dress? That shade of rose so becomes you."

"Besides which, it is a colour you dare not wear," her mother replied, "so I need not fear to discover you have 'borrowed' it."

Yolande laughed. "If I do—very occasionally—borrow your gowns, you have no one to blame but yourself, dearest. What other girl has a mother so youthful and slender she might well be taken for a sister?"

The compliment was well-founded. Lady Louisa had never been a beauty, but had, in her youth, been said to possess "a pleasing countenance," her appeal springing from an innate kindness, rather than from her looks. At five and forty, however, she outshone many a former Toast, for her hair, although an indeterminate shade of brown, had not begun to grey, her skin was clear and unwrinkled, and her merry disposition kept her as young in heart as in appearance. She was also a shrewd woman and, suspecting that she was being guided from an unwanted subject, said mischievously, "Oh, what a rasper! I must beware, for such tactics usually presage an outlandish plea I cannot then resist. What is it, my love? Are you going to tell me you have thrown dear Alain over in favour of some wholly ineligible young man?''

Yolande's smile faltered. She turned back to her contemplation of the horizon and said slowly, ''No, Mama. Of course I have not. I know how you and my father have always wished the match.''

Lady Louisa's hands clasped rather tightly, and for a moment she was silent. When she spoke, however, it was to ask in a mild way, ''Never say you have set the date at last? Devenish must be floating back to Aspenhill!''

''I . . . er— Actually . . .'' Yolande bit her lip. ''Oh—we had a small difference of—of opinion.''

''I see.'' Lady Louisa did not see. Were she twenty-five years younger, she thought, and Devenish had smiled her way, Sir Martin might have had a formidable competitor for her hand. As it was, the prospect of having such a son-in-law delighted her, and her husband's heart was quite set on it. He and Colonel Alastair Tyndale had been bosom bows since their schooldays, and it was well known that the Colonel's orphaned nephew, to whom he stood guardian, was his sole heir. Tyndale was not a man of great wealth, but the Park Parapine lands marched with those of his Aspenhill and that the two great estates should be merged by this marriage was the dream of both men.

Doting on her husband, Lady Louisa was in full accord with his wishes in the matter, but she also loved her daughter and therefore said gently, ''Dearest, you *do* wish to marry Alain?''

Yolande's lashes drooped, and the colour in the smooth cheeks was heightened. ''I—suppose I do,'' she answered, concentrating upon drawing the thong of her riding whip through her gloved hand.

''You—*suppose?* Good God! Do *not* you know?''

Yolande sighed and asked rather wistfully, ''Did *you* know, Mama?''

''Indeed I did! I had never met your papa, of course, although I had seen him everywhere. I was scarce out of the schoolroom when I was told he had offered and your grandpapa had accepted.'' She smiled reminiscently, her anxieties forgotten for a moment. ''I shall never forget when I was brought into the saloon and Papa took my hand and gave it to Sir Martin. I was so frightened, but his hand was shaking

3

harder than mine, and it gave me the courage to peep at him. And when I saw the smile in his eyes . . .'' She sighed again, then, meeting her daughter's intent regard, imparted, ''My heart was lost in that one moment.''

''Oh. And—have you never had—doubts? None at all?''

''Good gracious!'' thought my lady, but said serenely, ''Never. Oh, there have been times I might cheerfully have boiled him in oil, of course. Men can be so incredibly provoking. But he still has my heart, and I would do anything in my power to keep him happy. You must own he is a splendid gentleman, Yolande. And if you had but seen him when he was a young man . . .''

Yolande smiled. The portrait of her father that had been painted upon his attaining his majority still hung in the great hall of the house, so that she had a fairly accurate idea of how he had looked at four and twenty. He was a handsome man then, as now, although nowhere near as good-looking as Alain. It was easy to understand why Mama had fallen so completely in love with him. If only the same feelings were—A soft touch on her wrist roused her from her reverie.

''Dear child,'' said Lady Louisa in her gentlest voice, ''if you do not love Devenish, we will tell Papa. I am sure he would not wish—''

''Oh, no, no! I would not for the world— I *do* love Dev. He is the very dearest boy. It is only . . . that—''

''The years have a way of slipping by rather fast, you know, Yolande. If you love him, I would have thought—'' Lady Louisa did not finish that sentence, but added, ''He is *sans reproche* in so far as Family is concerned. And a more handsome young man one could not wish to meet.''

''Very true. But—but he is so *wild*, Mama! Only think of that fiasco at Cambridge.''

''Yes. Though I vow I cannot remember why he was sent down.''

''It was for putting glue on the soles of the Proctor's shoes. The poor man took up so much rubble when they went for their morning run, that he tripped and broke his ankle.''

''Dreadful!'' said my lady, sternly repressing a smile. ''But Devenish was honest enough to confess, no?''

''Oh, he is the soul of honour, who could doubt it? But—on the other hand—consider the whole picture, Mama. Expelled from Harrow; sent down from University; asked to resign his regiment—and then there was that frightful business in which he became involved last year with Tristram Leith and the

4

Frenchman. What it was all about I have never been able to discover, save that one has only to mention it and all the gentlemen become like clams, so it must have been very dreadful. One schoolboy prank after another! Do you know, I sometimes fear he will never grow up, for he is just like a naughty little boy!''

''Oh, just. I wonder you could still love the vexing fellow. He must be sternly guided by his lady, no?''

Yolande looked up, met the smile in the kind hazel eyes, and said with a small, wry shrug, ''Perhaps. But—my fear is, Mama, that I am, myself, not always very wise.''

My lady's heart sank. Still, she persisted gently. ''You have numbered his faults, but he has much to recommend him, do you not agree?''

''Yes, of course I do. I could say off a long list of good points. Only, he is so very . . . unlover-like.'' Yolande slanted a shy glance at her mother and, blushing, stammered, ''You will—will fancy me very foolish, I fear. But Alain has never once wrote me a love note, or vowed his devotion, or—or behaved like a man deeply attached.'' Having said which, she cast down her eyes in much confusion and turned her head so that her dark blush might not be seen.

Briefly, Lady Louisa was silent. How irksome, she thought, not to have foreseen such a development. She should have suspected it, Lord knows, for being a loving and concerned parent she was well aware of the many novels her elder daughter carried home from the various lending libraries. Certainly, a girl who shed tears over the pitfalls confronting Mrs. Radclyffe's much-tried heroines, and who had often fallen asleep at night with Lord Byron's poems still held in her hands, would find Devenish's breezy big-brother manner unfulfilling.

She gave her daughter a quick hug. ''Of course I do not think it foolish!'' she declared staunchly. ''I *do* think it most perverse of Fate to have made Alain so extreme handsome, and have given him so intrepid and dauntless a nature, only to then dump him in this modern age of ours!'' Yolande turned curious eyes upon her and, encouraged, she continued, ''Your cousin should rather have lived in the days when England was overrun with bold knights. He was meant to ride with lance in hand, and dragons lurking at every bend of his road through life!''

''Alain?'' said Yolande, awed. ''Heavens! I had never thought of him in such a light.''

"Perhaps because you have grown up together. I do assure you, however, that many other young ladies see him in *just* that light!" And wisely not belabouring the point, my lady went on, "Is it not typical that so dashing a figure should have no slightest vestige of the romantical in his outlook, whereas, beneath the stodgy exterior of some dull, lumpish young man, might burn a soul ablaze with romantic notions?"

Yolande smiled and nodded, and her gaze returned to the view, which she saw not at all. There followed a small, companionable silence, through which Lady Louisa watched her daughter hopefully. Her hopes were dashed.

"If only," Yolande murmured, "he had a steadier, less volatile temperament."

*   *   *

"Less volatile?" Sir Martin slapped one hand against his muscular thigh and gave a crack of laughter. "When did our flighty miss remark that, ma'am? This morning? She's known the boy all her days and only now is discovering he is no milksop?"

Lady Louisa put down the embroidery she had taken up several times during their conversation, and absently regarded her husband, outlined against the window of her private parlour. A big man who enjoyed the life of country squire and found town a dead bore, Sir Martin carried his years well. His colouring was slightly florid since he tended to burn in sun and wind rather than become tanned, but he was in splendid physical condition, his auburn hair still waving luxuriantly, the grey at the temples lending him dignity. His green eyes were only a little less keen than they had been when he was wed, and his countenance was so well featured that Yolande was flattered when her resemblance to her sire was remarked upon.

Neatly folding her embroidery, my lady asked mildly, "If Yolande was to reject Devenish, my love, should you be horribly disappointed?"

"Not *marry* him?" He frowned, all the laughter gone from his eyes.

"Oh, dear," murmured his lady.

"Why the deuce should she not marry him?" he demanded, a testy edge to his voice. "They have been promised since she was in the nursery, practically."

"True. But he has not offered. Formally, that is."

"Blast it all, why should he do so bird-witted a thing,

6

when it has been taken for granted these eighteen years and more!''

''Exactly so.'' She sighed, taking up the embroidery she had reduced to a neat square and shaking it out once more. ''Perhaps that is the whole trouble. I should have thought of it.''

Sir Martin departed on the first of several tours about the room, during which he animadverted bitterly upon the frivolity, thoughtlessness, and ingratitude of one's children. Never, he declared, would he have so vexed *his* parents. Especially when they had been nothing but good to him. It was a sorry world when youth today was so insensitive, so selfish. ''Devenish,'' he said, passing his meekly sewing wife on his third lap, ''is a splendid young fellow, of impeccable lineage.''

''So I told her, Sir Martin.''

''He has looks, charm, and a generally sunny disposition. The girls are fairly crazy over him. He owns a magnificent estate in Gloucestershire and will take control of a respectable fortune in a month or so, to say nothing of Aspenhill, for Alastair Tyndale is not like to wed at his age. Does *he* know about this nonsense, I wonder? Good gad! He would be heart-broken! All our days we've planned that the estates would be joined. What a splendid heritage to be whistled down the wind only because some silly chit decides Devenish is—what was it she said? Volatile? Volatile, indeed! The boy's high-spirited as any colt, is all. He's been in a few scrapes, I grant you, but conducted himself very well in that damned mess in Brittany last year, and by what young Leith says, is pluck to the backbone.''

''Yes, dear. But—'' She looked up at him and asked gravely, ''Could you compel Yolande to marry a man she does not love?''

''*Love?* Good God, madam! People of our order do not marry for love!''

Her ladyship said simply, ''I did.''

Sir Martin stared at her, snorted, stamped up and down, put his hands behind him, and stared at her again. Then, with a wry laugh he marched to sit down beside her, removed the embroidery and tossed it ruthlessly over his shoulder, and took his wife in his arms.

After a moment, Lady Louisa pulled back, straightened her demure lace cap, and said a trifle breathlessly, ''Now, Martin! Pray be sensible.''

''I am being sensible,'' he argued dropping a kiss on the

hand he still held. "You know very well, Louisa, that when you look at me in just that way, it always makes me feel—"

"Then I'll not look at you at all, sir," she said primly, withdrawing her hand, but submitting when it was promptly reclaimed. "Now, I have been thinking ever since I spoke with Yolande this morning, and I have a plan which I hope may work. Yolande must not marry Devenish only to please us, my dear."

He scowled. "Why not? Chances are that once they are wed she will settle down and be perfectly content."

"Oh, yes, that is very possible. And nothing would be more delightful than for her to discover she really is in love with Dev. But—suppose she should find to the contrary? She is scarcely the type to take a lover. And even if—" My lady paused, eyeing her husband with disfavour as he exploded into a hearty laugh.

"Apologies, m'dear," he said, patting her hand. "But I was just picturing Devenish's reaction to such a triangle." He chuckled again, "Lord! Can you not imagine that young volcano? Yolande may not know her own heart, but Dev has no such reservations. Yolande is his world. He would tear the man limb from limb!"

"He would, indeed. And I believe you are right, he worships her. What a pity he does not tell her so."

"*Tell* her so? Oh, gad! You ladies and your romantical vapourings! Dev comes over every day, don't he? He takes her riding, brings her gifts. Why only yesterday he—"

"He brought her that fox kit he found! A pretty gift! Not only did it keep Yolande up all night with its yelping, but it was full of fleas and bit one of the maids when she chanced to step on it while she was making the bed. She fell into strong hysterics and the kit raced out, with the cat in hot pursuit, throwing the entire house into an uproar!" Regarding her amused spouse with indignation, Lady Louisa said, "But you prove my point, Sir Martin. Alain has no more notion of how to treat the girl he loves than a Clydesdale knows how to dance a quadrille! And thus, I think—" She waited out another howl of laughter from her lord, who was fond of Clydesdale horses and could envision the scene she had suggested. "I think," she resumed severely, while he wiped his eyes, "that we should send Yolande to visit her grandpapa."

"What—in Ayrshire?"

"Since my own papa has gone to Paris, my love, I scarcely think such a journey appropriate."

"But why journey at all? Oh—do you think the old fellow might banish some of her silly megrims?"

"I think it is a very true saying that 'Absence makes the heart grow fonder,' and Mr. Alain Devenish has been taking your daughter entirely too much for granted."

"Well, if it's absence you want, m'dear, she could go to your sister in Town for a month or two. Don't have to travel all that way up to Scotland."

"I think she does have to," said Lady Louisa thoughtfully. "She must be far away. Where Devenish is not like to follow."

Despite his rantings, Sir Martin doted on his pretty daughter, but at this, he said with a slow smile, "I own no property on the moon, my love."

* * *

"To the moon, sir?" Mr. Alain Devenish blinked down into the cold blue eyes of the man who leaned back in the big chair behind the desk, and, running one finger around his elaborately tied neckcloth that suddenly seemed too tight, protested, "No, really, Uncle! I've not been gone *that* long, surely?"

Colonel Alastair Tyndale rested his elbows on the arms of his chair and regarded his nephew over interlocked hands. Twenty years separated the two men, and few, seeing them together, would imagine them to be related. Devenish was slender and not above average height, with curling blond hair, intensely blue eyes, and features almost too delicately carven for a man. Tyndale was tall and broad with a loose-limbed, athletic body, and a head of thick brown hair beginning to grey at the temples. His nose was strong, his chin a fierce jut, and his mouth a thin, uncompromising line. Only in the eyes was there a similarity, and that very slight and not so much a matter of shape or colouring as of expression. The eyes of both men were seldom without a humorous twinkle, and if in Devenish that twinkle could in a flash become a glare of rage, in his uncle it could as swiftly be replaced by inexorable purpose, a determination approaching ruthlessness.

"You have been gone," sighed the Colonel, drawing a rather battered timepiece from the pocket of his waistcoat and consulting it, "precisely eight hours and forty-five minutes. You doubtless forgot I had expressly requested that you return to Aspenhill by three o'clock so as to meet Lord Westhaven."

As always when his guardian was displeased, Devenish began to experience the unease that had afflicted numerous junior officers quaking before Tyndale during his years in India. Despite the fact that he and his late mother's younger brother were often at loggerheads, however, Devenish was fond of his uncle and chagrined by the knowledge that he had once again disappointed him. He took a turn about the pleasant, panelled room and stood frowning out across the lawns of this house wherein so much of his young life had been spent. "I was at Park Parapine, sir," he offered.

"So I had presumed. It was my understanding that you were to accompany Yolande on an early ride. One can but hope that the length of that—er, ride, indicates a satisfactory resolution of your—ah, problems."

"Lord!" muttered Devenish, under his breath. He swung about and returned to toss his slender body into a deep chair beside the desk and divulge that he had not spent the entire day riding. "I chanced to run into Harland," he said. "I think the old boy's lonely, now that Lucian is off honeymooning. Nothing would do but that I go over to Hollow Hill with him. He's leaving for Paris next week." He shrugged. "I forgot the time. And Westhaven." Flashing a contrite glance at Tyndale, he added, "Did I cause you to be embarrassed? My apologies, sir, but—I really have no interest in politics, you know."

"It would be enlightening to learn," the Colonel sighed, straightening a paper on his desk, "what *does* interest you. Besides Yolande Drummond."

Devenish flushed, his lips tightening with resentment, but he said nothing.

"From your demeanour," Tyndale went on, "I have to infer that my cousin's child has once again refused to set a date for your wedding."

The tone had not been unkind, but Devenish squirmed. "She says," he imparted indignantly, "that I am a here-and-thereian."

The shadow of a smile crept into the Colonel's blue eyes. "She is not without justification, would you say?"

"What, because I found University a dead bore? Because I did not—er, take to the military, or—"

"You were *sent down,*" Tyndale intervened, his voice suddenly holding a touch of steel, "because you played a childish prank upon the Proctor. You were *obliged* to leave the army because of just such another prank. Had you failed in your studies, having tried your best; had you been asked to resign your commission because of some blockheaded mili-

10

tary injustice, I could better have understood matters. You are five and twenty, Alain. In two months it will be time for my guardianship to end, and for you to take over the reins at Devencourt. It is past time you had moved back there. Oh, I know why you have not done so—my estates chance to march with those of the Drummonds. But your lands stand in need of an owner—a resident owner.''

''There is no cause for me to remain here now,'' Devenish grunted.

A frown twitched at Tyndale's brows. ''Good God!'' he exclaimed. ''Never say Yolande has cried off?''

''Lord, no! Never that, sir! But she has made it clear I must change my ways before—'' Devenish broke off. ''Oh, blast! I shouldn't have said there was no cause for me to stay. What a clunch I am!'' He leaned forward in his chair and, with the smile that had ensnared many a hopeful lady, said earnestly, ''You know I am more than grateful, sir. You know I've no wish to leave *you!*''

Tyndale's grim features were lit by an answering warmth. ''Thank you, Alain. And *you* know I've no wish to scold you. God knows, your conduct last summer in the Sanguinet affair made me very proud. Incidentally, have you heard from Leith? Is there any further word on the Frenchman?''

''I am in touch with Tristram, of course, sir. He feels that Sanguinet remains a menace to England. Somewhere—God knows where—he's up to his tricks. And—when we least expect it . . .'' He scowled. ''His scheme to kidnap the Regent was damnably clever, but if he strikes again, Tristram thinks it will be with men. An all-out thrust for power.'' His blue eyes ablaze, he drove one fist into his palm. ''Now, *there's* something I would be interested in, by Jove! I hope to God I'm about when the Frenchman does play his cards!''

''I cannot think he will do anything so unwise. He would have to be a complete lunatic to persist with plans about which he must know the authorities have been warned.''

''He *is* a lunatic! I believe he has some miserable scheme to take over where Bonaparte left off. He knows our warnings were laughed at. He knows Tristram was as good as cashiered and that both he and his bride are in deep disgrace. Oh, Sanguinet will not give up, I do assure you, sir. He will merely contrive again.''

''If he contrives, lad, it may be to your doom. He is a vindictive man. Have a care.''

Devenish's blithe response that he was sure Monsieur Claude

11

Sanguinet had more weighty matters on his mind than personal vengeance incurred Tyndale's displeasure. The Colonel embarked upon a lengthy discourse regarding the menace of the ambitious and wealthy Frenchman. At the close, Devenish said meekly that he would write out his will and carry a pistol the next time he left the estate.

Tyndale stared with suspicion at his nephew's angelic innocence and grunted, "Very good. Meantime, I've a task for you. A pleasant one, I hope."

"A task? For the military, sir?"

"Nothing so impressive." Tyndale stood and marched around the desk to perch against the edge. Reaching back, he took up a rumpled paper and glanced at the closely written lines that filled the page. "Westhaven brought me this letter. It appears to have had a rough journey, arriving at length in his hands and he was kind enough to deliver it whilst he was here. It concens your Canadian cousin."

Devenish glanced at the tattered letter curiously. "I was not aware I *had* a Canadian cousin."

"No? Yet you will, I feel sure, recall that I had a brother, Jonas."

"Oh, the firebrand who had to leave the country! Because of a duel of some sort, was it not?"

The Colonel's eyes clouded. He said broodingly, "We are none of us a very stable lot, I fear. But Jonas was rather more than wild. I have not gone into details before, because there seemed little likelihood we would ever see him again. Indeed, we will not, for he is dead, so I learn."

"Oh, I am sorry, sir. Were you fond of him?"

"I was deeply fond of him—as I was fond of your own father. It seems that his wife died a few years back, in childbed perhaps, for he has left a son, and the boy is on his way here to visit the land of his forbears."

A revolting suspicion had taken possession of Devenish's mind. Eyeing his uncle warily, he asked, "A boy, sir? Did *he* write that letter?"

"No." Tyndale replaced the sheet on his desk and explained, "It was written by Jonas's solicitor begging that we receive the little fellow and do all in our power to assist him. In what way, I could not determine, for the page is very travel-stained and some of the words were obliterated. I expect the poor child will find England strange and terrifying, as would anyone arriving orphaned and friendless in a new land. Therefore, I wish that you will—"

12

"Me?" With a sort of leap, Devenish rose. "Good God, sir! I know nought of children. And as for a brat who likely comes complete with leathern fringes and a furred cap . . .! Uncle Alastair! How can you even think—"

Tyndale stood up straight and, from his superior height, smiled into his nephew's aghast eyes. "You underestimate yourself, Alain. If you are capable of having aided Tristram Leith to outwit and outmanœuvre one of the most dangerous madmen of our time, you are certainly capable of handling a backwoods child. Now, I have other matters requiring my attention, and must beg that you excuse me." He lifted one hand as his nephew attempted a remonstrance, and returning to sit at his desk, said gently, "We will talk at dinner, Alain."

Devenish hesitated. The old fellow was devilish grumpy today. Probably the news of his brother's death had upset him, which was natural enough. What a clodcrusher, not to have thought of it! He murmured, "I am very sorry, sir. About my Uncle Jonas, I mean. I'll be only too glad to help the boy."

Tyndale voiced his thanks, but did not look up from the papers he was scanning. Devenish crept to the door and closed it softly behind him.

The instant he was alone the Colonel threw down the papers and sank his head into his hands. "Good God!" he whispered. "Perhaps I should tell him the truth *now,* and be done with it!" For a long while he stared, haggard-eyed, at the quill pen, turning the problem over in his mind. But in the end he decided his initial plan must be followed. "I will wait," he thought, "until he meets the child. It would be just like the young rascal to become deeply attached to the boy. Then, it will not be so hard to tell him."

* * *

From having known Mr. Alain Devenish since he was in short coats, none of the Drummonds fancied he would fall into a decline by reason of Yolande's scold. However, since he had announced at the conclusion of that unhappy interview that he meant to go on a walking tour, Yolande was mildly surprised to see him coming cantering up the rear drivepath the following afternoon. She had been gainfully employed for the previous quarter-hour in assisting her Aunt Arabella to unravel a piece of knitting and, glancing up, said a not displeased, "Oh, it's Devenish."

Mrs. Drummond uttered a despairing little wail. "But it

cannot be, for you quite distinctly told me he was going away! Alas, so it is! And now he will take you from me so that I shall never finish this jacket for your dear papa! You are so *very* clever at understanding complex instructions, Yolande. And I—as usual—am such a dunce."

A small, bird-like woman, Mrs. Arabella Drummond had been married when scarcely out of the schoolroom to Sir Martin's elder brother, Paul. She had early wilted before her husband's forceful personality, deferring to him in all things, and upon his sudden death on the hunting field at the age of two and thirty had fallen into a deep decline from which for a time it had been feared she would never recover. Lady Louisa had insisted on caring for the childless widow, and had nursed her so well that Arabella soon regained her health. The prospect of living alone in the Dower House had appalled her, however, and she had implored Sir Martin to be allowed to stay at Park Parapine, just until she was over the shock of her bereavement. She was not an invigorating companion, and her brother-in-law not only considered her a dead bore but marvelled often through the following years that his wife could endure so lachrymose a personality. His occasional efforts to dislodge her had invariably brought on an attack of the vapours, or palpitations, or a resumption of Mrs. Drummond's famous "weak spells," so that still the Dower House remained unoccupied.

Her aunt having been a fixture in the house for as long as she could remember, Yolande could not imagine Park Parapine without her and, although quite often she contemplated deliciously fiendish acts of retribution upon her vexing relative, she was nonetheless fond of her and said, with her kind smile, "You most certainly are not a dunce! You knit very evenly, dear, and if you will just be sure you do not turn to the wrong page of your instruction papers, all will be well."

Mrs. Drummond was little encouraged by these remarks. She hove a deep sigh and allowed the garment she held to fall into her lap, folding her hands upon it and saying mournfully, "I try so hard. And this time I really did think I might succeed. I own I fancied it odd to have that strange bump suddenly appearing in the middle of the back of your papa's jacket, but then I thought it was to allow for the width of the shoulders."

"No, dear," said Yolande, noting how cautiously Devenish swung from the saddle and thinking that his leg must trouble him, still. "It was for the heel of a sock."

14

Mrs. Drummond moaned. "You will be thinking I should have known," she sighed, becoming even more dejected. "But how could I, when I never have attempted a jacket before? You will recall the bedsocks I made for your mama last Christmas? Those were nice, were they not?"

Yolande had a clear picture of her father wiping tears of mirth from his eyes in Mama's parlour, when first Lady Louisa had tried on her new bedsocks. "They're big enough . . . for two men— and a boy!" he had choked. Struggling to preserve her countenance, Yolande assured her aunt that the bedsocks had been charming, and finished, "Pray excuse me, ma'am. I must go and welcome Dev."

She made her escape and found Devenish in the garden, holding a basket that her mother was filling with early flowers. Lady Louisa, wearing a becoming broad-brimmed straw bonnet, was saying, " . . . even just a few blooms will so brighten a room, especially if one is not feeling quite the thing. Oh, hello, my love! Here is Devenish come to visit you, and I have been telling him about little Rosemary."

Yolande smiled upon her suitor and gave him her hand. "Good afternoon, Dev. Is Rosemary still poorly, Mama? I had thought she just ate too many cheese tarts yesterday."

"I wish you may be right." Lady Louisa placed a daisy in the basket. "But Nurse says she is feverish. I do hope she is not sickening for one of those endless childhood ailments." And with a worried smile, a nod to Devenish, and a caution that her daughter stay out of the sun, she took the basket and made her graceful way into the house.

Yolande turned to Devenish and succeeded in releasing the hand he had firmly retained during her mother's remarks. "Really, Dev!" she scolded primly.

He grinned at her. "Still in a pucker, are you?"

"*Me!* You were the one went riding off yesterday like a thundercloud!"

A spark came into his eyes, but he had determined not to quarrel with her and, with an extravagant gesture, invited, "Madam—will you perambulate with me?"

She slipped her hand in his arm and they began to walk amongst the flower beds together. She knew that he watched her, but managed to appear unconscious of that fact, pausing to admire various blooms as they strolled along. "Only look at the poppies," she said. "Miller has such a sure touch and always knows just what will thrive in just which spot. Are they not a picture?"

His immediate, "Not so pretty a picture as you," shocked her. She must, she realized, have really alarmed him yesterday. The awareness that he was trying very hard to please, in some perverse way dismayed her, and she whirled away from him so that they were standing back to back. "Since you admire me so," she teased, "tell me, sir, what am I wearing?"

"Why—a dress of course, sweet henwit."

"Describe it."

Devenish groaned. "Oh, gad! It is—er, blue, I think. Yes. Blue!"

"And has it a ruffle? Are the sleeves long, or short?"

"Thunder and— What the deuce has that to say to the purpose?"

"You don't know!"

He gritted his teeth. " 'Course I do. Blast it! There is—ah, no ruffle. And the sleeves are those fat little things you women wear."

"You mean puff, I presume, Mr. Devenish?"

"My apologies, Miss Drummond! Yes. Puff."

"And have I a necklace today? Or ribbons in my hair?"

He was sure there had been no ribbons, so said triumphantly, "You wear a necklace. A blue necklace. To match your eyes."

"Oh!" With a cry of chagrin, Yolande spun to face him. She wore a gown of palest green muslin, the deeply scooped neckline having a demure inset white yoke laced together with matching green ribbons. The sleeves were tiny little puffs, as he had said, nor did she wear ribbons in her rich tresses. Horrifyingly, about her white throat was a necklace of jade beads. Which emphasized the green of her eyes.

"Oh— Lord!" Devenish clutched his fair curls in despair. "I am sunk quite beneath reproach!"

"Be assured of it! I could have forgiven you the colour of the dress, and my necklace, but—have you known me all my life and never noticed that my eyes are green?"

"I am the complete gudgeon," he admitted, peering at her from under his hand. "You would be perfectly right to reject me entirely."

She hesitated, but the mischievous quirk beside his lips brought a frown to her brows, and she tossed her head and started off alone. Devenish hastened to come up with her. "Yolande—for heaven's sake! I do not see what difference—"

"Oh, do you not!" She halted, the better to glare up at

16

him. "Considering, Alain, that you are so deep in love with me—"

"Dash it all! You know I am!"

"I know nothing of the kind! Does a gentleman truly care for a lady, he most certainly knows the colour of her eyes!"

"Yes—and I do, now."

She sniffed and started off again, and Devenish said with disastrous honesty, "It is only that I've known you so long, I simply did not notice."

"Not . . . *notice* . . .?" She turned back, frowning in that way he thought particularly delicious. "I will have you know, Devenish, that there have been odes writ to my eyes." The twinkle that came into his own deeply blue eyes vexed her into adding a defiant and rather inaccurate, "Dozens!"

"Oho! What a whisker! Only show me two and I shall rush home and write one myself!"

"How exceeding generous! But I would not so tax your abilities for worlds. Thank you *very* much, just the same!" Flushed, her head held high and haughty, she walked away, raging. And in a little while, finding that he did not follow, uttered a muted, "Huh!" and paced on. But she was deeply fond of him and gradually it dawned on her that they had been quarrelling like two foolish children, rather than lovers. The knowledge troubled her, as she had often been troubled of late, and she glanced back. Devenish was standing where she had left him, staring at the ground, hands thrust into his pockets. A pang that was as much remorse as sympathy went through her, and she retraced her steps, pausing before him.

The bowed, fair head was raised. The humour had left his face, and for a moment they stood looking at one another in a shared and yet subtly disparate distress.

Devenish stretched out one hand. "Yolande, my apologies. Truly, I did not mean to vex you. But—what *do* you want of me?"

"I do not know." She sighed and with a wry little shrug put her hand into his. "I—I suppose I want you to be more steady. To have a purpose in life, and not be always rushing off, helter-skelter."

They began to walk again, and Devenish said defensively, "I do not rush off! My uncle kicked me out when I was obliged to resign my commission, and—"

"You do! You know you do, Alain. Only look at—well, today, for example. You said you were off on a walking tour."

"And so I was."

"You did not walk to Park Parapine, you rode!"

"Oh, don't be a widgeon, Yolande! I changed my mind, is all."

She shook her head at him, then asked curiously, "Why? I thought you had really meant to go."

They had come to a stone bench, one of several grouped about a fountain, and she sat down. Devenish rested one booted foot on the bench and leaned forward. "I did, but—" His brow darkened. "Of all the bird-witted starts! I've to play nursemaid to some puling infant of a cousin I never even saw!"

Yolande stared into his indignant face, then broke into a silvery gurgle of laughter. "*You?* Oh, no! Who is it?"

"A Colonial." He took down his foot, dusted the bench carelessly and inefficiently with his riding whip, and sat beside her. "Some Canadian brat."

"But—how can that be? I thought I knew all the children in the family. Am I related to him?"

"Must be, I imagine. He is the son of my deceased Uncle Jonas."

Her eyes widening, Yolande breathed, "What, the black sheep? Oh, how fascinating! I must tell Mama. Now, let me see. The child is your uncle's son. And my aunt on Papa's side of the family married a cousin of your mother, so that makes me . . ." Her brow furrowed. "Oh dear, I do get bewildered by these family relationships."

"It will be much simpler when we are shackled," he pointed out. "You will be his cousin, too."

"Shackled! How I despise that odious expression!"

"Egad, how you take me up. Very well—united in the bonds of holy matrimony."

"Thank you. When is he coming? Or have you to go to Canada, Dev?"

"Hey! Would that not be famous?" Eyes alight, he said eagerly, "A great continent to be civilized. A whole new land to be cultivated and—"

She intervened dryly, "You have a great *estate* to be cultivated," and then, seeing the grimness come into his face, added, "You never have told me why you do not like Devencourt."

At once, he grinned boyishly. "Because there is nothing to tell, madam. I positively dote on the place. But I can scarce toddle off and leave the Old Nunks, now can I? Poor fellow

18

would likely fall into a deep decline were he deprived of my scintillating companionship and left lone and lorn.''

"But he will not be lone and lorn. Your little cousin will be here. Oh, Dev!'' She tightened her clasp on his arm. "Mama will be *so* titillated! When does he arrive?''

"Any day, I collect. Uncle Alastair wants me to take charge of him and get him settled down. If he stays, I fancy he'll be off to school so soon as he's old enough.''

"Stays? Dev, is he to stay with you? At Aspenhill?''

"Well I fancy he is. Dash it all, Yolande, the brat's an orphan. Cannot very well have a Tyndale on the Parish—now can we?''

She laughed, but then said in her warm-hearted fashion, "Poor little fellow. How strange everything will seem to him. *Do* let us go and tell Mama. Dev, I can scarce wait to see the child!''

Chapter Two

Mrs. Arabella Drummond carefully replaced the luxurious furred pelisse in its large box, folded the silver paper over it, and took the lid Yolande handed her. It was a trifle difficult to put this back on, for the landaulette, although very well sprung, jolted erratically over the rutted surface of the lane. "I really think it a sad extravagance,'' mourned Mrs. Drummond, as she tied the string about the box. "Likely Rosemary will be better in plenty of time for your mama to accompany you, and you won't need me at all. What a waste!'' She shook her head over the new pelisse, and sighed heavily.

"But it looked so nice on you dear,'' said Yolande, squeezing her arm encouragingly. "Besides, even if you do not come to Scotland you need a nice warm pelisse. You feel the cold so in the wintertime.''

Mrs. Drummond wiped away a tear. "Oh, I do, and how kind in you to remember that, dear child. But were I not required to chaperone you on your travels, I could not have allowed your papa to purchase so costly a garment for little me.''

"Well, do not worry about it now." Yolande looked up at blue skies, flying white clouds, the lacy branches of trees overhead, and the tall hedgerows that hemmed in the open carriage on either side. "Is it not a glorious morning?"

"It is indeed," agreed Mrs. Drummond, but added lugubriously, "I wonder if we shall have any sight of the sun whilst we are in Scotland. I do trust the weather is not too inclement. Rain is so lowering."

"It has been several years since last I visited my grandfather," said Yolande, struggling to remain cheerful. "But it seems to me that the weather at that time was delightful, and when I came home Arthur said it had rained in Sussex almost the entire time we were away."

"Dear Arthur," murmured Mrs. Drummond. "I pray for him every night. Only think how wonderful it will be does he come safely home."

Yolande blinked at her. "Good heavens! Why ever should he not? The war is over now. Arthur is unhurt and, to judge from his letters, does not find service with the Army of Occupation an unpleasant task."

"No, for he never has been one to complain. However miserably he may be circumstanced. And only think, my love, your poor brother was deep in that horrid fight at—er—"

"San Sebastian."

"Yes. Such a frightful ordeal! And then—that hideous Waterloo."

"Yet came through both unscathed, Aunt."

"Exactly so! And is it not just like Fate, that having lived through such murderous encounters, a man may slip on a cobblestone, or trip on a stair, and—when 'tis least expected—" She broke off with a shriek.

Yolande had a brief impression of a horseman hurtling over the hedgerow to land directly in their path. The horses neighed shrilly the coachman shouted, the landaulette lurched, swerved, and plunged into the ditch. Clutching desperately at the side, Yolande caught a glimpse of Aunt Arabella sailing into a clump of lupins. She thought they would surely overturn, but with a muddled sense of surprise discovered that the team was still running. The landaulette bounded and rocked. The wheels hit the lane once more, and the vehicle fairly flew along. For a moment Yolande was too stunned to notice anything more than that they were moving very fast. Then, with a gasp of horror she saw that Tom Bates no longer occupied the driver's seat. She was alone in the vehicle! Her teeth jolted together as the wheels hit a deep rut and the landaulette bounced into the air. Still clinging to the side, she leaned as far forward as she dared, but the reins were far out of reach, trailing in the dirt beneath the pounding hooves of the thoroughly panicked team.

The rush of air past her face had already torn the bonnet from her head, and the curls, which her maid had styled into a pretty tumbling about her face, had whipped free and were blowing wildly. She gave a gasp of fear as they shot around a bend in the lane. Two elderly gentlemen, taking an equally elderly spaniel for a dignified stroll, glanced around, saw disaster bearing down upon them and, with surprisingly agile leaps, followed the spaniel into the ditch. The team rushed past and passed also the turn that led to Park Parapine. A scant mile ahead was the approach to the busy London Road. To enter that crowded highway at this speed could only mean death. With a sob of terror, Yolande peered ahead. Her only chance was to find a clear patch of grass and leap from the speeding carriage. But there was no clear patch of grass, only the hedgerows flashing past in a dark blur, and the ditch beside the road that was at best rutted and uneven, and in places strewn with rocks and fallen branches.

Fighting for the breath that the wind snatched away, she screamed, "Whoa! Whoa!" But her voice, shrill with fear, served only to further alarm the terrified animals. With flying manes, rolling eyes, and pounding hooves, they galloped ever faster along the narrow lane. Far ahead now, Yolande could glimpse the signpost pointing to the highway. Once they reached it, there would be no possibility of stopping in time. She would be doomed! Her horrified eyes fastened on that fateful sign. The pointing finger seemed to leap towards her. She could see the letters. Beyond now were the shapes of wains and lumbering wagons; the swifter passage of a mail or stagecoach . . . "God!" she sobbed faintly. "Oh—my dear . . . God . . . ! Help me!"

The thunder of hooves seemed to deepen until it filled her ears. Then, she saw with a thrill of hope that a horse raced alongside. A tall grey horse with an unlovely hammer-head, eyes starting, and gaping mouth foam-flecked. But it was gaining slowly. It was level. Surely the man bent low over the pommel could not hope to stop the maddened team? But just the knowledge that someone was trying to help comforted her. She caught a glimpse of a grim face, light brown hair, whipped back by the wind, and broad shoulders. But—dear

21

heaven! The signpost was here! And past! Even above the rattle of wheels and the beat of twelve racing hooves, Yolande could hear the sudden frantic clamour of a coachman's horn.

The man on the grey horse leaned far over and with reckless daring grabbed for the trailing reins. Squealing, the panicked bay beside him swerved. The landaulette rocked perilously. The would-be rescuer was all but torn from the saddle, and fought to right himself. Yolande sobbed. "He cannot regain his seat now," she thought. "He will fall and be killed . . . with me!"

But somehow he managed to drag himself up. Again leaning to the side, he kicked his feet free of the stirrups, his narrowed eyes judging the distance, then launched himself at the bay. Incredibly, his gloved hands caught the harness. A lithe twist, and he was astride the terrified horse. Another instant and he had recovered the reins.

Yolande clung to the seat of the landaulette, numbed, and too afraid even to pray, for the London Road was dead ahead.

A stagecoach driver, his scared gaze on the runaways, was heaving at the reins, cursing the carter ahead of him and the stream of traffic to his right.

The man astride the bay made no effort to halt the team. Instead, he bent forward, gripping the reins with one hand, stroking the foam-splattered neck with the other.

The stagecoach seemed to leap at them. A welter of sound—shouts, wheels, neighing, snorting horses—filled Yolande's ears. The carter glanced back over his shoulder and saw the flying team and the rocking carriage. His eyes rounded with shock. He cracked his whip belatedly, with the result that his frightened horses promptly plunged off the road. In the same instant, Yolande's would-be rescuer succeeded in turning the team. They raced along beside the welter of traffic, but now the carter's heavy wagon was directly in their path. To have been so close to safety only to be faced with death again brought a choking sob from Yolande. Tears blinded her and she closed her eyes. She heard a male voice screaming profanities and a keening squeal as the wheels of the landaulette scraped those of the wagon. The wild, headlong gallop went on, but the seconds dragged past and there was no shattering crash, no hideous shock.

Opening her eyes a crack, she saw trees about them again. The cacophonous roar of traffic had faded. He had turned the team! Somehow, he had avoided the carter and the tragedy that had seemed so inevitable.

She knew a great surge of relief and at once also experienced an almost debilitating weakness. With an effort she relinquished her grip on the side of the landaulette. Her fingers were white and cramped, and she was temporarily unable to straighten them.

The horses slowed and stopped, and the gentleman who had mastered them swung from the back of the bay and strode to the vehicle. "Are you all right, ma'am?" he asked, scanning Yolande's white face anxiously.

He looked to be about eight and twenty. His hair was windblown and untidy about his tanned face. It was a strong face with a jut of a chin and a Roman nose that had evidently at sometime been broken. The mouth was wide and well shaped, the brow high and intelligent. A pleasant-looking person, she thought vaguely, whose best feature was a pair of long, well open grey eyes under shaggy brows. He had asked her a question, but she could not seem to reply. Concern came into the grey eyes. They were decidedly nice eyes, she confirmed, and very kind. She closed her own, and quietly fainted.

*　　*　　*

Something icy cold splashed into Yolande's face. She sat up, gasping.

"No! Please lie back, ma'am."

She was sitting on the rug from the landaulette, which had been spread out in the field beyond the lane. Her rescuer knelt beside her, water dripping from the handkerchief he held as he watched her with fearful anxiety.

"Oh, dear," said Yolande. "You have lost your hat, I'm afraid."

He bent to slip an arm gingerly about her shoulders. "It is of no importance," he declared in a deep, slow drawl, gently pulling her back down.

She struggled, protesting, "I do not want to lie down!"

Nonetheless, she was lowered to the rug. "Ladies who faint," he said firmly, "should always lie flat for a time, otherwise they become sick."

"You are very determined, sir!" She frowned a little. "And I do not faint. Usually. This is my first time, in fact."

A gleam of amusement crept into his eyes. "The more reason you should obey me, ma'am. I have had some experience, for my mama suffered from poor health and fainted frequently." He raised one hand to quiet her attempted response.

"You are exceedingly pale. I do trust you are not hurt, or badly bruised?"

"Oh!" she gasped, memory returning with a rush. "What nonsense I am talking! You saved my life!"

"Having first very stupidly endangered it," he said gravely, sitting down facing her and resting one arm across a drawn-up knee.

"You? *You* were the idiot who came leaping into the lane?"

He inclined his head. "Idiot, indeed. I wish I might deny it. I cannot tell you how sorry I am. I'd no idea there was a lane—thought it was just a hedge."

Incredulous, she stared at him. "But—you *must* have known! You are certainly aware that hedgerows—" And she stopped, the wry lift of his brows alerting her. Aside from a hint of the military about the cut of his coat, he was dressed as one might expect of a well-bred young man out riding. There was nothing of the dandy about him; his shirt points were not exaggeratedly high, his cravat was, if anything, rather carelessly tied, and the dark blue jacket that hugged his broad shoulders did not give one the impression that two strong men had struggled for half an hour so as to insert him into it. His light brown hair was a little longer than was the current fashion and, although it showed a slight tendency to wave, it was neither curled nor had it been brushed into one of the currently popular styles. A typical enough young Briton, yet—there was the faintest suggestion of an accent in his speech.

The grin that curved his mouth widened. "You've rumbled me," he chuckled.

"I—am not sure," she said hesitantly. "Are you—American, perhaps?"

"No, ma'am. I come from Upper Canada. Just landed at Dover yesterday. I haven't been astride a horse for—er, several months, so started off bright and early this morning."

"Oh! What a coincidence! I should like to sit up now, if you please, for I am not hurt and not at all dizzy. Thank you." Yolande freed her hand from his strong clasp and turned slightly, straightening her gown. "I am expecting a cousin to arrive from your country. Were there any little boys sailing with you, sir?"

"If there were, ma'am, I was not so fortunate as to have met any." He added a rueful, "I chance to be one of those

24

unfortunates who cannot tolerate water travel. I trust that will not give you a disgust of me."

"If it did," she said with a flash of dimples, "I should not know with whom I am disgusted."

"Oh, egad! What a simpleton I am! Please know that Craig Winters is humbly and most apologetically at your service, Miss—er . . .?" His gaze slanted to her left hand and was thwarted by the mitten she wore.

Yolande smiled. "It *is* Miss—Drummond. Yolande Drummond. My father is Sir Martin Drummond of Park Parapine. And I can sympathize with you about ocean travel, Mr. Winters, for I've another cousin who becomes violently ill if only crossing our little English Channel, though to look at him you would fancy him quite above such miseries."

How straightforward she was, he thought. No missish airs and feigned shyness because she was alone with a stranger. And had the good Lord ever created a more exquisite little creature? "I suspect," he ventured, "that you have a great many cousins and brothers, and such."

The deep eyes were steady and held an expression that made her feel unaccustomedly flustered, but she managed a teasing, "Why, yes. Everybody does, you know."

His smile held a trace of wistfulness. She asked curiously, "Have not you, sir?"

"To say truth, ma'am, I—"

A rapid drumming of hooves along the lane ceased abruptly, and Alain Devenish burst through a break in the hedgerow and ran towards them. "Yolande!" he cried, his face pale and strained. "Good God! You are hurt!"

"She is unharmed, sir," said Winters, standing with the fluid ease of the athlete. "I must—"

"Who the devil asked you?" gritted Devenish, glaring briefly at him and dropping to one knee beside Yolande. "My dearest girl! Are you all right? Mrs. Drummond said you were as good as killed. I have been fairly beside myself!"

"Oh, heavens!" Guilt-ridden, Yolande gasped, "I had quite forgot the poor soul, and the last I saw of her, she was flying through the air into some lupins."

Immediately diverted, Devenish grinned. "No, was she? I'll wager she was complaining all the way! Never fret, love, she's bruised and shaken, but no bones broken." He turned a suspicious stare upon Winters. "By Jove! Could I but lay my hands on the looby who jumped his horse over that hedgerow . . ."

"I should explain," began Yolande.

"That looby is right here," Winters drawled.

"What?" Leaping up, his hot temper flaring, Devenish raged, "You damnable hedgebird!" He at once regretted his choice of words, especially when he saw the responsive twinkle that came into the other man's eyes. "You'll answer to me for this atrocity!" he said, one hand lifting purposefully.

"No!" Yolande scrambled up and gripped his upraised wrist. "Alain, if you will but—"

"I'll slaughter any swine who endangers your sweet life!" he snarled.

Winters sobered. He glanced from Yolande's pale, anxious face to this astonishingly handsome young firebrand, and the hopes that had bloomed so suddenly, faded. "I quite understand your concern, sir," he said earnestly. "I can only beg you will accept my—"

"Well, do not, because I won't, damn your eyes! What the devil d'you mean by jumping your stupid hack onto a lady's carriage? Are you—"

"If you think—" Winters began, with the trace of a frown.

"He saved my life!" intervened Yolande, tugging at Devenish's arm. "He was superb! If—"

"If he hadn't pranced over the hedge, there wouldn't have been no cause to save your life! It's good that he did so, of course, but that don't excuse it! Fella must be disguised!" He glanced down at Yolande and appended a contrite, "Poor girl, you look worn to a shade."

"And shall be conveyed home at once," Winters declared, his own gaze lingering on Yolande.

Devenish noted that appreciative look. "Miss Drummond," he gritted, pacing a step closer to the much taller and more sturdily built Winters, "will *assuredly* be conveyed to her home. By me. And you, sir, will convey yourself off! And be damned glad I've the lady to care for, else I would undertake to beat some sense into your feeble brain!"

Winters' mouth tightened. "You would do well to temper your language before a lady, sir."

Devenish spluttered and his fist clenched.

Quickly turning her back on Winters, Yolande placed one small hand on her volatile cousin's arm. "Please do take me home, Alain, for I feel quite poorly."

His rage was forgotten at once. "Of course—what a gudgeon I am! Lean on me, m'dear. Or perhaps I should carry you? Very well—this way, then . . ."

He guided her tenderly to the break in the hedge.

Winters watched them go, then stooped, gathered up the rug, and followed.

In the lane, Devenish assisted Yolande into the landaulette. Silently, Winters offered the rug. Devenish snatched it fiercely, then turned back to his charge. He tucked the rug carefully about her. Suddenly very weary, Yolande settled back, content to be fussed over. "Rest and be comfortable, my sweet life," he murmured. "I shall have you safe home in jig time." He hastened to tie his horse on behind the carriage, passing Winters, who had located his tall grey and stood watching. "Should I ever come up with you again, sir," said Devenish in a low, grim voice, "I will call you to book for this day's work."

Winters swung into the saddle and returned no answer. This mercurial young man was obviously deeply attached to the lady. Still, she had said she was a miss. Nor had she indicated a betrothal. He had learnt her name; it should be a simple matter to discover her direction. But not today.

Devenish had mounted to the driver's seat of the landaulette, moving in rather a slow fashion for such a slim and dynamic gentleman. He stopped only to assure himself that his charge was comfortably disposed, then took up the reins and, without another glance at Winters, urged the weary team onward.

For a moment the Canadian sat looking thoughtfully after them. Then he leaned to stroke the neck of his horse and said fondly, "You old fool, you can still outrun anything on four legs." The grey turned to peer back at him, seemingly just as fondly. "Come on." Winters grinned. "Up and at 'em! We still might find the silly place."

He glanced up at the sun, squinting a little to that brightness, then turned the grey through the break in the hedge and across the field to the west.

* * *

For the third time since Yolande had been tenderly ushered to her bed, Mrs. Drummond had recourse to her vinaigrette. "No matter how he rode to her rescue," she gasped out faintly, "that dreadful foreigner might as easily have brought about the deaths of us all! Indeed, I wonder I yet live, for I vow I must be black and blue from head to toe!"

Devenish, seated in a chair in the bright saloon, eyed the reclining victim uneasily. Sir Martin, less impressed, said tartly, "Then you should be laid down upon your bed, ma'am.

I'm sure I do not know why you must persist in lying here on a sofa, when you could be resting comfortably, above stairs!''

Mrs. Drummond rested a look of long-suffering martyrdom upon her unfeeling brother-in-law. ''I refused,'' she sighed nobly, ''to add to my dear Louisa's burdens. As though she had not enough to bear with little Rosemary deep in the throes of a putrid throat—which could very easily turn into rheumatic fever, you know—and now—''

''Nonsense!'' snapped Sir Martin, rising. ''The child is perfectly healthy and there ain't no cause for all your doom and gloom, Arabella! I'll thank you not to alarm her ladyship with such megrims!''

Struggling to hide a grin, Devenish stood also. Mrs. Drummond was not at all amused. She said an aggrieved, ''As you say, dear sir. But even so, Louisa will scarce be able to accompany Yolande on her journey. If the poor child is *able* to undertake such a long—''

All but snarling his irritation, Sir Martin interrupted, ''Your pardon, ma'am. You are clearly in sorry case, and since you refuse to go upstairs where you belong, we will leave you in peace. Come, Devenish.''

He strode out before the resentful lady could utter another word, and stamped along the hall to the book room, muttering fierce animadversions upon distempered freaks and blasted idiotic martyrs. The last thing either he or his spouse had wished was that Devenish learn that Yolande was removing to Scotland for the summer. The boy would most certainly have pricked up his ears at the blathering Arabella's indiscreet remarks, so now he must be warned off. An unpleasant task!

''Blast the woman!'' he growled, ushering his prospective son-in-law into the room and slamming the door behind him. ''Why my lady wife tolerates her I shall never—'' He caught himself up, took a deep breath, and, hopeful of turning Devenish's attention, occupied a wing chair and indicated another. ''Sit down, my boy, and tell me more of this Winters fellow. From what Yolande says, he must be a jolly fine horseman. That was no mean jump, and how he managed to transfer from his own mount to a bolting team is more than I have been able to come at. Did you see it?''

Devenish himself was too keen a sportsman to find anything unusual in Sir Martin's apparent admiration for the man who had jeopardized his daughter's life. ''I did not, but I saw his horse, sir, and a more unlovely brute I've seldom beheld.

You'd doubt he had the ability to set one hoof before the next."

"Is that so? Bit of a dark horse, what?"

"Like his owner! They were undoubtedly seeking the nearest circus so as to exhibit their tricks!"

"Oho!" Sir Martin's eyes widened. "From Yolande's manner I had thought him a gentleman."

Devenish shrugged. "A Colonial."

"Really? We don't see many of them hereabouts. I heard the Beau had one on his staff. Fine chap. De-something. Got himself killed, poor fellow. DeWitt—was it?"

"Oh, you mean DeLancey, sir. Yes, he was American—killed at Waterloo. This chap is Canadian. An insolent devil."

Sir Martin decided he had done the trick and that it was safe to now call the discussion to a halt. He said, "Well, I am sure you put him in his place, eh?" Standing, he put out his hand. "You'll forgive me, Dev, but I'd best get upstairs and see how Yolande goes on."

Devenish stood reluctantly, and the two men shook hands. "Of course. But—"

"My regards to Alastair," Sir Martin said hurriedly. "You must come and take your mutton with us. Er, in a week or so, when we've quieted down a trifle."

"Thank you, sir. Is Yolande going away?"

The bedevilled father ground his teeth, but answered brightly, "Not today, at all events." He swung the door open. "As to the future, who can tell? These ladies of ours change their minds every time the wind blows from a different quarter. I remember once . . ."

His memories lasted until the safety of the main staircase was reached, at which point he clapped his balked companion on the shoulder, said heartily that there was no call to show him out since he'd run tame at Park Parapine since he was breeched, and made his escape up the stairs.

Devenish watched that retreat broodingly. "Humbugged, by God!" he breathed. Every law of proper behaviour dictated that he politely accept his dismissal. He had spent most of his life, however, breaking laws of proper behaviour. He therefore set his classic jaw, turned on his heel, and marched back to the saloon. There, he tapped gently on the door, waited through a sudden scurry of movement inside, and turned the handle.

A little flushed, Mrs. Drummond lay as before, save that the quilt which had been laid over her was considerably

29

rumpled, and on the air hung the distinct aroma of peaches. Devenish darted an amused glance to the teakwood credenza. A jade bowl held some grapes from the succession houses, but there was no sign of a peach. He thought, "Aunty nipped over there and found something to sustain her, the crafty rascal!" But he said, with appropriate if insincere gravity, "I came to see how you go along, ma'am. You suffered a very nasty fall."

Just as insincerely, Mrs. Drummond murmured, "Dear Devenish. How very kind. I expect I shall—come through . . . somehow. . . ."

It was a superb performance, he thought, and said wickedly, "Gad, ma'am! You are become so pale. May I bring you a morsel of food? A glass of wine, perhaps? A little sustenance might—"

"No, no!" She shuddered, wrapping the peach pit in her handkerchief under the shield of the quilt. "The merest thought of food nauseates me! But you have a kind heart. Pray sit down. Not everyone does, you know."

He hesitated. "If you prefer that I stand . . ."

"No," she giggled coyly. "I meant—not everyone has a kind heart."

He smiled and seated himself, prepared to guide the conversation to the questions he burned to utter. He was doomed. On the brink of extinction though she might be, Mrs. Drummond expounded at length on the evils attendant upon allowing foreigners to cavort unchecked through Britain, the terrible ills that had befallen several ladies of her acquaintance following accidents far less severe than the nightmare she had just experienced, and her belief that "this Winters man" was in reality an escaped lunatic. "No one in possession of his faculties," she stated unequivocally, "would have attempted such a jump, let alone failed to consider that a vehicle might be travelling along the lane, and although I grant you it is not as well travelled as it was in my dear husband's day, for then there was a far jollier life here— Oh, but you should have seen the balls and the boat parties and garden fêtes! I well remember those grand times!" She chose not to remember that her "dear husband" was known to have all but bankrupted the estates, so that his brother had been obliged to wage a desperate struggle to restore Park Parapine to solvency. She became so busied with her reminiscences, however, that she forgot the initial trend of her remarks and eventually paused in a little confusion.

It was the opportunity for which Devenish had been waiting with concealed but fuming impatience. "It must have been grand indeed, ma'am," he inserted swiftly. "And as for the fiasco today, I am more than thankful for your concern. But surely, Yolande will not attempt a journey—under the circumstances?"

"I do trust she will not," his foil replied, portentously. "She was quite knocked up, did you not think? She is a brave girl, and people fancy her stronger than she is, but to go all the way to Scotland so soon after a dreadful accident would be most unwise, and so I shall tell her mama. Dear Lady Louisa is not the one, despite *other* counsel, to dismiss as merest frippery the opinions held by family members." This vengeful theme pleased her, and she rattled on happily for some moments, slanting such veiled but slanderous barbs at her absent brother-in-law that she felt triumphant and was much more in charity with him by the time she had exhausted the topic.

Devenish waited politely, but did not attend her and, as soon as was decently possible, escaped. He rode home at a less neck-or-nothing rate of speed than was his usual habit, restraining his beautiful black mare's occasional spirited attempts to break into a gallop. His hand on the rein was, in fact, so unwontedly heavy that twice she rolled an indignant eye at him. Of this, also, he was unaware. He rode along lost in thought, his expression grave. For Mr. Alain Devenish was an unhappy man. Mrs. Drummond's volubility had apprised him of the fact that his chosen bride, aware that she was soon to depart on a long journey, had not only shown no slightest concern about being parted from him for a protracted period, but had failed to notify him of her impending removal. Further, her parents, with whom he had always stood on the best of terms, appeared to be part of what he could only judge to be a conspiracy of silence.

Frowning, he recalled his most recent disagreement (it could scarcely be rated a quarrel) with Yolande. For as long as he could remember he had taken it for granted— He grunted impatiently; well, not *taken it for granted*, exactly, but certainly *anticipated* that they would wed. The two families were so close; Arthur and John and little Rosemary were almost like brothers and sister to him. And he and Yolande had always been such fine friends. She had not, in fact, begun to grow skittish and flighty and argumentative until first he started to speak of setting the date for their marriage. She was

31

a lovely and sought-after debutante, and as such had the usual share of cow-eyed admirers, but he was willing to swear she cared for none of them and was merely, womanlike, being just a little, and quite charmingly, coquettish, before settling down to domesticity. He sighed wistfully. He had been more shaken than he would have cared to admit when she had told him with that suddenly troubled look that *he* was not ready to settle down. Such fustian! He was five and twenty, deeply in love with his lady, and had—as she herself had pointed out—an estate in Gloucestershire that had been too long neglected. Devencourt. His lips tightened. The haunted manor. It was ridiculous, but his childish feeling about the house persisted. His earliest memories were of a great estate standing deserted and lonely in the vastness of its own grounds. An estate crying out for its owner, seeking to entrap him into remaining there until he also became deserted and alone. . . . How foolish that such juvenile imaginings still caused him to avoid his heritage. Yet even now, he could not discuss his reaction to Devencourt; not with anyone. Especially not with Yolande! Still, she was quite in the wrong of it when she named him a here-and-thereian. Not so! He'd had his fill of adventuring, with Tristram Leith last year. He'd been lucky to escape France with his life, and if Claude Sanguinet had had his way, would not have done so. No, when he was wed he would be quite content to settle down to a peaceful and respectable existence divided between town and country, with nothing more exciting to anticipate than the arrival of two or three little Devenishes.

He shifted uneasily in the saddle. Sounded devilish dull. . . . He dismissed the thought hurriedly. The bitter fact was that he was being treated by the Drummonds as though he were a complete stranger! Was it possible that they had received a more flattering offer for Yolande's hand? Surely not! But he glared angrily at Miss Farthing's ears and thought that it would serve them right if Yolande rejected him only to choose some rank ineligible—such as that curst circus acrobat this morning! Blasted encroaching mushroom! The way the fellow had looked at her was alone cause enough to have grassed him! For all his mercurial temperament, however, Devenish was a fine sportsman, and it had already come to him that he had been less than fair to Mr. Winters. The fellow had meant no harm with that splendid jump; he had after-wards most certainly saved Yolande's life and been given precious little credit for it.

He shrugged his shoulders. The Canadian was far away by this time. The thing now was to get back to Aspenhill as quickly as possible and discover whether his Tyrant had also been aware of Yolande's proposed jaunt to Scotland. By God, if *that* wouldn't be the outside of enough!

He touched his spurred heels gently to Miss Farthing's sides, and she sprang eagerly into a gallop that took them rapidly across lush meadow and through shady copse until they reached the last hill beyond which sprawled the Tyndale preserves and the welcome of Aspenhill.

Chapter Three

Colonel Alastair Tyndale looked up in mild surprise when his nephew unceremoniously flung open the study door and strode in. Leaning back in his chair, Tyndale laid down the letter he had been reading and said, "I'm glad you came back, Dev. Your—"

"I was at Park Parapine," Devenish interpolated. "Sir, did you know that Yolande is going away?"

The Colonel pushed back his chair and came to his feet, standing very straight so that although the desk was between them, Devenish had to look up at him. "We can discuss that, together with your—ah—unfortunate manners, later," he said. "I must tell you that your cousin has arrived."

"Oh. Well, can the brat wait awhile, sir? What I would like to know is—"

"And," Tyndale continued inexorably, "had you not burst in here at such a rate, you might have noticed that he is sitting behind you."

"Eh?" Devenish swung around to meet his small and unwanted cousin. "I say, I apologize if—" The words died abruptly. He gasped, "The devil!"

The Canadian who sprawled in the chair behind the door may have been unwanted. Small, he was not. Mr. Craig Winters' long, booted legs were outstretched, his chin propped on the knuckles of one hand, while his amused eyes took in Devenish's stark horror. He came lazily to his feet and drawled, "The Colonial looby—at your service, cousin . . ." His bow was deep, flourishing, and decidedly mocking.

Devenish spun to face his uncle. "Sir! This is a confounded hoax! This beastly fellow ain't a little boy! Nor is he related to us!"

The Colonel's keen blue eyes drifted from tall, derisive Canadian to slender, fuming Englishman. "I see," he said dryly, "that you two have met." He moved towards the door. "Come, gentlemen."

"Uncle!" flared Devenish, his comely face flushed. "Be damned if I'll—"

"Colonel," drawled Winters, his accent very pronounced, "maybe I'd best get on my—"

"We will talk," said Tyndale arctically, "over luncheon." He opened the door. "You will both be so good as to join me in the breakfast parlour as soon as you've put off your riding clothes. Ah—there you are, Truscott. Where have we put Mr. Tyndale?"

Winters' heavy brows twitched into a frown. The butler, customarily suave and seldom at a loss, was apparently not at his best today. "Mr.—Mr. Tyndale, sir?" he echoed.

"My nephew. Mr. Craig Winters Tyndale. Wake up, man!"

"M—my apologies, sir. Mr. er—Tyndale, is in the blue guest suite." He turned glazed eyes to Winters and bowed. "May I show you the way, sir?"

"You may not," the Colonel intervened. "Devenish, take your cousin to his room, if you please. I want a word with Truscott."

"With pleasure, sir," lied Devenish. Ascending the stairs beside his new kinsman, and bound by the dictates of good manners, he added, "I collect you stand in need of the services of a valet, so—"

"Oh, no. Thank you for so kind an offer. But I sent my man ahead of me. He's here now."

Devenish raised one bored eyebrow. "Indeed?"

Had he put a quizzing glass to his eye and leisurely surveyed his cousin through it, he could scarcely have more clearly implied his scepticism.

That mischievous twinkle again lit the Canadian's eyes. "We Colonials do have *some* of the social graces." He glanced up. "Everything in now, Monty?"

Devenish lifted his scornful gaze to discover the doubtful merits of this "social grace." Scorn was routed. It was, in fact, all he could do to restrain his jaw from dropping to

34

half-mast. The man who stood on the landing, with one hand lightly resting on the banister, was tall and with a suggestion about him of the panther. His long hair was blue-black, tied in at the nape of his neck, and very straight. The skin that stretched over lean cheeks had a coppery glow, and his eyes were unfathomable pools of jet. He wore a tunic and trousers of soft leather that were as if moulded to his lithe form, and on his feet were intricately beaded moccasins. He met his employer's laughing gaze, and his features softened imperceptibly. Not into a smile, exactly, but a semblance of one that was a brief flash of gleaming white against his dark face. "Everything in," he confirmed in a deep rumble of a voice. "You come."

Lips quirking, Tyndale threw a quick glance at his paralyzed relation and went on up the stairs.

For almost a minute, Devenish did not move. A distant shout of laughter roused him from his trance. He tottered to the landing. "Now—by Jove!" he breathed, his eyes stunned. "Now—by Jove!"

* * *

An hour later, Colonel Tyndale blew a cloud of smoke into the air and, with an appreciative eye, regarded the cheroot he held. "A very good brand, Craig," he acknowledged. "From your native land?"

"No, sir. They're—er, from Spain, actually. Glad they please you."

Devenish coughed rather pointedly and waved smoke from his vicinity.

"Alain don't smoke," advised Tyndale. "It's a filthy habit, I will admit."

"Oh, absolutely," Winters agreed affably. "Good you don't allow it, sir. Perhaps, when he's older . . ."

Bristling, Devenish grated, "What the deuce d'you mean by that? I'm as old as are you, you blasted circus clown! And furthermore—"

Tyndale lifted a restraining hand. "Peace, gentlemen. Peace! I have heard you both out and, unless one of you is bending the truth a trifle, it must be apparent that Craig acted unwisely, but did his best to atone, and that you, Alain, behaved with your usual calm, good judgment and comforted Yolande."

"Oh, very well," Devenish muttered, reddening. "I'll own I may perhaps have neglected to properly thank you, Winters, for acting as fast as you did to rescue my lady, but—"

35

"Your—ah, lady . . .?" breathed Winters. "You and Miss Drummond are promised, then?"

"From the cradle." Eyes narrowed and deadly, Devenish went on, "Furthermore, I warn you, here and now, that—"

"I feel sure," put in Alastair Tyndale, "I need not remind you, Dev, that your cousin is—my guest."

His fists clenching, Devenish choked back his angry words and sat seething for a moment. "If Mr. Winters is indeed our kinsman, sir," he exploded, "why don't he use his rightful name?"

"My apologies, Craig," said Tyndale regretfully. "I'd not intended to be so blunt, but since the question has been raised . . ."

His head very erect, Winters answered, "I understood it was one of my grandfather's stipulations, sir. That if he paid my father's way to Canada, the family name would not be used."

Devenish uttered a barely audible snort. Winters turned suddenly glinting eyes to stare at him unblinkingly.

The Colonel, frowning at the upcurling smoke from his cheroot, pointed out, "That stipulation did not apply to you. The—the indiscretions of your sire are not part of your inheritance. I believe it would be appropriate for you to use your correct name."

Without removing his gaze from Devenish's bland hauteur, Winters said gently, "Your pardon, Uncle. But I have no wish to change."

"My regrets, nephew. But it is *my* wish that you do so," said the Colonel, just as gently.

Here, Winters shifted his attention to the older man, a troubled uncertainty in his eyes. "I have no intent to distress you, sir. Were I to change my name, it would be to take your own, I assume."

"Tyndale. Of course. What had you supposed?"

Winters shrugged. "I wasn't just sure: You Englishmen seem to change your names at the drop of a hat." He glanced at Devenish. "So long as it's Tyndale, I'll settle for that."

"Will you, by God!" raged Devenish. "And I suppose had it been *my* name, that wouldn't have been good enough for your backwoods clodhop—"

"That will do!" The Colonel's voice cut like a sabre through the tirade. "I suggest you apologize, sir!"

Devenish's blazing eyes fell. He was behaving badly, his awareness of which fact did little to mitigate his loathing of

36

his tall cousin. "Yes," he mumbled. "Quite right." And forcing his eyes upwards, met an unexpected glare in the grey gaze across the table. "Apologize, Win—Tyndale."

The glare faded into a grin. The Canadian drawled, "Thank you."

"Still, it might be better," said the Colonel, "did you find someone else to accompany you, Craig. I wish I might go, but I am—er, detained here by—by a matter that I cannot postpone just now."

"Think nothing of it, sir. I've done a little pathfinding through the mountains of Upper Canada. It should be simple enough for me to find my way round this little island."

From the corner of his eye Colonel Tyndale saw Devenish's lips parting, and said a fast, "It might be less simple than you think. The British countryside has a way of confusing people." He turned to Devenish. "Your cousin means to have a look at his property, Alain."

With sublime indifference, Devenish said, "Property? Some distance from here?" And he thought, "I hope it's in Siberia!"

The Colonel put out his cheroot and murmured, "I took you there once, when you were a little shaver—perhaps you recall . . .?"

A sudden sense of déjà vu seized Devenish. He frowned. "I do seem to remember something. A gloomy old place, no? I think I loathed it."

Winters had been admiring an unusual scarabæus ring the Colonel wore, and so it was that he noticed the strong hand tighten convulsively about the stem of the wineglass. Curious, he glanced at his uncle and would have sworn he saw sweat beading the man's upper lip before the Colonel turned away.

Devenish had also seen. He leaned to slip a hand onto the older man's arm and asked with a swift anxiety that betrayed his affection, "Are you all right, sir?"

"Perfectly, thank you." Nonetheless, Tyndale's hand trembled slightly as he took a last sip of his port. "Shall we adjourn to the terrace? Or have you something planned, Alain?"

The Tyrant was looking fairly pulled. With a twinge of guilt, Devenish wondered if his own hasty temper was the cause. He managed somehow to smile at the usurper. "As a matter of fact, I was hoping Winters would let me have a look at his horse."

"Yes, by gad!" exclaimed the Colonel, brightening. "And that reminds me, Craig. From all I hear, you must be a superb horseman. How ever did you manage to change mounts at full gallop? I'd give something to have seen it!''

Winters coloured. ''I was practically raised on a horse, sir.''

''Your papa taught you to ride? He was a grand sportsman, God rest him!''

Something at the back of the grey eyes became blank. ''No, sir. Matter of fact, an Iroquois Indian taught me.''

''I say!'' exclaimed Devenish, immediately intrigued. ''How dashed splendid! You said the horse was Spanish-bred. Imported, I gather. Did you bring him over with you?''

Winters' gaze shifted to his plate. ''Er—yes,'' he said.

* * *

''Come in, Mama,'' called Yolande, looking up from the pile of notes and invitations spread out on her quilt. ''I am wide awake, and would have got up hours since, save that I decided to indulge myself.''

''Very rightly, my love,'' nodded her ladyship, closing the door and crossing the sunny bedchamber. She kissed her daughter, scanned her face with the knowing eyes of motherhood, and perched on the side of the bed. ''I am so glad the sun came out for you. We have had such a wretched spring. Now tell me, should we call in the doctor? Be honest.''

''Oh, absolutely not, I thank you. I feel perfectly well.''

''Wonderful. And how grateful we must be to Mr. Winters. It was very naughty of him to jump the hedge, of course. But I could not help but dwell on the accident last night. You know how things always seem so dreadful during the hours of darkness! And I thought how much worse it might have been. Only think, it might have been Herbert Glick, for example. Not that I wish to imply a criticism of poor Glick,'' she added with a guilty dimple. ''But—oh, dearest, can you not picture him galloping to your rescue as did Mr. Winters?''

Both ladies succumbed to the deliciousness of the picture thus conjured up, and laughed merrily.

Yolande gurgled, ''I cannot imagine him jumping the hedge in the first place, Mama. And had he done so, he would most certainly have parted company with his horse and landed beneath the hooves of our team!'' She took up an invitation and said, ''A masquerade at Greenwings—oh, what a pity I must refuse. Has—anyone called? I cannot guess how I came to sleep the day away.''

''Oh, can you not? I can! You were thoroughly shaken, poor lamb! Yes, Devenish stayed a little while after you was gone up to bed. He was beside himself, naturally." She sighed. "Your papa was so vexed, for Aunt let fall a remark about your stay in Scotland."

"Oh, dear! How unfortunate! Whatever did Dev have to say?"

"He tried to worm the whole out of Papa, as you might expect, so soon as they were alone. Papa says he tried very hard to turn his train of thought, and for a time believed he had succeeded, but Alain harked back to the subject, and your father was obliged to be quite devious."

"Bother! Now he will come and take me to task for not having told him! He must have been very angry, for already he considered me his personal property."

"He did seem angry, I grant you. But I thought his rage was directed at Mr. Winters. Your aunt, I fear, has taken that young man in strong aversion. Do tell me, love—what was he like? Handsome?"

Yolande thought for a moment. "No. Not handsome, though any man would seem plain if compared to Dev. He is certainly not unpleasant to look at, and has the nicest grey eyes. His build is sturdier than Alain's and I would suppose him to be a fine sportsman, for he moves with much grace. But I had the impression he is a little pulled. There was a—a sort of tiredness about his eyes that made me wonder if—" She looked up and found her mama watching her with brows slightly elevated, and felt her cheeks become hot. "Good gracious, Mama! What are you thinking? I have but seen the man once!"

Lady Louisa smiled and remarked that she wished she had seen Mr. Winters once—if only to thank him.

"I wish someone had," said Yolande regretfully, "for I am very sure I failed to do so. I have a vague recollection, in fact, of ignoring him completely and driving away without so much as a glance in his direction."

"Perfectly understandable. Has the young man any sensibilities at all, he will have found nothing to marvel at—save that you were able to speak at such a time, when most girls would have swooned away!"

The door opened. Peattie, Yolande's abigail, waddled her stout way across the room and deposited a charming bouquet of spring flowers on her mistress's lap. "From a Mr. Winters, Miss Yolande," she announced, broad features wreathed in a grin.

"How—er, pretty!" stammered Yolande, her heart giving a quite unfamiliar leap.

"The gentleman must still be in the vicinity," murmured Lady Louisa, watching her daughter's pink countenance with a touch of unease.

"The flowers was sent over from a flower shop in Bex-hill," Peattie volunteered and, crossing to her ladyship, murmured, "The boy who brought 'em said they was ordered by a gentleman what's staying at Aspenhill, milady."

Lady Louisa's unease increased. "Did he now? Thank you, Peattie. Miss Yolande will ring when she needs you."

"Mama?" said Yolande, as the maid closed the door. "Are you provoked because Mr. Winters sent the flowers?"

Her mother started, looked at her rather blankly for a moment, then smiled. "Of course not, you silly goose. What does he have to say?"

"That he means to call this afternoon in order to apologize to Papa for the accident. And that if his unforgivable reckless-ness has not given me a distaste for him, he will beg to see me for a moment or two." She gave a mischievous giggle. "Prettily said, eh, Mama?"

"And very pretty flowers." My lady touched the waxy petals of a tulip. "Shall you receive him, Yolande?"

"No. For you object, I see. Oh, never speak me a far-radiddle, dearest. Something troubles you, I know, for you seldom frown."

"Was I doing so?" My lady put up one white hand to wipe away the frown. "What a shrewd little puss! However, I do not object. It is only . . . Yolande, you are quite *sure* his name is Winters?"

"Yes. Positive. Do you know his family, perhaps?"

"No. At least— It just seemed rather odd that he should be staying with Alain and the Colonel, and I wondered— But that is foolishness, of course."

"At Aspenhill?" Yolande exclaimed, not having heard the exchange with Peattie. "Why, how very strange. I had fan-cied he and Alain took one another in the strongest aversion."

The trouble returned to Lady Louisa's eyes, full measure. "Oh, dear," she muttered. "How very difficult that will be for poor Alastair!"

*   *   *

There was, among the saloons at Park Parapine, one rather smaller than the rest, and decorated throughout in shades of gold and cream. Cream brocade covered the dainty chairs and the Louis XIV sofa; cream velvet draperies were tied back by ropes of braided gold silk; and the fine Aubusson carpets were of cream, gold, and brown. It was to this saloon that Yolande repaired shortly after half-past two o'clock, by some happy circumstance clad in a robe of palest gold linen, opening below the high waist to reveal a paler gold silk slip. Her glowing curls were piled high on her head, the fine tendrils that curled down beside her ears emphasizing the faultless delicacy of her skin. For jewellery she wore the topaz necklace and matching topaz ring presented to her by Alastair Tyndale on the occasion of her twenty-first birthday, and a zephyr shawl of white with gold threads was draped across her elbows.

A very old embroidery frame stood in a well-lighted spot between two windows, a straight-backed chair before it. Yolande made her way to open the sewing box beside the chair, and spread several strands of embroidery floss across the inner tray, ready for use. She then seated herself (making sure that her draperies were gracefully disposed), and took up the needle that had been neatly tucked into the stretched linen.

It was here that her visitor found her, when a superior being in powder and satin ushered him to the saloon shortly after three o'clock. Pausing on the threshold, Mr. Winters gazed at the lady bending so gracefully over her needlework, and knew that never had he seen a more beautiful sight.

Yolande glanced up in pretty surprise and saw him standing tall and straight in the doorway, his head slightly to one side, watching her with an expression that took her breath away. She forgot affectation and came to greet him, holding out one hand in welcome. Winters strode to take it. For a moment, tongue-tied, he simply held her hand, looking down into her eyes with that faint, tender smile still lingering in his own. Then, he bowed and kissed her fingers lightly. "It was most kind in you to receive me, ma'am," he said in his quiet, lazy drawl. "You cannot know how relieved I am to see you so well recovered. I was fairly terrified when you were driven away yesterday, looking so very shaken. Can you ever forgive me for having brought it all about?"

Yolande was finding it difficult to regain her breath, and she made a business of taking up the fan that hung from her wrist. "Far from chiding you, sir," she said, opening the fan and studying the hand-painted parchment as though she'd not seen it a hundred times before, "I must crave your pardon for failing to properly thank you. Had you not galloped after me so gallantly, I am quite sure I should have perished.''

Shattered, he bowed his head. "And I the cause of such a tragedy! My God! It would have been past bearing!''

"And did not happen, so never blame yourself. The flowers are lovely. Thank you so much.'' She glanced to the door, wondering what Mama could be thinking, to allow her to be alone with this young man. "Pray sit down, Mr. Winters,'' she invited, indicating one of the gold chairs. "I understand you make a stay with Colonel Tyndale. We are related, you know.''

He waited until she had seated herself on the sofa, then occupied the designated chair. "Yes. And we also are related, Miss Drummond.''

With a surprised arch of the brows, she asked, "You and I, Mr. Winters?''

"Apparently, ma'am. You see, for—er, various reasons, I did not use my full name when first we met. Winters was my mother's name. I am Craig Winters Tyndale.''

The fan shut with a snap. *"You . . .?"* she gasped. "But—but—'' Mirth overcame her, and she relapsed into a flood of laughter. Daintily wiping away tears, she apologized. "Oh, whatever must you think of me! How dreadfully rag-mannered! I do beg pardon, Mr.—er, Tyndale.''

"Please do not,'' he said, delighted at having caused her to be amused. "Indeed, I could not be more pleased than to discover I have such enchanting relatives.''

She had decided he was shy and bashful, but at this was startled into looking straight into his eyes, which she had guarded against doing. Her gaze was locked with his, and once more that heart-stopping breathlessness dizzied her.

Mr. Craig Winters Tyndale said nothing. There was not the need.

*   *   *

At the same moment, Lady Louisa sat beside her husband in the book room, as stunned as was her daughter, though for a very different reason. "It is as I feared, then!'' Agitated, she placed one hand on Sir Martin's wrist, as though for support.

He took up that small hand and, finding the fingers cold as ice, squeezed them reassuringly, then returned his attention to Alastair Tyndale, who stood before the fireplace, staring down at the large brass Chinese dragon which occupied the hearth when the fire was not lit. "Alastair,'' he said, and paused to clear his throat. "Alastair, does Devenish know? Have you never so much as given him a hint?"

Tyndale passed a weary hand across his eyes. "Never."

The Drummonds exchanged worried glances. Lady Louisa said, "But, you do *mean* to tell him? Surely, now. Especially *now!*"

He said wryly, "It is for that very reason, Louisa, that I *dare* not tell him now! He believes I am upset solely because of the news of my brother's death. I've no need to remind you of how kind-hearted the dear fellow is. He was all eagerness to help, and more than willing to deliver a letter to my solicitor in Tunbridge Wells. He even invited Craig to accompany him. Not very heartily, but he *did* invite him. I succeeded in convincing him that Craig and I had much family business to discuss. Had he suspected we meant to come here . . ." He shook his head bodingly.

"And you say there was instant antipathy?" muttered Sir Martin. "How very strange."

Frightened, his lady scanned his grave features, then uttered a bracing, "Not so strange, surely, Drummond? Two healthy young male animals, snarling at one another over a lovely female."

"Perhaps." The Colonel nodded, accustomed to her frank ways. "Indeed, I pray you may be right. But—if Yolande is attracted to Craig—" He stopped.

"Lord!" Sir Martin muttered, half under his breath. "Add that to all the rest . . .!"

Colonel Tyndale eyed him apprehensively. "What do you think, my dear?" he asked, turning to Lady Louisa. "You, of all people, know how Yolande's heart is engaged. Is she in love with Devenish?"

My lady bit her lip. "She loves him, I know," she said haltingly. "She always has, but— Oh, *why* did Craig have to arrive at this particular time!"

"I see. We have an undecided heart, have we?" Tyndale said with reluctance, "I suspected as much. And what of young Craig? They've only just met, of course, but—I've a suspicion the lad received a leveller."

"Pshaw!" scoffed Sir Martin. "Love at first sight? I never believed in it! Attraction perhaps, but nothing lasting. Not in the wink of an eye! Fairy-tale nonsense! Do you not agree, my love?"

Again, Lady Louisa hesitated. "I feel sure you are right, Drummond," she said quietly. But she avoided the Colonel's

43

searching gaze, and his heart sank. "Nonetheless," she went on, "I cannot but think it would be best, Alastair, did Alain know the truth. If there is already antagonism between them . . . It would be so dreadful if . . ."

Colonel Tyndale stared in silence at the brass dragon. Lady Louisa did not complete her sentence, and Sir Martin looked from one to the other of them gloomily.

"Aye," the Colonel sighed, at length. "You are probably in the right of it, Louisa. But . . . heaven help me! How shall I tell him . . .?"

* * *

Yolande started as her name was uttered in a shrill, horrified screech. "Aunt!" she gasped, wrenching her eyes from Mr. Craig Winters Tyndale. "How you startled me! Whatever are you doing up and about?"

"Why, I crept from my bed so as to let out Socrates, for with little Rosemary so ill I would not dream of requiring anyone to come to *my* aid." Mrs. Drummond gathered her voluminous dressing gown closer about her and, looking at the tall young man who had risen respectfully upon her entrance, said, "Thank goodness I *did* come, dear Yolande. How shocking that you have been abandoned!"

Craig blinked. Flushed with irritation, Yolande responded, "Scarcely abandoned in my own home, Aunt. You will have noticed the door is wide, and Mama will be here directly, I am sure."

"I only arrived a few minutes ago, ma'am," said Craig, colouring up. "At least," he turned a betrayingly warm smile on Yolande, "I—er, *think* it was a few minutes ago."

A dimple appeared briefly and, he thought, adorably, in her smooth cheek, but Mrs. Drummond moaned. He moved at once to her side. "May I assist you to a chair, ma'am? You do not look—"

A small fox terrier, quite old and very fat, tottered into the room and, upon perceiving this enormous individual reaching for his mistress, gave vent to a piercing spate of barking, rushed forward, and dealt Craig a hearty nip on the ankle.

The Canadian exclaimed an involuntary "Ow!" and stepped back hurriedly.

"Socrates!" scolded Yolande.

"Dear little fellow," cooed Mrs. Drummond, bending to gather up her snarling pet. "He was only protecting his mama, wasn't you, love?"

Tyndale bestowed a smouldering look upon the "dear little

fellow." Hastening to him, Yolande asked a concerned, "Did he hurt you?"

A tall grey-haired woman in a flowing grey gown and snowy white apron hurried into the room. "Is my lady here, miss? Oh! Excuse me, sir!"

"Nurse," said Yolande anxiously, "Is Miss Rosemary not improved at all?"

"The fever gets higher, miss, no matter what I do. I fear she is sickening for something. There is the beginning of a rash, and—"

"Oh! My heavens!" wailed Mrs. Drummond, sinking dramatically into the nearest chair. *"Never* say it is the smallpox!"

Entering in time to hear those dread words, Lady Louisa blanched and clutched at the door-frame. "Smallpox? God in Heaven! Nurse—it isn't—?"

"Of course not, Mama," said Yolande, crossing to support her. "Aunt Arabella misunderstood."

"Oh, that poor . . . sweet, child!" cried Mrs. Drummond, a handkerchief pressed to tearful eyes.

Nurse, having slanted a disgusted look at these histrionics, vouchsafed that she could not tell what ailed Miss Rosemary, but she doubted it was the smallpox.

"Nonetheless, I must go to her," said Lady Louisa. "Yolande, pray ask your papa to send a groom at once for Dr. Jester."

Craig had moved quietly back to stand out of the way beside the mantel and now came forward, saying with an apologetic smile that he would take his leave and would gladly relay the message to Sir Martin.

"Oh, dear!" Yolande exclaimed. "I have sadly neglected you, cousin! How is your poor ankle?"

Mrs. Drummond's recovery was astonishing. *"Cousin?"* she bristled.

"What happened to his ankle?" asked Lady Louisa, distractedly.

"Socrates bit him," Yolande supplied. "Horrid creature!"

"Mr. Winters may have brought great suffering upon us," Mrs. Drummond said smugly, "but you really should not refer to him in such terms, my love."

Craig grinned at this excellent shot, but Yolande was not amused. She blushed scarlet and turned to her aunt with such anger that Lady Louisa intervened with a vexed, "Really, Arabella! Cousin Craig, my apologies, but—"

"But you must be wishing me at Jericho!" He took her

hand, patted it sympathetically, and said his farewells. His smile included Mrs. Drummond and Nurse, in addition to the brief but meaningful seconds during which it rested upon Yolande. Then he was gone.

An hour later, wandering onto the front porch in search of his wife, Sir Martin found her staring after the doctor's departing gig. "Are you coming in, m'dear?" he enquired. "Not worrying over a simple case of measles, surely?"

"What? Oh, no, of course not, Drummond. Though the poor child is so wretchedly uncomfortable. Yolande is with her, which she will very much like, you know."

He nodded, closed the door, and walked across the hall beside her. After a pause, Lady Louisa sighed. "She was right. He really does have very nice eyes."

My lady was in the habit of occasionally speaking her thoughts aloud, sometimes to the complete mystification of her listeners. For once, however, her apparently irrelevant remark did not confuse Sir Martin. He was perfectly aware she did not refer to Dr. Jester.

*   *   *

Two days later, clad in a dark green fitted coat that closed to the waist with large brass buttons, Yolande tied the grosgrain ribbons of her bonnet beneath her chin, surveyed her reflection critically in her standing mirror, and turned to the bed to take up her muff. "I cannot be easy in my mind about leaving you with Rosemary ill," she worried. "Mama—perhaps I should stay."

"And be the cause of a full-fledged duel?" Lady Louisa handed her an urn-shaped reticule of green velvet, embellished with pale green beads. "How very pretty this is. And goes with your coat and bonnet so nicely."

"Thank you. Mama, you do not really think . . .?"

My lady smiled into her daughter's aghast eyes, and sat down on the bed. "I think it would be as well for neither young gentleman to see you just at the moment. You look awfully fetching, dear. Come now, never be so worried, I was only teasing. They are likely the best of friends by now."

"I doubt that," Yolande sighed, pulling on one small leather glove. "Mr. Glick said that when he stopped to visit the Colonel yesterday, Alain was in a tearing rage because he had discovered that Cousin Craig had come here whilst he was in Tunbridge Wells!"

"Herbert Glick!" said my lady, with uncharacteristic

impatience. "The poor moonling! He likely exaggerated the matter out of all proportion. I should forget all about it, were I you."

Considerably troubled, Yolande argued, "Mama, I *cannot* forget about it. I am—most fond of—of both of them."

Lady Louisa shook her head. She did not say anything, however, but sat staring down at her clasped hands, her expression so pensive that Yolande went and sat beside her. "Dearest, why have I the feeling that you and Papa, and Uncle Alastair too, are terribly upset? Is it because of my—my procrastinating? Shall I set the wedding date before I leave? If it will put your minds at ease, I will gladly do so."

Her ladyship reached up to touch that loved and lovely face and say with a wistful smile, "Fate is very strange at times."

"Oh, *dear* Mama! What is it? I have never seen you so!"

My lady summoned her brightest smile. "Then I must be behaving in a very silly fashion. Now—your papa would like to speak with you for just a moment." Forestalling Yolande's next question, she said, "And—no, it has nothing to do with Rosemary, I promise you. It is just . . . it is something you should have been told of, long ago. Only—well, we never thought it would come to this, do you see?"

"I am frightened," said Yolande, a shiver creeping down her spine. "Is it very dreadful, Mama?"

Again, Lady Louisa looked down at her hands. They were gripped very tightly. She unfolded them. "I fear," she said, a tremor in her gentle voice, "that it really *is*—rather dreadful, Yolande."

Chapter Four

The morning was misty, lacking any trace of the warm sunshine of the past two balmy days. There was a smell of rain on the cool air and, as if glum in the face of more damp weather, even the birds seemed disinclined to sing, so that a deep silence lay over the lush and pleasant swell of the South Downs.

A large hare came hopping up the slope and at the summit

stopped, suddenly very stiff and still, ears upright and nostrils twitching as it stared back the way it had come. It darted away then, moving so fast that it was only a tan blur against the rich grasses, swiftly vanishing. And in its wake came the sound that had frightened the small, wild creature. A muffled tremor that at first barely disturbed the air, growing to a distant throbbing, a rhythmic beat swelling ever louder until it became a rapid tattoo of iron-shod hooves racing headlong through the quiet morning. Up over the rise they came, neck and neck, the ungainly grey gelding, the sleek black mare, the riders flushed and breathless, leaning forward in the saddles, fair men both, but one much fairer than the other, and both heads bare, for the wind had long since snatched their hats, and neither would stop to reclaim them. A thunder of sound, creak of leather and jingle of spurs and harness; the earthshaking pound of hooves, the snorting breath of striving horses. A buffet of wind at their passing. And they were gone, plunging down the slope, the grey gaining a little as they started up the other side.

They were out of the Downland now. A long hedge rose ahead, and Devenish grinned and glanced at his cousin as Craig bent lower. Lord, he thought, but the man could ride! And with a widening of that impudent grin he knew the Canadian would have to ride like a centaur to take this jump unawares. He leaned forward, patting the mare's sweating neck, preparing her with hand and voice.

Tyndale, narrowed eyes fixed on the hedge, was sure this time there was no lane, for there was not another hedge beyond, that he could see. "Come on, Lazzy!" he cried, and felt the great muscles tense beneath him as the grey shot into the air. Too late, he saw the gleam of water below and knew that the jump was too wide. The grey snorted with fear, landed with a mighty splash, and fell. Tyndale flew over his head and landed hard on the bank.

Laughing, as Miss Farthing landed neatly on the far side, Devenish glanced back. His laughter died. He swore, reined back, and swung the mare in a wide circle, dismounting in a flying leap. He staggered, gripped his right leg and swore at some length as he limped to his cousin, who lay sprawled at the water's edge.

Thus it was that a moment or two later, Tyndale blinked into a pair of disembodied blue eyes that gradually became part of features that were almost too beautiful for a man, but set into an expression of grim ferocity. "Jove," he breathed, with an unsteady grin. Then, in sharp anxiety, "Is Lazzy . . .?"

"Scraped one knee. No, lie down, you gudgeon! It's nothing serious."

"Poor old fellow."

"Yes," grunted Devenish, furious with himself. "I should have thought of that." His cousin slanted an amused glance at him, and he flushed and reached down. "Here."

Tyndale disdained the proffered aid, and sat up.

"Why the deuce," exploded Devenish, "did you not slow down? You surely must realize you ain't familiar with the lay of the land?"

"I also realize that because I am a stranger does not make you responsible for me," Craig answered calmly, his eyes fixed on his grey.

"Don't be so damned patronizing!"

Tyndale said nothing, but the cool stare shifted to Devenish, whose flush deepened. "Blast you!" he fumed. "I suppose I should have warned you. I knew you could not hope to negotiate such a jump." His angry gaze fell away. "It was—it was poor sportsmanship. I apologize."

It had obviously been a painful admission, thought Tyndale. But it had been made. "Thank you," he said gravely. "But I do not very often take a toss."

At once those fierce eyes lifted to glare at him. "It is very well to brag, cousin. But had you broken your neck, only think of my position. There'd be the devil to pay and no pitch hot, for everyone would say I had done it deliberately because I dislike you."

Tyndale smiled faintly. "I'd not have cared overmuch for such a development, I admit." He reached up.

Devenish stared.

Tyndale's eyes glinted. He said without expression, "Give me a hand, will you?"

Relieved, Devenish obliged, and Tyndale moved rather erratically to his grey. The big horse nuzzled him affectionately, and, watching as he bent to inspect the damaged knee, Devenish asked curiously, "What is it that you call him?"

"Lazzy. Short for Lazarus because he—after a fashion—rose from the dead." He felt the hock carefully, hove a sigh of relief, straightened, and reeled unsteadily.

"How?" persisted Devenish.

"Eh? Oh, there was a sort of a battle. At the edge of a rapids. Between Monty and me."

49

Awed, Devenish asked, "You mean, he was after your scalp? That sort of battle?"

Tyndale's mouth twitched. "That sort."

Waiting in vain, Devenish burst out. "Well? Go on, blast it!"

"Monty's mare had just foaled. We caromed into her and scared her so that she plunged about and the foal went over the edge and into the river. Monty and I were a bit—er, done up. So it took both of us to haul him out. When we managed it, Monty insisted the foal was mine and there was another—ah, discussion. We wound up having to doctor one another because the foal began trying to die. Between one thing and another . . . well, we've been together ever since. All three of us."

There was more to it, Devenish suspected. The Iroquois had exuded pride, yet he served Tyndale and was very obviously devoted to him. "Is that where you got that beast of a scar?" he asked. "I wonder you're still breathing."

Tyndale stiffened and his hand flew to his throat. His neckcloth had been removed and his shirt unbuttoned. Buttoning it, he evaded, "It has been said that I'm devilish hard to snuff. Speaking of which—I will concede you the race."

Devenish gave a gasp. "The devil! Did you think I was really trying?"

"To win?"

"To snuff you."

"Were you?"

"I should, by God! If only for that bacon-brained remark!" He stamped to the black, swung into the saddle, and demanded furiously, "Do you seriously think I would deliberately endanger another man's life over a stupid race?"

Interested, Tyndale inquired, "Why *would* you deliberately endanger another man's life?"

"Dash it all!" snarled Devenish, setting his mare to capering. "I did not deliberately— That is, I had thought it would— I —Oh, hell and the devil confound you!" And he cantered away until he was out of sight.

Craig chuckled. "Lord, what a fire-eater!" He found his neckcloth and replaced it, then mounted and bent forward to stroke the grey's neck. "I hope we can find our way home, friend, else—" He broke off as rapid hoofbeats announced his cousin's return. Hair windblown, cheeks flushed, and eyes shooting sparks of wrath, Devenish came up at the gallop and, as if there had been no pause, gritted, "Furthermore,

50

since I did *not* win, or if I had it would have been by cheating—''

"Cheating, coz?" Tyndale demurred mildly. "I would not say you cheated—exactly."

Devenish fixed him with a baleful eye. "We will call it a tie. Satisfactory?"

"Oh, perfectly."

They started off, side by side, Devenish stiff, Tyndale relaxed. After a few moments, Tyndale enquired, "What do you do, cousin?"

"*Do?* What the deuce do you mean '*do*'? A gentleman don't *do* anything."

"My apologies. Not being a gentleman, I didn't understand."

"Oh, Lord," groaned Devenish. "*Now* what fustian are you about? Of course you're a gentleman. You're a Tyndale, ain't you?"

"I'll admit that. But—I do not think I'll be a gentleman. Thanks just the same."

"Don't think you'll . . .!" gasped Devenish. "You *are* short of a sheet! Damme if you ain't!"

"Why? Because I don't choose to be a gentleman?" Tyndale laughed. "Gad, Dev, I couldn't abide it! The life of a do-nothing would drive me straight into the boughs! I'd a sight liefer be a coal-heaver!"

"Yes, and probably should be! And do not call me Dev! Only my friends call me that!" He thought, "Cousin's almost more than I can bear!" and added irritably, "Besides, I had not meant *nothing* exactly."

"Oh, I should have guessed. You've likely just come down from University, correct, er, Mr. Devenish?"

Turning in the saddle the better to direct a hard stare at that bland smile, Devenish refuted, "Incorrect. I was sent down."

"Wrong again, alas. Perhaps I had better have addressed you as Lieutenant Devenish?"

Gritting his teeth, Devenish imparted, "I was obliged to sell out of the military. Damn near cashiered. Does that satisfy you?"

"By all means. If it satisfied you, I've no quarrel with it."

"*Satisfies* me? Why, you Colonial clod-crusher! Is there no end to your impudence?"

Tyndale threw back his head and gave a shout of laughter. "My apologies, Sir Cousin."

"Do you know . . ." Devenish pulled his mount to a halt, and glowered at his tormenter. "I have been wondering of

51

whom you put me in mind, and now I know. It is Leith, by God.''

Briefly, Tyndale looked startled. Then he muttered, ''Leith. Oh, yes. Colonel Tristram Leith. A proper dirty dish, eh?''

The amusement that had begun to creep into Devenish's eyes, vanished. He sat straighter. ''Your pardon?''

''I said I had heard of Leith. What you people over here would call a wrong 'un, no?''

Devenish swung one leg across the saddle and slid to the ground. There was no trace of temperament about him now, but an icy coldness that, had he known his kinsman better, would have warned Tyndale. ''Will you favour me by dismounting for a moment,'' he invited with a smile.

Tyndale obliged.

Eyes of blue ice fixed themselves upon his face. Stripping off his gloves, Devenish murmured, ''You are likely at least a stone heavier than I, Tyndale. On the other hand, you just suffered a bad fall. That should, I think, even the odds.'' He flung his gloves into his cousin's startled countenance. ''Put up your fists, you damned scaly gabblemonger!''

''Hey! Wait! I only—''

Devenish jumped forward and with surprising power landed an open-handed blow to the jaw. Dancing back again, he shouted, ''Fight, curse you!''

Sighing, Tyndale took off his own gloves, tossed them aside, and crouched.

The battle was short-lived, but interesting. Never had two men fought in more diverse styles. His eyes ablaze with excitement, Devenish feinted, shifted, leapt in to unleash a lightning fist, and danced out of reach again. Tyndale, shoulders hunched, eyes watchful, moved very little, as unflustered by his cousin's antics as Devenish was elated. And somehow, as fast as Devenish undeniably was, as lethal the blows that he aimed, at the end of five minutes, there was not a mark on either man, but while Tyndale was as calm and easily breathing as at the start, Devenish was slowing noticeably, his face paler, his movements less springy, some of his enthusiasm replaced by grimness. ''Fight, you churlish clod!'' he raged. ''Do not just stand there like a lump! Fight!''

Tyndale smiled, but did not reply. And it was borne in on Devenish that when the bigger man did move, it was with amazing efficiency, his tall figure swaying easily and never more than was necessary to elude the blows flying at him. Tiring, Devenish's fists lowered, his shoulders slumped. He was breathing distressfully and, watching him, Tyndale dropped his guard a little. In that instant, Devenish sprang. His right rammed home to the jaw. Tyndale staggered and, hurt at last, retaliated immediately and instinctively. . . .

Flat on his back, Devenish smiled up at blurred skies. "Beautiful . . ." he sighed.

Standing over him, Tyndale asked, "Are you much damaged, Sir Cousin?"

"I beg leave . . . to tell you that . . . I shall lie here until my head rejoins . . . the rest of me and . . . be damned t'you."

Tyndale grinned and sat down also, feeling his jaw experimentally.

"Let us have no more of your . . . Canterbury tales," Devenish exhorted. "I know blasted well I scarce laid a fist on you."

"One. Whereby I seem to have several loose teeth."

"No, truly?" Devenish rolled onto his side and, supporting his cheek on one hand, said gleefully, "Egad, but I did mark you a little, at that! Coz—where in the name of all that's wonderful did you learn that left jab?"

"Oh, I sort of—er, developed it. With help. Here and—and there." Tyndale saw Devenish's mouth opening for an indignant retort and added a hasty, "Though why you attacked me so viciously is more than I can comprehend."

Reminded, Devenish sat up, clutched his head, and uttered a trifle thickly, "I do not suffer my friends to . . . to be slandered, in my hearing."

"Leith? But, from what I have heard, he's not worthy of—"

"Tristram Leith," Devenish stated deliberately, "happens to be one of my closest friends. And whatever you may have heard, quite apart from being as far removed from a rogue as it is possible for a man to be, he is a valiant and honourable gentleman. I owe him my life."

Tyndale stared at him. "Then surely it ain't proper that you should so dislike the fellow."

"Dislike *Leith*? Are you mad? I do not dislike him!"

"But—you distinctly said that I reminded you of him."

Frowning into the innocent grey eyes, Devenish declared, "Even Leith has a few mannerisms that are irksome."

"And those you detect in me, eh, sir? Heigh-ho. Life is a sorry thing!" He drew out his handkerchief and handed it over. "Your mouth is bleeding."

53

Devenish accepted the handkerchief and dabbed at his mouth. Tyndale helped him to his feet.

Setting one foot into the stirrup, Devenish muttered, "Coal-heaver, indeed!"

Tyndale laughed.

As the horses passed through the gate at the eastern end of the meadow, and entered the lane, a pink nose and then the rest of a large hare emerged with caution from beneath the hedgerow. For a moment it paused there, very stiff and still, nostrils twitching and ears erect, staring after the departing humans. The sound of Tyndale's laugh had not fallen unpleas-antly on its ears, and, reassured, the wild creature proceeded busily about his tasks.

*   *   *

Colonel Alastair Tyndale stood before the hearth of the book room, one booted foot on the gleaming brass fender, and brooding gaze on the flames. He had heard his nephews ride in some half-hour previously and, by means of a casual remark dropped to his omniscient butler, had culled the infor-mation that there looked to have been "some sort of dispute." His gaze lifted to the two neatly folded sheets of parchment that lay on the mantelpiece. When those letters were read, the very obvious and mutual dislike between the young men might well harden into all-out hatred, even before he—

The door swung open and Devenish entered, saying in his pleasant voice, "Good afternoon, sir."

Following, Craig offered the hope that they had not kept the Colonel waiting.

Alastair regarded them gravely. They had changed for luncheon and each in his own way was impressive. Craig wore a jacket of maroon that hugged his broad shoulders admirably, and if his neckcloth was less than expertly tied, his pantaloons displayed excellent legs, and his lack of jewellery did not earn him any censure in his uncle's eyes. Devenish, his curls carelessly tumbled, wore a navy blue coat of superfine, his neckcloth was a work of art, and although he lacked his cousin's powerful figure, his physique was in perfect propor-tion to his size.

Despite the fact that the morning had darkened, no candles were as yet lit in the room, but as the two men moved rather hesitantly towards him, Colonel Tyndale noted the darkening bruise along Craig's jaw, and Alain's puffy and split lip, and his own jaw hardened. He made no comment, however, wav-ing to the sideboard, and suggesting they help themselves

54

from the tray of decanters which the butler had left. "Before we go in to luncheon," he added when they all were seated around the fire, "there is something I must say to you." In silence, he handed a letter to each man.

Glancing at the superscription, Devenish muttered, "Yolande! What the deuce? Good God! Sir, it's not little Rosemary?"

The Colonel shook his head. "I doubt it. But read it—then we will talk."

To a point, the letters were similar, Yolande informing her cousins that she had departed for Scotland and would spend the summer at her grandfather's home in Ayrshire. The closing paragraphs, however, were quite different.

Craig's letter ended:

> I am most pleased that I was given the opportunity to meet you, and I take this opportunity to once again express my thanks for your gallant efforts in my behalf. You will, I am assured, have returned to Canada by the time I come back to Sussex. I wish you Godspeed in your long journey.
>
> Although we have been acquainted for so short a time, I think you may be interested to know that I expect to be married this year, and thus, by the time we meet again shall probably no longer sign myself,
>
> Yr. affectionate cousin,
> Yolande Drummond

Devenish, meanwhile, read:

> Papa has only now told me the true facts concerning your father's tragic death. I was never more shocked. As you know, I have always deplored violence, and I send you my sincerest sympathies, dear Dev. I can only beg you to allow the past to remain so.
>
> On a happier note, I mean to discuss our formal betrothal with my grandfather and, in the event that nothing untoward occurs by the time I return to Sussex, and if it is still your wish, I think we should at that time fix upon a date for the wedding. Until then, I remain,
>
> Yr. affectionate cousin,
> Yolande

His lady's willingness to pick a date for their wedding had the effect of lifting a great weight from Devenish's spirits. It was silly, of course, but lately he had been haunted by the fear that although she was undeniably fond of him, she meant to cry off. That terrifying spectre could now be banished forever, thank the Lord! He thought absently that he must buy a ring for the sweet chit; and that it would never do for her to jaunter about the countryside without his escort. The reference to his father's death shadowed his joy, however. He had always understood that Stuart Devenish had died as the result of a fall, and that the shock had caused his wife to miscarry and soon follow both her husband and stillborn child to the grave. A most frightful tragedy for two young lives to have been so suddenly ended, and a third never quite begun. But why Yolande should have been upset by it at this late date was as inexplicable as her remark anent allowing "the past to remain so."

Baffled, he glanced up, and was further disconcerted to find both his cousin and his uncle watching him.

Craig, his own hopes shattered, asked quietly, "Have I to offer you my congratulations, coz?"

"No law says you must, but I'll accept 'em, with thanks. Sir"—he turned blithely to the Colonel—"since Craig has proven to be out of leading strings and does not stand in need of my aid, with your permission I shall go and instruct my man to pack a valise."

"But you have *not* my permission."

Devenish had already started to the door and he swung around saying a surprised, "What? But, sir, you surely understand that I must go and—"

"And pester your betrothed? I see no reason for it."

The tone was unwontedly harsh. Taken aback, Devenish said, "Pester her? Why—no, I hope I will not—"

"I am informed on the best authority that Yolande is escorted by three outriders, is followed by her maid and personal groom, and accompanied by Mrs. Arabella."

"Oh, no! That prosing antidote? And if Aunty took her revolting animal along, poor Yolande will be driven to distraction. I must—"

"Learn to refrain from speaking disparagingly of a lady?" snapped his uncle.

Again shocked by that unfamiliarly cold voice, Devenish flushed scarlet. "I did not mean— That is, I intended no— Oh, gad, sir! You know very well that the woman is insupportable."

"To the contrary. I know that whatever her small failings, she is devoted to her niece. Now, have you by any chance forgot there was more to Yolande's letter than the matter of your betrothal?"

Stunned, Devenish returned to his chair. "No, sir. My apologies."

Colonel Tyndale thought, "Dammit, there was no call to hurt the boy!" And knowing his harshness was born of a dread of the next few minutes, he drew a hand across his brow and muttered, "I'm sorry if I spoke with unnecessary heat, Dev. But Yolande had told me part of what she intended to write, and I'll own I don't relish telling you of it."

Much embarrassed, Craig came to his feet. "You will be wishing for your privacy, sir. I am the one should go. Besides, I've a long journey before me and might as well get started."

"Journey?" echoed Devenish suspiciously. "To where, may I ask?"

"Why, it seems I have inherited my father's home in Ayrshire. I hope I may find it, but—"

"You mean Castle Tyndale?" Devenish sprang up, his eyes sparking. "The devil! That's less than ten miles from Steep Drummond! And I suppose you'd no idea you would be following the same route as my lady, had you?"

Craig's head tilted back a fraction, and his eyelids assumed a bored droop. "Since you appear to be betrothed to the lady, I fail to see your concern. No gentleman could approach her under such circumstances."

"No gentleman!" flared Devenish. "Why, you slippery Captain Sharp, you'll not pursue her while I live to prevent it! If you really seek your blasted inheritance, I'll ride with you, and let me tell you—"

"You—will—do—no—such—thing!" thundered the Colonel, standing and suddenly looking to be seven feet tall. "Sit down! Both of you!"

When his two dismayed nephews had complied, he went to the sideboard, fortified himself with a glass of cognac, and strode back to the mantel, blinking a little because of the unaccustomed haste with which he had swallowed the strong liquor. For a moment he stood there, swirling the brandy in his glass and frowning down at it. "You will not like what I have to tell you," he said slowly. "It should have been told long since, but from the contents of your solicitor's letter, Craig, I collect you have never been informed, and I'll own I have kept the truth from you, Alain." He looked deliberately from one apprehensive young face to the other, and sighed. "You were aware that my brother and sister were twins," he began. "I suppose of the two of us boys, I resembled my father more closely. I was the stolid plodder, while Jonas was

57

handsome and light-hearted, but with the devil's own temper—always into some mischief or other. Despite our different natures, we were deeply attached, but between Esme, your mother, Dev, and Jonas, Craig's father, there was a bond such as I have seldom seen between brother and sister."

Devenish said, "I knew they were twins, of course. And I believe you said they looked alike."

"Very much. Your mama was a singularly beautiful girl. I remember . . ." The Colonel frowned, his eyes becoming remote and sad. "I remember Jonas bragging that with her looks his twin would wed no less than a duke, and even he would scarce be good enough for her!"

"Instead of which," Devenish put in, "she married the younger son of an impoverished house. Her twin must not have thought much of my papa, eh, sir?"

Alastair's sombre gaze drifted to him. "Jonas was furious, and did all in his power to prevent the match. He even appealed to my father, but by that time—" He shrugged. "He was such a wild young rascal. He had already been out twice, and was obliged to flee the country and stay abroad for six months as a consequence of one of those meetings."

"Killed his man, did he, sir?" asked Devenish, his eyes sparkling. "By thunder, but he must have been a dynamic fellow! I wish I might have seen a likeness of him."

Craig threw a faintly bored glance at him. The Colonel, vexed by the interruption, said, "You would have, save that my father had every trace of Jonas destroyed, or so he thought. Esme kept a miniature of him, and after her death I acquired it." He walked to the small table beside his chair and opened the drawer. "I intend to bequeath it to you, Craig. But I will ask that you allow me to keep it until my death." He looked down at the small painting with wistful eyes, then held it out.

Craig glanced at it, his own eyes enigmatic. "I have a larger one in Canada. Thank you, sir."

The Colonel's brows lifted slightly, but without comment he handed the miniature to Devenish.

The result was a breathless exclamation. Paling, Devenish gazed down at a man that, save for the style of dress, might have been himself. The fair curling hair, the wideset deep blue eyes alight with laughing impudence, the straight nose and sensitive mouth were almost identical. Only in the set of the chin was there a difference; Devenish's inclined to be more square than that of his long-dead uncle. "The resemblance," he gasped, "is—is—"

"Uncanny." The Colonel nodded, retrieving the miniature and gazing at it. "I told you they were twins, and you take after your mama, rest her soul." He glanced at Craig, wondering if the boy might resent that close resemblance, but the strong face was without expression.

Devenish asked, "Sir, what happened? If the attachment between my mother and her twin was as deep as you say, I would have thought Uncle Jonas could have influenced her against the marriage."

"Do not imagine that he did not try." Tyndale replaced the miniature in the drawer and closed it, but remained standing, hands linked behind him, facing these two so dissimilar young men, and dreading what he must tell them. "Perhaps the most ironic thing about it," he went on, "was that Jonas had introduced them, for all through school and University, Stuart Devenish was his dearest friend. Jonas reproached himself bitterly for that, but it was too late; Esme adored her brother, but she had her share of spirit and determination, and nothing would sway her from Stuart. She told me once that the instant she laid eyes on him, her heart was given. And I am very sure it was the same with him. They delayed their wedding, hoping Jonas would come home for the ceremony, but he refused, and they were married in his absence. A year later, Alain was born. Jonas was still in Belgium. When he did return he seemed less vindictive towards Stuart. It was not his way to hold a grudge, for he was all fury one minute and sweet contrition the next, so I began to hope the breach might be mended. During Jonas's absence, Stuart's elder brother had been killed in a racing accident and Stuart had inherited Devencourt, the family's country seat in Gloucestershire. My dear sister delighted in the house, but she had never forgotten our happy days in Scotland, and it was there that you were born, Alain. You were at Castle Tyndale again when you were nearing your first birthday, and when Jonas came back from Belgium I told him I meant to journey to Ayrshire for the occasion. I could scarce have been more pleased when he agreed to accompany me."

He paused, smiling nostalgically. "Shall I ever forget that reunion? Stuart had been deeply troubled by the quarrel and was more than willing to let bygones be bygones, but I'll own I was a little apprehensive. My father was ailing, and was at that time dwelling in Cornwall because of the milder climate.

59

He had already announced the disposition of his estates. Because of his impatience with his heir, Aspenhill, which should by rights have gone to Jonas, had been deeded over to me, and Jonas was the legal owner of Castle Tyndale. As a result, he had every right to demand that Stuart leave. However, he marked the resemblance immediately he saw you, Alain, and when he learned they had named you after him, he was so proud it was— I see I have surprised you, Craig. Your cousin is called Alain Jonas Devenish, you were unaware, eh? Your own middle name is Winters, you said?''

Craig drawled with a touch of irony, ''To be precise, sir, Craig Stuart Winters Tyndale.''

''Now—by thunder!'' muttered the Colonel. ''So the affection held true—in spite of everything.''

Eager to hear the rest of the story, Devenish prompted, ''Not so unusual, surely? They had been friends in childhood and were now brothers-in-law. But something occurred to disturb this truce, did it, sir?''

Behind his back, the Colonel's hands tightened. ''Yes. The castle. Ah, you may well look surprised, but Jonas was possessed of odd fancies at times. He had always disliked the place, and had told me on several occasions that he never would live there, and that our father had given it to him out of malice because it was haunted; as indeed, legend has it. He could not be easy there, and once—God! Why did I not heed him?—he said he felt the Sword of Damocles poised above his head, and he had best get back to town before it fell!''

He was silent, lips tightly gripped together, eyes gazing into a past that only he could see. Watching him, Craig saw the gleam of sweat on the high forehead, and his own inner apprehension deepened.

''About a week after the birthday party,'' the Colonel resumed, ''Esme became slightly unwell. She was increasing, and at first none of us was too much concerned. It was just a cold, she said. But she was slow to recover. Jonas blamed the climate and asked Stuart if he could take Esme back to Town. In point of fact, I doubt his fears were justified. It was cold, but it was a dry cold, lacking London's penetrating dampness, and it was my impression that my sister throve in the place. Jonas, however, became more and more worried.''

''Was my father not concerned at all, sir?'' Devenish asked curiously.

''He was willing that Esme should come back to Town. He worshipped her and would have done anything she desired.

60

But Esme wanted her child to be born in Scotland. As I said, she was a strong-minded girl, and she only laughed at what she called Jonas's 'fey fancies.' As the weeks went by, Jonas grew more and more irked by Stuart's refusal to order his wife to leave Castle Tyndale, and I must admit I also was becoming anxious for Esme's welfare. Jonas began to sneer that Stuart dwelt under the cat's foot—that sort of nonsensical talk. It was I think inspired partly by worry for your mama, Dev, and partly by his own fear of the castle. Fortunately, Stuart's disposition was amiable, and he could usually tease Jonas out of his dismals. But one day . . .''

Again he paused. The room was hushed, and the soft rain which had begun to fall sounded very loud as it pattered against the window. The cousins exchanged an uneasy glance, already half guessing what was to come.

"Stuart," the Colonel said heavily, "loved the sea, and it was his habit to go up to the battlements every day, weather permitting, and look out over the cliffs. He was there one afternoon when Jonas came to me in great agitation, saying that Esme had fainted in her dressing room, and that with or without her consent he intended to take her down to London at once and place her under the care of a most excellent physician. I was alarmed, naturally, and I made haste to my sister's room, while Jonas went rushing in search on Stuart. I found Esme laid down upon her bed, with her woman fussing over her. I could hear Jonas and Stuart shouting. I remember thinking, 'My God! What a time to quarrel with poor little Esme lying here so ill!' and I started up to the battlements to try to quiet them.''

His voice shredded, and when he resumed his tale, he spoke in so low a tone that his hearers were obliged to lean forward to hear him. "There is," he said, "a side stair that winds up around the northwest tower. And there are occasional windows . . . narrow, and very deep." He turned abruptly, to stand with head down and shoulders hunched. "I see it . . . still . . . So terrible. A sudden—darkness, passing the window. And this—this awful, despairing scream . . .''

White as death, Devenish sprang up. "God in heaven! Sir—what are you saying? Was my father—*murdered?*''

For an interminable moment, the Colonel did not answer. Surreptitiously, he dragged his handkerchief from his pocket and wiped it across his face. With a deep, quivering breath, he turned to face them again, his lean features drawn and haggard. "We found Jonas lying in a dead faint on the battlements. For two days he was as one in a daze; quite unable to tell us what had happened. When he at last could speak of it, he admitted he had flown into a passion and warned Stuart he would hold him personally responsible if anything happened to Esme. Stuart, it seems, turned on him at last, and demanded he cease frightening his sister with his morbid imaginings." The Colonel sighed. "I knew Jonas so well. It would have taken no more to inflame him."

"And because—because of that perfectly justifiable remark," gasped Devenish, "he flung my father from the parapet?"

"He swore he did not. He said he struck Stuart with his open hand only, and at once repented the blow, but that Stuart leapt back, stumbled, and fell."

His fists clenched, Devenish admitted reluctantly, "I suppose that—could be so."

The Colonel said nothing.

Watching him tensely, Craig probed, "There is more, I think, sir?"

"How I wish there were not," groaned the Colonel. "Some of the men Jonas had set to clearing debris from the beach saw Stuart fall. They insisted he had not stumbled, but that they had distinctly seen him hurtle backward as though violently pushed. That he had, in fact, been struck with such force he'd had no chance to catch at the battlements or attempt to save himself, but had soared straight back and down, to his death."

His face set into a grim mask, Devenish fought rage and horror, to ask brusquely, "But the battlements are crenellated, are they not?"

"True, lad. But the crenels atop Castle Tyndale reach to the floor." The Colonel glanced at Craig. "A crenel is the space between the merlons atop battlements. In many instances, the crenels are constructed a few feet from the floor."

"But at Castle Tyndale," Devenish rasped, "they have no lower wall. My poor father had not even that slight chance of saving himself."

The Colonel pointed out miserably, "It would not have helped, Dev."

Devenish swore and turned a contorted face to his cousin. The Colonel was also watching Craig, and he was startled when the bowed head was raised to reveal the cheeks streaked with tears. "I wish," the Canadian said painfully, "I only wish to God—I had *known*."

"Well, *I* know!" Devenish stood and glared down at him. "From the first moment I saw you, I loathed you! I thought it was because you had hurt Yolande. And later, I supposed it was because of the way you ogled her! But it goes far deeper! Your miserable wretch of a father murdered mine! And the hatred between us is—"

Craig had also come to his feet, his expression only a little less enraged than that of his cousin. "Foul-mouthed clod! What proof have you of his guilt?"

"It was proven long ago! Murder, cousin! Murder most hideous! And I swear that I—"

"*Be still!* Both of you!"

Colonel Tyndale's cry knifed across that savage room. Devenish flung around to face him, rebellion written clearly in his face. Craig started and drew a hand across his wet brow.

"By your leave—*gentlemen*," the Colonel said angrily, "I will finish my unhappy tale and be done with it!" The cousins remaining silent, he went on, "Within two months of the tragedy, my beloved sister suffered a miscarriage and died. The doctor tried to ease the blow by saying she would have died in childbed at all events. It was untrue. Esme had lost all will to live. When Stuart was killed, her heart broke. The most . . . pitiful thing was that"—his voice became husky with emotion again—"that she blamed *herself*!" That sweet, gentle child who was born to love and to be loved. If she had not wed in the face of Jonas' opposition, she used to cry, if she had only obeyed him—none of it would have happened. But that was not the truth of it!"

He paced to stand before Devenish and glare at him until his nephew recoiled a step, his own fury giving way to consternation. "The crime—if such it was," the Colonel grated, "grew from my brother's ungovernable temper! And be warned, Dev! *I will not* stand by and see it happen again! So help me, God, I swear it!"

Devenish said a cautious, "Surely, you are confused, sir! It was Stuart Devenish, *my* father, who was foully murdered. It is Craig on whom your wrath—"

"No! It is very apparent to me that Craig has little of Jonas in him. *You* are the one has inherited that unpredictable temperament!" He jabbed a finger at his aghast nephew and accused, "You—as I told you at the start—take after your mama. My brother's twin. In you, I see again his undisciplined impetuosity, his fierce pride and swift rages. I have

63

struggled these twenty years and more to break you of those tendencies. I have watched irresponsibility drive you from one disaster to the next. I'll not now stand by and see you exact vengeance upon your innocent cousin! No, by God! Sooner would I have you clapped up in Bedlam!''

Devenish gasped and, shaking his head speechlessly, shrank away until he stood against the wall, staring with stricken eyes at this relentless stranger he had known so many years, and knew not at all. "But—but, Uncle," he faltered, "you know—you *must* know that I never deliberately— I mean, a few practical jokes, I—I admit. But I would not—intentionally—really hurt anyone, save in self-defence.''

"No more, I doubt," Craig's quiet drawl intervened, "did my father."

Two distraught faces jerked towards him. The Colonel exclaimed, "You knew all of this?"

"I would to God I had! I might have understood him better. I might even have been able to help him.''

Colonel Tyndale stepped closer. Devenish did not move, but demanded, "Then what do you mean?"

Craig looked from one to the other, and asked hesitantly, "How old—do you suppose me to be?"

Watching the Canadian narrowly, the Colonel said, "Three and twenty, though I'll own you appear older.''

"I am twenty-eight.''

"That's not possible!" flared Devenish. "Unless—" With a surprising degree of eagerness, he asked, "Do you tell us you are adopted? That you were my uncle's stepson, perhaps?"

"No. I do not say that. You remarked, sir, that my father was obliged to flee the country because of a duel, just before his twin married Stuart Devenish. My mother was the cause of that duel.''

"Was she, by thunder!" breathed the Colonel. "He knew her—*then?*''

"She was his wife.''

"That is not possible, by God! Jonas may have been ramshackle, but he'd not—I cannot believe that he—" The Colonel checked, scowled, drew a bewildered hand across his brow, and groaned. "He *would!* Devil take him! I loved the young fool, but . . . he would! And yet—why the secrecy? Was she—your pardon, boy, I mean no disrespect but—was she—''

"Rankly ineligible?" With a prideful smile, Craig said, "She was fair as the morning, my father used to say. A tall, softly spoken, serene lady. The daughter of a—Yankee merchant." He heard a muffled exclamation from Colonel Tyndale and went on scornfully, "She was everything any man could ask in a wife, but my father knew well what his family would think. The daughter of a foreigner. Worse, a foreigner engaged in trade. No background; no title; no ancient name! He was already in deep disgrace. It was more than he dared do to acknowledge his marriage at that time; his father would have cut him off without a penny. Always, he hoped to redeem himself. He used to tell my mother that if he could win the old gentleman over, he would broach the marriage to him, gradually, and that once my grandfather met Mama, and me, he would have to acknowledge us."

"But . . ." faltered the Colonel, "the—duel . . .?"

"A rascally acquaintance of my father's discovered that Mama was, as he thought, Papa's mistress. My mother had been sent to Paris for 'a European finish' prior to wedding a wealthy man of her father's choosing. The aunt to whom she was entrusted knew of the marriage, but had agreed to keep it secret." He frowned, and said thoughtfully, "I think she was not very wise. Be that as it may, this rascal threatened blackmail. When Father threw him out, he came to England. My mother was beside herself with fear. She was sure the old gentleman would disown him, and if they were both cut off, she did not know how we could live. Her terror enraged my father. He followed the man to England and, before he could speak with Grandfather, called him out and shot him. It was a fair fight, sir. You may remember that my father was wounded in the encounter?"

"Yes, I . . . good heavens!" said the Colonel, still amazed by these disclosures. "Then—you must have been . . . three years old when Alain was born?"

"About that, sir."

"All very interesting," put in Devenish, brusquely, "but I'm damned if I see what it has to do with your belief that he was innocent of my father's murder."

"After we went to Canada," Craig explained, "he was a man tormented. Often I heard my mother striving to comfort him. The truth was kept from me, but I did know that he had been forbidden ever to return to England, or even to use his family name, and as boys will, I imagined all manner of terrible crimes lurked in his past. Mama knew, but she never spoke of it to me. I watched my father age long before his time. Always, he was homesick and flayed by conscience. I sup-

65

pose it proved more than the poor man could bear. He took refuge in drink, and I—all prideful intolerance—despised him for it. The lower he sank, the deeper was my mother's grief, and the more I—May God forgive me! If only I had known!''

The Colonel shook his head. ''You were not to blame, boy. Do not scourge yourself.''

''I could have been more understanding,'' Craig muttered. ''He had so many fine qualities, I should have reasoned that—'' He cut off that useless grieving and drew his shoulders back. ''In some things, we do not get a second chance, do we, sir?''

''No,'' the Colonel sighed. ''Is this why you feel Jonas was innocent? Guilty men can be flayed by conscience too, you know.''

''True. But once, in one of his bad moments, I heard him tell my mother repeatedly that he was not guilty of something. I knew from his manner that it must have been something very bad.'' He hesitated, as if reluctant to continue, then added, ''I do not know how it was in his youth, but all my life I found him a deeply religious man. I—I confess that it disgusted me. To see him in his cups on Saturday night, and at church first thing on Sunday. I did not—understand. But I do know that he believed in God, and felt that there is another life beyond this one. I was in the room when he lay dying, and the Vicar asked him to repent his sins. My father roused and said, quite proudly, 'The worst sin of which I was ever accused, I did not commit.'''

Craig paused, looked into his uncle's intent face, and said earnestly, ''I suppose, naïve though I was, I loved my father, and could not bear to see him—as he became. But, I *did* know him, sir. And I know he would not have lied at such a moment. I will take my oath that my father did not intentionally cause his brother's death, Devenish—'' He stopped. Devenish was gone.

Chapter Five

"I can only beg of you," said Mrs. Arabella Drummond, absently stroking the dog who sprawled beside her on the rocking carriage seat, "to put the matter quite out of your mind. I believe Dr. Jester to be a very fine man. You will recall, my love, that when I took that horrid chill last winter, he was so obliging as to come to the house in the middle of a most frightful storm."

Her nerves rather strained, Yolande pointed out, "He thought you had the pneumonia."

"Yes." Her aunt giggled. "It was naughty of Sullivan to give him that impression, though she was motivated by loyalty to me, you know, and I am sure that as a physician and healer, he must only have been glad I had instead nothing worse than a cold. I think I must have been *close* to pneumonia, however, for I suffered so that poor Sullivan thought it would put a period to me. But Dr. Jester's medicine—though it tasted ghastly! I wonder why medicine must always taste ghastly . . .? Not that that is either here or there, of course. The medicine was most efficacious, and I particularly recall that the doctor was not in the least irked, in spite of being so young a man, and having drove such a distance. And only think, my naughty boy bit him when he came up to my bed!" She pulled the fox terrier's ear, and cooed, *"What* a scamp you are, to be sure!"

Socrates opened one eye and peered around to discover if it was time to eat. Disappointed, he lay down his head and went back to sleep.

Her attention having wandered, Yolande made no comment. Mrs. Drummond slipped her hand into her muff once more, tilted her head, and frowned. "I do not think that was quite the point I had meant to make."

"We were speaking of Rosemary," said Yolande, stifling a yawn.

"So we were. And although you may think Jester is young and inexperienced, and only a country doctor after all, for I agree he is not to be thought of in the same breath as Lord Belmont, still, I do not doubt his ability to recognize measles when he sees it. It was so silly of Nurse to frighten us all by saying it might be the Pox! Why, I knew very well that could not be, for I distinctly recall that when I was a child . . .''

Again, Yolande's attention drifted. The journey had been slow and although they had left Park Parapine before noon, they had not yet reached Tunbridge Wells. The carriage was cumbersome and not speedy at best, and their stops at various stages to change teams did not, it would seem, coincide with the needs of Socrates, thus making it necessary that more stops be undertaken. At this rate, it would take well over a week to reach Grandpapa's great house. That prospect did not particularly distress her, but she felt oddly heavy-hearted, probably because of leaving her friends and family; or perhaps because Aunt Arabella was not a very enlivening companion. She closed her ears to that lady's unending stream of chatter and at once her thoughts flashed to her new cousin. They did so of late with a frequency that was most disquieting. Therefore, instead of resolutely striving to oust him from her mind, she decided to assess the matter. Dispassionately. And thus reduce it to the proportions it deserved.

Mr. Craig Winters Tyndale, she concluded, had little to recommend him. Aside from his gallantry in having come to her rescue, and the fact that he was a superb horseman, he had a fine athletic figure, an excellent leg, and a pair of shoulders that would probably cause most tailors to exclaim with joy. But, even were Devenish not so well featured as to cast any other man into the shade, Mr. Tyndale could not be termed handsome. She thrust away the image of a pair of long-lashed grey eyes and hastened to the next point in her evaluation. Tyndale was of a more reserved nature than his ebullient cousin. He was also, to a great extent, an unknown quantity; why, one did not even know where the Colonial gentleman had gone to school! As for fortune, Papa had said he could aspire to a modest competence left him by the grandfather he had never met, and an estate in Scotland, dominated by a castle that had stood lonely, and largely unoccupied, since Stuart Devenish's tragic death there. She had never been inside the castle, but she had seen it often and it had always seemed to her to be a fairy-tale place, soaring as it did at the cliff edge, its conical towers rising high above the battlements and sometimes the only parts visible above the mists that drifted in from the sea. She sighed dreamily. What a romantic setting for a deeply in love couple starting their married—

Shocked by a sudden awareness of such impractical digressions, she returned to her clinical appraisal. Cousin Craig had burst into her life like a comet. A rather blinding comet, although one had to face the fact that her initial attraction to him had been founded in gratitude and admiration. (Hadn't it?) She frowned at an inoffensive hayrick they were passing. She *was* attracted to him. And that was perfectly dreadful and must not be encouraged! Much as she might yearn for romance, she was not a foolish girl. She was bound by invisible but very real ties to a man she had known all her life. Devenish was not vastly wealthy, but he had inherited the respectable fortune his papa had not lived to enjoy. He owned a large and beautiful, if somewhat neglected, estate in Gloucestershire that could, with very little effort, become a showplace. He was both loved and approved of by her parents, to whom the match represented the culmination of years of joyous anticipation. Mrs. Alain Devenish . . . Her eyes softened. Dear Dev; so staunch and fearless for all his harum-scarum ways. How many girls adored him? How many men thought him the best of good fellows? And he was! Despite his swift temper and fierce jealousies, he loved her with all his honest heart, and would care for and cherish her all her life. If she allowed him. And if, being such a romantic figure (as Mama had pointed out), he had no thought of romance, why it was a small fault surely. If one truly loved a man.

A pair of fine grey eyes again played havoc with her precise common sense. Eyes so full of tenderness . . . She thought in desperation, "Very well, dear sir. If intrude you must—what have *you* to offer me?"

The answer was immediate. An inevitable duel between him and Devenish, with consequences that could not be less than disastrous for all concerned. More tragedy for Colonel Alastair, and the dear man had already known too much of tragedy. Grief for her parents, who hoped she would make not only a good match but one that would not be tainted by scandal. And as for herself, removal from the family she loved and the only way of life she knew; a new home which, despite her romantical imaginings, actually consisted of a mouldering castle perched on a cliff and (understandably!) rumoured to be haunted; and a future in which loneliness and poverty went hand in hand. She had a mental picture of herself, a bucket in one hand and a mop in the other, toiling at an endless flight of clammy stone stairs, while Craig dug turnips from the stony ground, preparatory to entertaining Grandpapa to dinner. Horrors! she thought, shuddering.

"Why, you naughty little puss! Here have I been prosing on and on, and I do believe you've attended me for not one single minute!"

Seldom had Yolande been more relieved to be wrenched back to the here and now. She sat up straighter and turned a repentant face. "Oh, but I assure you, Aunt, I heard all you said. I do apologize for allowing my attention to wander, but—er, it is this black chaise that comes up so quickly behind us. I have been watching it reflected in the brass of the lamps. Do you suppose the driver means to pass? He seems very impatient."

Mrs. Drummond turned to the window. "Good heavens! I trust he has not that intent, for the road is much too narrow. But—oh, my! Indeed, it seems he does mean— A gentleman, driving his own chaise. No! He must not! Oh, sir! Stay, I beg!" These dramatics were accompanied by alarmed little gestures, culminating in a desperate flapping of her muff at the approaching driver, who paid her not the least heed, but as he drew level, glanced with sardonic amusement into the carriage.

The glance became an intent stare. He removed his tall beaver and bowed his dark head with patent admiration.

Yolande ignored him, and the chaise shot past, pulling in before them just barely in time to avoid the Royal Mail that thundered around the bend of the road and made its stentorian way southwards.

"How very rag-mannered," Mrs. Drummond exclaimed with justifiable indignation. "Did you know him, Yolande?" And, contradictorily, "He doffed his hat to us. Such pretty curls. I was ever fond of a dark-haired gentleman, and especially one so well favoured. He looked familiar. I wonder who he can be."

"Now how can this be, dear Aunt?" Yolande teased. "The gentleman is one of Prinny's particular cronies and was, until her recent betrothal, most assiduous in his pursuit of Lisette Van Lindsay."

"What? That high-in-the-instep creature? I vow I was never more amused than to hear she is to wed Justin Strand. I can scarce wait to meet her starched-up mama and offer my felicitations. Everyone *knows* the poor girl was as good as

70

sold to that nobody on account of her papa's debts. Ah! Now I have it! Our Mr. Impatience is no less than Mr. James Garvey, no? A most desirable *parti* for any lady of the *ton*, and if I dare be so bold as to venture my humble opinion, my love, a far more appropriate suitor for you than young Devenish. And I will own I could not like the way Mr. Winters, or Tyndale, or however one is now supposed to address him, was looking at you when I came upon you both in the small saloon the other day. Not that there could be anything to *that*, of course, for the man is beyond the pale, entirely. Nonetheless, dearest, I must caution you against ever giving cause to be thought fast.'' She glanced to each side as though eager dowagers clung to the exterior of the carriage, ears straining to hear what went on inside. ''I know your dear mama,'' she said, for once picking up the threads of her monologue where she had left them, ''has done all in her power to instruct you, but—''

A stormy light had begun to gather in Yolande's green eyes, so that it was perhaps fortunate that Socrates chose this moment to sit up and by means of a series of piercing yelps, yowls, and shrieks, make known his desire to alight. Mrs. Drummond sighed that she also would appreciate a respite from this eternal driving, and since Yolande was beginning to feel the pangs of hunger, it was decided to stop for luncheon at a charming old posting house called The Little Nut Tree that lay just ahead.

Mine host hurried onto the front steps of the thatch-roofed structure to greet so luxurious a carriage, and when he perceived the three outriders and liveried coachman and groom, his eyes lit up. The arrival of the second carriage which conveyed the luggage and the abigails of the ladies, brought visions of enormous largesse, and mine host was happy indeed.

The Little Nut Tree was a welcoming establishment that shone with cleanliness. The ladies were shown to a bright chamber under the eaves, where they refreshed themselves before going down to the private parlour where Yolande had required that a light luncheon be served. At the foot of the stairs, the host awaited them, all apologies. His good wife, quite unbeknownst to himself, had already promised the parlour to another traveller. It was unforgivable, beyond words distressing, but the coffee room was unoccupied at the moment. There was a pleasant corner from which the ladies could observe the gardens, and he would see to it that they were not in any way disturbed during their luncheon.

At this point, a cool voice intervened, "Nonsense, host. I am acquainted with these ladies."

Yolande turned to encounter a pair of eyes as green as her own that smiled down at her. "Mr. Garvey," she murmured, inclining her head slightly and holding out her hand. "I believe you have not the acquaintance of my aunt. Mrs. Drummond, allow me to present Mr. James Garvey. The gentleman who swept past us at such a rate a little while ago."

Mr. Garvey was delighted to meet Mrs. Drummond, and made her an impressive bow. He was, he vowed, devastated to think he might have startled two such lovely ladies by driving very fast along the highway. It was his habit; admittedly reckless. And as for their being compelled to dine in the coffee room, such a thing was not to be thought of. Save for his servants, he was travelling alone, and they would be granting a solitary gentleman a great favour would they consent to share the parlour with him.

Yolande hesitated. She knew Mr. Garvey only slightly, but they moved in the same circles, and she had from time to time attended functions at which he was also a guest. No one could deny that he was of the first stare: His birth was impeccable, his close friendship with the Prince opened useful doors to him, he was extremely good-looking, still a bachelor at five and thirty, and his fortune far from contemptible. Indeed, one wondered that the Van Lindsay family, in dire financial straits, had not jumped at the chance when he had shown an interest in their daughter. The fact that they had instead chosen a wealthy young man of dubious lineage had puzzled Yolande, and she had wondered at the time if some whispers anent Mr. Garvey's reputation were well founded. Mrs. Drummond suffered no such qualms. She was charmed by his smile and what she later described as a most insinuating address, and she signified in a lengthy speech that they would be very willing to accept Mr. Garvey's generous offer since a common coffee room was not a proper place for Miss Drummond of Park Parapine to sit down to luncheon.

Yolande waited patiently through the ponderous monologue. Looking up, she found Mr. Garvey watching her with an understanding twinkle in his eyes. She had known from the start, of course, that her aunt was not going to be an altogether salubrious companion, and it occurred to her that their having met up with this polished gentleman might not be such a bad thing, after all.

With hands loosely clasped between his knees and head down bent, Alain Devenish sat on the bench in the shrubbery and contemplated a very small yellow caterpillar that was busily engaged in inching its way up a strand of grass. He had known there was tragedy in the early deaths of his parents, but he'd not dreamed how stark that tragedy was, nor that it had touched so many lives. He was not a young man much given to introspection, being quite willing to travel whatever path Fate offered, and accepting good-humouredly, if not resignedly, any buffets that came his way. He was not insensitive, however, and his heart was wrung by the picture of his young and lovely mother grieving herself into an early grave following the loss of her husband. "Poor little soul," he thought, and could not but wonder how his life might have been changed had she lived. The influence of a gentle lady might have softened his nature. Perhaps he would not now be scorned as a person of "undisciplined impetuosity and swift rages." He flinched a little. Devilish accurate with his lances was the Old Nunks.

His tiny acquaintance had by this time found its way to the top of the strand of grass, and stopped. "Now what are you going to do, foolish creature?" Devenish enquired. "There is nothing for it but to go down again. Had you a single brain in your head, you would know that!" The caterpillar paid him no heed. Probably, he decided, because it had *no* brains in its head. It was better off in such a deprived state. If one had brains, one cared about people. And just when one least expected it—just when one might, in fact, have felt in need of a little sympathy and support—those same people turned on one like angry serpents. "I have struggled these twenty years and more . . . I have watched your irresponsibility drive you from one disaster to the next. . . ." The fair head ducked lower. It was true, of course. And Uncle Alastair had been angry before. Very angry. But had not glared with such a look—a look almost of . . . contempt. . . .

"He loves you, you know."

Devenish frowned at the quiet drawl. Not looking up, he growled, "I came out here to get away from you."

"I know." Craig settled his shoulders against a convenient birch tree and folding his arms, said, "Still, I must talk with you."

Devenish sneered, "I wonder you dare. Are you forgetting that I have inherited your father's murderous inclinations?"

"That is not possible."

"Devil it ain't! You saw the likeness the moment we met. At the time I thought it was impudence when you stared so. But it was shock, was it not?" He had brought a frown to those controlled features and, bitterly hurt, wanting only to hurt in turn, laughed. "Was you afraid, cousin? Did you fear I might seek vengeance for my youthful, slaughtered father, my heart-broken mother?"

"No."

"I'd be within my rights, by God, but I would! Yet—you heard him. *You* have the taint of murder in your veins. But *I* am the one from whom people will shrink in horror! I am the one who is—his greatest trial!" He swung his head away, but Craig noted how his hand gripped the bench until the knuckles gleamed white. And with sudden and unexpected sympathy, he offered, "He has cared for you for twenty years; naturally, he—"

"I need no reminders of that, damn you!" Devenish jerked around to reveal a haggard face and eyes that blazed. "You likely think me too selfish to be aware of my uncle's self-sacrifice, eh?"

"Yes."

"Well, blast your smuggery, I am *not* unaware! I have disappointed him a hundred times—and worried him twice that often, belike. But I'll repay him, never doubt it! He is growing old, but his old age will not be lonely, I do assure you."

"Nonsense!"

With a swift, fluid movement, Devenish came to his feet. "Your *pardon?*"

"He is not old. I doubt he's much past forty."

"Five and forty, if you must know, Master Impudence."

"And have you never noticed, my Lord Arrogance, how fine looking a man he is? What he needs is a loving wife—not a repentant would-be martyr."

For a moment Devenish was so taken aback that hurt and rage left him and he stared his astonishment. Then, "*M-marry?*" he gasped. "Uncle *Alastair?* Damme, but you *are* wits to let! I might have known you sought me out to mouth some such fustian!"

"Aye, you might!" Pushing himself away from the tree, Craig said a disgusted, "And I might have known you were too set up in your own conceit to listen to aught that did not concern your all-important self!"

Devenish seized his arm. "Confound you! I'll make you eat those words!"

"Yap, puppydog," Craig taunted.

Devenish's fist swung up. Craig's hand flashed to catch his wrist. For an instant they stood there, eye to blazing eye, the Canadian's fair young might straining to hold back the Englishman's slighter but powerful arm. And then, with a sweep, Craig released his grip and moved back.

"Do you see now? D'ye see how easy it would be? I came out here to bid you farewell, and only look at us! Another moment and—"

"And you would have done—what? Murdered me?"

"Did *you* mean to kill *me?* Think, man! Did you?"

"Don't be so blasted ridiculous! Pummel your cloddish head, perhaps. No more. For Lord's sake, Tyndale, do you really believe I've murder in mind?"

"No more than I believe my father had. But this morning when you attacked me—"

"Dash it all, did you fancy your life in danger then?"

"No. But when you tricked me and I grassed you, you went down mighty hard, cousin. Suppose your head had hit a rock? With what lies between us, who would have believed I did not deliberately put a period to you?"

Devenish avoided that earnest gaze and said an uneasy, "Very few people know what lies between us."

"It would all come out, certainly. And what would that do to your uncle?" After a brief silence, Craig went on, "I came to tell you that I am leaving. While I am in Scotland, I mean to find out whatever I may about the death of your father. And I swear—so long as I live, should we ever meet again, no matter how you may provoke me, I'll never raise my hand against you!"

For a long moment they stared at one another in a silent measuring, both faces grim until a twinkle dawned in Devenish's eyes. He said, irrepressibly, "How relieved I am. I shall be safe."

Tyndale's lips tightened. "Goodbye, then. I mean to leave at once. I have already sent Montelongo ahead with my chaise and luggage."

Devenish nodded. Craig started off, hesitated, then turned back. "We will not meet again, cousin. Will you not at least say goodbye to me?"

"No need," said Devenish cheerfully, coming up with him. "I ride with you."

"You—*what?* In spite of all I have said, you still think I pursue Cousin Yolande?"

"No. But since you raise the question, I'll have no interference in that quarter."

"Naturally. Unless the lady should—er—change her mind. After all, no formal announcement has yet been made, so she is not irrevocably bound."

"*Bound?* Why, you insolent bumpkin, I—" Devenish burst into a laugh. "Off we go again! Lord, it will be a miracle do we not come to blows before the day is out. But by hedge or stile, I go with you. I mean to prove to my uncle that, however aggravating you may be, I can rise above such petty annoyances. That I can control my—ah—natural instincts and travel beside you, turning the other cheek to your boorish ways and smug fatuities, and maintaining always my usual calm dignity."

Tyndale demonstrated how aggravating he could be. He gave a shout of laughter.

*   *   *

"What a perfectly lovely morning," said Yolande from beneath the protection of her sunshade. "I am so glad you suggested that we walk back to the hotel after church."

Mr. James Garvey directed a glance from the vibrant blooms of the gardens through which they strolled on this balmy Sunday, to the lovely face of the lady beside him, framed as it was in a very dainty high-poked bonnet of cream straw, with pale blue velvet ribbons that tied demurely under her dimpled chin. "I had at first thought we might go for an early ride," he said. "But then I supposed you have had sufficient of riding."

She smiled up at him. "I have indeed. You are a most thoughtful escort, sir."

"It has been my very great pleasure, ma'am. Indeed, I am most gratified you do not visit relations along your way, else I should be sent packing, I do not doubt."

"As a matter of fact, we had intended to, but—" She checked and said a careful, "It is—er—imperative that we reach Ayrshire as quickly as possible, and you know how it is with family—you stop to visit for just a little while, and perhaps have dinner, but they are so eager to entertain you that a week passes in a twinkling. Papa decided it was best that we travel straight on."

"And most fortunate for me."

She blushed prettily. "I am assured you will find a way to

contradict me, sir, but I cannot continue to take you out of your way."

"I should not presume to contradict so lovely a lady, but will point out, rather, that since I also am bound for Scotland, I would certainly travel the Great North Road."

"Yes, but you must have noted, Mr. Garvey, that we do not make rapid progress. You could travel much faster alone."

"And much less happily!" He drew her to a halt. "Miss Drummond, am I encroaching? These past three days have been a delight for me, but I pray you believe that you have only to say the word and I will leave you in peace."

Yolande scanned the anxious features of this most eligible bachelor and could only like what she saw. Rumour had it . . . But rumour was so often based on petty jealousy. He had been more than kind and, while openly admiring, had not once stepped beyond the bounds of good manners. Aunt Arabella was captivated, for Mr. Garvey spared no effort to show her every attention, never—as was so often the case with gentlemen—granting the older lady the barest of civilities while attempting to ingratiate himself with the younger.

"Our journey must have been a great deal more tedious without your many kindnesses, sir," she said. "For instance, our dinner last night and the play were both so enjoyable."

"You are too kind. I had feared the farce might offend your aunt—it was a little broad. But the play was well done, I thought."

Mrs. Drummond had privately expressed herself as considerably scandalized, but Yolande, no mean judge of character, had suspected that both her aunt and Mr. Garvey had by far preferred the rather naughty comedy of the farce to the melodrama of *The Milkmaid's Secret—or—A Tattered Tinker*. She kept these conclusions to herself, however, continuing to chat easily with Mr. Garvey as they made their way along the sun-dappled paths of the little park and thence to thoroughfares busy with open carriages, their elegantly garbed occupants out for a Sunday drive. Several people recognized her companion and waved a greeting. He was very well acquainted, naturally, thought Yolande, and wondered again why he was going to so much trouble to escort two ladies he scarcely knew. Early in their journeying he had said that he was bound for Stirling, but Aunt Arabella had remarked in private that the gentleman was obviously bewitched, and that she would not be in the least surprised did he persist in escorting them all the way to Steep Drummond. Yolande was too level-headed to believe this suave Corinthian was exactly bewitched. It was said sufficient handkerchiefs had been dropped for him that he would stand knee-deep in them were they all gathered around him at once. Still, he was evidently willing to slow his own progress, and she had been sincere when she'd thanked him for relieving the tedium of their journey. His cheerful presence had done much to divert Aunt Arabella's tiresome chatter and had enabled Yolande to relegate her own perplexities to a far corner of her mind—at least during the hours of daylight.

The afternoon was growing warm by the time their walk was concluded, and Mr. Garvey was handing Yolande up the front steps of their hotel when the diminutive and ferocious boy who served him as tiger approached. He was, as always, very smart in his scarlet-and-gold livery, but Mr. Garvey eyed him with just the trace of a frown. The boy, he ruefully admitted to Yolande, had been bred up in the gutter and, despite all his own efforts, still used such language as must shock any gently nurtured lady. Despite this unenthused reception, the tiger knuckled his brow and bestowed a meaningful look on his employer.

"I collect," sighed Mr. Garvey, "you have got into some mischief from which I am now expected to extricate you. Is it something you can manage to convey without offence to the ears of Miss Drummond?"

The tiger glanced at Yolande and hung his head.

Mr. Garvey nodded. "As I suspected. I fear I must investigate at once, ma'am. If I know this rascal I am quite likely to find the town beadle awaiting with a warrant for my immediate arrest! May I have the honour of escorting you down to dinner? Six o'clock? Or is that too countrified?"

Yolande said that six o'clock would be just right, favoured both Mr. Garvey and his tiger, who bore the droll name of Lion, with one of her brightest smiles, and made her way to the suite she shared with her aunt.

"Here I am at last, dear," she said, opening the door to the parlour that separated their rooms. "Have I been—" She checked, and stood motionless on the threshold.

Two young men had sprung up at her entrance. Two men dissimilar in everything save their fair colouring and something indefinable that she had not quite been able to place. Her wide gaze dwelling a shade longer on the taller of the pair, she gasped, "Alain . . .! And—Craig! What on earth . . .?"

78

"Discovered you was here, my fair." Devenish beamed, striding over to claim her hand and drop a proprietary kiss on her brow.

"B-but," she said unsteadily, freeing her hand so as to extend it to Tyndale, "how? That is— I thought—" Her hand being taken and bowed over, she was struck by some invisible lightning bolt and so unnerved that she at once summoned a fierce frown and levelled it at the unfortunate Devenish.

"Oh, but this is too bad of you, Alain. You know full well my parents wished me to be free from all entanglements so that I might—"

"Entanglements, is it?" he protested with righteous indignation. "Now, see here, Yolande, I ain't no entanglement! I've come rushing here purely so as to escort you—"

Striving to appear collected, when he was in fact badly shaken, Craig drawled, "I thought you were escorting *me!*"

"Yes, but Yolande is so much prettier." Yolande was also obviously astounded by this apparently amicable exchange, and Devenish grinned, swung the door to, and imparted, "Ain't no need for you to be in a pucker lest I slaughter our Colonial bumpkin, coz. We have declared a truce. Now why in the world would you do so shatter-brained a thing as to journey to Scotland for the summer?"

"I do not see that it should be judged shatter-brained if I visit my grandpapa." Yolande removed her lacy shawl as she spoke and, Craig, being closest, at once took it from her.

Devenish leapt forward and all but tore the reticule from her hand. "You did not tell me you meant to go!" he complained, with a fierce scowl at Craig.

"No. Nor do I need an escort, Dev."

"'Course you need an escort! A single lady jauntering about—"

Mrs. Drummond made an entrance at this point, hurrying from her bedchamber, proclaiming that she had sent Sullivan out with 'him,' and that he would soon feel better. She gave a little squeak of surprise when she saw Yolande. "Oh! You are come back, love. Did you have a nice walk? Was not the sermon inspiring this morning?" She cast a stern glance at the gentlemen. ' "Vengeance is mine, saith the Lord!' "

Happily misinterpreting the quotation, Devenish soothed, "Do not get up into the boughs, ma'am. Tyndale's becoming accustomed to it."

Puzzled, Yolande asked, "Accustomed to what?"

"Good old Socrates went after some Canadian beef again. Aunt Arabella had to struggle to restrain him."

"Oh, my goodness! That wretched little beast!" Yolande moved to sit beside her aunt on the rather faded sofa. "You really should keep him on a lead, Aunt Arabella."

"No, but it was famous," Devenish exclaimed, blithely ignoring the thoughtful gaze Craig turned upon him. "That was how we discovered you was here."

Mrs. Drummond said a surprised, "You did not know? But I had supposed you were seeking to come up with us."

"No, ma'am." Tyndale settled himself against a side table. "Devenish guides me to my inheritance. At least, he says that is what he's about."

"Your inheritance . . .? Surely you never mean that horrid old haunted castle on the edge of the cliffs?"

"Aunt!" gasped Yolande, her apologetic glance flying to Craig's impassive features. "What a thing to say!"

"It is truth, after all," said Devenish, suddenly grim. "I understand you have been put in possession of all the hideous facts, Yolande?"

"I marvel that you two gentlemen can be so convivial," Mrs. Drummond interposed. "Now in *my* young days—"

"I am delighted you are so *civilized*," Yolande interjected swiftly. And in a desperate attempt to change the subject, "Only think, Aunt, we shall now have *six* escorts!"

"If the arrival of your cousins does not discourage our charming gallant," Mrs. Drummond pouted.

Devenish and Tyndale exchanged taut glances. "Gallant?" Tyndale murmured.

"What—has some impertinent fellow been annoying you?" asked Devenish, bristling.

Mrs. Drummond tittered. "*Annoying?* An odd way to describe a gentleman who is all consideration. Quite, in fact, the most courteous and charming man I have met this twelve-month and more!" Her sharp eyes rested fixedly on Tyndale as she spoke, and he reddened and looked away.

Devenish experienced an odd surge of resentment. His unwanted cousin was a clod, and Lord knows he had reason to detest the fellow, but—he *was* family. With a hauteur that startled Tyndale and astonished Yolande, he said, "Then I'm obliged to him. Perhaps I may have the name and direction of this paragon?"

For a second, Mrs. Drummond fancied it had been the Colonel who spoke and she was shocked into silence.

Yolande said, "His direction is here, for he stays at the hotel. I fancy you are already acquainted, Alain, for he is very highly regarded and you may see him everywhere. He is Mr. James Garvey, and I—"

Devenish, who had disposed himself with careless grace upon an arm of the sofa, uttered a muffled exclamation and shot to his feet. *"Garvey?* By God! Why the deuce is *that* loose fish hanging about you?"

Mrs. Drummond uttered a shriek and clapped protecting hands over her ears. Yolande frowned upon her suitor. Intrigued, Tyndale waited.

With no more than a rageful look at Mrs. Drummond, Devenish started for the door.

"Wait!" Yolande ran to stand before him. "Whatever is wrong? Mr. Garvey is the best of good *ton!*"

"Much you know about it! Stand aside, miss!"

"No! Are you run quite mad, Dev? Mr. Garvey is a close friend of the Prince, and—"

"Which of itself should tell you something! Move, I say!"

"I shall *not* move!" She leaned back against the door, barring her suitor's way, her eyes flashing with rare anger. "Devenish, I warn you! Do you embarrass me with your unsufferable jealousy, do you insult a gentleman who has been all that is helpful and conciliating—"

"I'll conciliate the b—" Devenish gritted his teeth as Mrs. Drummond again squealed.

Yolande threw a frantic glance at Tyndale. "Cousin Craig! He is insupportable! You must see that!"

"I do, indeed, ma'am," he drawled with his slow smile.

"Oh, do you? Damn you!" snarled Devenish.

A moan arose from Mrs. Drummond.

"Then—stop him!" Yolande implored.

Craig said gently, "Your wish is my command. At any other time. But now, I think it would be best that you should stand aside, Cousin Yolande."

"So much for your promises and declarations!" Her temper thoroughly aroused, Yolande did not pause to reflect that the only promises and declarations that had passed between them had been silent ones, conveyed by the eyes.

Devenish fired up at once. "So you've made promises and declarations, have you? You'll answer to me for that treachery, bumpkin! Yolande—blast it all! Move aside!"

"Profanity will not move me!" she declared, assuming an

Early Christian Martyr pose that must have made the great Sarah Siddons envious.

"In that case," he said, grimly determined, "I'll go out the window."

He strode across the room. Knowing him to be quite capable of doing just that, Yolande uttered a shriek and ran after him. He eluded her by means of a lithe spring over the sofa, drawing a faint yelp from Mrs. Drummond, and was to the door and in the hall in a flash.

Callously ignoring her aunt, who was flapping a handkerchief feebly at her face, Yolande ran wildly after Devenish. "Do *not!* Alain! If you do, I *never* will speak to you again!"

"Silly chit!" Devenish shouted, racing down the stairs.

Distraught, Yolande turned and pounced upon Craig. "Stop him! Oh, you *must* stop him! This is utterly disgraceful! I shall be humiliated beyond bearing. Can you not see that he is crazed with jealousy? And—poor Mr. Garvey has done nothing! Nothing!"

"From what I have heard, cousin, Mr. Garvey has traits you could not be expected to—"

"Why do you not help me?" She tugged at him distractedly. "*Do* something!"

He took up her hand and kissed it gently. "Do not worry so. I very much doubt it will come to a duel."

Sudden tears blinded Yolande. Frightened by the unfamiliar emotions stirring in her heart, she took refuge in anger. "A duel! Oh, you are just as bad as Devenish! I think you both utter—utter *boors!* I had sooner be escorted by—by warthogs! And so you may tell Dev!"

The corners of his mouth twitched suspiciously. "I suppose," he sighed, "it's no great distance from a clod to a warthog. Very well—I will go and try to keep Devenish from throttling your beau ideal."

"Oh! He is not! How dare you!"

Craig looked at her affronted beauty with a rueful smile, bowed, and left.

Mrs. Drummond who had viewed the exchange with interest, soothed, "Never fear, my love. Dear Mr. Garvey will be quite capable of defending himself against those two uncouth creatures."

Yolande choked out, "Oh—Aunt!" and burst into tears.

Chapter Six

"*One thing,*" *said Devenish savagely, sauntering back across* the cobbled stableyard, "according to the ostler, the silly court card will be back before evening, and you may depend on it I shall soon nip in the bud any plans he may have to escort Yolande in to dinner."

Tyndale glanced curiously at his cousin's set scowl. "Is he?"

"Taking her in to dinner? Doubtless he thinks so. It is perfectly obvious that he has made a strong bid to engage her affections, which only proves what a ramshackle cawker he is! Only a few weeks back he was in a passion because Justin Strand is to wed Lisette Van Lindsay."

"And this Garvey admired the lady?"

"Fairly slathering for her."

"Hmmm. He would appear to make a fast recover. However, you misunderstood my initial question. What I meant was, is this Garvey a silly court card? Yolande seems to rate him high."

"He's a damned slippery customer is what he is! Trust a woman to see no further than a handsome face!"

Tyndale shot him an amused glance.

Devenish growled, "Do not dare say it!" and stamped in through the door a boy ran to swing open.

Chuckling, Tyndale tossed the boy a coin and followed his cousin into the cool and fragrant hall. Devenish sniffed. "Ale. By gad, but it tempts me and I've no wish to go upstairs, at all events."

Tyndale accompanied him into the dim old tap and they occupied settles on either side of an oak table that was dark with years. Tyndale called an order for a jug of ale. Turning back, he was met by a cold stare and lifted one eyebrow enquiringly. "Are you still raging about my alleged promises and declarations?"

"I shall take your word as a gentleman that you did no more than offer any service you might to my lady. Nonetheless, I wonder that you do not gallop above stairs and charm her with the news I could not find Garvey.''

Tyndale smiled thoughtfully. ''She was not encouraging.''

''So I should hope!''

''She said, in fact, that she would sooner be escorted by—warthogs!''

''Did she now. Er—plural . . .?''

''Decidedly plural.''

Awed, Devenish murmured, ''By . . . Jove!'' Then broke into a shout of laughter. ''What a termagant she can be! But it only adds spice to her charm, bless her! I shall have to spruce up a bit for dinner and try to mend my fences, if— Oh, my God!'' He directed a dismayed gaze at Tyndale. ''This morning we sent Monty on to Northampton with the chaise and all our luggage! Damn! I shall have to send a groom after him!''

A message having been despatched to the stables, the two men settled down to enjoy their ale. Sighing his appreciation, Tyndale set down the tankard and asked, ''How is our friend Garvey, a . . . er, slippery customer?''

''Why, he's supposed to be such a bosom bow of Prinny's, ain't he? Oh, Lord! I keep forgetting you don't know anyone! Well, he is. But—'' Devenish glanced around the empty tap.

Tyndale said an amused, ''State secrets, cousin?''

Devenish met his eyes gravely. ''After a fashion. I mean to tell you some of it, because there's just the barest chance Garvey may have seen me and made himself least in sight. If that is so, I'd not put it past him to—'' He frowned. ''Never mind. But one of us must be here to keep an eye on Yolande.''

This was a side of his cousin he'd not seen before. Intrigued, Tyndale leaned forward. ''Has he 'done a deed whereat valour will weep'?''

''So you did go to school! I am all admiration.''

''And I am all ears.''

''You had better be part discretion. I'll have your word you won't repeat any of this, Tyndale.''

''You have it.'' There could be no doubt but that Devenish was deadly serious. Impressed by this calm stranger, Tyndale begged, ''Please go on. He's more than silly, I take it.''

''I judge him by the company he keeps. You will remember our earlier discussion regarding Tristram Leith? As I told you, Tris is a grand fellow. He was at Waterloo and rather badly mauled. An English lady named Rachel Strand found and tended him, and he fell head over ears into love with her. Unfortunately, it turned out she was already promised.

84

To a Frenchman. A quiet little fellow named Claude Sanguinet, richer than Golden Ball, up to his eyebrows in international intrigues, and as safe to annoy as any Bengal tiger."

Tyndale's brows went up. "And—Leith annoyed him?"

"Considerably. Tristram was shattered, you see, when he fancied Miss Strand lost to him." His gaze becoming reminiscent, Devenish went on, "At about that same time, my governor and I having had—er, a slight misunderstanding, I was drifting about Sussex. Tristram came back to England, and we met and joined forces. I won't go into the details— suffice it to say that Tris discovered his lady's betrothed, this Sanguinet fellow, was up to some very dirty work indeed. A scheme that threatened the safety, perhaps the very life, of our Fair Florizel."

"The Regent?" Tyndale whistled softly. "The plot thickens. Did Miss Strand know of all this?"

"Not a glimmer. And when Leith realized what she was getting mixed up in, he went to her home to warn her. Unfortunately, Miss Strand had already gone to Brittany for her betrothal ball."

"I doubt that would stop him," muttered Tyndale. "He followed, eh?"

"We both did. I—" Devenish checked and, scanning his cousin's faintly amused expression with a suspicious frown, demanded, "See here—do you know Leith?"

Tyndale blinked at him. "How the devil could a simple Colonial be acquainted with Colonel the Honourable Tristram Leith?"

"I suppose not, but—Hey! I didn't say he was a Colonel! Nor an Honourable, neither!"

"Did you not? Gracious me. Told you I've heard about him. He's quite famous, after all. Do go on, Sir Coz."

Devenish regarded him dubiously. There had been some talk, of course, despite the Horse Guards' struggles to keep everything quiet, and there was no knowing how many people Tyndale may have met before he'd come to Aspenhill.

The picture of interested innocence, Tyndale prompted, "You were saying that Leith followed his lady to Brittany, and that you accompanied him."

"Yes." Devenish nodded, still frowning. "And never in all my days have I seen a chateau so beautiful as Sanguinet's, nor one filled with a more unsavoury lot of guests. We had walked into a veritable hornets' nest of intrigue, and had our hands full getting the girl and her sister out of it, I can tell you!"

85

"But you did get them out? How? Come on, coz! You're leaving out all the meat of the tale."

"It is too long a story for me to relate now. The point is . . ." Devenish paused, all this chatter having increased his thirst. He attended to the matter, set down his tankard and resumed. "The point is, my clod, that in amongst that nasty little clutch of ruthless, scheming connivers was our own James Garvey, Esquire. The Regent's bosom bow."

"Now was he, by God!" breathed Tyndale. "And what did you and Leith do about that nasty little gathering?"

His eyes dancing, Devenish said with choirboy meekness, "Do about it? Why, we enjoyed a dish of Bohea with Sanguinet, pointed our toes in a stylish quadrille, and toddled back home with the ladies."

"Damn you, cousin! I want the truth of it."

"So do a lot of others." Devenish grinned but shook his head and said firmly, "No, really, Tyndale, I've told you the only part that need concern you, and enough that you should understand why I take a very dim view of our dandified Buck."

"I can, indeed. But—no! For Lord's sake, you cannot leave me in this puzzle! Did you not warn the Horse Guards, the Foreign Office?"

Devenish stared at the tankard he turned slowly on the table, and said dryly, "We did. Wherefore Leith is no longer a Colonel." He looked up and met his cousin's incredulous stare. "True. He was—er, it was politely suggested that he resign his commission."

"The devil!"

"Precisely. Our Monsieur Claude Sanguinet is a *very* powerful gentleman!" He glanced around again and, although there was no other within earshot, murmured, "And you will not forget you gave me your word?"

"Of course not. But we must keep Garvey away from Yolande."

"I mean to. But, just in case—" Devenish broke off as a groom came in, peered through the dim room, then wandered over to their table.

"Beg pardin, sirs," he said, touching his cap respectfully. "Be ye the gents as was wishful to look at Sir Aubrey Suffield's team, s'arternoon?"

"Wrong gents," replied Tyndale with his pleasant smile.

His blue eyes alight with excitement, Devenish asked,

"*Suffield*, did you say? Sir Aubrey is never selling those bays of his? To whom?"

The groom shrugged. "I dunno, sir. He said the gents would be waiting in the tap. I thought as it was you. I'd best see if I can find my proper party." He begged their pardon again, and departed.

Afire with eagerness, Devenish jumped up. "What a bit of luck!"

Standing also, Tyndale asked, "You know this Suffield?"

"Everyone does. Except you, of course. He's a regular Top Sawyer! A member of the Four Horse Club. Drives to an inch. No man living is a keener judge of horseflesh. I'll wager its Lucian St. Clair who's after those bays! I just may steal a march on him!"

Starting into the hall, they encountered Mrs. Drummond, a leashed Socrates panting along beside her.

"Well, gentlemen," she sniffed. "And did you find poor Mr. Garvey? Does the poor soul lie out under the sun somewhere, with a broken head?"

"Good God!" muttered Devenish, *sotto voce*.

"He was gone out, ma'am," imparted Tyndale, accompanying the lady to the stairs.

"One can but hope that by the time he returns, you both will have thought better of your violent inclinations. Come, Socrates! Mama's little boy can manage these stairs, surely? Up we go!"

"Mama's little boy" struggled up the first step, planted his front paws on the second, and waited. Grinning broadly, Devenish leaned against the wall.

Ever courteous, Tyndale asked if he might be of some service.

Mrs. Drummond eyed him without appreciable gratitude. "Well," she said grudgingly, "perhaps you may, at that. The poor darling ate rather too much nuncheon, I fear, and he is a trifle feeble these days."

Mindful of his earlier encounters with "darling," Tyndale asked uneasily, "Should you wish me to carry him, ma'am?"

"No. He does not like to be taken up. He is too proud, aren't you, my love? He only needs a helping hand, poor fellow. If you would be so kind as to just give his little rumpty a lift up each step, he can be spared embarrassment, and I expect we shall go on nicely."

This declaration brought tears of appreciation to Devenish's eyes. Enjoying himself hugely, he waited. Socrates, still maintaining his stance, turned his head and watched Tyndale's cautious approach, a glint in his beady eyes.

Tyndale liked dogs, but this particular animal he would sooner have shown his boot than a "helping hand." Nonetheless, Mrs. Drummond was Yolande's aunt. . . . He bent, therefore, and with one eye on the dog's still sharp set of fangs, supplied the required boost. The stairs were long and winding, and Socrates' progress was not rapid. Several interested onlookers gathered, sniggering. Under other circumstances, Devenish would have howled his mirth, but as it was, he clapped a hand over his mouth and succeeded for the most part in stifling his hilarity. Tyndale sensed that his subjugation was being observed by appreciative eyes. He darted a mortified glance downward. As a result, his boost was too precipitate.

"Oh!" wailed Mrs. Drummond. "You made him hurt his dear little nose."

Socrates was less vocal. His head darted around and he gave the hand that helped him a good nip.

Tyndale jerked his hand back and clutched it, his narrowed eyes registering his wrath. Socrates hopped nimbly up the three remaining stairs and stood at the top, grinning his defiance. Devenish, wiping tears from his eyes, fled.

"Did he nip you a little?" asked Mrs. Drummond. "Oh, see that—it is scarcely bleeding at all. If you will just twist your handkerchief around it, I will bathe it for you. Come along, little rascal! Much you care for all the bother your poor mama is put to!"

Ten minutes later, his injury having been bathed, sprinkled with basilicum powder and not very neatly bandaged, Tyndale strode along the hall, lips tight and eyes glittering with mortification. He could only pray that he might not encounter any of those people who had witnessed that ridiculous scene upon the stairs. The very thought made him grind his teeth, and to add to his chagrin, despite having made a complete cake of himself, he had not been rewarded by even a glimpse of the delectable Yolande. Mrs. Drummond had said accusingly that her niece was laid down upon her bed, resting, and much upset by the actions of her cousins. And, glorying in her grievance, she had expounded at great length on the peculiar manners and morals of today's young people, so that by the time her ministrations were completed he had been both irritated and eager to make his escape. He gripped his right wrist; his hand felt bruised to the bone and smarted like the deuce. That blasted little cur had caught him fairly. And it served him right. It was pointless to yearn for a last sight of Yolande. She was hopelessly beyond his reach; the sooner he accepted that fact, the less miserable he could be. He sighed and ran lightly downstairs.

The stableyard was deserted at this drowsy hour of the afternoon, and he crossed it briskly. In certain quarters he was accounted quite a judge of horseflesh, and he was every bit as eager as his cousin to see Suffield's famous team. He slowed his steps as he entered the coach house, narrowing his eyes to adjust to the dimness. Someone called, "Over here, sir!" and he started towards a stall where he could discern a gentleman engaged in inspecting the teeth of a horse. Too tall for Devenish, he thought.

A soft footfall behind him brought with it the sense of danger, sudden and strong, and he reacted with an instinctive swing around. He was too late. He did not feel the blow that struck him down; rather, it seemed that the gloom was rent by a searing explosion. He had a brief, confused thought that one of poor Whynyates' rockets had found him. . . .

*   *   *

Mr. James Garvey, resplendent in a jacket of maroon Bath suiting and a cravat that had caused Yolande to wish that her brother John (an aspiring dandy) might see it, frowned thoughtfully at his empty plate. "I fear I must disagree with you, my dear lady," he said. "Rackety, Devenish may be, but as your niece says, it does seem a trifle odd that he and his cousin should have departed with word to none." He looked with grave sympathy into Yolande's anxious eyes. How very pretty she was in that misty green evening gown, and how wisely she had chosen to wear no jewellery, allowing the eye to dwell undistracted upon her fair skin. She was not as lovely as his adored Lisette, of course, but very pretty indeed. And useful, for anyone chancing to see him on his northward journey could now read nothing more into it than that he escorted two ladies. Perfectly innocuous. And with the threat that Devenish constituted now happily removed, he could proceed to his destination with perfect equanimity. "You said, I believe," he murmured, "that you last saw your cousins early in the afternoon?"

Yolande nodded. "Soon after we returned from church. I will own I was a trifle annoyed by—by a small disagreement, but I had not thought they would just leave." She added worriedly, "It is so unlike Devenish."

"Perhaps the Canadian fellow was upset because Socrates bit him," said Mrs. Drummond, off-handedly.

"I doubt that, Aunt Arabella. He did not seem angry when I arrived home from church."

"Oh, that's right! I had forgot that time."

"Good heavens! Never say it happened again?"

"While you were resting, my love. I brought Mr. Tyndale, for somehow I cannot endure to call him 'nephew,' or Craig, he seems so—so *alien!* Where was I? Oh, yes—I fetched him up here and tended him, though it was not a bad bite at all, and soon stopped bleeding."

"*Bleeding!* Oh, Aunt Arabella! I wish you had not brought Socrates! He has the most horrid disposition."

At once firing up in defence of her pet, Mrs. Drummond wailed, "How *can* you blame it on my poor doggie? If truth be told, Mr. Tyndale brought it on himself, for had he not hurt Socrates' little nose, the dear pet would not have bitten the clumsy creature!"

"Craig hurt Socrates?" gasped Yolande, considerably taken aback. "But—but, why?"

"You may well ask, though I'm sure it is all of a piece. He is, after all, from a wild frontier, and obviously more accustomed to deal with savages than civilized ladies and gentlemen. Only think of how he almost brought about your own death, my dear."

"Did he, by thunder?" ejaculated Mr. Garvey, straightening in his chair. "It would seem that you are well rid of the fellow, Miss Drummond."

Irked, Yolande said, "It is not quite as it sounds, sir. There was an accident, true, but Mr. Tyndale rescued me from it most gallantly."

"Oh, *very* gallantly, I am sure!" said Mrs. Drummond, huffily. "And not a thought for *me,* lying senseless in a ditch! It's a wonder my neck was not broke, and indeed I still suffer so many aches and pains that I feel sure it will be found I have taken some grievous inner hurt!"

"Of course Craig thought of you!" Yolande flared hotly. "We both did! I am assured he would never have left you had there not been others to aid you, whereas I was helpless, with the team bolting as they were. I truly am sorry you were so badly shaken, Aunt, but Craig—"

"No, no, never apologize, dear love," Mrs. Drummond inserted in honeyed tones, but with her eyes sparking. "In-

90

deed, I can but marvel at the forbearance that leads you to intercede for the crude fellow. Under the circumstances."

Flushed with vexation, and looking, or so thought James Garvey, exceedingly lovely, Yolande fell into the trap. "Circumstances? What circumstances? The circumstance that having unwittingly endangered my life, Cousin Craig proceeded very bravely to save it?"

"Why—no, dearest," purred her aunt with sublime innocence. "I had meant simply the circumstance of your being promised to dear Alain Devenish. And the Colonial being so obviously—however presumptuously—enamoured of you!"

Thoroughly angered, Yolande prepared to retaliate with the remark that since she *was* to wed Devenish and that Craig was aware of the fact, her defence of him was as devoid of interest as it was impartial. But she could not speak the words and, tongue-tied, her face flaming, she knew why. Her feelings for Craig Tyndale could, under no circumstances, be described as being devoid of interest.

Mrs. Drummond had little use for Alain Devenish, but she was aware that he was a peerless suitor if compared to his Canadian cousin. Triumphant, she smiled a faint but smug smile through a brief, pregnant pause.

Hiding amusement, Mr. Garvey reached out to place his well-manicured fingers over Mrs. Drummond's hand, lying upon the tablecloth. "Poor little lady," he soothed gently. "How worried your niece must have been for your sake. And how pleased I am that you have effected such a remarkable recovery, so that I may beg you will both accompany me this evening. It would seem there is to be a lecture in the Parish Hall upon the words of Lawrence and a young fellow called Constable. I am no connoisseur of the arts, but I understand the paintings of several local artists will also be on display, and it might prove an entertainment to suit the sensibilities of such gentle ladies as yourselves."

Mrs. Drummond was pleased to accept. Turning to the quiet Yolande, Mr. Garvey gave her a surreptitious grin so full of mischief that her disturbed heart was eased. "You are too kind to us, sir," she protested gratefully.

He shook his head and said with perfect, if oblique, honesty, "Miss Drummond, you cannot know what it means to me to be allowed to keep such charming company."

"Such graciousness," sighed Mrs. Drummond, as she climbed the stairs to prepare for the outing. "Such an air! Oh,

Yolande, how it would gladden my heart to see you wed so perfect a gentleman as Mr. Garvey."

Yolande scarcely heard her. "I wonder," she muttered, "wherever they can be."

Mrs. Drummond tossed her head. "If I know anything at all in the matter," she said tartly, "they are likely carousing in some tavern in an intoxicated condition, and will awaken with fearful headaches, wishing themselves dead!"

* * *

Fervently wishing himself dead, Alain Devenish dragged his unco-operative body out of the ditch and again sprawled, face down, at the side of the lane, too nauseated to move another inch. He had, he told himself fuzzily, probably felt worse in his life. He could not remember when. His head ached dully, he felt wretchedly ill, and his leg was pounding so that he clutched at it miserably. Dimly, he was nudged by a sense of urgency; of something vital he must accomplish with the least possible delay, and obedient to that spur he struggled upwards, fighting the nausea until it overwhelmed him and he sank down and was very sick. For a while he lay still, not thinking at all, drenched in a cold sweat and lacking the strength of a newborn kitten. But gradually he began to feel less limp and, after what seemed a very long time, he crept slowly to his knees and thence to his feet. The lane, the dark loom of hedges, the violet skies of evening, tilted slowly to the right. He closed his eyes, gritted his teeth, and hung on. When he peeped through his lashes once more, the countryside had righted itself. His first few steps were uncertain, but in a little while he was going along less erratically. Still, it was several more minutes before he began to wonder why he was here, and where "here" was.

Puzzled, he slowed, then stopped. A large badger, very wet, trotted busily into the lane, paused to shake itself, then froze, petrified, as it saw the human so near to it. There was water nearby, then, thought Devenish. The badger watched, undecided as to whether a retreat or an attack was indicated. Devenish started to bow, thought better of it, and said softly, "Good evening, Mr. Badger. Alain Devenish at your service." The badger abandoned its deliberations and waited fearlessly. Devenish put it in possession of the fact that he had been properly hornswoggled. "I was," he advised, "half suffocated, drugged, and tossed into a ditch. And let me tell you, sir, that if the party I suspect of this dastardly crime was in truth responsible, it is a miracle I yet live!" The badger took a few unhurried steps. "Off to your club, eh?" said Devenish. "Then, if you've no objection, I do believe I shall avail myself of your bath." The badger paused, twitched its long whiskers, and went upon its way.

Devenish watched it, a faint smile lurking about his mouth, then turned aside, crossed the ditch, found a break in the hedgerow and emerged into a wide meadow that sloped downwards to a distant gleam that was the river. Starting thitherward with quickening step, he tensed and stopped. *Yolande!* His lovely little lady was at the mercy of that miserable libertine, Garvey! Trusting him! Supposing him to be—what was it she'd said? "All that is conciliating!" He thought, "*Conciliating!* My God!" He must get to her, and as fast as may be! But starting off, he again checked, the sense that he was followed bringing a recollection of the vicious assault in the stable. He swung around, ready for battle, his keen eyes scanning the quiet loom of the hedge. But there was no movement this time; no rush of dark forms, no sickly-smelling rag to be clapped over his nostrils with the resultant and immediate weakness that had been so swiftly followed by unconsciousness. Perhaps it was only the badger, who had decided to come this way after all. He resumed his route. "Not too sociable creatures, badgers," he advised a field mouse as it scampered past. "But far more decent," he went on, his usually humorous mouth settling into a stern line, "than many of us who walk on two legs!"

The evening air was sweet with the scents of damp earth and honeysuckle, and vibrant with the small, myriad voices of the night dwellers; the warning call of an owl, the pattering progress of some water rat or mole, countless chirps and rustlings that ceased abruptly as Devenish approached the river. Coming to the bank, he sat down, pulled off boots and stockings, divested himself of coat, cravat, and shirt, rolled up his breeches, and stepped gingerly into the water. He gasped and danced a little to that icy immersion, but waded deeper, bent, and with the aid of his handkerchief managed to wash himself quite well. The cold water took his breath but set his skin to tingling and his head began to throb less viciously. When he felt sufficiently cleansed, he trod rapidly up the bank, and then stood very still, listening.

The sounds of the night had resumed when he'd begun to take off his clothes, but now all was very silent. The breathless hush was of itself a warning. He thought, "So I was right the first time!"

"You might as well have taked off the lot," said a clear, childish voice. "You're all over wetness."

Devenish, who had jumped at the first word, now continued up the bank, peering at the small, dark outline beside his discarded garments. "Who the deuce are you?" he enquired, then hopped as he trod on a sharp pebble and added an exasperated, "Dammitall!"

The small figure backed away.

"My apologies. No—do not go away," Devenish pleaded. "What are you doing out alone after dark like this? You should be laid down upon your bed."

"Never mind about me," said the child with surprising firmness. "I may be all of my ownness. But I is not touched in the upper works."

Devenish was beginning to shiver. "N-no more am I. Are you a boy?"

"'Course. What are you going to dry on?"

"My shirt." He took it up and began to scrub vigorously. "It will dry as I go along. And because a fellow bathes in the river, don't mean he's a looby."

"Anyone what puts his whole self—or most of it—into the river at night, is crazy. But it ain't 'cause of that I thought it. I heered you talking to the badger."

Beginning to feel a little warmer, Devenish laughed, pulled the shirt briskly back and forth across his shoulders, then shook it out and began to put it on. "So you were watching, were you? I thought someone was. As for the badger—well, when a fellow's alone he talks to all manner of things. I didn't frighten him, you know."

"I know. You got Rat Paws."

"I've—what?"

The child shrank back behind one protectively upflung arm. "Don't ye clout me! Oh, don't you never clout me!"

"Curse and confound it!" fumed Devenish. "I'm not going to hit you. Put your blasted arm down at once!"

With slow caution that guarding arm was lowered. A scared voice whimpered, "Lor', but you get so cross, so quick! I be afeared!"

Devenish winced. Even from this unknown child! "My wretched temper," he muttered contritely. "I'm sorry, boy. Now, tell me why you made that revol—er, that unkind remark about my hands." He held out one slim, neatly manicured member and peered at it by the light of the rising half-moon. "They ain't that bad, surely?"

"Rat Paws don't mean *hands!* Cor!" the scorn was apparent. "Don't you know *nothink?* It means as you understand the little people. Animals."

"Does it, by Jove!" Devenish pulled on his jacket. "Well, I'll be dashed! Rat Paws, eh? And how did you know, my elf, that I've a way with animals?"

The child sighed and shook his head at this inexplicable obtuseness. "Because of the badger, 'course," he explained patiently. "He would've either runned off or gived you a good bite if you didn't have the Rat Paws. Not many does. I don't. But I seen it before. Among the Folk."

"Aha!" Devenish felt in his pockets. "So you're a gypsy lad, are you?"

The child sprang up and crouched, hissing furiously. "Go on! Count it! Count it! See if I cares! I didn't prig nothink!"

"I doubt there was anything to prig. Someone was before you, I fear."

The boy sniffed and sat down with the unaffected, loose-limbed slump of childhood. "I bean't surprised. You deserve it for being indecent."

"Good God!" Devenish abandoned his hopeful but doomed search for any kind of cash or pawnable item still remaining about his person. "*Now* what are you accusing me of? Because I took off my shirt? Did it offend you to look upon my nakedness, Master Virtuous, you should have continued about your probably nefarious pursuits!"

There was a brief pause, then the boy remarked thoughtfully, "I don't know what all them jawbreakers means. But I heered you say the badger he was more decent than what you is. And badgers are not always nice."

Devenish chuckled. "Well, that wasn't quite what I meant. Now, sirrah, I think I shall walk with you so far as your cottage—or do you dwell in a caravan, perhaps? Anyway, I'll see you safe home. Which way? And by the by, where are we?" The small stocking-capped head turned to him with incredulity. "I was robbed in St. Albans," he explained, "and thrown in a ditch not far away from here, but I've no least idea where I am."

"Lawks! A rank rider?" The boy moved a step closer and looked around uneasily.

"Something like that." Devenish dropped a reassuring hand onto a very frail shoulder. "Never fear, laddie. He's far off by this time."

"I hopes as how he is. We're on the outside of Cricklade."

95

Devenish knit his brows. "Oh, then that's the Thames, is it? Jove! I've a school friend lives nearby, just past Tewkesbury."

"Tewkesbury!" The boy gave a muffled snort and began to move off. "It's this way. There's a sign at the crossroads."

Following, Devenish scanned him narrowly. How thin he was, poor shrimp. Likely half-starved, and although he moved along well, his stride was short and cautious as he picked his way across the meadow. It was too dark to see the face and, beyond noting how peaked it seemed, the eyes dark shadows in that pale oval, Devenish had no clear impression of his looks. There was an inconsistency about his speech that was intriguing. Although he used cant terms and his grammar was atrocious, the h's and g's were largely intact, and just now he had said with surprising precision, "badgers are not always nice." Odd. Recalling his last succinct exclamation, Devenish enquired, "What's wrong with Tewkesbury?"

"Nought. Be ye going to walk?"

"*Touché!* I suppose . . ." he frowned, "I've no choice." And then, resenting a scornful "Hah!" he demanded, "And why should that disgust you?"

"'Cause you be a nob. And nobs don't walk better'n thirty miles."

"Surprising as it may seem to you, young sir," said Devenish loftily, "I have been on the padding lay before. Now then"—he indicated the row of shabby cottages they were approaching— "is this where you live?" The boy nodded and led the way to a gate that drooped in a picket fence sadly lacking paint.

Devenish closed the gate behind him, waved cheerily, and went on his way. "Strange little duck," he mused, then glanced back curiously. It was stranger that a gypsy should live in a cottage, but perhaps the child's parents had tired of the nomadic life. At all events, it was none of his bread and butter. But, by gad! when he and Yolande set up their nursery the children would not be permitted to wander about the countryside after dark! Yolande . . . His eyes softened to a surge of tenderness. God love her sweet soul, already he missed her damnably! He squared his shoulders. "Tewkesbury. Thirty miles. Lord!"

He stepped out briskly and soon came to the fork in the lane, the signpost pointing south to Swindon, and northwest to the Cotswolds, beyond which lay Tewkesbury and the home of Valentine Montclair. Perhaps he might advance faster by retreating, for Swindon, on horseback at least, was not far from the Leith's country seat, Cloudhills, where he could be sure of a warm welcome and the loan of a chaise and pair, even if Tristram was from home. But he *had* no horse, and Cloudhills was as far as Tewkesbury and in the wrong blasted direction! He'd never visited Montclair's country place, but Val had been a fine fellow at Harrow, and would most certainly do all he might to aid a former schoolmate.

Not until he had walked a long way did it occur to him that Craig might be the villain who'd had him abducted, so that he might dishonourably pursue his cousin's lady without fear of interruption. He halted, scowling, but almost immediately grinned and shook his head. Never. Tyndale, whatever else he might be, was a gentleman.

*　　*　　*

The gentleman in question was at that very moment lowering himself to the ground, having accomplished which, he stretched out his long legs and leaned back against the stone wall, closing his eyes. The cut above his right temple had stopped bleeding, but the blow must have jarred halfway down his spine, and each hair on his head seemed to throb. He had not the remotest idea of where he was, but considering England was such a tiny island, it was amazing he'd not walked clear across it. The lanes went on and on, one succeeding another, the occasional signposts all too often extending invitations from towns he'd never heard of, and only his small knowledge of celestial navigation enabling him to constantly head north. He sighed. He'd endured worse pain than that which he now suffered, but, Jupiter, he'd be glad to be rid of it! Still, he mustn't lounge here for long. If what Devenish had said was true, and as far-fetched as it seemed, Dev was not the kind to lie, then the beautiful Yolande was in real peril. A man who would betray his country was capable of any villainy. Tyndale sighed again. He was so very tired. He could not guess at the hour, and his watch was gone, along with his ring. He didn't mind the watch so much, but the ring had belonged to his father and carried the family crest. Blast those . . . misbegotten . . .

He awoke shivering and soaked. More rain! It was a wonder this little island stayed afloat! He knew he'd slept only a short while, but it was very cold now, and the rain becoming a downpour. He struggled up and trudged through the puddles, concentrating on Yolande's lovely eyes, and the proud rage that had flashed in them so adorably yesterday. . . . Or was it yesterday? Gad, but he was cold, and to add to his misery, a chill wind was rising, cutting icily through his wet clothes. A gate banged to a sudden gust. His teeth beginning to chatter, Tyndale drew his jacket closer, tucked his hands under his arms, and kept moving. A flickering glow of lightning illumined a cluster of distant, dilapidated farm buildings. The gate slammed again and he saw that it was not a gate, but the door to a small shed located only a few yards from the lane. Part of the farm, no doubt, but hidden from it by a stand of trees. He halted and scrutinized the shed with interest. A glance at the house verified that not a light shone. They would certainly be asleep at this hour. He scaled the low wall in a quick leap and again searched the gloom for irate men, or dogs. He'd had enough truck with dogs to last him for a while. But all was quiet, save for the depressing beat of the rain. He crept to the swinging door and peered inside. A toolshed, having among all the muddy impedimenta, a pile of dry sacks.

Five minutes later, the shed door tight closed, his head comfortably settled on two of the folded sacks and the rest disposed over him, Tyndale smiled into the darkness. It was not the Clarendon, precisely, but it was no worse (a sight better!) than many a night he'd passed with Timothy Van Lindsay and his maniacs. Thunder bellowed, closer this time, and lightning shone through the many cracks in the dusty old shed. Tyndale grinned and yawned sleepily. "Just like Spain," he thought. "Good old . . . Tim . . ."

*   *   *

Devenish awoke to the touch of watery fingers creeping down his neck. He swore and sat up. The roof of the barn had a large hole, this flaw revealed by the glare of lightning. "A fine thing!" he snorted indignantly. The two cats who had curled themselves up beside him opened yellow eyes to blink through the gloom. *"Madame et Monsieur,"* he said, "I regret the necessity to disturb you, but—" The light words ceased, and he stared in stark shock at a fourth inhabitant of the old barn. A small figure, cuddled so close against his back that he'd not seen it when he awoke. "Well, here's a fine start!" he exclaimed. "Who the deuce asked you to attach your—" He ceased to speak as lightning flashed again. His breath was held for an instant, then released in a slow hiss. He'd noted a lantern hung on a nail against the wall, but had made no attempt to light it for fear of betraying his presence. Now, he stood cautiously, groped his way to it and was lucky enough to discover a tinderbox lying on the

98

workbench. When he had ignited the wick, he turned the flame very low and tiptoed to the intruder, lying just as before and breathing with deep, soft regularity. He bent, and held the lantern closer. The shirt was too large for the child, the breeches tattered, and the thin sandals frayed, but it was not these that widened Devenish's eyes. During the night, the stocking cap had shifted and a strand of hair had escaped. A long, dark, curling strand. He uttered a faint moan, reached down, and gently pulled the cap away. Thick, dark, matted curls tumbled down. "Oh, my God!" he groaned. "A female!"

She had not been as fast asleep as he supposed. The long curling lashes flew open. Great eyes at once becoming wild with terror gazed up at him. The pale lips opened in a scream the more horrifying because it was soundless, and she sprang up. Devenish put down the lantern hurriedly, and leapt after her. He caught her at the door; a small, writhing madness.

"No!" she sobbed. "Oh, no! Let me be! Gawd! Let me be!" And between sobs and cries and entreaties, came a thin keening shriek that he swiftly muffled.

"Quiet!" he hissed. "I will not harm you, child! Just be quiet, or we'll be put out in the rain, to say the least of it!"

He glanced down when she ceased to struggle. Her eyes were half closed, the thin features like paper. "Egad! Am I suffocating you?" he gasped, removing his hand.

"Let . . . me . . . be," she whispered threadily. "Do not—oh, do not touch me!"

She looked on the verge of a swoon. What in heaven's name would he do if she committed so dreadful a thing? He released her hurriedly. "Just *please* do not scream," he implored.

She did not scream, but she swayed, an awful moaning escaping her. In a burst of sympathy, Devenish forgot her plea, put an arm about her bony little shoulders, and led her back to the pile of straw and the two cats. "Sit here," he urged, drawing her down beside him. "There—that's better. Poor creature. Was it a nightmare? I've had a few of them m'self."

Those haunted eyes watched him with a sort of dulled pleading, and he smiled his kindest smile and added, "I will not touch you. Promise."

Still looking straight at him, she began to weep; a helpless, undisguised sobbing that smote him to the heart, but when he edged back, horrified, the thin claw of a hand came out to clutch his own, and she gulped, "And—and you ain't like—like Akim ... or Benjo?"

"I most certainly hope not, if they affect a little girl in this way." A frown crept into his eyes. He asked in a different tone, "Is that why you ran away? From Akim and Benjo?" The tangled, greasy curls bounced as she nodded, and teardrops splattered. Devenish's jaw set. "Are they little boys?"

She shook her head. "Men. And I be eleven—I think."

Eleven. She looked no more than seven or eight. . . . Dreading the answer he might receive, he asked, "What did they do?"

"They started to . . . to look at me." Crimson swept over the pinched cheeks, and she threw grubby hands up to cover her eyes. "And—and one day Benjo catched me washing of myself in the stream. He took hold of my hair when I tried to cover up myself. And—and he laughed and said . . . he said they'd get a good price for me soon, from . . ."

"From whom?"

"From . . . Oh! From one of the *Flash Houses!*" Her eyes, agonized, were fixed on him, and Devenish gritted his teeth over the oaths that surged into his throat. By thunder, but was there anything lower than some men? He'd never been in a Flash House, but he'd heard of those hellish traps in which girls scarcely having known childhood were forced into prostitution and kept thereafter more or less permanently drunk to ensure they continued their trade; a trade from which they reaped only the benefits of food and warmth while their soulless procuress grew rich and fat at the expense of their degradation. Boys fared little better in those dens of vice: if they refused to steal and deliver up their spoils, they were cast out into the street, penniless, where the chances were that they would be hauled off to gaol, flogged, and thrown into the streets once more to begin the whole vicious circle over again.

A small cold hand creeping into his own recalled Devenish from his bitter thoughts. The child was watching him beseechingly. He looked into the tear-streaked face of this helpless piece of jetsam caught in a relentless tide that must only lead to— Cutting off that terrible strain of reasoning, he demanded harshly, "What is your name? Have you no parents?"

"They call me Tabby. And I don't know about me mother or father. I was stole."

He looked at her clinically. Her hair was very dark, but he

saw now that her skin was extremely pale beneath the dirt, and her eyes, although dark also, had flecks of hazel in them. She was a dirty, wretched, plain little girl, all skin and bone, but he saw the same promise in her thin form that Akim and Benjo must have seen, and his rage at those crude spoilers grew. Forcing himself to speak calmly, he asked, "Why Tabby?"

" 'Cause I scratched 'em when they tried to touch me like— like Akim did once. And they said I was a wildcat, and after that they all laughed, and teased me, and—and called me all kinds of horrid, ugly things. I hates 'em all." The bony fists clenched. She repeated through her teeth, "I *hates* 'em! So I didn't say nothink, but last night when Akim's mort was asleep and Akim and Benjo was drunk, I creeped away. And I'm *never* going back!" Her angry flush died away, her lips began to tremble pathetically, and her eyes blinked up at him, aswim with tears. "You won't make me go? Oh, please— *please!*" She knelt, cowering before him, hands upstretched in supplication. "I'll do anything! I'll cook for you and scrub your floors when you get some. And when I grows up in a year or two, if you likes me a bit, I'll—"

Devenish gave a gasp and pulled her to her feet. "Hush! Poor child. Now, sit properly and do not even think such things."

Trembling, she whispered, "It would be better, sir . . . than a Flash House, but— Oh! Now I've gone and made you cross again! You do get very awful cross, mister . . ."

"Devenish. Alain Devenish, at your service, madame!" He rose and swept her the most stately bow of which he was capable with his leg throbbing so. The child was delighted, laughter returned to her eyes, and her hands clapped joyously. "Now," said Devenish, "we must find a name for you, for Tabby I will not tolerate."

"A name? A new name? Oh, sir—do that mean as you will keep me?" And she clasped her hands before her thin breast with such an intensity of hope that he feared to hear those fragile bones snap.

"I cannot keep you, child," he pointed out gently. "It wouldn't be proper, for I've no lady wife to care for you, but—"

Undismayed, she said, "Well, if you don't got a wife, you prob'ly have a—"

"No! I have not one of those, either! Now—what am I to

101

call you?'' He ran through his mind the names of every lady he could recall. "It must be a pretty name . . ."

She said timidly, "If I was to think of a speshly lovely name, p'raps *then* you might keep me?"

"No. But I shall see to it that you've a decent chance in life. One of my aunts, or cousins—some kind lady will take you in, and perhaps train you for her abigail. Would you like that?"

The child tried to answer, but could not. And to his horror, flung herself down and began to kiss his muddy boots.

"Good God!" he gasped, again hauling her up. "Never do such things!"

She dragged one torn sleeve across her small nose, and sniffed, "I can't help it. You be so good to I. Does you like 'Josie'?"

He said dubiously, "Josie? Why? Do you like it?"

"I don't know." She shrugged. "It—sort of comes into my head sometimes."

Devenish had been considering the merits of Antonia but—"Well, it's better than Tabby!" he said. "Very well, Josie it shall be." He looked about as a sudden flash was followed by a great rumbling bump of thunder. "Josie Storm! How's that?"

"Lovely!" The newly christened Miss Storm hugged herself ecstatically. "I feel new all over! Josie Storm . . . *oooh!*"

Chapter Seven

"*I* was sure they would be here for breakfast, Aunt," said Yolande, her worried glance travelling for the hundredth time around the emptying coffee room of the hotel. "I wonder if we should not send one of the outriders in search of them? Or perhaps call in the constable?"

"Yes, and a pretty figure we should cut when they were discovered roistering in some ale house!" her aunt sniffed. "The host told you, my love, that neither Devenish nor Tyndale—or whatever he calls himself—signed the guest register."

"No, but they stabled their horses here, and they were still here when we retired, for I sent Peattie downstairs to enquire. You know how Dev loves that mare. And Craig values Lazzy most highly."

"Goodness only knows why, for a more unattractive beast I seldom beheld. Oh, mercy, here is dear Mr. Garvey! Perhaps he can set your mind at ease."

James Garvey, looking very well in a dark brown riding coat and buckskins, came to join them, his grave "May I have the honour?" drawing an immediate and dramatic "Oh, *pray* do, sir!" from Mrs. Drummond, and a welcoming smile from her niece. His polite enquiries as to their night's rest were brushed aside, Yolande replying almost impatiently, "Very nice, I thank you. Mr. Garvey, have you seen anything of my cousins Devenish and Tyndale? I hope you will not think me foolish, but I am becoming most anxious for them."

He rested an appreciative gaze upon her. "Your concern does you credit, dear lady. As does your gown. Dare I be so bold as to remark how pleasingly that shade of peach becomes you?"

Irritated by what she considered a pointless digression, Yolande was also struck by the thought that Dev would have said carelessly that her dress was orange, if she'd asked him, and Tyndale would probably merely have observed that she looked charmingly. She smiled politely, but decided she would soon find Mr. Garvey's suave manners a dead bore. Yet— how kindly he was regarding her, and only think how willingly he had spared them from what must otherwise have been a dull journey. "What a wretched, ungrateful girl I am!" she thought penitently.

Her aunt had willingly jumped into the pause resulting from Yolande's brief hesitation and was exclaiming over Mr. Garvey's unending kindnesses. As soon as she paused to draw breath, Yolande cut into this welter of gratitude. "I echo my aunt's sentiments, sir," she said warmly. "You have been too good."

He looked a little solemn then. "I do have some news," he said with marked reluctance. "I trust it will not distress you. The head ostler tells me that your cousins have departed, ma'am. They came to the stable late last night, apparently, claimed their mounts, paid their shot, and rode out."

Stunned, Yolande stared at him. She had, she knew, been out of reason cross with both of them. But could Dev have been so offended he would leave in such a way? Would Craig

103

take himself off without so much as a farewell—a note, at least? A pang pierced her heart, and suddenly she felt miserable and betrayed.

"Typical!" snorted Mrs. Drummond. "It would be asking too much of you, dear Mr. Garvey, to enquire if they left a *billet-doux* at the desk, perhaps?"

"I did so, ma'am. That is, I asked of the clerk. There was nothing."

Mrs. Drummond cast her niece a smug "I told you so!" look.

Yolande pulled herself together. "How foolish in me to have worried," she said, striving not altogether successfully to sound lightly amused. "Well, dear, you were very right to tease me. I expect Sullivan has given Socrates his exercise by this time, so perhaps we should collect our cloaks and be upon our way."

*   *   *

Sadly in need of a shave, and looking considerably tattered and weather-stained, Devenish lay back against the tree trunk and sighed beatifically. "How strange it is," he mused, "that a dinner of bread and cheese eaten in town would be plain fare, but bread and cheese eaten under a tree is always so dashed magnificent."

Bathed in the golden rays of the late afternoon sun, Josie scratched her head and regarded her protector doubtfully. "Does that mean as ye liked it?"

"Nectar of the Gods!" sighed Devenish. He stood and reached down to help her up. "We've still far to go. Are you tired? We've come a long way today."

"I be a better walker'n you," she said pertly. "Though you're padding better'n what you did last night. Has you got blisters? Them boots is pretty, but they don't look like walkers."

Devenish peered ruefully at his top boots. "They're not. But I shall do, never fear. *En avant, mon enfant!*"

"Très bien, monsieur," giggled Josie.

Devenish, who had been about to explain what he'd said, caught her skinny shoulder and pulled her to a halt. *"What,"* he breathed, "did you say?"

"Nothing bad! Not nothing bad, sir! Oh, don't be cross again! You was talking French, wasn't you?"

"Why—yes. Do you know what I said? What it means?"

"It means 'let's go on' or something, don't it?"

Marvelling, he released his hold and nodded. "What did you answer? In English, that is."

"Very well, sir." He didn't seem cross. Reassured, she tilted her head to one side and watched him curiously. "Why? Does you hate all Frogs, like Akim and Benjo does?"

Starting on again, but still regarding her askance, he said, "Gad, no. I merely wonder, my small conundrum, how it is that your English is appalling, yet you know French. Where did you learn it?"

"Don't remember." Her brow wrinkled, but at length she concluded, "Prob'ly heered a body say it. And my English ain't—what you said. I speak good. Even Akim and—"

"I know. Akim and Benjo. But I doubt they are authorities, elf. We must improve your grammar are you to obtain suitable employment."

She stared at him. "But—she's dead. And even if she wasn't, I don't see why you'd want to mess about with *her* to get me a sittyation."

At first puzzled, Devenish eventually comprehended. "*Grammar*, Josie," he explained laughingly. "It means your use—or misuse—of English."

"Oh." She flushed scarlet. "All right. Go on, then."

"Me? Good God, no! I do not excel in that line myself. But when we reach Tewkesbury—"

"Tomorrow," she inserted, pulling a face.

"Oh, no. I think we can do better than that. If a carter chances by, I shall bribe him into taking on two paying customers."

Josie looked regretfully at his jacket, now bereft of two of its three handsome silver buttons. "You shouldn't have let that tinker gull you out of both them pretty buttons for his bread and cheese. He likely thought you was a proper pigeon for milking. And 'sides, carters isn't s'posed to give rides."

"Listen to Miss Prim." He grinned. "I doubt your sensibilities will be offended, however, for this road seems to attract very little traffic. Still, if one ventures this way I mean to try him, for I'm in a hurry, Miss Josie. I must get myself hooves or wheels—preferably both—as soon as may be."

The child smiled but said nothing, and Devenish's concern returned to his adored Yolande. Whatever must she have thought of his absence? In view of their earlier disagreement and his confounded temper, it was all too likely she supposed him to have ridden off in a huff. He scowled and thrust his hands deeper into his pockets, and the threat of James Garvey heightened his worries so that he did not notice that the afternoon was growing colder and the skies becoming heavy with clouds. Not until a gust of wind cut chillingly through his fine linen shirt was he recalled to the present. He glanced down and saw the child's head bowed, and her feet scuffing wearily at the damp surface of the lane. Contrite, he exclaimed, "What a clod I am!" and dropped to one knee, reaching back invitingly. "Come aboard, madam."

She looked at his shoulders with longing. "No. Thankee, but you'm tired. And your feet hurt, too. I can tell."

"Nonsense," he lied. "You, m'dear, are in the company of a former military man. Why, when I was in the army we used to tramp about all day long—sometimes half the night—just to keep our Colonel amused. This is nothing. Come now—don't dawdle about!"

He waved his arms imperatively, and with a giggle she ran to clamber onto his back. He stood, his arms cradling her bony legs. She was heavy as a bushel of feathers, poor mite. "Gad!" he groaned. "What a lump!"

She laughed and said gratefully, "Oh, this is such fun, and I be warmer already!"

Devenish warned, "You realize, m'dear, that I shall want my own turn at piggyback?"

Another merry little laugh greeted this sally, but she pointed out that he was not going so fast with her on his back.

"Remorseless taskmaster!" He broke into a run, but soon had to slow again.

After a little while, Josie asked "Be she pretty, your lady?"

"Very pretty."

"Is that why you want to marriage her?"

He smiled, Yolande's vivid loveliness very clear before his eyes. "Not entirely. I've wanted her for my wife for as long as I can remember. She is kind as well as pretty. And she has a happy nature and a quick, merry laugh. She is generous and charming, and—oh, all the things a man wants in the lady he marries."

"Oh." A thoughtful pause, and then, "Mr. Dev, why does some gents have wifes and some have—"

He said hastily, "It's—er, all according to—ah— Well, a gentleman usually—"

He was reprieved from this quagmire as they came around a bend in the lane and Josie interrupted in a scared voice, "Mr. Dev, what are those people doing?"

A burst of shouting broke from a group of burly men engaged in dragging a struggling individual across the field a short distance ahead. Devenish halted and moved into the shade of the hedge. They looked a rough lot and he'd no wish for the child to witness a brawl. A roar of laughter arose and, with it, the body of their victim, soaring into the air to fall heavily onto the muddy lane.

"The deuce!" exclaimed Devenish.

A bullet head appeared over the top of the hedge as the unfortunate sprawling in the dirt commenced a feeble attempt to rise. "That'll do fer'ee," quoth the farmer, grinning from ear to ear. "Next time as ye fix fer to trespass in some 'un's shed, ye best ask perlite-like, fust!" And to the accompaniment of another roar of laughter, his head was withdrawn and the loud voices began to diminish.

"Oh, the poor cove!" cried Josie pityingly. She slid from Devenish's hold and scampered along the lane, her ragged breeches flapping.

Following, Devenish quickened his pace as the man in the road turned on his side, got one elbow under him, and lifted a blood-streaked fair head.

"Well I'll be— Tyndale!" said Devenish.

"Give us your hanky, Mr. Dev," Josie demanded, kneeling beside the victim and extending an imperious hand. Receiving this grubby article, she began to wipe carefully at Tyndale's battered features.

Her patient managed to sit up, and leaning back on both hands peered blurrily at her. "Dev . . .?" he said, bewildered.

"Over here, you clunch." Devenish bent over him. "Lord, what a mess! Did they run the cows over you?" And, as Josie gently parted his cousins's thick hair, he added, "The devil! Who did that?"

"An admirer . . . in the hotel stable. I thought perhaps you . . ." Tyndale flinched back from Josie's busy hands.

"You would, blast you!" snapped Devenish, considerably irked, and forgetting that he had cherished the same suspicion of his kinsman.

"Try not to wriggle, please, sir," said Josie. "There's a perishing great splinter here."

An amused gleam lit Tyndale's strained eyes, but Devenish groaned, "Josie! For heaven's sake, child, you must not use such terms."

She bit her lip and threw him an anguished look.

Tyndale asked, rather faintly, "Who is my small angel of mercy?"

Josie gave a quick, firm tug, and a little whimper of

sympathy. Tyndale's eyes became slightly glassy, and a white-ness under his eyes was intensified, but he made no sound.

"You'm brave," she told him, touching his cheek gently. "And I'm new today. I was Tabby, but now I be Josie Storm. When I grows up I going to be Mr. Dev's—"

"Abigail!" yelped Devenish, and then fumed, "And re-move that damned smirk from your face, or I'll shove this hunk of wood back in your thick skull! Josie is going to be *trained* for an abigail is what I mean!"

"You should not swear," scolded the "angel of mercy." "And if I had a friend what was so big and strong and brave, I wouldn't shout at him like what you does."

Devenish scowled. "He ain't a friend. He's my cousin."

"Cousin! I thought relayatives liked one another." She added, "I never had no cousins or nothing."

Devenish stared at her small, wistful face, flashed an un-comfortable look at the grinning Tyndale, and had the grace to redden. "Enjoy your gloating," he grunted. "That's not going to stop, Josie. Give me the handkerchief."

She turned away, holding it apart. "*I* know how!" she declared loftily. "I done it for Akim's mort when he hit her with a gin bottle."

"Did you, by God!" Impressed, Tyndale lowered his head so that she might more easily perform her task.

She folded the handkerchief, by now considerably the worse for wear, into a diagonal strip, tied it around his brow, then inspected her handiwork critically. "It ain't high enough," she admitted, "but at least it will keep the bleedings out of your eyes."

Tyndale assured her that it was splendid, and thanked her for her efforts. Devenish slipped a hand under his arm. "Can you stand? Good man. Up with you."

Tyndale swayed, but the rain was beginning to come down now, the air was chill, and Devenish's supporting arm ena-bled him to remain upright until the dizziness passed.

"He should rest," said Josie, indignantly.

"No—thank you, Miss Josie, but—I shall go on nicely," Tyndale gasped.

And so on they went.

The rain proved of short duration. The wind blew the clouds apart and, unexpectedly, the lowering sun shone be-nignly upon the odd little trio, the two battered young men, and the child, tattered and dirty but, after the fashion of youth, now skipping merrily beside her new friends, her weariness forgotten.

As Devenish expected, his questioning elicited the information that Tyndale's capture had been accomplished shortly after his own, the main difference being that his cousin had been more crudely struck down. "I rather fancy," he growled, "that they had only enough of that revolting ether for me."

"Likely you're right." Tyndale said slowly, "They seem to have gone to no little pains to separate us. I wonder why."

"Perhaps they wanted us to be further delayed in searching for one another. They wasn't to know we—er, would not give a hoot."

Tyndale was briefly silent. "I didn't mean quite that. I collect you fancy Garvey was behind it?"

"I don't *fancy*, cousin! I know da—er, dashed well he was!"

"But—why? Do you think he was that desperately smitten with Yolande?"

"Well, I'd like to know why the devil he would not be! Yolande is—Yolande!"

"I'll not argue that point. But did you not mention that he was, until recently, deep in love with another lady?"

"The Van Lindsay. An accredited Toast. What I may have failed to mention is that rumour has it he's under the hatches."

Tyndale stiffened. "And the Van Lindsay was an heiress? I understood you to say the family was in Dun territory."

"True. But there is a grandmama who's as full of lettuce as she is full of years, and who dotes on the girl." His eyes grim, Devenish growled, "That hound lost her, so now pursues a lady of greater fortune! There's no knowing how desperate he may be, but he travels with an expensive set; Carlton House, no less! And if he does mean to snare Yolande, I pose a double threat. Not only am I known to be betrothed to the lady, but I could tell her much that Garvey would prefer she remain unaware of."

Tyndale nodded. "It is motive enough, and yet—I still cannot fathom the attacks upon us. At most, Garvey will only buy himself a few days in which to ingratiate himself. He surely realizes you will rumble him, and will tell Yolande when—" He broke off. "By Jupiter! You never think . . ."

"That we were supposed to have been dished?" Devenish gave a cynical snort. "I'd not put it past the rogue!" He lengthened his pace. "Now perhaps you can appreciate why I am so anxious to come up with them! Can you walk a shade

109

faster, cousin? I appreciate you ain't in the habit of marching, but—''

It was as much as Tyndale could do to set one foot before the other, to conceal which, he said laughingly, ''Not like you dashing Hyde Park soldiers, eh?''

The more infuriated because it was truth, Devenish whirled to face him. ''Now, damn your impudence, I'd like to know what *you* did that was so blasted much more useful!''

Tyndale shrugged. ''Not my war, cousin.''

''No,'' gritted Devenish, contemptuously. ''And I can well believe that even if it had been, you'd not risk your precious hide to—''

Slipping between them, her pointed little face set into a daunting frown, Josie demanded, ''Why don't you both dub your mummers! Blessed if ever I see such a pair of shagbags!'' She glared up at Devenish, whose face was a study in disbelief. ''You ain't no better than a windy wallets, and he—'' She turned about to fix angry eyes on the startled Tyndale. ''He's too top lofty to admit he's in queer stirrups!''

Tyndale laughed unsteadily, but staggered even as he laughed. Jumping to steady him, Devenish fumed, ''And you, my girl, should have your mouth washed out! Dammit, Tyndale—if you cannot walk, why in the deuce did you not say so?''

''Can . . .'' Tyndale muttered. ''I'm just as eager to reach . . . Yolande as are you. It's—it's just . . . this blasted head, is all.''

''And those yokels gave you more rough handling. What in the world did you do to rate such treatment?''

Leaning on him, despite his reluctance to do so, Tyndale tottered on and said wryly, ''Well, it was raining, and I came upon a snug toolshed by the road and made myself comfortable. Woke up find a dashed blunderbuss aimed at my head, and the farmer and his sons mad as fire because I'd trespassed.''

''Mad as fire! It was likely a trap. I was once caught in just such a shabby scheme. They put you to work, I collect?''

''I never worked so hard in my life! That mean old curmudgeon even berated his daughter for bringing me a drink of water. This afternoon, old Nimms, the farmer, came out and watched me, guzzling at a tankard of ale, and laughing while I dug every weed and rock from the most miserable field you ever saw.

''What—did they not even give you a crust, or a hunk of cheese?''

"No, and there was all the time the most mouth-watering smell of the stew his poor wife was cooking. When I asked him if there was some way I could work for a meal, he thought it hilarious, but I finally talked him into allowing me to instruct his sons in fencing."

Devenish said a surprised "You fence?"

"A . . . er, a little. I told old Nimms I was accounted not paltry in the art, and he said in his crude way that he thought there was little of art in a man's protecting himself. At all events, I was allowed to go into the kitchen and eat, after which largesse I commenced my first lesson." He was feeling steadier and relinquished his grip on his cousin. "Thank you. I can go on now."

"Good. How did your lesson go on? From the look of those louts I'd have thought they'd scarcely know point from grip!"

"Very shrewd of you. They didn't." Tyndale drawled wryly, "Our problem, it developed, was with communication rather than skill. My fine farmer had apparently not thought I referred to fencing with foils."

"With swords? A first lesson? Fella must be queer in his attic!"

"Not with swords."

Devenish frowned. "Then—what the deuce else could—" Comprehension dawned. *"Fencing?"* He grinned, in huge delight. "No, not really! With—*wood?*"

"My good Nimms," Tyndale sighed, "had once seen a picture of an Italian villa surrounded by an ornate fence he particularly admired. He thought I would know of some simple and inexpensive way to build it, and—Now, blast you, Dev!"

"Sorry," wheezed Devenish, wiping his eyes. "So—so when he discovered you'd hoodwinked him, he was—put out, eh?"

"Hoodwinked him? I didn't hoodwink the clod! At least, not intentionally. Much chance I had of convincing him of it!"

"So I should think. What did he say?"

"That he was going to push my face in the dirt and step on it."

"Whereupon," said Devenish, his hilarity fading, "you attempted to show him the error of his ways?"

"Correct. The trouble was he had three stalwart sons. No brains, you understand, but muscles—and to spare."

"And so . . .?"

"And so—they pushed my face into the dirt, and Nimms demanded I admit to being a lying, cheating Captain Sharp. My response, alas, did not please; besides which I had managed to deal him a bloody nose during our little tussle. His sons proceeded to pick me up and run my head against a fence post a few times. So I would know what a fence was, they said. You saw the last act."

"Well, I think it was plain horrid!" Josie said indignantly. "Four to one! They was cowards, sir!"

"Dashed unsporting!" Devenish frowned from his cousin's rueful smile to the blood that slowly crept down to stain the handkerchief about his head. "They must have known you was already hurt."

"From what I saw of the Nimms clan, coz, I rather fancy that would have added spice to their enjoyment."

"Would it! Well, it occurs to me that the family honour has been sullied. And we cannot have that, now can we?" Devenish halted, lost in thought, while his companions watched him wonderingly. "Nothing for it," he said, looking up with a grin. "We must go back."

"Back!" echoed Tyndale. "But—why? Even together we couldn't hope to—"

"Oh, I do not propose to take on the Nimmses. Not—ah, exactly. After all, they did not play fair, so we have a little more—er—scope."

He looked, thought Tyndale, like a small, mischievous boy. "What do you mean to do?" he asked.

Devenish regretfully inspected his last remaining silver button. "Part with this." He wrenched it off. "I had meant to use it to bribe a carter. Still, honour must be served. Josie, my elf, do you recall that last village we trudged through? Do you fancy we can reach it by nightfall?"

She nodded. "If Mr. Craig can walk so far. Oh, what fun it would be! I wonder if the man with the performing bear be there still."

Tyndale, whose eyes had widened during this innocent revelation, turned to his cousin. "Devenish, you never mean to . . .?" he breathed in awe.

Devenish chuckled. "Don't I just!"

*   *   *

It was very cold that night and, although it did not rain, the men of the Nimms family were not without optimism as they advanced in a roseate dawn towards the toolshed.

112

Edgar, the eldest, was inclined to temper hope with reason, however. "It ain't likely as we'd catch another noddicock this quick," he pointed out in a hoarse whisper. "We should've never let that big cove go, Pa. He could've finished the west field by now."

"Ar," the patriarch agreed. "I were a sight rash there, son. Still, by the time we was done, he wasn't good fer much. And ye can never tell. With all this ragtag soldiery creeping about the roads, we might— Hey! Look there! The door be shut so tight as any drum. What'd I tell'ee? We do have hired ourselves another volunteer!"

Exultant, the four big men bore down upon their cunning trap, never dreaming that they were watched by four pairs of eyes, each alight with anticipation.

Farmer Nimms tightened his grip on the serviceable cudgel he carried. "Ready, lads?" he hissed, one hand on the door. His sons grinned and nodded. Movement could be heard from within the toolshed. "Sounds like another big'un," gloated the good farmer, and his sons brandished their clubs, eager for the fray.

Swinging the door wide, Farmer Nimms stepped inside. "You worthless scum!" he roared. "Get—"

The movements in the shed became more pronounced. A strange voice rose in irate protest. The voice of Farmer Nimms also rose. To a shriek. He left his shed far more hurriedly than he had entered it. So hurriedly, in fact, that he ploughed into the three stalwart offspring who pressed in behind him. The fame of the Nimmses had spread far and wide, and it would have been difficult to determine whether they were best known for their truculence, their dishonest dealings, or the brutality they visited upon the unfortunates they caught in their strategically placed toolshed. They took care never to engage in a fair fight, with the result that it had been many a day since they had been bested. They were bested now. The trespasser looming in the doorway was enough to strike fear into the heart of any reasonable man. The bear was extremely large, brown, and annoyed. It reared onto its hind legs, toppling the toolshed in the process, and letting out another roar of displeasure.

Filial affection went by the board. Trapped by the burly figures of his nearest and dearest, Farmer Nimms damned them for knock-in-the-cradles and fought tooth and nail for freedom. Hurled back, the brothers caught sight of the monster looming above them. None of them could seem to move quite fast enough and in their frenzy they collided. Their shrieking profanities did little to improve the temper of the bear, who had taken a very dim view of the toolshed, but had been mollified by the pot of honey Devenish had had the foresight to provide, and into which the good farmer had been so unwise as to put his foot. Since Nimms did not seem inclined to stop and remove the honey pot from his boot, the bear saw his prize being made off with, and sprang in hot pursuit.

Thus it was that Harry Oakes, the apothecary, driving his pony and trap on an early call, beheld such a cavalcade as was to delight the patrons of The Duck and Drake for months to come. Farmer Nimms was well out in front, head and elbows back, legs pumping vigorously, albeit the handicap of a strange pot wrapped around one foot. Behind him, racing at a good rate of speed, were his three boys, their squeals of terror rivalling his own. Next came a large and angry bear (causing Mr. Oakes to turn hurriedly into the trees), and bringing up the rear, a lean individual who waved a long chain while imploring Bruin to stop "like a good boy!"

Not until the procession was fading into the morning mists did Mr. Oakes discover that others had witnessed it. Two young men and a little girl lay in the ditch beside the toppled Nimms toolshed. He was unable to get any sense from them, however, for they were equally overcome, their howls and sobs of laughter having reduced them to near-imbecility and a complete inability to either stand or converse intelligently.

Mr. Oakes abandoned his attempts to communicate and joined in their hilarity.

*　*　*

Despite the relatively fair weather, the progress of Yolande's party was slow. This was in part due to the habits of Socrates, and in part due to the habits of his owner, who could never be convinced of the benefits to be derived from an early start. Mrs. Drummond was of the opinion that none but commoners ventured abroad before noon, and it was only by dint of long and patient representations that Yolande was able to prevail upon the lady to take her breakfast at "the heathen hour" of nine o'clock.

Two days after leaving St. Albans, Mr. Garvey was still escorting them, a circumstance for which Yolande could only be grateful. All her protests that they delayed him were waved aside, and when she again pointed out that he should be travelling eastwards to Stirling, he said he merely altered his plans so as to take the westerly loop on his way north instead of on the way back down to London. "For I have an aged pensioner dwelling in Kilmarnock," he averred suavely. "A devoted old fellow I am promised to visit. I can deliver you and your aunt to Castle Drummond, continue to Kilmarnock and take the Glasgow road east to Stirling. I gave my friends no definite date for my arrival, so you see, dear lady, your worries are quite without foundation."

If Yolande's concerns were unjustified in that sense, they also appeared unwarranted in another. Mr. Garvey was charming, and his assistance of real value, yet there was something about the gentleman she could not like. She had made up her mind therefore, that if she saw signs of his having developed a *tendre* for her, she would be firm in refusing his escort. It soon became obvious, however, to herself if not to her aunt, that he actually derived much more pleasure from the company of the elder lady than from that of her niece. Since the two of them shared both a wide acquaintanceship among the *ton*, and an inclination to gossip, they were in no time at all the very best of friends, chattering away the miles in convivial, if scandalous, fashion, and thus allowing Yolande to indulge her own thoughts in peace.

Those thoughts were far from peaceful, however. Try as she would, she could not banish her anxiety concerning her cousins. However irresponsible Devenish might be judged, she had never had the slightest doubt of his devotion and, while it was true that she had been very cross with him in St. Albans, he was scarcely the man to be easily daunted. As for Craig . . . Her heart gave that odd little jolt that any thought of him seemed to precipitate. She glanced guiltily at her aunt, sitting beside her in the carriage, and was startled to find that lady's enquiring gaze fixed upon her.

"My apologies, dear ma'am," she said hastily, having a vague recollection of some half-heard remark. "I fear I was wool-gathering."

"So I imagined, dear child," her aunt agreed in a faintly martyred voice. "I was urging dear Mr. Garvey to instruct the coachman to make a small detour. I should so much like to see the new construction at the school, should not you? And since we pass this way so seldom . . ."

Yolande blinked, striving to gather her scattered thoughts. "School?"

"We are coming into Rugby, ma'am," volunteered Mr. Garvey with a kindly smile.

Yolande glanced out at the lush, rolling countryside. "Oh—yes, indeed. So we are. But why should we detour? We have no relations at the school, Aunt Bella, have we?"

"Not presently, but you know that all four of your Aunt Cecily's boys came here. I have not seen the new structure Hakewill designed. The school was rebuilt about seven years ago, Mr. Garvey," she added, turning a warm smile upon their companion, "and my brother-in-law tells me the work was most attractively accomplished."

"I am sure you are right, dear," said Yolande. "But perhaps we might stop here on the way home. I am eager to reach Steep Drummond."

"Oh, but this rushing and tearing about is so exhausting," pouted Mrs. Drummond. "I do not complain, for it is not my place. But Mr. Garvey *told* you that Devenish and that Canadian person had turned back, so you need not worry so."

Yolande blushed to think that her distress had been so shrewdly noted and interpreted, but she persisted, "Perhaps they did, at first. But Dev is a very stubborn young man, as you should certainly be aware, Aunt. And Craig is eager to see his inheritance, besides which—"

"Besides which, he was behaving like any love-struck moonling from the moment he saw *you!*" Arabella gave a shrill little titter. "You would scarce credit the impertinence of the fellow, dear Mr. Garvey. No sooner had he all but put us in our graves, than he must come to Park Parapine, trying to ingratiate himself with Sir Martin! I wonder my brother did not at once show the door to the presumptuous upstart, rather than—"

Her own rare temper flaring, Yolande exclaimed, "I think you must forget that Craig Tyndale is my cousin, ma'am, else you would not designate one of our family a presumptuous upstart! Nor can I suppose Mr. Garvey to be in the slightest interested in such matters."

Mr. Garvey's well-shaped brows lifted in faint amusement. Mrs. Drummond, however, stared at her niece in astonishment, clapped a handkerchief to her eyes, and dissolved into tears.

Aghast, Yolande strove to mend matters; a long struggle that ended, of course, with her agreeing that they should detour to see the famous boys' school.

Mr. Hakewill's architectural designs had yielded impressive results, and Mrs. Drummond and Mr. Garvey were vociferous in their admiration of the new buildings. Yolande wandered about reacting politely to their remarks. Inwardly, however, she was as disinterested as she was disturbed. To have lost her temper with an older lady was very bad. And even worse, she had done so in front of a comparative stranger! She *never* lost her temper. Well, almost never. She would not have done it, of course, save for the fact that she was so worried about her two suitors. Guilt struck again and her cheeks flamed. Craig was not her suitor! "And neither is he a presumptuous upstart!" she thought with a flare of irritation. He might be a Colonial, and perhaps he had a shocking blot on his name, and a sad want of fortune, but . . . She sighed, seeing again the concern in his grey eyes as he had bent over her while she lay on the rug after the accident; feeling again the firm clasp of his hands as he made her lie down when she had striven to rise. Such strong hands and yet, so gentle . . .

"Wake up, dearest!"

Yolande started. Her aunt and Mr. Garvey were watching her smilingly. Good gracious! She had drifted off again, like some silly thimblewit! Whatever was wrong with her intellect?

"I declare," said Mrs. Drummond, "one would fancy you fairly enamoured of that door, for you have looked at it this age, and with such *tenderness!*"

Mr. Garvey chuckled. "I think your niece's thoughts were not with the door, dear lady."

"Clever rascal," trilled Mrs. Drummond, giving him a playful tap with her fan. "And you are perfectly right, of course. My dear niece is enchanted! 'Absence, that common cure of love' did not prevail. Alas. Yet—oh, to be young—and in love . . .!"

Yolande could have sunk. She was rescued when Mr. Garvey proceeded to recount an amusing episode of his schooldays, but walking along, her emotions were chaotic. Had she really been gazing tenderly at a door? If so, she had no least recollection of what it had looked like. "Oh, to be young and in love . . ." What stuff, when she had only been thinking of . . . Craig. An even sharper pang of guilt made her squirm. Despite her procrastinations she knew very well that she would eventually marry dear Dev, just as he knew it. To allow her thoughts to wander to another gentleman in so foolish a way was wickedly disloyal.

Raising her eyes she found that Mr. Garvey was watching her with faint curiosity. He must think her a thorough widgeon! She forced a smile, but her cheeks were so hot she knew they must be scarlet.

Chapter Eight

*Far into the morning, Devenish and Tyndale were still chor-*tling over the rout of the Nimmses. The day lived up to its early promise and by mid-afternoon the sun was so hot that the small pilgrimage began to slow. The men took turns carrying Josie until she complained that she was quite able to walk and didn't want to be "babied."

"Why not?" laughed Devenish, setting her down and inwardly relieved to do so. "You *are* a baby"—he ruffled her tangled hair—"and must be coddled."

She scowled at him ferociously. "I is not! You think I'll be a great nuisance, but I knows how to take care of myself and I don't need carrying! You just see if I don't walk so good as what you and Mr. Craig does!"

She ran out ahead, defiance in every line of her. "Revolting grammar!" called Devenish, teasingly.

"What the deuce are you going to do with her?" asked Craig.

"Lord knows. Gad! I keep thinking of how old Nimms shot out of that shed! It was worth the loss of our funds, damme if it wasn't!"

"Yes." Craig grinned. "The family honour is restored."

Devenish sobered. "In part, at least," he said pointedly.

Reddening, Craig was silent, but after a while he chuckled. "How in the world you were able to control that bear is quite beyond me!"

"Nothing to it. I've got the Rat Paws, you see."

"The—*what?*"

"Josie says it means I've a way with animals. I do, as a matter of fact, and it stood us in good stead today, I'll allow. I wonder if poor old Schultz ever got his bear back? His legs were going a mile a minute the last time we saw him."

They went on, talking more or less companionably, but progressing ever more slowly, and not noticing when Josie dropped back to walk with them, and gradually fell behind.

"Jove," sighed Tyndale, drawing a sleeve across his perspiring brow, "I didn't think it ever got hot in England. Have we far to go, yet?"

"Eight or nine miles, at least. I only hope Val is not from home. He's a dashed good fellow, but—his family!" Devenish grimaced. "His brother's a decent sort, but he has a cousin I'd as soon—"

A shrill scream cut off his words. Whirling, he caught a glimpse of Josie, her hair clutched in a large, grimy fist. From the corner of his eye he saw just such another fist clutching a whizzing branch. He ducked, but the branch caught him across the base of the neck and for a little while he saw nothing but wheeling lights.

He aroused to a scuffling sound; an irregular thudding, short heavy breathing, and an occasional gasped-out curse. A dark shape shot past. Not quite sure of what was to do, Devenish gathered that he was missing a jolly good brawl. How it chanced that he was lying down, he could not remember, but he commenced a dogged struggle to get to his feet.

A crowd was involved in violent dispute. "Yoicks!" croaked Devenish, and launched himself into the fray. The crowd thinned, and he blinked and found that Tyndale was battling two men whose head scarves and swarthy countenances proclaimed them gypsies. Even as his vision cleared, a knife was plunged at Tyndale's back. Devenish jumped into action and sent the weapons spinning off.

Tyndale panted, "Thanks . . . coz!"

The knife wielder however, was indignant, and Devenish blocked a hamlike retaliatory fist. "Akim and Benjo, I take it?" he shouted.

"And—Rollo," said Tyndale, jerking his head to the side and a heavily built man sprawled on the grassy verge.

"You took our—Tabby!" snarled Tyndale's opponent, his dark face twisted with passion.

"Yus, and we'll 'ave the law on yer!" shouted his comrade, rushing Devenish, who dodged adroitly.

"Good . . . idea!" Tyndale feinted, then drove home a shattering jab that staggered his sinewy adversary. "We might discover from whom you stole her!"

Patently offended by such tactics, the gypsies abandoned talk in favour of a concentration upon the business at hand. The recumbent member of the trio also surged back into the fray. It was a short but fierce struggle. Tyndale, as Devenish noted with admiration, was a splendid man with his fives, but he was not at the top of his form and was tiring visibly. The

119

impromptu bandage had already been dislodged and the cut over his temple was bleeding so that he was compelled to wipe hurriedly at his eyes. Devenish grassed his man with a well-aimed right, but was sent sprawling by the third gypsy, who had timed the attack nicely. Winded, Devenish cried out as a heavy boot rammed home. Tyndale saw the kick that had savaged him and with a shout of rage leapt astride his cousin. He would have little chance alone, Devenish thought dazedly, and if they were bested, these ruffians would take the child. He fought to rise. She must not end her days in a Flash House, poor mite! She *must* not! He got to his knees, but was unable to stand, so threw himself at the legs of the tall Rollo, and clung doggedly. It was all the chance Tyndale needed. With one blindingly fast uppercut he sent Akim to join Benjo, turned in time to see Devenish crumple again and, seething, drove a fist into Rollo's midsection, then finished him with a powerful chopping blow to the back of the neck.

Hobbling to his cousin, he wheezed, "You . . . all right . . .?"

"Quite," gasped Devenish, clutching his leg. "Good scrap . . . what?"

A small, weeping shape hurtled at them. Frantic hands reached out to stroke back Devenish's tumbled hair. "I thinked ye was . . . cross with me!" gulped the child. "And then Benjo got me and—and I thinked I was going to be . . . sold to the Flash House, surely! Oh, Mr. Dev! You won't never let 'em take me? Don't let 'em! Promise Josie you won't!"

He sat up and pulled her into a hug. "Silly elf," he said gruffly. Her arms flew around his neck and, sobbing, she pressed tight against him. Over her shoulder, he said, "I rather fancy you saved me from getting my ribs . . . stove in, cousin."

"And you—diverted the knife that would have split . . . my wishbone."

It was said so reluctantly that Devenish flared, "I collect you would prefer I had not?"

"No, but . . ." Tyndale hesitated, frowning.

Devenish burst into a breathless laugh. "A trifle awkward, eh?"

"A trifle."

"No matter. We're even, at all events." Devenish put the clinging child from him. "Come, Miss Storm." He gave her hair a slight tug. "There's work to be done. I think our friends yonder would be the better without their boots. Can you pull 'em off?''

She dashed her tears away with the heel of one grubby hand, smiled tremulously, and flew to do his bidding. Tyndale helped him to his feet and, as soon as the boots were removed from the unlovely trio, the two men and the child set forth once more, each carrying a pair of the purloined articles.

For a space they were silent, all three, Tyndale seeming to ache from head to toe, and Devenish's limp becoming ever more pronounced until Tyndale halted and said, "Friend Rollo dealt you a leveller, did he not?"

Snatching back the hand that was unobtrusively gripping his right thigh, Devenish said brightly, "Pooh! Fustian! I shall do nicely."

"He was limping 'fore Rollo kicked him," Josie put in anxiously. "Don't he allus?"

"No, child. Dev, let me have a look."

"Certainly not!" Devenish threw up a restraining hand as Tyndale stepped closer. "I am a most private type and will suffer no one to inspect my—er—limbs."

Tyndale glanced at Josie.

"I seen legs before," she revealed scornfully. "And once I see Akim's—"

"Never mind!" said Devenish, retreating. "No, really, cousin, what do you take me for? Some kind of Spartan slowtop? If there was anything could be done, I'd have yelled for help long since."

"An old injury?" asked Tyndale.

"Yes. Rollo's boot chanced to find it, is all."

"The war? Oh, no—you said you did not get to the Peninsula."

"True. This was another kind of battle. I suppose it was one of the details you complained I left out, when I told you how Tristram Leith and I got the girls away from the chateau in Dinan."

They started to walk on again, and Tyndale asked curiously, "What kind of 'detail'? A pistol ball?"

"Crossbow bolt." Tyndale's jaw dropped, and Devenish said wryly, "Our Frenchman has a taste for medieval weapons."

"Does he, by thunder! Then we had best—"

Her small face sharp with fear, Josie warned shrilly, "Some 'un be coming!"

Devenish pulled her behind him and both men turned to face the cart that came rattling up.

Clinging to Devenish's jacket, Josie gave a sudden glad cry. "Tinker Sam! Oh, Tinker Sam!" She ran to greet the newcomer. "It be *me!* Tabby!"

The cart halted. A round-faced, round-eyed, friendly-looking little man exclaimed, "Tabby? Why—so it do be! And two gents what look, as they say, very much the worse fer wear. There's a tale here, I do expect. And one thing as I loves is a tale. So—come aboard, gents and missy. Where be ye bound fer?"

"Hallelujah!" breathed Devenish.

"And amen," agreed Tyndale.

More practically, Josie said, "Tewkesbury. In exchange for three pair of smelly boots!"

*   *   *

With an eye to his own affairs, Mr. Garvey so charmed Arabella Drummond that for the next two days she was induced to rise very much earlier than was her usual custom, with the result that they reached Leeds in good time. Mr. Garvey directed the coachman to a fine posting house just south of the city and procured excellent accommodations. Having ordered up and enjoyed a superb dinner with his two weary charges, he then accompanied Yolande while she took Socrates for a brief outing in the gardens. He returned her safely to her bedchamber, and took himself off to his own room.

Opening the door, he froze. A lamp burned beside the curtained window, and the wing chair was occupied. The gentleman seated there had a fine head of neatly curled dark hair untouched by grey; his build was slight, his age indeterminate, and his elegance considerable. He raised a pair of warm brown eyes from the pages of the periodical he was idly scanning, and revealed features that were good, if not remarkable. "Do pray come in, my dear James," he murmured in French. "One never knows who might pass by."

Garvey hurriedly swung the door shut, advanced into the room to toss hat and gloves on the bed, and demanded, "Are you mad? If we were seen together! *Up here!*"

The Frenchman shrugged. "Yet you were on your way to see me—is it not so?"

Garvey's cloak followed hat and gloves, and he drew a chair closer to his unexpected visitor. "Yes. But I was in-

122

credibly fortunate in chancing upon an excellent means of explaining my journey, Claude, and—''

Monsieur Claude Sanguinet smiled. His soft voice and gentle manner were at odds with the fact that he was held by many knowledgeable men to be one of the most dangerous plotters in Europe. Garvey, knowing him very well indeed, knew that smile also and quavered into silence.

"Ah," said the Frenchman, laying the periodical aside. "But I think it must be that you are unaware of something, *mon ami*. Namely, that your—er, 'excellent means' chances to be betrothed to an old and so dear friend of ours, one Monsieur Alain Devenish."

"No, but I *am* aware," Garvey asserted eagerly. "And you must be very pleased, Claude. I have disposed of him!"

Sanguinet rested his elbow on the chair arm, and his chin upon the fingers of one slender white hand. He murmured, "Then I am of a surety indebted to you, my dear James. Dare I ask how this—necessity—has been accomplished?"

Garvey glanced to the closed door and lowered his voice. "That rogue of a tiger of mine hired some ruffians to abduct him, carry him away, and put a period to him." He grinned triumphantly. "You can count yourself avenged for—" In the nick of time he stopped himself from saying "for Devenish having kicked you last year!" Monsieur Sanguinet did not care to be reminded of embarrassments. Therefore, he finished, "for his interference."

"But, how charming. And what a great pity it is that your, ah, hirelings bungled the job, my dear."

Garvey's jaw dropped. "But they did not! They could not have! Devenish would have been hot after us if—"

"They appear to have decided," purred Sanguinet, "that the penalty for murdering two aristocrats was too great. At all events, I have it on the most reliable authority that our intrepid friend and his cousin are on their way north at this very moment. I fancy they mean to stay at Longhills, near Malvern. I discover that Devenish has a friend whose country seat is located there."

Dismayed, Garvey muttered, "Longhills? Oh, Montclair's place. I am acquainted with his cousin, Junius Trent."

One of Sanguinet's brows arched. "Is important, this?" He shrugged smiling sweetly.

Garvey reddened and retreated into bluster. "Now, damn those bucolic clods! They took my gold and left the business undone! By thunder, but—"

Sanguinet waved his hand in a gracefully arresting gesture. "But, as is usual, I must do the thing myself."

Staring at him, Garvey went to the round table before the window, and unstoppered a decanter. "You . . .?" he echoed, disbelievingly. "You, personally, will—"

"You are ridiculous, James, do you know? Ah, thank you. I wondered if ever I was to be offered refreshment. As you should surmise, I shall be the—how you say?—master-mind. My hands I do not foul. Dear Monsieur Devenish has dwelt on borrowed time these many months. It was not my intention to attend to him as yet. However, once again he is drawn into my orbit, and this time with *très* convenient the cousin. Do you know aught, my dear James, of Devenish's Canadian cousin?"

Sipping his wine, Garvey proceeded to occupy the other chair and replied, "Only that he comes at a curst inopportune time! They mean to go to *Castle Tyndale*, Claude. Did you know *that?*"

"But of course. I know everything." Sanguinet chuckled suddenly. "And do you know, James, our fine Colonial's arrival may be most fortuitous. Almost one might say Fate plays into our hands. With a little manipulation, perhaps, a *soupçon*, merely, our task yet may be very tidily accomplished, and all explained away for us." He raised his glass. "How sadly puzzled you look, James. Trust me. I really think that this time I have our Devenish in a quite delightful trap. Let us drink to its closing with finality. For do you know, if this foolish Englishman should elude me once more, I believe I might be . . . most vexed."

His manner was as languid, his smile as gentle, as ever, but the glow in the brown eyes contained a red shade that sent a chill down Garvey's spine. He lifted his own glass and said hurriedly, "To our dear friend."

Sanguinet nodded. "And his cousin, James. We must not forget the so charming Colonial cousin!"

* * *

Longhills was a beautiful estate, the great Tudor house being situated on a rolling knoll that commanded a fine view of its extensive park, meadows, woods, and rich pastureland dotted with fat brown cows and threaded by the gentle curve and gleam of the river. The travellers received a hearty welcome from the Honourable Valentine Montclair, a slight dark young man to whom Tyndale warmed at once. That his cousin's old school friend was a man of great wealth and social position was obvious, but there was no trace of height in his manner, which was quiet and so unassuming as to be almost humble. However surprised Montclair may have been to have three tattered and disreputable-appearing visitors thrust upon him, he evinced no sign of anything but delight. A considerably less delighted butler was commanded to provide suitable changes of clothing for the new guests, a frigid-mannered housekeeper was required to prepare suitable apartments, and the great house became a bustling beehive of activity as water was heated, linens allocated, and the cook apprised of the need to adjust his dinner plans. Upon learning that his guests had been obliged to abandon their horses in St. Albans, Montclair sent two grooms riding southward with instructions to reclaim the animals and take them to Castle Tyndale by easy stages.

Upstairs, a kindly abigail took charge of Josie. The child was bathed, her hair brushed until it shone, and an old flannel nightdress was hurriedly cut down to more or less fit her. When he himself had bathed, shaved, and donned the clothes Montclair had somehow conjured up, Devenish went in search of Josie and was slightly nonplussed to discover that her bedchamber was quite small and cheerless. She, however, considered the accommodations little short of palatial, and confided to Devenish that she'd not have dreamed she ever would occupy so lovely a bedchamber. She sighed ecstatically, "Never in all me kip!"

Devenish bade her good-night and returned to the quarters he shared with Tyndale. He found his cousin brushing his hair before the standing mirror, clad in rich, if ill-fitting garments, and looking much more civilized than when he had left him. Watching the Canadian thoughtfully, Devenish perched on the arm of a chair and wondered why the housekeeper had found it necessary that they share this bedchamber and the small adjoining parlour. Certainly, the rooms were luxurious, but it did seem odd that in so enormous a house they might not have been assigned individual apartments.

As if reading his thoughts, Tyndale said with his slow smile, "Have you the impression that Montclair is not the master of this house? I think I'd not trade places with him for all his wealth!"

"Nor I, poor devil! His aunt and that old curmudgeon of a husband of hers rule Val with a rod of iron. And if you think our arrangement miserly, coz, you should see what Josie has been offered."

"Well, it's a sight better than any of us had last night. What d'you mean to do with her, by the bye?"

"God knows. I fancy Yolande will have some solution. Or Lady Louisa."

At this point, the door opened and Montclair enquired if they were comfortably bestowed. Coming into the room, he was very obviously taken aback to discover they shared it, but not wishing to cause a commotion, Devenish lied that they had requested the arrangement because his cousin walked in his sleep. Tyndale concealed his indignation admirably. Montclair's dark eyes glinted with anger, but he kept himself in hand. His aunt, Lady Marcia Trent, had returned from visiting in the village, and would join them for dinner. "She is," he said, "eager to meet you, Tyndale. It seems she is acquainted with poor Lady De Lancey, who has often spoken of you."

"Oh," said Tyndale, slanting an oblique glance at his cousin.

"De Lancey?" Devenish repeated. "Wasn't he that American fellow who was Wellington's Quartermaster General at Waterloo?"

Montclair nodded. "Splendid chap. He was killed, you know, and only been married—what was it, Tyndale? A few days?"

"A little over two weeks when he died, I think. A terrible tragedy." It was a tragedy that had touched him closely, so that Tyndale forgot himself and said broodingly, "Poor Magdalene . . . but he died in her arms—she has that, at least." He sighed, sat down, and began to wrestle with his boots.

Staring at him in stark astonishment, Devenish exploded, "The devil!" How do *you* know?"

"Er . . . well," said Tyndale awkwardly. "It, er—"

"Of course he knows," Montclair interposed in no little bewilderment. "Who should know better? He was *there*, you gudgeon! Damn near stuck his spoon in the wall as a result, and only—"

"*There . . .?*" breathed Devenish. "Tyndale was—at *Waterloo?*"

Montclair stared from one to the other. "Well, of course! He used the name Winters then, but he was a major with the—"

"A . . . *Major . . .?*" Soaring rage banished Devenish's stunned expression. "Why, you dirty . . . lying . . . bastard!" With a howl, he leapt for his cousin. Tyndale's chair

126

went over and they were down in a flurry of arms and legs, while Montclair gave a whoop and sprang clear.

"Miserable *cheat!*" Devenish snarled, locking his hands about Tyndale's throat. "So it wasn't *your war,* eh?"

"Dev! Now, Dev!" Tyndale laughed, tearing at Devenish's wrists. "I never said—"

"No, damn you! But you gave me to—ow!—to understand that—"

"Well—let be! You were so blasted ready to—to believe me a worthless clod, that—"

"Good gracious!" A clear feminine voice cut through the uproar. Sitting astride Tyndale, Devenish jerked his head around, then scrambled to his feet, running a hasty hand through his dishevelled locks.

Lady Marcia Trent stood on the threshold, a tall young exquisite holding the door for her. Tall herself, and angularly elegant, my lady's face had a pinched look, the thin nostrils and tight, small mouth not softened by icy blue eyes, prominent cheekbones, and a pointed chin. Montclair presented his friends with a marked lack of apology for their antics. Nonetheless, as they went down to dine, Lady Trent was soon chattering happily with Tyndale. Her son, Junius, was not so amiable, his sardonic stare repeatedly wandering from one to the other of their unexpected guests while he made few attempts to contribute to the conversation. This was not a cause for dismay, however, since it developed that his mother's notion of "a pleasant cose with the gallant Major" consisted of her complete domination of the conversation, her piercing voice overriding the efforts of any so bold as to attempt a side topic, and only her son daring to interrupt her occasionally.

These tactics neither disturbed nor bored Tyndale. He was very tired and quite content to let the odious woman prose on while he murmured appropriate responses and allowed his own thoughts to wander. Inevitably, they wandered in one direction. He had hitherto known little of affairs of the heart and, although he longed for a loving wife and children, he had begun to fear that either his nature was cold, or his standards too high, for never had he met the lady who could awaken in him any more than a sense of liking or admiration. Until a certain morning in a lane in Sussex. Until he'd seen Miss Yolande Drummond. . . . Yolande, beautiful, sweet and proud, and dainty and brave, and desirable. His sleeping heart was awake and with a vengeance, but what a bitter twist of Fate that of all the girls he had ever met, he must fall desperately in love with a lady who was hopelessly beyond his reach. Not only was she promised, but she was to wed a man who had just this afternoon turned aside the knife that might have killed him! A man who had every right to despise him, and who would likely have been considered justified to have looked the other way rather than saving his life. Not that it made much difference, for no gentleman could pursue a lady already promised. Besides, even had she been free as air, his chances would doubtless have been nil. That lovely and desirable girl would certainly not be permitted to marry a man whose name was so horribly besmirched.

He must, he thought drearily, put her out of his mind. Difficult, if he stayed at Castle Tyndale, for Devenish had said that Steep Drummond was only ten miles distant. To run the risk that occasionally in the empty years to come he would see her—as Mrs. Alain Devenish—was too daunting a prospect to contemplate. No, it would not do. He must strive to clear his father's name, and then either go back to Canada or settle somewhere at a safe distance from his adored but forbidden lady.

He was very quiet for the balance of the evening, and despite his weariness, slept fitfully.

They left Longhills early the following morning, Devenish and Josie occupying the chaise Montclair had insisted they borrow, and Tyndale riding a magnificent blood mare. Their host accompanied them to the northernmost border of his far-flung preserves, then watched rather wistfully as they left him, Devenish turning back to wave and promise the chaise and horses would be well cared for and promptly returned.

Montclair called, "Keep them, old fellow, until my grooms come with your own horses. They can bring back my cattle then."

"Right you are!" Devenish lifted the reins. "Off we go, Josie Storm," he said joyously. "Egad, but I can scarce wait to see Yolande!"

The chaise picked up speed.

Tyndale gazed after it for a moment, then followed.

*   *   *

Steep Drummond was constructed of red sandstone and, perched on the top of its hill, turned a defiant eye to the rest of the world as though it were a fortress, maintaining stern guard over its domain. It was a large house, uncompromisingly square, and with gardens so neat and trees so uniformly

128

spaced they gave the appearance of being prepared at all times for a tour of inspection.

On this grey spring morning, smoke curled from several chimneys, one of which led from the morning room where the fire blazed merrily. Standing before the hearth, hands clasped behind his back, General Sir Andrew Drummond's craggy face did not, however, look in the least merry. As was the way of his house, he was a tall man, and his well-built frame was as lean and erect as ever, although the thick, once-red hair was now iron-grey. He had the Drummond chin, which had lost not one whit of its belligerence and was, at the moment, decidedly aggressive. "Yon wee hoond," he proclaimed, "has seen fit tae sink his fangs intae ma mon, and nip twa o' the hoosemaids! I've held ma peace the noo, Arrrabella, but enough 's as guid as a feast! 'Tis a chancy business tae lure a decent chef up here, forbye. I'll nae hae him run off by any scrrruffy mongrel! Do I make m'sel' clearrr, ma'am?"

The question was debatable. Blinking at him, his daughter-in-law asked uncertainly, "Yolande, what did your grandfather say?"

Exasperated, the General's fierce green eyes rolled at the ceiling, his moustache bristled, and he uttered a sound midway between snort and groan—a sort of "och-unnh!"—while reflecting that from among all the women in the world, his eldest boy had seen fit to choose *this* silly widgeon!

Regarding him with fond amusement, Yolande said, "I see you still become pure Scots when irked, sir."

"All Scots are puir!" he asserted.

"Their whisky, at least," his irreverent granddaughter chuckled, winning an immediate answering grin. "It would seem, Aunt Bella, that Socrates has been partaking of the servants, and Grandpapa's chef has threatened to leave. You really will have to muzzle him, if—"

"Muzzle him!" exploded the General. "I'd a sight sooner shoot the wretched pest oot o' hand!"

This, it developed, Mrs. Drummond did understand, for she uttered a shriek and clapped handkerchief to tearless eyes. "Oh! How could you be so—so unkind?" she sobbed. "My d-dear little Socrates! All—*all* I have left in the . . . whole, wide world!"

The wiles that worked so well with Lady Louisa did not so much as check the General. "Then," he said dourly, suddenly becoming punctiliously English, "do you wish your worldly goods to remain intact, madam, I would suggest you confine your pestilent pet to a leash!"

"Cruel!" wept Mrs. Drummond. "Cruel!" And wailing, departed.

"Whisht!" the General erupted as the door closed behind her. "How do you abide that caper wit, Yolande? I'd have thought you could have delayed your visit until one of your brothers could escort you. Or at least, that young scapegrace, Devenish—though I canna abide the boy!"

A frown shadowing Yolande's eyes, she said, "Papa would have come, save that poor Rosemary is miserably ill with measles and Mama draws so much support from him at such times, you know. As to Aunt Arabella, why, I suppose the poor soul needs to be needed. And I needed a chaperon."

"At your age?" he snorted, tactlessly. "Gammon! Besides, you'd that fella Garvey to escort you, in addition to the outriders and your abigail. I'd have thought 'twas an ample sufficiency."

"We met Mr. Garvey quite by accident, sir, and it was indeed good of him to stay with us for the rest of the journey. Although he denied it, I suspect we took him out of his way."

"Very likely. Young Hamish MacInnes told me he saw the man bowling along north of Kilmarnock, so he canna have stayed long with his retired servant, if indeed there is such a creature. He probably told you he was to visit there purely to set your mind at ease. He seemed a well-bred sort of man, for all he cries friends with that Germanic clod who'll next usurp the throne."

Yolande threw up her hands in mock horror. "Heavens! Treason!"

"Fiddlesticks! Well, miss? Well?" He glared ferociously at her, even while thinking how pretty she was, gracefully disposed on the green damask sofa, wearing a morning dress of palest lime muslin, and with her hair arranged into glossy curls, soft about her face. "I suppose I'll next be forced to play host to your would-be spouse, eh? Chances are he's hot after you, as usual!"

"Perhaps not, sir," Yolande answered quietly. "We had a small—er, difference of opinion and Dev seems to have gone off in a huff."

"Good! You're well rid of him. He's no more ready to settle down than Brummel would be to wear Petersham trousers!"

She smiled. "You make it all sound very simple, Grand-papa."

"Aye. Well, so it is. If ye dinna care for the laddie, ye shouldna wed him. And—if ye *do* care for him, ye shouldna wed him. Hoot-toot, whar's the hair-tearing in that?"

Laughing, Yolande reached out her hand to him and, as he came to take it and sit beside her, scolded, "Alain is truly a fine young man, dearest. Why do you so dislike him?"

A frown tugged at his bushy brows. "Partly," he said softly, "because he is all frivolity and foolishness, and has never stuck to, nor accomplished aught in his ne'er-do-well life."

"I shall be so bold as to pull caps with you on that score," she argued in her gentle fashion. "Alain is, and I know this for a fact, a brave and fearless fighter, who stood by Tristram Leith when they were hopelessly outnumbered in Brittany last year. When he was hurt, he endured a great deal of misery with no complaint, so Leith told me. He is full of spirit, and if he has not yet settled down to managing his estates and—and setting up his nursery, why, it is for no worse reason than that I have made him wait so long."

Watching her narrowly, he said, "Which brings me to my other reason. I collect you must care for him very deeply, lass. And I'll own I've heard a few things of late to his credit. Yet, I've a wee suspicion that you have been pushed into this promise because my son and Louisa wish it. And that is an utter folly that I'll no—" He checked, glancing with irritation at the door as it opened and his stocky little butler entered to announce, "Mr. Devenish, Mr. Tyndale, and Mistress Storm, General."

Yolande started, and her heart began to pound in a most ridiculous way. *"Mistress Storm . . .?"* She turned, gave a gasp, and came instinctively to her feet as she saw the signs of battle on the faces of the two young men.

Standing also, General Drummond welcomed Devenish with cool dignity. Upon being introduced to Tyndale, he stared, frowned, and said, "Tyndale? Strange, I'd not even known of your existence until my granddaughter told me of you. Yet I feel we've met before. Gad, but I know we have! Wasn't it—"

"At the Horse Guards, I believe, sir. Though I was presented to you as—"

"Winters! Major Craig Winters! Right you are!" The General extended his hand. "Heard great things of you, young

131

fella, but never dreamt you was a Tyndale! Don't use the family name, eh?"

Tyndale smiled, his eyes very empty, and moved to shake hands with Yolande.

Quite bewildered by these disclosures, she said, "Why cousin! I'd not the faintest notion you were in the army."

"And at Waterloo, m'dear," said Devenish, coming up jealously to claim her hand and press it to his lips. "I was fairly bowled over when Montclair told me of it. Never heard such wicked deceit!"

Sir Andrew's sharp glance at the Major surprised a wistfulness in the lean face. "Oho!" he thought. "So that's the way the land lies!"

Yolande was still striving to recover from the all too familiar lightning bolt that had again struck her the instant Tyndale touched her hand. She said in pretty confusion, "Well, well—never mind that now. How glad I am to see you both! But how naughty of you, firstly to have vanished, and now to come here!"

"You never thought to keep me away?" Devenish grinned, squeezing the hand he still held. "The fact is, Tyndale and I were set upon. Robbed, carried off, and dumped miles from anywhere!"

"By Jove!" fumed the General, his whiskers bristling alarmingly. "Do not just stand there, laddie! Set ye doon. You too, Major. Yolande, never loiter about with your mouth at half-cock! Pour these fellows some cognac! Now, Alain, tell us of it!"

Devenish obliged in his usual exuberant fashion, Tyndale inserting an occasional quiet remark of his own. Listening with indignant incredulity, Sir Andrew variously smothered oaths, snorted his outrage, or applauded the cousins' resourcefulness. Just as intent, Yolande was soon very pale, her horrified gaze darting from one young gentleman to the other. Devenish was only halfway through his tale, however, when the General suddenly flung up a hand. "Lord! Where is my mind? Devenish—do we not neglect someone?"

Devenish blinked. "Eh? Who?"

"The child!" Tyndale exclaimed in dismay. "By gad! What's become of her?"

"I be here," came a scared little voice, and Josie, her eyes huge and fearful, peeped from around the back of a tall wing chair.

"Jupiter, but I forgot her," cried Devenish. "Come here,

elf, and make your curtsy to Miss Yolande Drummond and General Sir Andrew Drummond.''

Trembling with nervousness, Josie crept out and essayed two clumsy curtsies.

"Really, Dev!" Yolande scolded. "You could at least tell us the poor child's name.''

"Enderby announced her," he said defensively.

Josie flushed. "I be Josie Storm now," she piped. "I was Tabby, but Mr. Dev found me and when I grow up I going to be his—''

"Housekeeper!" Devenish inserted, in the nick of time.

Tyndale chuckled, and a corner of the General's stern mouth twitched appreciatively.

"*Found* you?" echoed Yolande, much intrigued. "Dev, whatever have you been about? You've never kidnapped the child?''

"'Course he hasn't!" said Josie scornfully. "I followed Mr. Dev because I don't want to be sold to no Flash House. He didn't want me, but he's going to train me for a abigail if *he* don't want me when I be growed.''

Devenish sank his head into his hands. The General gasped. Tyndale turned away, smothering a grin. Yolande, her warm heart touched, stroked the child's dusky curls and, not deigning to pretend unawareness of such horrors as Flash Houses, said gently, "Poor little girl, what a dreadful time you have had. Are your parents living?''

Kindness was a blessing Josie had known but seldom, and at this, tears blinded her. Dashing them away, she blinked up at this fairy princess of a lady and divulged huskily that she had been stole and didn't, if you please, know who her parents had been.

"The devil!" muttered Drummond. "You did perfectly right, Devenish. What d'you mean to do with her?''

"I was hoping Yolande or Lady Louisa could advise me, sir.''

Yolande, whose grave regard had not left the child, said, "Did you and Cousin Craig buy her this dress, Dev?''

"Yes," he answered proudly. "Jolly good—what?''

Yolande shook her head at him in the time-honoured sympathy of a woman for a helpless male, and asked, "Josie, would you really like to be an abigail?''

"I'd like to be a lady, like you." The child sighed wistfully. "But I'd a sight liefer be an abigail than be sold to some bloody Flash House!''

133

Tyndale and the General dissolved into mutual mirth. Devenish groaned and clutched his locks. Yolande, her face scarlet, was momentarily struck dumb. Horrified, Josie threw both hands to paling cheeks, and her gaze darted to her god. "Oh," she wailed, "I said something drefful again! Don't ye be cross with Josie, now! Don't ye!"

"Of—of course he will not," stammered Yolande. "It is only, er—you will soon learn. Dev, excuse me, please. I will hear the rest of your tale later. Come, Josie, we will see what we can do about that—dress."

She extended one dainty and exquisitely manicured hand. Staring from it to Devenish, Josie demurred, "If you please, ma'am, I'd like to stay with Mr. Dev."

"Castle Tyndale," cautioned the General softly, "is no place for a child, Devenish."

"No, sir," Devenish agreed. "And what's more, my elf, you'll be a sight better off with Miss Drummond than jauntering about the countryside with two rogues like Tyndale and me." He threw up one hand, silencing the forlorn attempt at a plea. "Do as you're told! Lord, but I am surer than ever that I should have left you in Cricklade! Which reminds me— Yolande, where is that reptile, Garvey? Still trying to fix his interest with you?"

She frowned. "Oh, never start that again! Mr. Garvey was the essence of courtesy, which is more than could be said for you, Dev! Only see how you have made the child weep! Truly, you should be spanked!"

"Don't you never cut up stiff with him!" sobbed Josie, turning on her in a flame. "He can make me cry if he wants. He don't mean it. It's just—he don't want me. And why should he? I ain't got a pretty face, and I'm just—just a nuisance to . . . to him. . . ." Her voice broke, and she stood there in choked silence, the tears coursing down her gaunt little face.

With a muffled cry, Yolande pulled the child into her arms. "Of course he wants you! We all want you!" Over Josie's shoulder, she flashed a fuming glare at the hapless Devenish, then murmured, "Come, dear. We'll visit the kitchen first, for I'm sure you would like a glass of milk and there may be some cheese tarts left. Then I'll take you down to see our new filly—should you like that?"

Her woes forgotten, Josie dragged one skinny arm across her eyes, and said eagerly that she would like that very much, adding an anxious, "Providing Mr. Dev do not go off without me."

Devenish, his own eyes rather inexplicably moist, promised gruffly that he would not desert her.

"All right," said Josie sunnily, accepting Yolande's hand. "I'll go with you, miss. I loves animals. Though I ain't got the way with 'em like what Mr. Dev has. Did you know," she went on chattily, "that he's got the Rat Paws?"

As an amused Tyndale closed the door behind them, Devenish turned to find the General's fascinated gaze upon his hands.

"Be dashed if I ever noticed it," said Sir Andrew. "Let us have a look—poor fellow."

Chapter Nine

The clouds had lightened, but a brisk wind blew Yolande's pelisse and tumbled her hair as she leaned against the paddock fence, watching Josie romp happily with the two-week old filly. She could scarcely wait to see Devenish and hear the rest of his adventures. From what she had heard, Tyndale had been quite brutally beaten. Her heart turned over as a picture of his pale bruised face came into her mind's eye. Whatever must he think of England, being so newly arrived and so savagely dealt with? But, he was not newly arrived, of course. He was a major, and had survived the terrible Battle of Waterloo. She thought with a sudden surge of irritation, "Oh, how I wish they had not come here! I wish Dev had not brought Craig!" But in the next breath she was wishing that Devenish would hurry to her.

The child did not look so scared any more, poor mite. And they would soon find some decent clothes for her. That awful dress! How could those two great moonlings have thought it became her? It was at least three sizes too large, and that hideous red-and-white check was downright ghastly! Already Peattie and Sullivan were quarrelling happily over an ell of cambric and several pattern cards, and if she knew those two redoubtable women, their nimble fingers would have fashioned a far more attractive frock for the little girl by morning.

"Here you are, my delight!"

She jumped and, relieved to see that Devenish was alone, reached out both hands in welcome.

Devenish took them strongly and kissed each. "Lord, but I've missed you!" he said with unusual fervour. "Are you ready to go home yet?"

"I just arrived, silly boy," she laughed. "And you have no business to have come!"

Deliberately misinterpreting, he said a blithe, "Oh, I slipped away as soon as I could in good conscience do so. Luckily, Tyndale's taken your grandfather's fancy, and they're jawing like a couple of old campaigners." His merry eyes slipped past her. "Josie found a friend, I see. Gad! What a fine filly! Who's the dam? Is she—"

"Never mind the filly, sir," said Yolande, trying to look stern, while thinking how hopeless a case he was to take it for granted so breezily that they had nothing more important to discuss than that Molly-My-Lass had dropped her foal. The marks of combat were very evident upon his classic countenance and, touching his perfectly straight, slim nose, she murmured, "It never ceases to amaze me that through your many battles you've managed to keep this article from being broken."

"Tactics," he asserted, seizing her finger and kissing it. "I was born to be a general, but the Horse Guards lacked the sense to snap me up."

Despite his light manner, she thought he looked tired and said gently, "Poor Dev. What a dreadful time you have had." And then, teasing him, "Are you quite sure it is not all a hum designed to cover up the fact that you and Craig fought all the way up here?"

"You're not so far out, at that," he chuckled, reluctantly relinquishing her hand. "Though not one another. We've both—more or less . . . er, taken vows not to—to come to blows. Ever." As always when he was in earnest, he stumbled and flushed, and darted a self-conscious glance at her. "Curst n-nuisance, ain't it?"

"Indeed not! I think it splendid! And splendid that you rescued the child. Did you ride Miss Farthing all the way up here?"

"Oh, no. She and Lazzy grow fat in St. Albans. I fancy we will have a very large reckoning at the posting house."

Dismayed, she cried, "But—Dev! Your horses were taken from there. Did not you and Craig call for them?"

"Devil we did! What d'you mean—taken?"

"Well—oh, heavens! We all thought— Oh, you never think they were stolen? Craig thinks the world of that queer animal of his, and Miss—"

"That slippery rogue!" raged Devenish. "I'll call him out, by God! Where is he? Not too far from you, I'll warrant!"

"What? Who? If you mean Craig—"

"Not Craig, m'dear! Not this time!"

"Then— Dev, do you *know* who is responsible for these dreadful things?"

"Assuredly! Your gallant, conciliating escort! And as for—"

She stiffened and stepped back a pace. "*James . . . Garvey?*" she whispered, staring at him incredulously. "Oh, but . . .you cannot be serious?"

"Oh, can I not!"

"Then you must be all about in your head! No, really— you allow jealousy to go too far. My aunt and I—"

"Were properly gammoned," he rasped, flaming with wrath over the loss of his beloved mare.

"I was not 'gammoned,' as you so crudely put it," she declared angrily. "I am truly sorry you were set upon, but since you were last seen in the tap you were probably very well to live, and—"

"Well, if that don't beat the Dutch! Here I've been lured into an ambush, drugged, robbed, tossed into a ditch and left to wander over half England with not so much as a groat in my pockets. And every moment half out of my wits with worry for you! And you meanwhile, allow that treacherous scoundrel to—"

Her chin lifting haughtily, Yolande countered, "Since you are so sure Mr. Garvey is a treacherous scoundrel, one must presume he introduced himself before clapping the drugged rag over your face."

"No, he did not," he fumed. "Nor did he hand Tyndale his calling card before breaking his head! But that don't mean he wasn't behind everything! And if you was half as shrewd a judge of character as—"

"Then dare I ask, O infallible judge, upon what—save your despicable suspicions—you base this wicked slander?"

Devenish marched closer, grabbed her shoulders, and held her firm despite her struggles. "My opinion, ma'am, is based not upon suspicions, but upon something that happened whilst I was in Dinan last autumn."

Shock came into her eyes, and her struggles ceased abruptly. Any lover with an ounce of wisdom in the ways of women would have allowed those ominous words to sink in. Devenish, however, was as inexperienced in courtship as he was swift in temper, and swept on disastrously. "And furthermore, I have every right to be both concerned and jealous as bedamned over you! As soon as you stop playing off your coquettish airs and set a date, we will—"

"*Coquettish . . . !*" she gasped, wrenching free. "Why, of all the—"

"Well, dash it all, Yolande, when *are* you going to permit me to announce it?"

Her heart fluttering, she said, "Perhaps never, if I must face a future in which you are ready to call out every gentleman I chance to speak to!"

"*Never?* My God! You do not— Dearest girl . . . you never mean to cry off?"

She felt miserable now and close to tears, and darting a glance at him saw that he was very white, a stark desolation in his face. She loved him dearly and, struck to the heart, reached out her hand. "Forgive me. That was very bad. But, you know, Dev, I have almost as—as nasty a temper as do you."

He clasped her hand between both his own, scanning her beloved features anxiously. She had spoken in the heat of anger, merely. She had not truly meant that she might not wed him. For a moment, the prospect of a future in which Yolande played no part had stretched out, bleak and terrible before him, but that was silliness. They were meant for each other; they always had been meant for each other. He must learn to handle her more gently was all. It was difficult sometimes, when one had grown up with a chit, to see her as anything but a pigtailed schoolgirl. . . . But Yolande was far from that now, and other men—too many, blast them!—saw her with far different eyes. "I'm a crazy clunch," he said repentantly, "and you are perfectly right, I'm jealous as a link boy's torch. I love you, you know. Very much. But—I wonder you tolerate me, much less accept me as a husband."

The declaration was as clumsy as it was rare. Overwhelmed, Yolande tightened her grip on his hand and smiled mistily.

Devenish knew a great surge of relief. Her affection was plain to see. He was reprieved! Offering his arm, he said with his engaging grin, "A stroll around the riding club, m'dear?"

She took his arm, and as they strolled along together he told her most of what had transpired. He spoke lightly, but at the finish she halted and stood regarding him in no little perplexity.

"However can you laugh at it? You might very well have been killed! I can certainly understand your aversion to Mr. Garvey, and I will be honest, Dev, and admit I cannot quite like him, although I have no complaints as to his treatment of us. I assure you he made no attempt to engage my affections. He was kind and considerate, and apparently with no other object in view than to be of help to us. He said his adieux very politely when he delivered us safely here, and I've not seen him since. Why would he have gone to the trouble and risk of having you abducted, as you suspect, if he did not mean to try and fix his interest with me?"

"Perhaps he had another motive." He thought, "Perhaps he was hoping to please Sanguinet," but he knew that would sound farfetched, so said nothing more.

Yolande eyed him uncertainly. "Are you thinking that Craig might pose a threat to him? But—how could he? Craig knows so few people over here."

"I wouldn't refine overmuch on that, m'dear. That varmint knows a sight more people than he'll admit to."

"Now *that*,—" she smiled—"sounds much more like dear Dev."

"How so?"

"Why, when last I saw you it seemed only a matter of time before you two were at it with sword and dagger! Yet just now, when you were telling me of your adventures, one might have thought Craig your dearest friend."

"Good God! How could I give you so revolting an impression! Only because he saved my life, I'm not like to change my opinion of the rascal."

"Saved your life? Heavens! When?"

"During our scuffle with Messrs. Akim and Benjo. I told you of it."

"You did not say your *life* was endangered!"

"Oh. Well, I was downed and just for a minute or two knocked clean out of time. Old Craig stood over me when one of the louts made to kick my ribs in, and fought like a lion till I could hop up again."

Her eyes glowed. "How splendid!"

"Yes. I'll admit it was, rather. I was surprised to see how well he handled himself, for he's such a quiet type. I was never more shocked than to hear he'd served at Waterloo."

"It does seem incredible. And at first he was at pains to make us think he had only just arrived in England."

"Well, I suppose he had. He likely joined up in Belgium.

139

Never look so doubtful. He was at Waterloo all right, and got himself properly stove in."

"He was wounded? Are you sure there can be no mistake?" And she knew that there was no mistake, but that she asked purely to learn more of Craig.

"Quite sure. For one thing, I saw the scar on his chest—beast of a thing! For another . . ." He frowned a little. "When we was at Longhills, Montclair's place, you know, Craig and I were given a room to share—if you can credit it."

"My goodness! They must have been very full of guests."

"Lord, no! There was only Montclair and the Trents—and Selby was from home, thank God! But, never mind about that. The point is that Craig started to talk to me in the night—or so I thought, only it turned out he was dreaming. Had the deuce of a time with him. He kept saying that he was 'all right' and that they must hold their position at all costs. There wasn't much doubt what he was re-living, and I'd judge the real thing to have been—" he kicked at a clump of dandelions—"rather grim."

For a moment Yolande stood silent and very still, staring also at the dandelions. Then, drawing a deep breath she said, "I see. No wonder you name him a shifty scoundrel! He deceived us all."

Devenish glanced up, met her smile, and grinned responsively. "Didn't he just! Which—"

"Mr. Dev! Oh—Mr. Dev!"

Mounted on the back of the filly's mother, Josie ambled towards them.

"My Lady Fair," Devenish laughed. "How did you manage to get up on that mighty charger?"

"By Jove!" exclaimed Tyndale, wandering up to them with the General. "What a magnificent animal! A Belgian, sir?"

"Clydesdale," said Drummond, proudly. "The breed was founded in my father's youth. That's Molly-My-Lass you're looking at."

They all walked closer to the fence, and Tyndale reached up to stroke the neck of the great horse, who suffered his caress for only a moment before moving to nuzzle at Devenish.

Nodding at Josie, the General observed, "That must have been a large climb for you, little lady."

"Oh, I loves horses, sir," said she brightly. "And they like me. Mostly. I just climbed up the fence and then hopped on. But I think I'll come down now please, 'cause her back's so wide it's making me legs stretch awful!''

Devenish put one hand on the fence, but hesitated. Craig swung with lithe ease over the bars and into the paddock, and lifted the child down.

A part of Yolande's mind registered the fact that poor Dev's leg must be troubling him again, which was natural enough after so long and violent a journey. Most of her awareness was centred on Craig, however. How kind that he had moved so quickly to spare Dev any possible embarrassment. He was smiling at something Josie had said, the wind ruffling his light hair, the sunshine bright on his face, accenting the laugh lines about his eyes.

The filly came flirting over, and Josie made a dart for the pretty creature, but with a flaunt of her tail and a roll of saucy eyes, the filly bounced off again. Craig swept Josie up and settled her on the fence, and Devenish reached up to collect her. Climbing the rails, Craig swung one leg over the top, glanced at Yolande, and paused, struck into immobility as his eyes met hers. The clear grey gaze seemed to pierce her heart and she could not look away. Time had halted. Yolande seemed scarcely to breathe and was so entranced that it was all she could do not to move towards him, and Craig sat astride the topmost rail as one hypnotized.

Devenish whirled Josie around, and the child's shrill joyous squeal shattered the spell. Tyndale gasped and jumped quickly to the ground.

Her breathing very fast and her cheeks very pink, Yolande called, ''Josie, I think we should go inside now and change for luncheon.'' Not daring to look at Tyndale, she asked, ''Are you gentlemen coming?''

Devenish was beside her at once. Tyndale declined, however, saying with a somewhat fixed smile that he would like to know more of the Clydesdales, if the General would be so kind as to tell him of the breed.

Sir Andrew was more than willing. ''A Dutch stallion was the founder,'' he began. ''They brought him up here from England, and we've bred many fine animals since. Molly's one of the larger specimens—weighs in the neighbourhood of two thousand pounds. Did you mark her fetlocks, and . . .?''

As she walked back towards the house, listening with only half an ear to Josie's merry chatter, Yolande's eyes were troubled.

* * *

Tyndale now found himself in the unenviable position of longing to be near Yolande, yet dreading each moment he spent in her company. In an effort to end his misery, he remarked in a casual way that he would start for the castle after luncheon. Sir Andrew, however, had taken a liking to the tall young Canadian, and was determined he should stay on, at least for a few days. In this he was abetted by his widowed daughter, Mrs. Caroline Fraser. This angular, kind-hearted, but rather sharp-tongued lady ran the Drummond household with inflexible efficiency. She mistrusted Devenish and had privately advised Yolande that no gentleman possessed of such extraordinary good looks could be expected to be a faithful husband. Mrs. Fraser had no use for "foreigners" in the general way, but Craig's rather shy smile and gentle manner had made an impression on her. Sensing that Yolande was not indifferent to him and aware that Arabella Drummond (whom she detested) loathed him, she joyously added her own voice to that of her father in urging that both men make Steep Drummond their temporary headquarters.

Desperate to escape, but dreading to offend, Craig suggested that he should go on alone, while Devenish remained. Mrs. Fraser brushed his hesitancy aside, and the General's eye began to take on a frosty glare, so that Craig had no recourse but to accept the hospitality so generously offered. He did so with sufficient grace that the old gentleman's suspicions were lulled. Delighted, he clapped him on the shoulder, admonishing, "Dinna fash ye'sel, laddie, we'll nae demand ye don sporran and kilts!" this drawing a laugh from almost all those present. The exception was Yolande. She sensed the real reason behind Craig's attempt to leave, and directed a sober glance at him that caused his beleaguered heart to cramp painfully.

Contrary to what others might think, sporran and kilts were not unknown to Tyndale, but to Josie they were both new and vastly intriguing. It was the custom at Steep Drummond for the colours to be taken down with full ceremony each dusk, and when the child's eyes first rested on one of the General's retainers in all the glory of kilts, tartan, and bagpipes, she was speechless with awe and astonishment. They all followed to the roof and the small platform around the flagpole. The pipes rang out their unique song, the Scot marched proudly, the cold wind blew, and the kilts swung. A glint of curiosity grew in Josie's eyes. She edged closer and, her watchfulness unrewarded, appeared to experience some continuing difficulty with her shoe. When the flags were down, folded, and being reverently borne away, the child contrived to head the small procession and was obliged to pause on the stairs and again attend to her recalcitrant shoe buckle. Craig, his mind burdened with other matters, did not notice this behavior. Devenish was both aware of and amused by it. Coming up with Josie, he gripped her elbow and propelled her along beside him.

Scarlet, she gulped, "I was—only wondering—"

"I know just what you were wondering," he said *sotto voce*. "And they *do*, so have done, wretched little elf!"

She saw the laugh in his eyes and knew he was not angered, so accompanied him cheerfully enough, but at the foot of the stairs was evidently still fast gripped by curiosity, for she murmured, "Then they must be awful tiny not to show under that—"

"I beg your pardon, dear?" asked Yolande.

"I said, if that great big man wears—"

"She—ah, said she didn't—er, know about tartans," Devenish blurted.

His beloved turned an impish smile upon him. "Oh," she said meekly.

There were many tartans at Steep Drummond that evening. Word that the General's lovely granddaughter was visiting him had spread lightning fast through the Scottish hills. Several dinner guests had found their sons extraordinarily willing to accompany them, and by nine o'clock a steady stream of chaises and sporting vehicles was bowling up the drive, well escorted by riders. Yolande, clad in a gown of creamy crepe, wore also the plaid of her house, held at the shoulder by a great sapphire pin. The soft blue, green, and rust of the tartan became her, lending her a dignity that enhanced her beauty. She was hemmed in by ardent young gentlemen and a few just as ardent but less youthful. Devenish was as admired by the ladies as his love was worshipped by the gentlemen. He was impatient with what he described as "doing the pretty" and parties bored him, but he was much too well mannered to show it. His pleasant laugh rang out often; he managed to convince all about him that he was thoroughly enjoying himself, and when Mrs. Fraser sat down at the pianoforte in the music room and an impromptu hop came into being, he danced politely with Yolande's very good friend, Miss Hannah Abercrombie, who had red hair and a high-pitched giggle; and next with Miss Mary Gordon, a dark pretty girl who, harbouring a secret *tendre* for him, trembled so much that she succeeded in conveying her nervousness to him, so that at the first decent opportunity he contrived to wend his way to Yolande's side.

With equal determination, Craig stayed as far from his lovely cousin as manners would allow. Having carefully rehearsed a means of escape when he should ask her to dance, Yolande was denied the opportunity to put it to use. She knew perfectly well why he did not approach her, and told herself she should be grateful for his common sense. But she was woman enough to be disappointed. She was not alone in this. Craig fell short of being a handsome man, but no one could have denied that he was attractive, and many a feminine eye turned to the corner of the room where his tumbled fair hair could be glimpsed above the heads of the other gentlemen. He, however, was quite unaware of this attention, and had anyone told him of it, would have laughed and decried it as rank flattery. Embroiled in a discussion of the quarter horses that were gaining much popularity in Canada, he was asked by a well set-up gentleman with a fine military moustache if he had as yet seen Scotland's Clydesdales.

"I have," he replied, his eyes kindling. "And they are magnificent, if I do right to judge by Molly-My-Lass."

"Och, ye do, laddie," said his new acquaintance with enthusiasm. "Did ye hear that the noo, Drummond? 'Tis a bonnie braw laddie ye've claimed for a guest. We'll make a good Scot oot o' him yet, eh?"

The General smiled and rested one hand on Craig's broad shoulder. "I don't know about that, Donald, but he's a fine soldier, that I do know. He was at Waterloo. Served with—was it the Forty-Third, Tyndale?"

An admiring crowd had gathered at these magical words. Flushing, Tyndale stammered, "Thank you, but—er, that's not quite it, sir. I was—"

"With a line regiment, perhaps?" asked young Hamish MacInnes, who had his own aspirations for the fair Yolande's hand and would have given his ears to have been at Waterloo.

Tyndale said quietly, "I was with the Union Brigade."

MacInnes opened his eyes. The General muttered, "Were you, by God!"

"And—your regiment, sir?" persisted Mr. Walter Donald, eagerly.

"The Scots Greys."

Shouts and cheers arose. Grinding his teeth, MacInnes

retreated. There was no fighting that! Tyndale was the hero of the hour. When the uproar eased a trifle, General Drummond drew the uncomfortable cause of it towards the door. "Tyndale," he murmured. "There's a wee favour ye can grant me—if ye'll not find it unco' ghastly!"

Thus it was that, half an hour later, leaving the floor on Devenish's arm after a country dance, Yolande was surprised by a sudden quieting in the noisy room, followed by a crashing chord from the indefatigable Mrs. Fraser.

All eyes turned to the General, who was ushering a new-comer from the hall—a tall young Scot, with unruly fair hair, but who was elegant in his kilts and plaid and black velvet jacket, with lace foaming at throat and wrists. He halted and looked up, and Yolande stared in disbelief. It was Craig, his grey eyes flashing across that silenced room to meet her own, a tentative smile trembling at the corners of his wide mouth. She thought numbly, "Oh, how superb he is!" and, choked with pride, went to him. Never knowing how her eyes glistened, nor how fine a sight they were, the two of them, she said huskily, "My goodness, how grand you are!"

"Aye, he is that!" The General laughed, vastly pleased with himself. "What d'ye think of our 'good Scot' now, Donald?"

"Why, I think ye're a muckle old fool, Drummond," scoffed his friend. "Ye've wrapped the boy in the wrong plaid!"

"Lord, what a sight!" Much amused, Devenish came over to them, his manner earning an irate scowl from the General. Taking Tyndale aside, he added murmurously, "You've won the Fairs with your boney knees, coz. But—I give your fair warning—look out for Mistress Josie Storm!"

Tyndale's answering smile was strained. Looking sharply at him, Devenish detected a hunted look in the clear eyes. He uttered a crack of mirth. "Don't care to be the centre of attention, eh? Well—" He checked to glance around curiously for the cause of a new commotion that arose in the hall. Two footmen and the butler were remonstrating with someone. Devenish glimpsed a sleek, blue-black head towering over the throng, and grinned hugely. "Beastly luck, coz," he commiserated, "but your glory is about to be considerably eclipsed."

He was right. The footmen were sent reeling back. The butler chose discretion as the better part of valour and effaced himself. Through a sudden awed hush, Montelongo strode across the floor, tall, bronzed, pantherishly graceful, totally out of place, yet ineffably proud as he made towards his employer.

One swift glance told him that the Major had suffered a few hard knocks since last they met. He stopped before him. In an oddly measured way, his dark head bowed very slightly. He said in that deep rumble of a voice, "You very fine?"

Recovering his own voice, General Drummond stalked over to demand, "What the deuce is all this? Who is that—fella to come bursting in here, flinging my servants about?"

Behind him, the ladies were whispering excitedly behind their fans. The gentlemen, only slightly less intrigued, had missed no part of the Iroquois's leathern garments, the long knife that hung, sheathed, at his lean waist, or the beaded moccasins.

Tyndale smiled into his man's keen eyes. "Perfectly fine, thank you," he answered, before turning to his irate host. "My apologies, sir. Montelongo is of the Iroquois Nation. He is a chief's son, but has been so good as to look after me for some years. I ask your pardon for this intrusion, but I've no doubt he was concerned when we did not rendezvous as I'd instructed. May I present him to you?"

Sir Andrew's brows bristled alarmingly, and his outraged eyes shot sparks. Tyndale met those eyes and said in cool challenge, "Monty, this gentleman is General Sir Andrew Drummond. Sir—Montelongo."

Some small titters arose behind him. The General's jaw set. He gave a frigid nod. Untroubled by protocol, Montelongo put out a broad, bronzed hand. To one side, Devenish grinned his delight, while beside him Yolande wondered if Craig had lost his mind. Slanting a molten glare at Tyndale, Sir Andrew encountered steady eyes of steel. A reluctant grin took possession of his strong features. He took the Indian's hand and wrung it, but could barely refrain from gasping at the answering pressure that was, he suspected, carefully restrained.

Montelongo's lips parted in the brief, white flash that served for a smile. "Proud to meet great warrior," he rumbled. And again, his head nodded in that quaint suggestion of a bow.

"Jove!" chuckled the General. The look in Tyndale's eyes had softened to a mute "thank you." "Rogue!" said Sir Andrew. "Off with you. I'm sure the butler will know where to put him." And turning to his entranced guests, he remarked, "What a night this has been, eh?"

Making his way through the curious and admiring throng, Montelongo stalking behind him, Tyndale led the way out. Once they were in the hall, he said urgently, "Monty, I'll tell you what happened, later. I cannot guess how you found us, but—have you brought the horses?"

The Iroquois emitted a grunt, the timbre of which indicated an affirmative reply. "When you no come, me go back to St. Albans. Desk man say you leave. Me trail. Find horses with thieves. So take Lazzy."

"Good God!" Tyndale checked his stride. "They must have been Montclair's people! But—no. That couldn't be, they've not had sufficient time to get down there as yet." He frowned thoughtfully. "I wonder who the devil they were."

"Bad men."

Tyndale scrutinized the impassive features. "For Lord's sake! You never killed them?"

"Bad men," Montelongo repeated. A twinkle lit his dark eyes. "But very good runners. Me and Lazzy find this place. Have mare of beautiful man, too."

Tyndale laughed, but threw a quick glance around. "Don't ever let Mr. Devenish hear you say that! No matter how he looks, he's a splendid fighting man, Monty. He saved my life."

The Indian was briefly silent. "Him Monty's brother. Why you wear petticoats?"

It was a term that had been used in Belgium to describe the Scots. It was also a term of high respect, for none had so endeared themselves to the Bruxellois as the Scottish regiments. Nonetheless, leading his man down the hall to the kitchens, and happily unaware of how many awed household eyes were watching, Tyndale carefully explained it was an expression that might better not be used. At least, in front of the uninitiated.

Montelongo grunted.

* * *

The night was crisp and clear, a half-moon illuminated the walkways, and Yolande followed them aimlessly, lost in thought, her plaid wrapped about her shoulders. The attraction she had felt when first she met Craig Winters Tyndale had not diminished. To the contrary, the sight of him tonight in all the glory of formal Scots attire had stirred her heart in most disquieting fashion. Even now, to visualize him, the way his grey eyes had sought her out, that charmingly uncertain smile, made her pulses leap and brought a warmth to her cheeks. Were these emotions merely the result of gratitude because he had come to her rescue? Was this rapid heartbeat brought about by admiration of his military record, or interest because he was different from any other man she had ever known? She closed her ears to the wretched voice that sought to whisper "nonsense!" and, not a little frightened, decided resolutely that she was not falling in love with Major Tyndale. She *must not* be falling in love with Major Tyndale! The difference in their stations could not be ignored, and there were other loves—Devenish and her parents, for instance. And as for Grandpapa—she shuddered. No, it was quite impossible. Besides, the Major had paid no more attention to her than would be required by the dictates of good manners. How foolish to be constantly mooning over a Colonial gentleman who had made not the slightest push to court her—and should not of course, do so, when she was promised to dear Dev. The chastisement did not seem to make her either more sure, or less miserable, and yet it was the only possible verdict.

Thoroughly irritated with herself, she swung around very suddenly and gave a little cry as she came face to face with the very object of her thoughts. "Oh, my!" she gasped. "How you frightened me!"

"My most humble apologies, ma'am," said Tyndale, remorsefully. "You passed me by just now and I—er—had been hoping for a word with you, so I followed. Will you permit that I walk with you?"

"Of course, though I must return to the house. Had you come out for a breath of air, cousin?"

"And a smoke," he nodded, holding up the cheroot that glowed in his hand. "A wretched habit I picked up in Spain."

"I was indeed surprised to learn that you had served with our army over there. I'd no idea you were a military gentleman."

"How should you?" He said awkwardly, "We—er, scarcely ҅ow one another."

"True. And have had scarce two words together since you arrived. I had, in fact, begun to think you might be avoiding me." And she thought in dismay, "Oh! Now, why did I say *that?*"

"Perhaps I have," he admitted, his grip on the cheroot tightening. "Devenish is—well, he's a good man and—and, you and he are— That is, I mean—you are to be wed. No?"

Even in the moonlight she could see that the cheroot was now quite badly bent. Her own heart was thundering, which

148

was too ridiculous. She said with desperate calm, "It has been understood for many years that we will—will marry."

"I see."

He did not, to judge by the hesitant words, and, wondering vaguely at the need, she felt obliged to add, "Our estates march together."

Their progress had become very slow. Tyndale halted to drop the wreckage of his cheroot and grind it into the dirt. "Not a compelling reason for wedlock," he remarked, gravely.

Flustered, she answered, "No. Of course. I did not mean to imply— Suffice it to say he is my choice. And—and that choice is much applauded by my family."

"Very wisely," he said. But he thought, "And how horrified your family would be did you wed a Colonial about whom all they know is that his father was a murderer!"

Watching him from beneath her lashes, she saw the bitter twist to his mouth and her heart was wrung. Fighting an inclination to burst into tears, she said with forced lightness, "You seem to like my grandpapa, sir."

"I do. He is such a fine old fellow."

"Yes, he is. I wish he lived closer to us, but he loves this old house."

"I can see why he would. It has great character. I am—very glad he invited me to stay. Though—I'm surprised he did so. Under the circumstances."

She caught her breath and, dreading what he would say next, yet longing to hear him say it, faltered, "Cir-circumstances, cousin?"

The moonlight on her lovely upturned face was driving him to distraction. Clenching his fists, he mumbled, "My—er, father. And—and Devenish's father."

"Oh." Of course that was what he had meant. What a ninny she was! "But, you see, Grandpapa does not know about that."

"No?" Tyndale's heavy brows drew together. "I thought everyone knew."

"Only those who were there at the time knew. It has been kept very quiet down through the years. I did not know of it myself until very recently."

"But—there must have been dozens of people—servants, workers on the estate . . .?"

"They were loyal, and were well paid to hold their tongues." She smiled. "Besides, Scots tend to be a secretive people. They have had to be."

Somehow, they had stopped walking. Not speaking, they stood gazing at one another.

The wind sighed softly through the trees. In the stables, a horse stamped and snorted restlessly. High on the hill, the windows of the house shone bright amber, and from them came the distant sounds of laughter.

Tormented by Yolande's nearness; by the faint scent of her perfume; by the terrible temptation to sweep her into his arms and kiss those sweetly curved lips, Tyndale wrenched his eyes from her face and stared down at the path. He thought, "My Lord! I *must* get away from here!" And he said, "If your grandfather *did* know that my father is believed to have murdered Stuart Devenish, would I still be welcome?"

She did not answer. He raised his down-bent head and looked at her gravely. Her eyes fell away, and she turned from him.

"Yolande," he persisted, softly. "Would I? Would he give me the benefit of the doubt? Or—would he be outraged?"

With slow reluctance she answered, "He would be outraged. He has introduced you to so many of his friends. And they would—would feel . . ."

He stiffened. "Insulted. I see. Then I had best be upon my way as soon as may be."

Spinning around, not wanting him to go, she protested involuntarily, "Why? After all these years, the secret is not likely to suddenly become public knowledge."

"It could." Ah, but how sweet, how unbearable to see the concern in her dear face. "Our presence here might awaken old memories; set people to talking."

It was true. She could only ask miserably, "Then—what shall you do?"

"Tell the old gentleman I simply *must* leave tomorrow. But there is no reason why Devenish should accompany me."

"If he promised to go, he will," she said, adding stoutly, "he is the soul of honour and will not break his word."

He said with a wry twinkle, "His honour may be severely tested. If the castle has not been lived in for twenty years and more, it must be in a sorry state, and probably beastly damp into the bargain."

"Oh, no. I doubt it is that bad. Colonel Tyndale comes up at least once a year, and there has been a caretaker of sorts, until recently. I know most of the furnishings are under Holland covers, and I suppose you will find the carpets rolled up, and the linens stored away. I will ask our housekeeper to

150

pack some bedding for you, but I believe you will find cedar chests very amply supplied with linens needing only to be aired.''

"You are too kind, Cousin Yolande," he said gratefully.

She thought, "No. I am only afraid," and avoiding his gaze, she began to walk on once more. "Well," she responded, "you are, after all, one of the family. And—you have, I believe, become a good friend of Alain's, no?"

He hesitated, then said slowly, "Not exactly. There is—ah, too much between us, you see."

Yolande glanced at him and found in his eyes a smile touched with sadness. Her face flamed. She knew suddenly that she herself was one of the reasons why the cousins could not be friends. And she knew also that Craig Tyndale loved her. She thought numbly, "What a fine bumble broth it would create did I love him also. Dev would kill him!" Fear closed an iron fist around her heart. She said something, heaven knows what, and hurried back to the house, Tyndale silent beside her.

Chapter Ten

The morning dawned clear but cool, and by the time they were ready to depart the sun was growing warmer, giving rise to hopes for a nice day. The General had been at first amused, then irked by Tyndale's quiet insistence that he must leave, but had capitulated at last. Since Devenish would not draw back from his promise to accompany his cousin, the end result was that they all would go. "If only," grunted Sir Andrew, "to detairmine if yon pile o' rubble is fit fer human habitation, regarrrding which, I hae me doots!''

It had been decided that Josie would stay at Steep Drummond until Devenish returned, and he would then take her back to England with him, hoping to obtain the benefit of Lady Louisa's wisdom in the matter of her eventual disposition. Meanwhile, however, she formed part of the small cavalcade, her peaked face bright with happiness as she nestled beside Yolande in the open curricle Devenish drove.

151

Yolande was outwardly as bright as she was inwardly disturbed. The ravages of a sleepless night had been concealed by Peattie's deft hands, and she was radiant in a primrose muslin dress buttoned high to the throat, a beautifully embroidered yellow shawl about her shoulders, and the poke of her bonnet a foam of primrose lace.

Despondent because he was leaving her, Devenish rallied when she smiled at his glumness and assured him she would anxiously await his return. She was so affectionate in fact that he was soon in high gig, all his dismals flown.

Sir Andrew led the parade, riding a fine bay gelding, with on one side of him, Mr. Walter Donald, his friend of many years who had over-nighted at Steep Drummond, and on the other, Tyndale, astride his big grey. Next came the chaise containing Arabella Drummond and Caroline Fraser, who quarrelled politely all the way, each convincing herself she was scoring the most hits. Following, Devenish drove the curricle, and, bringing up the rear was a landaulette bearing two footmen and various hampers and bottles that promised an excellent luncheon.

Yolande exerted herself to maintain a cheerful façade, responding with every appearance of gaiety to Devenish's easy banter. Josie, impressed by his proficiency with the reins, eventually interjected the observation that he was "a regular top-draw-yer!"

He laughed. "That's 'Top Sawyer,' my elf. Where did you learn that term?"

"Benjo," she replied, gazing up at him, ever hopeful of bringing the approving smile to his eyes. "He said I could manage the pony and trap so good because my old man was a Top Draw—I mean, Top Sawyer."

Yolande murmured, "Dev, we really *must* try to discover something of her background." She lifted the child's hand that was confidently tucked into her own and, marking the fine bones and long, slim fingers, said, "There's good breeding in her, I'm sure of it."

"*We* must?" he said eagerly. "Yolande, does that mean you're ready to allow me to announce our betrothal, at last?"

Yolande shifted her glance from the child's hand to Devenish's handsome, hopeful face. Dear Dev. She *did* love him. And surely countless women had married gentlemen with whom they were not deeply *in* love? She knew she could make him happy, unless . . . "Dev," she said, watching him steadily, "are you quite *sure* you are in love with me?

152

No—do not answer so quickly! Think on it for a moment. You love me, of course, just as I love you. But—is there no one else? Are you really *in love* with me?'' And, realizing what she had said, she could have bitten her tongue.

Devenish had suspected that his passion was not as fully returned, but the confirmation was like a knife being turned in his breast. He managed to keep his face from revealing his hurt, and said staunchly, ''I really am, m'dear. But if you ain't in love with me, it's only to be expected, and I don't mind. That you love me at all is far more than I deserve.''

It was the most romantic speech she had ever heard him utter, and she reached across the child to him, her heart touched.

Taking that small, gloved hand, Devenish searched her face, waiting.

''Yes, you may announce it,'' she murmured, smiling at him. ''We will settle the details when you return from the castle.''

He gave a whoop of joy that brought the heads of the riders twisting around, and so alarmed his horses that he had to relinquish Yolande's hand and give his full attention to his driving.

''Jove!'' he said with a guilty grin, succeeding in quieting the teams at length. ''Almost had us in the chaise with your aunts! A fine set-to that would have been!''

Josie's head was bowed. Yolande stroked the dark curls and asked gently, ''What is it, dear. Are you sad?''

The child nodded. ''Josie *is* sad. If Mr. Dev marriages you, you won't never let him have me fer his—''

''Abigail?'' Yolande inserted swiftly.

Devenish chuckled. ''Perhaps Miss Drummond will let you be *her* abigail,'' he suggested, buoyant at the promise of a glowing future.

''She's got a abigail.'' Josie sighed. ''I'll be all growed in a year or two.''

''Or ten,'' he qualified.

''Even when I be *that* old, Peattie might not be dead.''

''Good heavens!'' gasped Yolande. ''What things you do say! Oh—see, Dev! There is Castle Tyndale!''

They had passed through a hilly area of lush pastures dotted with black-faced sheep and threaded by the hurrying sparkle of the river. Ahead, the hills fell back to reveal, far off, the wider sparkle of the sea and a distant misty looming of islands. The skies were threatening over the Firth of Clyde, creating a fitting background for the castle that soared at the top of the cliffs. A tall structure, its three conical topped towers upthrusting stark and grim against the clouds, its Gothic windows dark holes against the massive grey walls, it presented, from this distance, a desolate picture of brooding power.

"Jupiter!" Devenish exclaimed. "Old Craig cannot mean to dwell alone in *that* great pile?"

"It could be spectacular, were it brought up to style," mused Yolande.

"Yes, but that would take a mountain of blunt, and—What's wrong now, elf?"

Clinging to his jacket, Josie whimpered, "I don't like it! It's a bad place! I don't want to go there!"

Devenish experienced a deepening of his own inner apprehensions. Those were the battlements from which his youthful father had plunged to his untimely death. Within those walls his heart-broken mother had lost her babe and grieved herself into an early grave. He shivered suddenly.

He was not alone in his apprehensions. Surveying his birthright with troubled eyes, Craig was deeply shocked, not because it looked so forbidding, but because it was so exactly as he had pictured it. He had no sense of strangeness or unfamiliarity, but rather a feeling of inevitability; of a homecoming that had been planned and long awaited—not by himself, but by that great grey pile of stone and mortar and memories. He turned to find Walter Donald's keen brown gaze fixed upon him with so gravely speculative a look that he flushed and was seized by the feeling that the gentleman knew more of the tragedy at Castle Tyndale than he had said.

They still had several miles to drive before they came to the heavy lodge gates and the winding drive that led up to the castle, and with every mile Devenish's unease increased. When Tyndale dropped back to ride beside the curricle, he said, "Well, there's your ancestral pile, coz. What d'ye think of it?"

His face expressionless, Tyndale countered, "What do *you* think of it?"

"I don't like it!" whimpered Josie, holding tightly to Yolande's hand. "I got a bad tummy about it!"

"It's—rather grim," said Devenish.

Tyndale nodded. "Certainly not Prince Charming's castle."

"Lord, no!" Devenish elaborated tactlessly, "More like

Bluebeard's demesne. I pity the poor princess who was carried in through those doors!''

Yolande kept her eyes on the child. "Pity the poor princess, indeed!" she thought.

They soon came to the gates, hanging rusted and broken upon massive pillars. The lodge house was abandoned, the windows boarded up, and a padlock upon the door.

"Small need of a lock!" the General snorted.

"None at all," Mr. Donald agreed, watching Tyndale.

Tyndale met that grave regard squarely. "Why?" he asked curtly, his chin well up, and irritation gnawing at him. If this man fancied he was ashamed, or held his father guilty, he was vastly mistaken!

Donald smiled and said rather apologetically, "Your pardon, but—it *is* said to be haunted, you know."

They passed through the gates and began to clatter up the winding, neglected drivepath.

The General declaimed his friend's fears as "gilliemaufrey nonsense!" To which Mr. Donald responded by asking Sir Andrew if he had ever been inside. "I have," he went on, "and I'll no deny it had me shaking in me shoes, and I'm no a supairsteetious mon! Not," he went on in purest Oxford accents, "that I mean to deter you, Tyndale."

"You would be wasting your time, sir," said the Canadian determinedly.

The General grinned his approval. "And that gave you back your own, Donald! Gad, it's no wee cottage, is it?"

It was not. And the closer they came, the larger loomed the castle until they were in the dark shadow of it, as it towered above them.

With a stirring of pride, Tyndale thought, "How grand it is! The home of my ancestors! And it is mine now."

His thoughts taking a different direction, Devenish noted that there were no small boys intrepidly exploring the great pile. And how odd that a hush seemed to have fallen upon their own small party, even the shrill titters from the chaise having been silenced.

The General pulled his mount to a halt beside the spread of some great old trees, and swung from the saddle. "Shall we picnic here?" he called with rather determined gaiety. "What d'ye say, ladies?"

Tyndale dismounted to hand Mrs. Fraser from the chaise. "It's well enough," she allowed, her shrewd eyes flickering over the bulk of the castle.

Following, Mrs. Drummond clutched nervously at Tyndale's arm. "Oh, my!" she twittered. "I think I shall not awaken Socrates. The dear little fellow would be petrified."

Mrs. Fraser threw a disdainful glance at the terrier, who snored on the seat. "'Twould take a mighty fearsome bogle tae scare that wee grouch!"

Innocently watching Arabella, the General asked if the ladies would prefer that they picnicked inside.

Mrs. Drummond uttered a small squeak. Mrs. Fraser cast disgusted eyes to heaven, and the General chuckled.

Yolande shook her head at him. "Wicked rascal!" She slipped her arm around her aunt's trembling shoulders. "We will do nicely out here. There is still plenty of blue sky, but if it begins to rain you and the gentlemen may go inside and light a fire for us."

"May we?" the General said with an amused chuckle, "Well—let us have the baskets down! I'm famished." The two footmen busying themselves at once, Sir Andrew said that the ladies could supervise the disposition of the picnic whilst the gentlemen took "our new property owner to view his home, the noo." He and Devenish led the way. Walking beside Mr. Donald, Tyndale asked softly, "Am I mistaken, sir, or do you know something of my . . . background that causes you to hold me in aversion?"

"Let us say rather that I have recently learned that which causes me to believe Drummond will be vastly incensed when *he* hears it."

Tyndale drew a deep breath. "I see. I trust you will believe me, sir, when I tell you that when I first arrived here, I thought everyone knew the—the details."

"And when did you find your assumption to be incorrect?"

"Last night. Which decided me upon leaving this morning."

"You do not mean to return to Steep Drummond?"

"No, sir. My man was packing and is likely already following."

Donald nodded and said a judicial, "As well, perhaps."

Angered, Tyndale lifted his chin, and, noting that prideful gesture, the older man said, "When the word gets out, you'll be cut—I warn you."

"And I warn *you*, sir. Whatever you have been told is not truth!"

A twinkle coming into his eyes, Donald said mildly, "If ye dinna ken what I've heard, laddie, how can ye know it for a lie?"

156

Tyndale flushed, his mouth tightening.

Taking pity on him, Donald gripped his shoulder briefly. "I'll tell ye what I *do* know, which is precious little. I was acquainted with your sire. Oh, never look so hopeful, lad! Not well acquainted. But enough to know that if Jonas brought about Stuart's death, it was because of a blow dealt in anger. Not a deliberate attempt at murder. Of that I am perfectly sure."

Mollified, Tyndale said, "Thank you, sir. But—may I ask who told you of it? And when? Yolande thinks it a deep buried secret."

"Aye. It was, that. For four and twenty years. Who let the cat oot o' the bag, I dinna ken. But oot it is! And—whisht! I'd as soon not be nigh when Andy learns of 't!"

Before Craig could respond, the General called a testy summons, and they hastened to join him atop the debris-strewn steps before the main door. The castle rose from a veritable jungle of overgrown shrubs and trees. Several window panes were broken, but it did not now appear to be in as sorry a state as it had seemed at a distance. It was perched at the very edge of the cliffs, and from below came a steady booming as waves broke against the great rocks offshore that rose as if to shield the bay from further inroads of the hungry tide. Devenish gazed up at the soaring battlements. Donald glanced meaningfully at Tyndale, who flushed darkly, drew from his pocket the heavy key his solicitor had given him, and fitted it in the lock. He had expected the door to prove recalcitrant, but it swung open smoothly enough, and like guilty schoolboys, they did not at once enter, but all stood at the top of the steps, peering inside.

They looked into a great, flagged, baronial hall. About forty feet distant, there was a gigantic fireplace, with beside it a steep flight of stone stairs, leading to a railed balcony. To the left of the fireplace an enormous door, half-open, offered a glimpse of a long corridor, and in the right-hand wall was a similar door that they later discovered led to the kitchens, servants quarters, and stableyard. Several well-preserved bishop's chairs were grouped about the hearth, and the walls were hung with occasional large and faded tapestries. At the foot of the stairs, a suit of armour had toppled, and lay rather pathetically strewn on the dusty flagstones.

Tyndale gathered his courage and walked inside. The General and Mr. Donald followed, but Devenish stood as one frozen, making no attempt to accompany them. He had never fancied himself to harbour a belief in the occult, but now he was gripped by an all but overpowering terror, so that it was literally impossible for him to put one foot before the next. It was as much as he could do, in fact, not to dash madly back down the steps.

"Jove," Tyndale murmured, considerably awed, "but it's big!"

"It was a bonnie sight when I was a lad," said the General. He turned to Donald. "D'ye recollect when—" He stopped and, following his friend's gaze, called, "Well, Devenish, d'ye not mean to come inside?"

Devenish wet his lips. Glancing at him, Tyndale said, "I fancy the ladies are ready. We can leave this until later."

"Hoot-toot!" exclaimed Sir Andrew, irascibly. "What ails the boy? He's no afraid o' ghosties, I—"

Donald frowned and leaned to murmur something in his ear, and Sir Andrew looked mortified. He said contritely, "My apologies, Devenish. I must be getting daft in my dotage! I'd clean forgot that both your parents died here."

"It was—just an odd sort of—feeling." Devenish gave a ghastly grin. "I shall do very well now, thank you." Nonetheless, to make himself walk forward was one of the most difficult things he'd ever had to do, and it seemed an age before he stood beside Tyndale, who was inspecting one of the tapestries.

"I would really as soon look over the castle by myself," the Canadian muttered. "And I am sure you would rather be with Yolande, so—"

"Stuff! I mean to stay and lend you a hand. Besides, I want to see—" The words ended in a yelp of shock as Socrates shot between his legs and disappeared into the dimness beyond the half-open door.

"That imp o' Satan!" growled the General. And then, brightening, "Happen a bogle'll get him!"

"I would never be forgiven," Craig said, going over to swing the door wide. There was no sign of Socrates, but he went into a broad corridor that gave onto several large rooms, some provided with heavy doors, and others having only broad archways to afford entrance. The first of these latter led into a formal dining hall that boasted two modern chandeliers above a fine oak table lined with about thirty ponderously carven chairs. There were fireplaces at both ends of this large chamber, and daylight shone dimly through three sets of closed curtains.

Devenish wandered in, remarked that the atmosphere in the room was less frigid, but dashed gloomy, and went over to fling back the draperies. He was at once enveloped in a dense cloud of dust, his resultant explosion of sneezing amusing the General and Mr. Donald, who mocked him gleefully.

Tyndale, however, paid no heed to his cousin's plight, but stood staring down at the oaken table top, his brows drawn into a thoughtful frown.

* * *

Clouds began to drift in from the sea while they were still sitting around the luncheon cloth, but the sunshine, although not constant, was sufficiently warm to take the chill off the air. The chef had provided a varied and tempting repast, to which they all did justice. Yolande was surprised to find herself hungry, despite the fact that she was heavy-hearted. Josie was prey to no such affliction, and soon forgot her initial fear of the castle. Not for as long as she could remember had she eaten as well as during her travels with Devenish, and she applied herself to the food with joyous appreciation, yet with a mannerliness that brought curiosity to Sir Andrew's eyes.

"I'd give a few guineas to know where you hail from, Mistress Storm," he said, waving a bannock at her.

"So would I, sir," she replied, serenely unafraid of this old gentleman before whom grooms trembled and maids were tongue-tied.

"D'ye hear that?" he demanded of Donald. " 'So would I, sir.' Proper as you please! D'ye recall nothing, child? Nothing of your lady mother, or a fine papa, belike?"

"I only remember Akim telling me I'd fetch a good price at the Flash House," she said. And watching Mr. Donald choke on the tart he'd just sunk his teeth into, went on, "Only Benjo said I might not, 'cause I ain't pretty."

"Whatever is a—a Flash House?" enquired Mrs. Drummond naïvely. "A place where they manufacture gunpowder, I suppose. Though," she tilted her head dubiously, "why one should be pretty for that occupation, I cannot understand."

Devenish gave a muffled chortle of amusement.

"Your supposition is incorrect," said the General, irritated. "And never mind what it *does* mean!"

"Ladies," conveyed Mrs. Fraser grandly, "are not supposed to know such things, my dear Arabella. Or so the gentlemen hold."

159

"Then that would certainly explain why it is I know nothing of such a term." Mrs Drummond replied with a smug smile. "For indeed, I have been sheltered by gentlemen all my days. My late husband, God rest his soul, would have flung up his hands in horror had any unsavoury remark soiled my ears." She raised her brows, all arch innocence, and enquired, "You, certainly, do not comprehend what the poor waif said, do you, dear Caroline?"

Mrs. Fraser fixed her with a look of searing contempt. "Ay, I do. *My* late husband was not one to value a widgeon."

The General, his thoughtful regard on the child, now daintily wiping greasy fingers upon her petticoat, asked, "How would ye like to stay at Steep Drummond, girl? My housekeeper could instruct you in the ways of a parlourmaid, I don't doubt. 'Twould be a good life. A clean life, y'ken. And ye'd not go hungry or abused—I'd see to that!"

Josie stared at him and wondered what Peattie would wish her to say. Mr. Dev was gazing at an apple he held and gave no sign of having heard the offer. She thought it a grand one, but sighed, scrambled to her feet, and dropped the old gentleman a curtsy. "Thank ye, sir General," said she. "But I'd liefer stay with Mr. Dev, if you please."

"I do not please! And nor will Colonel Tyndale, let me tell you. Ain't fitting! 'Tis a bachelor's dwelling, and they'll no be needing a young female growing up there."

The child paled, and her lips trembled. "No, b-but—I will *soon* be growed! I won't be no trouble!"

"Mama may be able to help, sir," Yolande put in kindly.

His own heart touched, Mr. Donald suggested, "Or perhaps Devenish will make her his ward."

The General slanted a glance at Devenish, who still tenderly contemplated the apple in his hand, wholly unaware of this conversation, torn between joy that he had secured his lady's promise and unease because of his reaction to that blasted great castle wherein he'd given his word to remain for a few days.

"Well?" fumed the General, eyebrows bristling. "Well, sir?"

Tyndale nudged his cousin and Devenish jumped, saw every eye upon him, and gulped nervously. "Eh? What's to do?"

"God! What a block!" snorted Sir Andrew.

Laughing, Tyndale said, "General Drummond is interested in Josie, Dev, and wants to know what you plan for her."

160

"Me? I have not the vaguest notion. Lady Louisa will have some splendid scheme, I expect."

Close to tears, Josie pleaded, "But, I want to stay with *you!*" And turning to the General, explained, "He don't mind if I'm not pretty, do you, Mr. Dev?"

"Lord, no. I don't mind if you're plain as a mud fence," he said, carelessly.

"Really, Dev!" scolded Yolande.

The General glared at him. "Insensitive puppy!"

These words exercised an extraordinary effect upon Mrs. Drummond. Her eyes widened alarmingly, and she became rigid. She squawked, "My sweet love has gone!"

"Been gone for twenty years at least, Arabella," the General pointed out, viewing her askance. "Don't go into a funny turn, now!"

Ignoring this, the distraught dowager, her eyes searching about frantically, wailed, "He was but now nibbling my fingers!"

"Nibbling . . . your fingers?" gasped Sir Andrew. He drew back a little and glancing to Donald, muttered, "She's off the road! Suspected it this twelvemonth and—"

Mrs. Drummond, lost in anxiety, shrieked, "My angel! Where are you?"

"Good God!" whispered Drummond, goggling at her.

His daughter-in-law's cry rose shrilly "Soc-ra-*tees*—? Oh! Surely he has not fallen over the cliff?"

The General cast her a look of both relief and disgust, and muttered something about "unlikely blessings."

Tyndale stood. "I think he is in the castle, ma'am. I'll go and find him."

Reaching out to be helped up, Yolande said, "Dev and I will come with you."

He lifted her to her feet but when she attempted to pull away, his grip tightened. He said a quiet, "Thank you. But Dev or Mr. Donald will help."

"What's this?" asked Devenish, belatedly becoming aware that something was brewing. "Who needs help?"

"Socrates!" wailed Mrs. Drummond. "My poor baby is lost, and Mr. Winters just stands and talks. And you sit! Will *no one* help the poor darling?"

"Lord save us aw'!" The General snarled.

Devenish promptly joined the search party, and Yolande again voiced her willingness to assist. "Famous!" Devenish nodded brightly, ignoring his own unease. Noting Tyndale's

161

dark frown, he added hastily, "But it is dusty in there, m'dear. Might spoil your pretty frills and furbelows."

"Pooh!" said Yolande.

Side by side, they walked up the steps and into the Great Hall. As before, Devenish was seized by the same unreasoning terror. He felt the blood drain from his face and, dreading lest he betray his craven fears in front of the girl he loved, forced his rubbery knees to obey him, and walked briskly to the rear door. The corridor stretched out in a dim, chill menace. Clenching his teeth, he walked on and began to call the missing dog.

In the Great Hall, Tyndale looked after his cousin, his lips a thin line of vexation. Yolande, uneasily alone with this disturbing gentleman, said brightly, "Why, it is not near so bad as I had feared." She started forward. "Whilst we are here, we can find where the linens—"

A firm hand seized her elbow, drawing her to a halt. She swung around, her heart thundering, her brows raised enquiringly.

Craig said a soft but determined, "No. I thank you."

He was very near, and yet the grey eyes were devoid of expression, telling her nothing. Puzzled, she demanded, "But, why ever not, sir? Do you fancy me thrown into a pucker by a little dust?"

"No, ma'am. But—I could not endure to see that very pretty frock sullied. Castle Tyndale is—is not yet ready to receive you." Brave words, spoken with the most honourable intention, but his heart cried out to her, and he did not remove his hand from her arm.

Yolande knew that she should leave. Hastily. Instead, she murmured a vague "Most . . . inhospitable . . . Major."

For Craig, all other matters and individuals had ceased to exist. "Why must you be so unforgivably lovely?" he thought yearningly. "I shall never see you again, my dearest, my darling girl . . ."

Yolande did not know that her lips were slightly parted, her eyes dreamy, but she saw the emptiness in Craig's eyes change to an expression of tender worship that took her breath away. It seemed to her that he was bending to her, but she neither moved, nor experienced the least desire to break this spell. The seconds slipped away and not one word was spoken. But two hearts met and the message they exchanged was as clear as though it had been shouted from the battlements.

And then, somewhere close by, Devenish whistled for Socrates.

Craig started. Dismayed by his shameful weakness, he said brusquely, "You had best wait outside—cousin."

His words restored Yolande to reality. Equally shocked, she turned from him and, without a word, walked across the Great Hall and onto the steps.

Craig watched her go. He whispered, "Goodbye, my lovely one . . ." and, sighing, went to assist in the search for Socrates.

The sky had become white. Yolande lifted a shielding hand against the sudden glare and walked as slowly as she dared down the steps and along the path. Her head was a whirl of confusion, impressions chasing one another at such a rate she could scarce comprehend them. She knew only that she was very unhappy, and that her once neatly mapped-out life had become a chaotic muddle. But she also knew that if she betrayed the slightest sign of discomposure, one of her aunts was sure to notice. She must bring her rioting emotions under control or there would be anxious enquiries with which she was in no state to cope.

Luckily, however, Mrs. Drummond had other matters on her mind and, before her niece had quite come up with them, was calling anxious questions as to the whereabouts of her pet.

"I can be of no help, alas," Yolande answered. She summoned a smile for Mr. Donald, who stood courteously to assist her to sit beside her aunt. "I have been banished."

"Would not let you stay, eh?" The General chuckled. "Speaks his mind, does Tyndale. Fine young fella, but he bears little resemblance to his sire. You'll recollect Jonas Tyndale, Donald?"

"Aye," said Mr. Donald, laconically.

"Wild as any unbroke colt." Sir Andrew nodded. "'Tis Devenish takes after him, had ye noted that, Donald?"

"Aye," said Mr. Donald.

"He has nae a mean bone in his body," observed the General, glancing covertly at Yolande. "But he's a feckless, reckless laddie, just like his uncle was, and no good end will come to him does he not bend his energies to something better than—er—"

"Than—murder?" interposed Mrs. Drummond, her anxious gaze on the castle.

Yolande gave a gasp and dropped the lemon tart she'd just

taken up. Mr. Donald directed a fuming glance at the bereft dog lover, and the General frowned, "Losh sakes, woman! What cockaleery nonsense are ye blathering at?"

Alarmed, Mrs. Drummond prattled a defensive, "Why—why, what's in the blood will out! And you yourself said that Alain takes after his Uncle Jonas!"

"And what has that to say to anything? Jonas Tyndale may have been wild, and fought him a duel or two. But he didnae murder!"

"I seed a duel once," Josie began, reminiscently. "It was—"

"Of course not," Yolande put in, fixing her aunt with a look of desperate warning. "You must be thinking of someone else, Aunt Arabella."

"No such thing!" retorted that lady huffily. "No one was *supposed* to know, of course, but I chanced to hear Mrs. MacInnes speaking of it to Sir John Gordon at the party last night. Jonas slaughtered poor young Stuart Devenish in cold—"

"Aunt!" Yolande blurted, her heart hammering with dread. "You really must not say such things!"

"Losh! What a prattle box!" Mrs. Fraser muttered scornfully.

Mrs. Drummond's gaze darted from Yolande's white face and imploring eyes, to her sister-in-law, to the General's intent glare. "Oh, dear! Have I . . . spoke out of turn?" she wailed.

"Now—by God!" breathed the General. "Have I been kept i' the dark all these years? Damme, but I'll have the straight of it the noo! *Be still*, Yolande!" He turned glittering eyes on his friend. "Donald? D'ye ken aught o' this? Caroline . . .?"

Mr. Donald scowled at his plate. Mrs. Fraser put up her chin, pursed her lips, and finally announced that she was not, nor ever had been a gabble-monger!

Walter Donald met Yolande's distraught gaze and shrugged helplessly. "'Tis nae use, lassie. The word's oot, I fear. Hamish MacInnes told me 'twas all over the county, yesterday, so—"

"You mean *it is truth?*" Drummond's voice cut like a knife through those reluctant words. "Jonas Tyndale *murdered* his fine young brother-in-law? And 'twas put out as an accident?" His face purpling, he sprang to his feet, Mr. Donald and the ladies following suit. "Now—blast it all! Why was I not told? Am I held too senile—too decrepit and irresponsible a gabble-monger to be trrrusted wi' family secrets?"

164

"You were in India," Yolande said faintly. "*Nobody* knew—save a few servants. And—my mama, because she went to nurse poor Aunt Esme, but—"

"Do ye tell me, girrrl, that my blithering idiot of a son fancied I must nae be trusted wi' the truth?" raged the General, beginning to pace up and down like a hungry tiger. "That puir wee lassie! Her ain brother had murrdered her husband! 'Tis nae wonder she lost her babe! My Lord! What infamy! Stuart was in every way a fine gentleman, wherefore that wild creature Jonas hated him with a passion and judged him unworthy! How did he do it? Shot? Steel? Poison? I'd nae put it past the scoundrrrel! Well? *Answer* me, someone! The cat's frae the bag—no use trying to wrap things in clean linen at this stage!"

Josie had slunk away and was cowering behind the landaulette with the two footmen who had speedily made themselves least in sight—and were listening eagerly. Mrs. Drummond, cringing before her father-in-law's wrath, mumbled, "Jonas p—pushed him from—from the battlements! And old Mr. Tyndale banished him to the Colonies and forbade him ever to use the family name, or return to England. Which is the shameful reason his son used the name Winters!" Encountering Yolande's seething glare, she wailed, "Now—never be cross, love! By what Mr. Donald says, your grandfather must soon have heard it, at all events. Better it should come from one of the family, than—"

"Aye," snarled the General. "And better yet had either of those two alleged gentlemen had the decency to have owned to it!"

Mrs. Drummond gave a joyous cry as Socrates reappeared and raced to fling himself, shivering, into her eager arms.

Tyndale and Devenish were also returning. Yolande's attempt to speak was cut off by a savage, "You will be *silent*, girl!" And her grandfather, tall, austere, and rigid with anger, ground out, "So ye found the pesky creature!"

"He found us, more like, sir." Devenish grinned blithely. "Shot down the stairs like the devil himself was after—" The tension of the group conveyed itself to him, and he stopped speaking, looking uncertainly from one to the other. "Something wrong? Cousin Craig and I wasn't gone too long, was we?"

"Nae, laddie," purred Sir Andrew with an awful smile. "'Tis only that I'm a mite fashed that ye'd address yon deceitful upstart as 'cousin'!'' His chin thrust forward. ''The *son* of the man who *murdered your sire!*'' he roared.

Devenish stiffened. Tyndale, the colour receding from his face, snapped, ''There is no proof of that, sir!''

''Is there not? I am told that your father deliberately pushed young Stuart Devenish from the battlements of yon accursed castle!'' The General threw up an authoritative hand to silence Devenish's attempted intervention. ''Donald''—his contemptuous gaze seared past Tyndale and Devenish—''I know *you* to be an honourable gentleman. If you will be so good as to tell me what you have heard I shall not question the truth of it.''

Tyndale clenched his hands and flushed darkly, but said nothing. Devenish, his own colour rising, flung up his head and frowned, waiting.

With a commendable paucity of words, Donald sketched the tragedy that had occurred here twenty-four years earlier. And all the time, Sir Andrew's cold gaze drifted from one to the other of the young men standing so silently before him.

''And that,'' Donald concluded regretfully, ''is all I know, Andy. I might add that I only learned of it yesterday afternoon.''

''Would I had done so!'' said Sir Andrew, shooting a brief, angry glance at him. ''I'd have known better than to introduce these two—individuals—to my friends, or allow either of 'em to make sheep's eyes at my granddaughter!''

''Sir,'' said Tyndale, with his share of hauteur, ''I can understand your anger, but—''

''Then ye're in the wrong of it tae starrrt with! I've no anger towards you, Tyndale. Ye've my sympathy, rather. Aye, my deepest sympathy for the black shame that has been handed doon tae ye! No, sir! Ye'll no speak till I give ye leave. Which is not yet!''

Tyndale subsiding, though he was white and trembling with rage, the General turned his attention to Devenish, who fronted him pale but proud, a slightly condescending droop to his eyelids that served merely to further infuriate the old gentleman. ''As for you,'' snorted Drummond, ''what manner of man is it cries comrade with the son of the rogue who killed his sire? I knew you for a wild young scalliwag. I dinna ken ye were withoot honour! Ye're just like Jonas! Ah, ye've heard *that* before, I see! Well, ye've heard the truth on't! And had I known ye for the man ye are, ye'd no hae set foot in my hoose! Either o' ye!'' Scarlet with wrath, he spun around to

166

shout, "Verra well, you two skulking behind the coach there! Come and clear this away as fast as may be!"

"Grandpapa!" Yolande began tearfully.

"By your leave, ma'am," Tyndale intervened in a voice she had never heard. "Sir, you have judged on hearsay. I shall not. Somehow I mean to prove my father innocent of intent to do murder. And Devenish—"

"Will speak for himself, if you please," said that individual his tone as cold as his cousin's. "General, my initial reaction to the truth of my father's death was very similar to your own. I have since discovered my cousin to be a gentleman. One to whom I probably owe my life. I mean to help him come at the real truth of the tragedy, but whatever comes of it has little to do with the fact that I have offered for your granddaughter, and been given reason to believe she—"

"Well, she don't!" Drummond overrode harshly. And loftily disremembering that two of his sons had married Englishwomen and that Yolande was half-English, said, "I would suggest that since ye've very little Scot in you, sir, you hie yourself back to your homeland and wed a girl closer to your own unfortunate background! Ladies—into the carriages, if you please!" With sublime arrogance and a spate of snapped-out orders, he marched towards his bay, but turned back, coming full circle to announce, "The bairn is innocent and can stay at Steep Drummond until you, Devenish, are ready to return to England. Then, you may come and collect her." Not so much as glancing at Tyndale, he finished a brittle, "Alone!" and stamped to where the grooms were saddling his horse.

For an aching moment, Tyndale looked squarely at Yolande, then he strode off to find Lazarus.

Wrenching her gaze from his tall, erect figure, Yolande faced Devenish, who came to her side, one cautious eye on the General. "Whew!" he breathed. "What a devil he can be. Bad as my own tyrant, and worse! Understandable, I suppose, but—not entirely justified. Craig's a good enough man, Yolande."

She smiled wanly. "He said the same of you. Dev, whatever shall we do?"

He took her hand and gripping it with a confidence he could not feel, said firmly, "You will do nothing. Don't let the old fellow scare you. He's all huff and puff, you know. Chances are he'll go off the boil and begin to think he was a shade hasty. At all events, I must stay with Tyndale—for a

167

while at least. When I come to get Josie, you'll—you'll not back off from what you promised?''

Suddenly, he looked very anxious. Yolande returned the pressure of his hand and said staunchly, ''I'll not back off, dear Dev.''

Chapter Eleven

*The skies darkened while Devenish and Tyndale were explor*ing the castle, and soon rain was pattering down, the gloomy weather and clammy chill adding to the forbidding aspect of the great, silent, high-ceilinged rooms.

Scanning a vast bedchamber, the bed hangings and furniture swathed in Holland covers, Devenish remarked, ''You know, coz, Yolande spoke truly—it could be jolly fine if you was to bring the place up to style. It would cost a mountain of blunt, though.'' And he wondered which of the rooms his parents had occupied, and how it had all looked when his gentle mother was alive.

''Might be worth it,'' Tyndale mused. ''I wonder what scared Socrates so badly.''

Following him from the room, Devenish did not voice his thought that the scruffy hound was not alone in finding Castle Tyndale daunting. ''A cat, probably,'' he said lightly. ''A black one, of course!''

The next corridor they came upon was dim and very chill. Tyndale opened the first door, ''Perhaps,'' he agreed. ''I must—'' He stopped. A pleasant bedchamber was before them; a room of painted ceilings, soaring leaded windows, a graceful canopied bed, its blue silken hangings free of dust covers, and a fine carpet of great size laid down in readiness for the new occupant. A stone fireplace was between the windows, and hanging over the mantel the portrait of a lovely fair girl, looking down with proudly tender eyes at the infant she held: a tiny infant, richly gowned, and having tufts of golden hair and deeply blue eyes. There were portraits of Esme Devenish at Aspenhill, and an impressive family group at Devencourt, but this portrait had a rare charm and warmth and, captivated, Devenish gazed up at it. Beside him, Tyndale was again struck by the stark pathos of the tragedy. He glanced from the radiant joy in the face of his long-dead aunt, to the awed features of her grown son, and guilt fastened steel claws in him. Only a short while ago he had been standing beside this man's love, wanting nothing so much as to sweep her into his arms and claim her for his own. The slightest encouragement from Yolande would have been all the impetus he would have needed to speak his love and try to win her from Devenish. Disgraceful behaviour in any man, but especially dishonourable in his own case, to attempt to steal the betrothed of a man who had already been so cruelly wronged, whether deliberately or accidentally, by the Tyndales!

"Was she not lovely, coz?" breathed Devenish.

"Indeed she was. I collect the caretaker must have been told you would wish to have this room. I suspect it was occupied by your papa when he—" It seemed to him that he heard something odd, and he stopped abruptly.

Devenish seized his arm and hissed, "Listen . . .!"

At first, the silence was absolute save for the faint drumming of the rain on the high Gothic windows. And then, faint and stealthy, came a soft shuffling, followed by a muted thump. Aghast, the two men looked at one another through a moment so intensely still that the air seemed to throb in their ears. All too soon another sound disturbed the quiet: an echoing wail, muffled with distance, but unutterably forlorn. The hair lifted on the back of Devenish's neck. His eyes grew dim, and his breath was snatched away. Of a less imaginative nature, Tyndale's calm was considerably shaken. Then, "Oh, good gad!" he exclaimed bracingly. "It must be that fool, Montelongo! Likely having the deuce of a time with our trunks and never dreaming his howlings would petrify us!"

Very aware that he had betrayed terror, Devenish coloured up and disclaimed, "I trust you apply that term to yourself, Tyndale!"

"Oh, but of course." Tyndale held open the door and bowed with a flourish. "You were perfectly controlled." But as Devenish sauntered past, he added mischievously, "A little green, perhaps."

His cousin's head tossed upward. "Your own colour was a trifle off. Though I doubt you would be honest enough to admit you were afraid."

There was a glint of anger in the blue eyes, and Tyndale made a disarming gesture. "No, seriously, Dev. I *was* uneasy,

169

I'll own, but I must confess I am out of charity with such flights of fancy as shades and goblins, witches and warlocks, and their brethren. Childish nonsense; or the promptings of an uneasy, er—'' And he checked, dismayed by the bog into which he had blundered.

"Conscience?" flashed Devenish, partly infuriated by those tactless words, and partly sickened by a terror that, instead of fading, became ever more compelling. "Faith, but you surprise me! Here I had thought *your* conscience would rest less easy than mine—in *this* place!"

Tyndale's lips tightened and for an instant he experienced a pressing need to apply his fist to that high-held jaw. Then he shrugged and stalked out of the room and towards the main staircase.

Montelongo was halfway up the first flight, struggling with Tyndale's heavy trunk.

"Idiot!" his master scolded affectionately. "Small wonder you howled. Mr. Devenish and I thought for—''

Propping the trunk, Montelongo leaned on it, panting. "I not howl!" he denied vehemently. "I think *you* do that!"

His blood running cold, Devenish grinned and said a forced, "Well, that's hell's own jest!"

"Tell you what," said Tyndale. "Let us leave the trunk on the landing for the present, and bring the rest of the paraphernalia inside. It seems to have stopped raining—for a minute."

He helped Montelongo deposit the heavy trunk on the landing, and they all started down the stairs. Glancing uneasily about him, the Iroquois muttered, "Me no like big wigwam. Me sleep out. Under stars. You too, sir."

Sighing as they crossed the great hall, Tyndale remonstrated, "Why must you persist in using that pidgin English?"

Montelongo responded woodenly, "I shall take my rest *à la belle étoile*."

Devenish halted, staring his astonishment.

"I engaged a tutor," Tyndale explained, "to help Monty learn English. It turned out he has a very quick mind. Speaks fluent English, French, and German."

With a shout of laughter, Devenish asked, "Then, why in the deuce do you do it, Monty?"

The Iroquois shrugged. "It is expected of me. You sleep outside, sir?"

Still chuckling, Devenish said that he might just do so.

"In that case," grunted the Iroquois, "me stay in the—er . . .''

170

"Heap big wigwam?" Tyndale offered, helpfully.

His minion's dark features broke into a broad and rare grin.

"Faker!" Tyndale scoffed and, coming to the chaise and the groom who waited on the drivepath, he walked to the rear of the vehicle and began to work at the straps that held the second trunk. "Devenish," he said softly, "there is no reason for you to remain here. Do you prefer to return to—"

"What you are saying, I think," said Devenish, bristling, "is that you take me for a poltroon!"

Tyndale glanced at him and ventured with caution, "I have heard it said that certain types of men have—er, perhaps more awareness of things that are not quite so—ah—readily apparent to—to others."

"And you do not believe one word of it!" His anger flown as swiftly as it had come, Devenish laughed. "Jove! What a windy wallets! My thanks for the offer of a gracious escape, but I shall stay. If you hear a drumming sound in the night, however, it will likely not be your Indian friend here, but my knees."

Montelongo, who had carried a large box of bedding from the interior of the chaise and stood watching, grunted his approval, and put down his burden.

Tyndale said, "Good man, Dev! I'd hoped you would stay. But—tell me, do you *really* believe the old pile haunted, or were you hoaxing me?"

Devenish hesitated. With his eyes lowered and stubbing one boot at the uneven drive, he said slowly, "My uncle and Drummond both say I'm the living image of your father. I—begin to fancy I do indeed take after him—in more than looks."

"He held the castle to be an evil house." Craig nodded thoughtfully. "Is that what you mean?"

"You will think me daft, but . . ."

"But—so do you."

Devenish looked up in a shy, shamefaced fashion. "I expect it sounds purely crazy but—but there *is* something here. Something not of—this world."

Montelongo folded his arms and, having privately made up his mind to stay as close to Tyndale as was possible, rumbled, "You speak of Evil Spirits! Me *very* sure me sleep out!"

"Well, before you do, you Friday-faced fraud, pick up your box!" said Tyndale. "I can manage this trunk. Dev, can you bring the greatcoats and dressing cases?"

Laden, they started back to the castle, Tyndale calling to

the groom to take the chaise around to the stableyard which he supposed to be further along the drive, beyond a stand of elm trees. It began to rain again as they were climbing the steps, and the wind blew up gustier and colder.

"First thing—" Montelongo shivered—"me build one fine campfire."

"Hey!" shouted Devenish, stumbling forward with his load.

He was much too late. The door slammed shut before he reached the top step.

"Oh—damn!" he groaned. "Hurry and fish out the key, Tyndale!"

Craig set down his trunk and began to grope in his waistcoat pocket.

Montelongo offered a disgruntled, "Me lay twenty pounds you no find it! This place bad magic!"

"Nonsense! I'm sure . . . I put it— No! By Jove! I left it in the lock!"

Montelongo uttered a triumphant exclamation. Tyndale said indignantly, "I didn't take your bet! Put down that box and help find the thing, you pagan mushroom!"

Amused by this appellation, Montelongo put the box down and began to prowl about, keen eyes searching. Fearing the worst, Devenish dumped the greatcoats atop the bedding and made his way to a window. Shielding his eyes with both hands, he peered inside. "Never mind the key," he called. "It's lying on the floor just inside the door. Craig, you dolt, you must have dropped it!" He tried the window. "Locked, blast it! Well, we'll have to try the others."

Up to a point, the idea was a good one. A few windows could be reached from the wide front steps; the rest, however, proved to be set too high to be investigated. At some time in the recent past the castle had been fitted with comparatively modern windows, but the three that were accessible were also securely locked. Montelongo was dispatched to the stables in search of a ladder, while Devenish and Tyndale roamed the building, looking for a likely means of entrance. By the time Montelongo reappeared, carrying a serviceable ladder, they were all soaked, but no closer to entering Tyndale's new home. It was, in fact, another half-hour before they were able to do so, having been obliged to break one of the panes so as to reach the lock.

"An inauspicious beginning," grumbled Devenish, peering around the dimness of a cold, shrouded saloon.

"It will be more inauspicious did someone see us creeping in and fancy us to be burglars," Tyndale pointed out, crossing to the door.

Montelongo hurried to unlock the main door and carry the boxes inside. He and Tyndale then took up the large trunk and prepared to haul it upstairs. Devenish, his arms full, kicked the door closed and followed them to the stairs. "I hope there's some food about," he remarked. "Ain't too hungry now, but by—"

"Look out!" shouted Tyndale. He and Montelongo dropped their burden and leaped aside. The trunk they had earlier deposited on the first landing had apparently not been securely settled. It had gradually yielded to the pull of gravity and now came hurtling down the stairs to fetch up with a crash against its fellow, missing Devenish by a hair. It was a sturdy trunk, metal-bound and heavy, and he whistled his relief that it had missed him.

"Are you all right?" Tyndale asked. "Why in the deuce didn't you jump for it?"

"I was behind you, if you recall. Did not see the blasted thing coming. What the devil made it shoot down like that?"

Tyndale glanced up to the landing. "I suppose we must have failed to anchor it securely. We were in such haste to bring the things in out of the rain."

"Almost," grunted Montelongo, "Mr. Devenish got brain box broken."

"Yes." Tyndale scanned his cousin frowningly. "And I wonder what people would have said of that!"

"Oh, pshaw! You would scarce murder me with a trunk, coz! Besides, Monty was here—he could swear it was purely accidental."

"You think folks believe word of ignorant savage?" Montelongo uttered a scornful, "Hah!"

"And if my pagan was Caucasian as you or I," said Tyndale grimly, "this little island is largely populated by people who consider those dwelling in the next *county* to be 'foreigners' and as such, quite untrustworthy. Can you not imagine how much confidence they would repose in the word of a *Canadian?* A man in *my* service, known to be very loyal to *me?*"

The cousins looked at one another.

Devenish said rather uncertainly, "Well—nothing happened."

"No. But do you know, I begin to think your presence is a

decided hazard. To me! Are you quite convinced you'd not prefer to return to your gentle Sussex?''

''Perfectly sure. All you have to do, coz, is make very sure nothing happens to me.''

''That may well prove to be a two-edged sword,'' Tyndale warned, his eyes sombre.

''Fustian!'' Never one to remain glum above a minute, Devenish scoffed, ''We shall likely go on comfortably enough.''

The evening that followed was, however, somewhat less than comfortable. As a result of their perfunctory tour of inspection, the book room was selected as the initial head-quarters. The dining room was warmer, but the long table was rather daunting, and Devenish had taken an aversion to the tapestry that hung above the long oak credenza against one wall. This monumental work depicted a boar hunt under-taken by a number of individuals caught in unlikely poses, their flat, pale faces and gory pursuits causing him to express the conviction that never had he seen such a set of rum touches, and that to spend an entire evening with them staring at him was more than he could endure. The book room, despite a pervasive odour of mildew, was a large chamber made considerably less forbidding by the addition of a mod-ern pegged-oak floor and, when some fine Sheraton chairs were unearthed from dusty Holland covers, was pronounced more the thing.

While Devenish and Tyndale embarked on a search for candles, Montelongo descended into the lower regions in the hope of finding firewood. He returned in a great hurry, clutching a scuttle full of logs and shavings, and with his bronzed features markedly pale. He insisted that he had been ''watched'' throughout his foragings, and advised Tyndale that much as he appreciated his situation, if the Major decided to dwell permanently at Castle Tyndale, he would be obliged to find himself a new valet! Tyndale laughed at him, and said his megrims were the result of the roast pork they had en-joyed at dinner last evening, but he noted that the Iroquois was even less loquacious than usual, and that often during the balance of the evening, his dark gaze would flash uneasily to the dimmer corners of the large room.

As soon as the fire was established, the box of bedding provided by the housekeeper at Steep Drummond was brought in to be set by the hearth. By that time, the pangs of hunger were at work and a small table was also borne over to the fireside to serve their dining needs. Thanks to the friendship

Montelongo had struck up with General Drummond's irascible French chef, they were enabled to eat quite well. The chef had provided a basket containing slices of a fine ham, some excellent cheeses, two fresh loaves with an ample wedge of butter, a cold roast chicken, some grapes from Sir Andrew's succession houses, and two bottles of a fair Burgundy. The inroads made on this fare by three healthy young men served to impress upon them the need for Montelongo to journey into the village next morning. A discussion as to the supplies needed resulted in the compilation of a list, at the head of which were a cook, housekeeper, footman, and two maids, these prospective employees to repair to the castle immediately.

The food, wine, and warmth produced a pleasant feeling that all was not as black as had at first appeared. Evening deepened into night, and they chatted drowsily, but always at the edges of two minds nibbled the sly demons of unease. Devenish, his easy grin and cheerful commonplaces giving no least sign of his inner apprehension, could not dismiss the grievous cry they had heard that afternoon, and Montelongo alternately pondered the rapid and unexplained descent of the heavy trunk and his persistent sense of being under constant but invisible surveillance.

The candles were burning low before Tyndale stood, stretched, and said he was going up to bed.

"Up where?" asked Devenish, staring at him.

"I think I'll take the large bedchamber on the west front. It has apparently been prepared for me, and I fancy it must have been the master suite."

"But—it will be freezing up there! Why not bed down here tonight, and—"

"I will be damned," said Tyndale, "if I'll allow myself to be scared into bivouacking in my own house!"

"Who said anything about being scared?" Devenish demanded, jumping up and snatching up blankets and sheets. "It just seems stupid to leave such a fine fire."

With a broad grin, Tyndale shrugged. "Then by all means, stay down here."

Devenish glared at him and stalked from the room.

The bedchamber he had selected was next to Tyndale's. The large canopied bed was free of Holland covers but not made up. Grumbling to himself, Devenish began to spread his blankets atop the mattress. Montelongo stalked in, stared from the blankets to Devenish, and with one sweep of his long arm cleared the offending articles away. Devenish meekly assisted him in the business of sheets and blankets and eiderdown, each in its correct order of business, until a very tidy arrangement had been completed. The Iroquois departed while Devenish was disrobing, and came back a few minutes later, carrying a warming pan which he tucked between the sheets while eyeing the young man appraisingly. "You," he imparted, "peel good. For small white man."

Devenish stiffened and prepared to devastate him with some well-chosen words. There was a twinkle in the unfathomable dark eyes, however, and it was dashed difficult to devastate anyone while one's teeth chattered so. Clambering hastily between the sheets, his feet encountered the comfort of the warming pan and he forgot indignation. "You," he shivered, "are—are a j-jewel! If ever you l-leave my cousin, come to me. My own man stayed with the m-military when I—er—left it, and now that I'm to be sh-sh-shackled, I'll have to find myself a valet."

Montelongo thanked him gravely and went off to the adjoining room, where he advised Tyndale he meant to stay by him all night, just in case an uninvited guest should put in an appearance. Tyndale chuckled and enquired as to who was protecting whom, but he was disturbed, nonetheless. He had never before seen the proud Indian show fear.

Devenish had set his candle on the table beside his bed and had instructed Montelongo to leave it burning. The room was so large, however, as to make the circle of light pathetically small. He found himself straining his eyes into the surrounding darkness, whereupon he closed them and tried to go to sleep. It had been a long, tiring day, and downstairs he had almost dropped off several times, but now that he wooed slumber his brain became fiendishly wide awake, his thoughts whirling helter-skelter fashion from one worry to the next. The shadows of past events weighed heavily on his mind until he felt crushed by sympathy for the mother he had never known, and for his father's sad death.

Outside, the night seemed full of movement and noise; the rain pattered, the wind sighed in the chimney and set the windows to rattling. Normal noises, of course. Certainly nothing to cause alarm. He concentrated on his beloved Yolande . . . her sweet face, and those heavenly eyes that could be so tender, or . . . sometimes, so vexed with him. . . .

He could not have said what woke him, but he started up suddenly, his heart thundering. The candle was out, the room oppressively dark with only the lighter squares of the windows relieving the gloom. The storm was still blustering. Perhaps a branch had come down, or a gate had slammed somewhere. He pulled the eiderdown closer around his ears and settled down again.

"Alain . . . Alain . . .!"

His breath congealed in his throat. His eyes shot open and he lay tensely unmoving. Tyndale never called him by his Christian name. Monty certainly would not. And besides—it had been the voice of—*a woman!* How stupid! He must have dreamed—

"Alain . . . oh—Alain . . . my son . . ."

His mind reeled. He thought dazedly, "My God! My *God!*" And leaping out of bed, grabbed for his tinderbox, only to pause, frozen with new terror.

A faint glow shone from the mantel. By that unearthly light, he could see his mother's portrait distinctly. His own infant likeness and the rose arbour wherein they had posed was gone, and there was only her face, transformed into a nightmare countenance like some hideous caricature of the beauty that once had been. The eyes stared from great, hollow sockets. The cheeks were sunken, the mouth gapingly down-trending as if in a despairing scream. Only the hair was as lovely as before, of itself seeming to render the other features even more ghastly.

Devenish wet dry lips and battled a sick weakness. "M-m-mama . . .?" he croaked.

"Avenge me . . ." came the poignant moan. "Alain . . . avenge us . . .!"

The outer door crashed open. Tyndale, holding up a branch of candles, and with Montelongo's dark face peering apprehensively over his shoulder, said, "Dev? Are you all right?"

The familiar faces seemed to ripple before Devenish's eyes, like reflections on the disturbed surface of a pool. "The—the portrait . . ." he managed, gesturing towards it.

Tyndale walked closer, holding his candelabra higher. Devenish saw the puzzled expression on the strong face and, dreading to look again, turned his own gaze to the mantel.

The portrait was just as he had first seen it, his mother smiling lovingly down at the babe she held.

Dimly, he thought, "I am going mad . . ."

Tyndale gave a cry of alarm, and Montelongo ran to steady Devenish as he swayed uncertainly. Considerably unnerved, the Iroquois demanded, "When we go home, Major? We got no haunted teepees in Montreal!"

*   *   *

For many years General Sir Andrew Drummond had served his country with distinction. He had left the military when the death of his elder brother brought him both the title and estates and, although he sometimes remembered the camaraderie of army life with a nostalgic sigh, his most bitter battles had been fought and lost behind a desk in Whitehall, so that he had never really regretted his decision to resign. He had proven a conscientious and just landlord, a fair-minded employer, a good neighbour, a bruising rider to hounds, and an excellent judge of horseflesh, the which sterling qualities had won him both liking and admiration. He was also, however, a man who drove a hard bargain, his manner was brusque, he was impatient with foolishness (of which he had been heard to remark the local society had more than its share), and his temper was notorious. Further, he had an unfortunate habit of refusing to bow to the dictates of protocol: he attended the social functions which pleased him, rather than those to which it was expedient to respond, and invited to his home people he enjoyed, not necessarily those who might some day prove of use to him. Needless to say, these praiseworthy practices had aroused a good deal of ire, albeit subdued, in certain quarters.

Nonetheless, General Drummond was the last man one might have suspected of improper conduct, and the entire County was astounded to learn that he had committed a horrifying social solecism. Unsuspecting guests, lured to his home so as to renew their acquaintanceship with his granddaughter, had been introduced to two young gentlemen distantly related to their host. Never dreaming that these same two men figured prominently in a shocking scandal, trusting parents had allowed their daughters to be presented to the newcomers and had watched indulgently as those carefully nurtured flowers flirted, chatted, and danced with them. Prominent citizens had greeted them cordially and had deigned to introduce them to their own friends. And then, after four and twenty years of lies and deceit, the sordid truth concerning the tragedy at Castle Tyndale had exploded through the county.

When the first wave of shocked incredulity abated, it was reasoned that the General must certainly have been aware of the long-kept secret, and had deliberately sponsored the son of a murderer into society. Young Tyndale had a fine military record, even if he was a Colonial, but that was no justification for allowing him to mix with the cream of the local

178

gentry. His blood was tainted with the dread stain of murder, his house was disgraced, and he must forever be a pariah. As for Alain Devenish—surely *his* behaviour was utterly beyond the pale! By all the laws of Polite Society, he should have faced Tyndale across twenty yards of turf, aimed down the barrel of a duelling pistol, and done what he might to obliterate the scion of the man who had orphaned him. Instead, he appeared to regard his dastardly cousin with an affability that was, opined several indignant gentlemen, sufficient to turn the stomach of any honourable, God-fearing man!

Thus, having arrived at their variously damning conclusions, the County, deliciously scandalized, proceeded to beat a path to the door of the miscreant. Such honeyed sympathy was extended by reason of his having been "hoodwinked" by the pair of young scoundrels; such heartfelt condolences offered upon the "unfortunate proceedings" at the castle; and such bland amazement expressed that the tragedy had been "so artfully concealed all these years," that General Drummond became almost purple in the face with rage, even as he parried thrust with block, and attack with evasion. "Curse and confound the pack of 'em!" he raged to his stoical daughter. "I canna fight back, y' ken? That's what galls, Carrroline! I canna say a worrrd in me ain defense! And if one more sanctimonious hypocrite comes fawning here wi' his treacly grin and sairpents' teeth, I'll chop him tae bits and stuff him intae his own sporran! And be damned tae him, if I dinna!"

Life at Steep Drummond was thus become a tense business of late. Mrs. Drummond, never at ease with her father-in-law, avoided him as much as possible and took care to say nothing at the dinner table that might provide fodder for his simmering rage. Yolande, having endured a thundering scold all the way back from Castle Tyndale on the fateful day of the picnic, had since refused to discuss the matter, regarding her grandparent with cool but respectful silence whenever he attempted to take her to task for not having informed him of the true state of affairs. He had, he snarled at her, written to his bacon-brained son, and in such a way that he had no doubt but that her father would "soon come posting up here to see what he might do to make amends." Yolande replied calmly, "How lovely," which drove her grandpapa into strangled choking sounds and grimaces that might have alarmed her, did she not know the old humbug so well.

She had her own share of callers and did what she might to

point out that for whatever had occurred four and twenty years ago, Craig was in no way responsible, and that Devenish would be a clod indeed, if he refused to give at least a hearing to the man who had saved his life. Not surprisingly, her most sympathetic listener was her friend Mary Gordon, whose dark eyes would glisten with tears at the very thought of "dear Mr. Devenish" being so unjustly accused. "How very said it is, Yolande," she mourned. "And you just aboot to announce your betrothal. Do you suppose your papa will be able to bring the General about his thumb?"

Yolande said that if Sir Martin was unable to do so, her mama would probably succeed, for Lady Louisa had so much charm her fierce father-in-law was usually putty in her hands. "It is not that which worries me, Mary," she confided one day, as they took tea together in the drawing room. "There are things I simply cannot understand. The real facts of what happened between Stuart Devenish and Jonas Tyndale have been buried for all these years. Yet within days of the arrival of my cousins, the entire County was fairly buzzing with it! Do you have any notion of who set it about?"

Miss Gordon shook her sleek head. "Hamish MacInnes told my brother, and Jock gave him a rare setdown for spreading such vicious gossip, I can tell you!"

"And spread it a little farther," said Yolande, dryly. "Oh, never fret, dear. I cannot blame Jock. It's just—" She hesitated.

Miss Gordon slipped a consoling arm about her. "Of course. I understand. You must be fair daft with worry, to have the love of your heart dwelling in that dreadful old pile and never knowing if yon Colonial wild man has taken it into his head to exact vengeance by pushing poor Devenish off—"

"Do not *dare* to say such wicked things, Mary Gordon! Or I shall positively shake you!" raged Yolande, springing to her feet and rounding on her startled friend like a fury. "Craig is as honourable as he is brave, and would no more attack Dev than raise his hand against—against little Josie!"

"Oh—I'm s-sure you are perfectly right," quavered her friend, variously frightened and elated. "Is a fine man, Major Tyndale. I never meant aught but to console you, and pray you will forgive me for being such a great gaby."

Yolande saw the gleam in the big eyes and knew what her friend was thinking. Scarcely caring, she resumed her seat, apologized, was forgiven, and sat staring miserably at the great bowl of sweet peas on the occasional table. What were Dev and Craig doing at this moment? Were they cold and uncomfortable, and not eating properly? Or had that strange man of Craig's managed to find them some servants? And what possible hope had they of ever proving Jonas Tyndale's innocence?

A warm little hand was placed over her own. Mary said softly, "I've known you a good many years, dearest, and never seen you sae doonhearted. Can I no help ye?"

Such warm understanding brought a lump to Yolande's throat. She pressed her friend's hand responsively. "Cousin Craig holds his father died swearing his innocence," she sighed. "I believe him, but—how he can hope to prove it, after all this time . . ." And she sighed again.

"Well, it certainly wouldnae hurt to try. And twenty-four years is not sae very long, Yolande. At least, so my papa holds. The older you get, says he, the faster pass the years." She added with rather doubtful logic, "To people of *his* age it likely seems no more than a year would seem to you and me."

"Yes," said Yolande dubiously. "But even so, a lot has changed since then. The only people who have even a glimmering of knowledge about what really happened that day are the servants who worked in the castle. And many of them may have moved away, or gone to their reward."

"Fiddle! Who would wish tae move from Ayrshire? Or leave their families? They are likely most of them within a few miles of here at this very minute. At least, Major Tyndale must be of that opinion, for he seems to have been pester —I mean—questioning everybody he can reach, and those he misses, Devenish finds."

"Oh!" cried Yolande, encouraged. "How wonderful if they learn something to help! Do you know if they've done so, Mary?"

"I—I hae me doots, Yolande. Sorry I am tae say it, but," she smiled wryly, "they're a close-mouthed lot at best, and from all I can detairmine, are not being—well, they seem to hae put up a—a wall of silence."

Yolande's hopes died. It was no more than she had expected, really. The Scots country folk with their fierce pride, their unyielding sense of family, their stern adherence to proper behaviour, had judged both Tyndale and Devenish and found them wanting. "What a frightful mess!" she thought. "No one will help them."

Moved by her friend's despairing attitude, Miss Gordon said a tentative, "If there is anything I can do, I'll nae hesitate. There may be old folks knowing something of it all who would never be found by Tyndale, but who my papa might be able to approach.''

Brightening, Yolande clasped her hand tighter. "Oh, bless you, Mary! I shall ask my Aunt Caroline, also. She is well acquainted.''

"Nae—d'ye think ye should?" Mary demurred. "Will she no tell your grandpapa?''

"Why, she's a dear, despite her gruff ways, and I feel sure . . . Oh, my! It would put her into a difficult position, wouldn't it? And my poor dear old gentleman is so upset just now. There must be *someone* I could ask. . . .'' She knit her brows, then exclaimed a triumphant, "Yes! There's Mrs. MacFarlane, the gardener's wife. She has the dearest little girl who sometimes plays with Josie, and I believe the family has been here for centuries. I'll go and see her at once!'' She stood, the bloom back in her cheeks again. "Mary—how good you are! Thank you, thank you!''

On the front steps they embraced and parted, Yolande to hurry into the garden and walk across the park towards the copse of trees beyond which was the gardener's cottage, and Mary to be driven home, her pretty head full of wonderment that Yolande Drummond, whom she had always thought a sensible girl, could have such a *tendre* for that lanky Canadian boy who was well enough in his quiet way, but had not one jot of Alain Devenish's looks or personality.

Yolande, meanwhile, was diverted from her route when she heard childish voices coming from the new summer house that was the General's pride. Sure enough, Josie and her friend were inside, solemnly conducting a tea party with two elderly dolls and a large black cat that seemed not to mind the dress it wore.

"Miss Yolande," called Josie gaily, waving the hand of the doll seated next to her. "Come and have a cuppa tea. These are Maisie's dolls. That's Mrs. Crump, and mine is Lady Witherspoon. Ain't they lovely?''

Yolande was suitably impressed with the company and, having been presented to the cat (first) and to Maisie, said with her kind smile, "Never look so frightened, dear. I'll not hurt your dolls.''

The child, rather frail and all eyes and elbows, backed away, remarking in a breathless fashion that she didn't mean no harm and that "Mum said I wasna tae play wi' Miss Josie.''

"No, did she? We must see if she will not relent. Meanwhile, I'm sure she would not object if I joined you."

Fears were forgotten, and the two junior matrons welcomed their guest and plied her with lemonade "tea" and broken biscuits. The black cat, who went by the odd name of Mrs. Saw, considered the newcomer at some length before deciding that she had an acceptable lap and occupying it.

"Oh, dear!" said Maisie, alarmed. "He's kneading your pretty dress, ma'am."

"It doesn't matter," Yolande reassured her. "I like cats, and she's such a lovely one, aren't you, Mrs. Saw?"

"It's a 'he.' And he doesn't like nicknames," Josie corrected primly.

A dimple peeping, Yolande said, "My apologies. But why do you call him 'Mrs.'?"

Both girls dissolved into shrieks of laughter, and when Yolande was at length able to enquire the reason, she learned that she had "said it so funny."

"We *don't* call him 'Mrs.,' " giggled Maisie.

"His name's *Methy-slaw!*" Josie elaborated with a shake of the head for the density of some adults.

For a moment Yolande was unenlightened. Then, she exclaimed, "Oh—Methuselah! A biblical name."

Josie nodded. "Like Mr. Craig's horse."

Intrigued, Yolande said, "Lazzy is short for Lazarus, then? Do you know why?"

"It's because when he was a wee colt, he was caught in a flood or something," said Maisie, all importance. "He almost drowned, but Mr. Craig jumped in and got him out, and that's why that funny Red Indian follows him all over the world, even to Waterloo."

Yolande blinked. Josie, incredulous, demanded, "How do *you* know all that?"

"Me mum told me. She knows all about Mr. Tyndale. I heard her tell me dad that we ought to make it our business to find out—"

"Maisie! Whatever be ye doing, child?" A thin, nervous, dark-haired little woman hurried up the path, wiping her hands on her apron.

"Good afternoon, Mrs. MacFarlane," called Yolande. "Will you not join us?"

Mrs. MacFarlane not only would not join them, but was apparently most distressed. "I *told* ye, never to come up

183

here, you bad girl!'' she chided. ''Do ye ken what happens to bairns that do nae heed their mums?''

Beginning to cry, Maisie picked up her doll.

Yolande stood and walked forward, pleading ''Pray do not scold her, m'' 'am. I am the culprit, for Josie is so short of playmates I asked your daughter to stay. It would be lovely if Maisie could keep her company now and then.''

The lady fairly clutched her child and, standing very stiff and straight, replied a frigid, ''We thank ye, Miss Drummond. Is best they dinna meet.'' She bit her lip and added with a sort of desperation, ''And besides, we'm moving away verra soon noo. Good day tae ye.''

She bobbed a curtsy and backed away, her attitude all but fearful.

Josie snatched up the other doll and ran forward. ''Don't forget Lady Witherspoon,'' she said sadly.

Maisie ran to retrieve her doll. A ball that had shared the chair with ''Lady Witherspoon'' fell to the floor. Yolande took it up. ''Catch,'' she called, and threw it to Josie.

Mrs. MacFarlane, standing just beyond the little girl, uttered a piercing shriek and sprang back, throwing up a protecting arm.

Astonished, Yolande cried, ''Oh, I do beg your pardon. Did I startle you, ma'am?''

The distraught woman returned no answer, but burst into tears, took her frightened daughter by the hand, and all but ran back across the park.

It was very apparent, thought Yolande, that she could expect little help from that quarter. Maybe Mrs. MacFarlane thought they were *all* murderers!

''Now,'' said Josie forlornly, ''I got no one to play tea party with.''

''Not only that, you have no tea party left.'' Yolande nodded at Methuselah who was on the table, busily crunching the remaining biscuits, with the empty cream pitcher overturned beside him.

''Silly creature,'' Josie giggled. ''There wasn't no cream in it. And cats do not like biscuits!''

Yolande smiled, ''I suppose no one has ever told him,'' she said, thus awakening a little peal of laughter.

As they started back towards the house together, Yolande thought, ''I wonder how Mrs. MacFarlane knew so much about Craig. . . .''

Chapter Twelve

The village of Drumdownie had seen many changes during the march of the centuries. It was thought to have been extant during the Roman military occupation, it had endured through the wars of the tribes, the Norman invasion, and a mighty battle with Norwegian hosts. It had known Robert the Bruce with pride, and Oliver Cromwell with hatred. But it had never as yet seen an Iroquois Indian clad in leathern tunic, trousers, and moccasins, and riding bareback with the demeanour of a conquering monarch. As a result, Montelongo's progress along the cobbled old street became more a procession, with children, dogs, and a growing number of adults following in his train, many of the latter, greatly diverted, calling out eagerly to learn where was the rest of the circus.

Ignoring the uproar, Montelongo drew his bay mare to a halt outside the blacksmith's shop where were seated several of the village elders. He swung one leg across the mare's back, preparatory to slipping down, but stopped as an ancient man tottered to his feet, his rheumy eyes as wide as his toothless mouth, to pipe in broad Scots, "The puir savage will be needin' a body tae translate. Now dinna everyone press in—he's nae tae be trusted too close, like as not!"

Montelongo decided this old gentleman was as unintelligible as most of the other Scots he had met, and eyed him imperturbably.

"Dinna fash ye'sel' laddie," urged the aged one. "Me name be Roberts an' I ask ye tae light ye doon and open y'r budget wi' us. How much will they be chargin' fer tickets? And d'ye ken whar the tent will be pitched?"

Very little of this was clear to Montelongo, but one word stood out. "Tent," he said in his deep, resonant voice. "Where big wigwam? Where Chief?"

Mr. Roberts cackled. "Not sae fast!" he admonished. "Show us some tricks, first."

An eager chorus echoed this request, shouts of "Aye, gie

us a show!'' . . . ''Whar's a skelpie?'' . . . ''Will ye nae dance fer us?''

The minister, a mild gentleman with a soft heart and patient eyes that blinked behind thick spectacles, managed to work his way through the throng. ''Och! A Red Indian, is it?'' said he admiringly. ''Will ye no stand back and give the puir chappie air. They're accustomed to great spaces, d'ye ken. Are ye lost, me guid mon?'' And then, misinterpreting Montelongo's incredulous stare, he said with careful articulation, ''You . . . come here . . . for . . . why?''

The fathomless gaze of the Iroquois drifted up and down the good minister and his black robes; around the circle of faces, variously grinning, mocking, curious, or awed; and returned to the reverend gentleman. ''I have come here,'' he said in flawless English, ''to hire servants for Major Win— Tyndale.''

A new chorus of astonishment arose, a markedly less friendly outcry.

''What manner o' jiggery-pokery be that?'' quoth Mr. Roberts, indignant.

''A iggeramous aping his betters!'' the baker sneered.

''Servants, is it?'' laughed the butcher. ''Tae worrk at Castle Tyndale, eh?''

A sharp-faced matron asked snidely, ''Why hae ye come all this way? Could ye no hire at Drumwater, or Kirkaird?''

Ignoring this unfortunate question, Montelongo proclaimed, ''Major pay well. We need housekeeper, cook, parlourmaids, a footman. A gardener, perhaps. People come early tomorrow morning.''

''Ye'd best hae the gates wide, big Chief,'' chortled the blacksmith, ''else they'll like to be beat down by the rush!''

This witticism sent the crowd into whoops, the following derisive comments causing many to become so hilarious that there was much side holding and moaning that no more mirth could be endured.

And the end of it all was that Montelongo returned to Castle Tyndale, a thunderous scowl upon his face, to inform his employer that everyone in the village of Drumdownie was crazy as a loon, and there were no servants to be had there, either. ''Them say,'' he imparted with a disgusted glance around the great hall, ''castle is bogle-ridden and they'll not set foot in it!'' And taking himself gloomily to the pile of dirty dishes in the kitchens, reflected that he was much in agreement with the locals, loony though they may be.

* * *

186

"It passes all understanding!" Mrs. Arabella Drummond tilted her parasol against the afternoon sun as she wandered with her niece along the village street. Following, Josie was obliged to adjust her pace to the meanderings of Socrates since that pampered darling paid little heed to tuggings at the red ribbon that served for a leash. "Simply," Arabella went on in high dudgeon, "because my sweet baby chanced to forget himself in the greengrocer's shop, one might have thought the world would come to an end! I shall speak to your grandfather about that wretched man, I do assure you! Never have I been so insulted!"

In Yolande's opinion the shopkeeper had been quite restrained, especially in view of the fact that they had entered his neat establishment in an attempt to gather information, and not as customers. The greengrocer had been able to supply little more than had been garnered from her previous informants. Of the inside servants who might be able to shed new light on the happenings of 1792, few were still in the neighbourhood. There was the Hewitts, he said thoughtfully. "But Mrs. Hewitt was a sickly woman who passed to her reward three years ago, and Mr. Hewitt went for head groom to a gentleman in India. Their daughter stayed, but she was only a wee bairn at the time of the tragedy."

Reflecting that it all seemed hopeless, Yolande murmured something placating to her aunt. That lady, her feathers still ruffled, remarked that she could not for the life of her see why Yolande must make all these enquiries. "It is downright embarrassing," she declared. "Had I known you meant to do so, I should not have accompanied you, for to be connected even remotely with such persons as Major Winters, er, Tyndale, is stigma enough, let alone to remind others of it! Were you wise, my love, you would allow him to do his own investigating. Much good will it do him, for the locals are not likely to tell him anything, even was there anything to tell!"

"Which is exactly why I am trying to help," said Yolande. "They think of—"

"Oh—only look at that darling doggie!" Mrs. Drummond interrupted, rapturously eyeing a china spaniel in the window of the draper's shop. "How that would brighten my poor little room at Park Parapine! Not that I mean to appear critical of the quarters allotted to me, for I am after all only a poor relation, and your dear mama is more than kind to allow me to serve as her constant stay and support, so I can scarcely expect to be given a chamber suitable for family or guests,

187

can I? Of one thing, Yolande, I am very sure; none can brand me ungrateful. Not a night passes but that I remember your dear mama in my prayers! As indeed I should, for it must be so tiresome for her there, all alone with the children. Save for your father. Sir Martin is not a garrulous man. Often have I remarked how little he contributes to the conversation when I am with your mama, which must make her life just now so very dreary. Though that was not what I had intended to remark, and . . ." She paused, at a loss to know what she *had* intended to remark.

Yolande seized the opportunity to remind her aunt of the china dog (which she herself thought quite revolting, for surely no dog had such enormous and soulful eyes, or hair the colour of raw liver). "Should you like to go inside, dear? I can wait out here with Socrates, if you wish."

Mrs. Drummond did wish. Yolande and Josie remained outside, but it developed that the lady proprietor was both an ardent faunophile and overjoyed by the patronage of one of the ladies from "up tae the hill." As a result, in a very little while Socrates had to be taken inside to be exclaimed over and, Josie also soon succumbing to the fascinations of the cluttered little shop, Yolande was left to her own devices.

It was a beautiful afternoon, the warm sunlight causing the old sandstone cottages to stand in sharp relief against the blue of the skies, and a light breeze flirting with the trees and swinging the weathervane atop the minister's cottage next to the quaint old church. The door of the church stood wide and, as Yolande passed a woman came out, head bowed and handkerchief pressed to tearful eyes. Wondering if she could be of some assistance, Yolande hesitated. The woman looked up, and Yolande thought she had never beheld so desolate a countenance. Her kind heart touched, she moved forward, stretching forth one hand and saying, "Mrs. MacFarlane! Oh, my dear ma'am, whatever is wrong? Is there anything I can do for you?"

But the gardener's wife only shrank away, uttered a gasping, unintelligible remark, and hurried past.

"Puir wee lassie," said the minister sadly, walking to join Yolande. "She carries a heavy load, Miss Drummond. A crushing load, indeed!"

Yolande nodded. "So I have thought," she agreed, still looking after that frantic retreat. "I know you cannot betray a confidence, but—is there any way in which I could help her?"

He sighed heavily. "In company wi' the most of us, ma'am, puir Mrs. MacFarlane's best help can come frae but one source. Her own self!"

He was probably in the right of it, thought Yolande, and she said no more. Just the same, when she returned to Steep Drummond, she sent a note down to the MacFarlane cottage, in which she reiterated her offer to be of any assistance, and urged that if Mrs. MacFarlane ever felt the need, she not hesitate to come to her.

*   *   *

"Six days!" Devenish observed wrathfully, following his cousin down the main staircase. "Almost a week in this miserable damned pile, and what have we accomplished? Nothing! Not a word! Not a hint! Not a clue!"

Tyndale frowned. "It is not a 'miserable damned pile'! In fact, I think the architecture superb for the period. Most edifices of this type are stately and impressive from the outside, and like a rabbit warren inside. Castle Tyndale has large, bright rooms; corridors that are straight and functional; and ample storage facilities."

"As you should certainly be aware," grumbled Devenish, "since you've paced off and sketched every blasted room we found."

"I really fail to see why that should so annoy you."

But it did annoy Devenish, because he judged it to be a bourgeois pride of ownership. His disgust had been so obvious that one day his cousin had met his irked glance, paused in his pacing, and murmured, "You certainly understand why I do this, Dev?" He had replied disdainfully, "Oh, it is quite obvious that you cherish every brick and stone in the place!" To which Tyndale had retaliated, "And, like my father, you do not." The reminder of his close resemblance to Jonas Tyndale had further infuriated Devenish. His head flinging upward he had snapped, "Very true. I am also becoming more aware of the murderous side of my nature of late. You had best never venture onto the battlements in my company, cousin!" and stamped away, fumingly aware that their relationship was fast deteriorating.

Now, however, knowing he was very tired and overwrought, he turned from an argument, saying merely, "I would think you had better things to do, is all, when we accomplish so little of what we'd hoped for."

"No, but I think we have accomplished a good deal."

"The devil! All we've managed to do is alienate the whole

189

damned county! The yokels mistrust you, and now they've turned on me because I'm trying to help you."

"Yes, I know. And I wish you will go back to London. You do not look at all the thing."

Devenish was silent. That he did not look well was very true. There were dark shadows beneath his eyes and a drawn look to his pale face. His nerves were taut, his temper flaring more frequently these days, his frustration over their lack of success finding expression in an irritability that he was at times unable to contain.

Watching him, Tyndale said, "You have spent too much time in the saddle."

"And learnt nothing! But they know—damn them! Some of 'em, at least! They know *something*, but will tell me nought!" He added moodily, "Besides, you have ridden as much as I."

"I do not have a game leg." Tyndale saw the immediate drawing together of the slim, dark brows, and went on hastily, "And *I* sleep. Why you must sit up half the night when you come in worn out, I cannot fathom."

Again, Devenish returned no answer. The truth of the matter was that these six days had been a nightmare such as he had never before experienced. Despite his carefree demeanour, his life had not been completely free from care. He had endured a good deal of merciless mockery because of his good looks, and although his friends were numerous, he had also made bitter enemies, many of these because some admired lady's eyes had wandered wistfully in his direction. He had known deep disgrace, and a prolonged siege of physical suffering that had not entirely left him. None of these experiences, however, had served to extinguish his ebullient optimism, or to daunt him for very long. But he was close to being daunted now. Just as, with every day that passed his cousin admired his heritage the more, with each hour that passed his own dread and loathing of it was increased. So long as he was inside Castle Tyndale, whether by day or night, he was tormented by the instinct that he was watched by other-worldly eyes. Often, he'd had the sensation that something stood so close beside him that his skin would creep with the fear of being touched by some cold, invisible hand. Prompted by the conviction that he was followed, his glance flashed constantly over his shoulder. His hesitant attempts to explain his experiences to his cousin had been met with a faintly incredulous simulation of understanding, but the sensitive Devenish had thought to detect amusement beneath Tyndale's gravity, and pride forbade him any further reference to the matter. If Tyndale thought him either over-imaginative or a poltroon, he would be driven into his grave sooner than add to either suspicion.

His terror of betraying cowardice forced him to retain the same bedchamber despite his first ghastly night in the castle. Each evening he lingered by the book-room fire for as long as he could manœuvre either his cousin or Montelongo to remain with him. When he did seek his bed, it was as much as he could do to open the door, and he avoided looking in the direction of his mother's portrait until shame forced him to glance at it. Only once, on the third night, had the gruesome transformation been repeated. He had sat up in bed, determined to keep his eyes upon the portrait to see if the change would take place while he watched. But he had dropped off to sleep and awoken, as before, to find his candle extinguished but the room illuminated by that soul-freezing glow emanating from the ghastly portrait. His teeth chattering, his limbs weak as water, he'd somehow driven himself to spring from the bed and rush to the painting, but he had tripped over some unseen object and by the time he'd picked himself up, all was normal again. The second and fourth nights had been entirely free from any manifestations, but he had been unable to sleep, his ears straining for the first sound of his unwelcome visitors. On the fifth night he had slept at last, only to awaken to a man's voice calling his name repeatedly, this swiftly followed by the sound of a woman's heart-rending weeping. Sick with fear, he had pulled the covers over his head and slept again from pure exhaustion, to awaken half suffocated when dawn lit the tall windows.

Even the memories were sufficient to make him shiver, and he was horrified to find Tyndale eyeing him curiously. Flushing, he said, "Instead of worrying about my sleep, cousin, you would do better to reflect on our failure to prove what we came here to prove. Dash it all, here we stay, achieving nothing, freezing with cold, victims of Monty's 'cooking,' ghost-ridden, and—"

"Nonsense! I have seen no ghosts, and if Monty has good luck in Kilmarnock today, we may soon have some servants to provide you with the comforts without which you evidently cannot exist."

They had reached the main floor and were starting across the echoing vastness of the Great Hall. Devenish wrenched Tyndale to a halt and expostulated angrily, "I have existed without comforts before this, blast your eyes! But it was in the good clean open air, not cooped up in a clammy, brooding—''

"Well, God knows you have often enough been invited to leave!''

"D'ye take me for a flat? I'm well aware of how eagerly you would gloat and sneer and spread about that 'poor old Devenish's nerve has gone!' Well, it has not! I can last as long as can you—and longer!''

His own nerves somewhat the worse for wear, Tyndale grated, "Devil take you! I would do no such thing!''

They stood in the middle of the big room, glaring at one another, and were both shocked when a discreet cough warned that they were not alone.

Mr. Hennessey, an Irishman who owned a small farm nearby, stood just inside the front doors, hat in hand, and an embarrassed expression on his ruddy face. "Sure and 'tis sorry Oi am did Oi disturb yez, gentlemen,'' he said in his soft brogue. "Oi've fetched the eggs your haythen—Oi mean, your man ordered. And some bacon and pork and chickens, besides. Oi'll bring 'em insoide if 'tis convenient and will not disturb yez at your brawling.''

The tension eased. Devenish laughed, and explained, "This was one of our quieter discussions, Hennessey. By all means, bring in the provender.''

"Well, Oi tried, y'r honour, so Oi did. But 'tis beyond me poor powers to get the kitchen door open. If you could be so kind as to unlock it, Oi'll be fetching the stuff.''

The cousins at once proceeding to the kitchen found the outer door not only unlocked, but standing open, a fact that caused Mr. Hennessey's dark eyes to become very round and his mouth very solemn. He carried in the supplies with marked rapidity, so eager to be away that he all but drove off without the flimsies Tyndale offered.

"So much for your 'large, bright rooms'!'' grunted Devenish as they loaded the food into the stone pantry. "Do you decide to live here, you are not like to be pestered to death by company!''

"Gammon! Hennessey said he'd been trying to get the door open. Likely he had got it almost free by the time he came for aid, and the wind did the rest. As for living here, I may very well do so. There must be *some* rational folks hereabouts who do not shiver and shake and fancy every sound the work of shades and goblins!''

Devenish flared, "You refer, perhaps, to me, sir?"

"Good God!" groaned Tyndale, swinging shut the door of the pantry. "He's off again!" He turned, half laughing, but was given pause by the stark fury in Devenish's blue eyes. His own eyes narrowed. After a silent moment, he said thoughtfully, "We have been here almost a week. Time we looked at the battlements—if that would not cause you to be overset."

Why he would choose this of all moments, Devenish could not comprehend, but he was damned if he would show alarm, and so followed his cousin into the hall.

In stern, unsmiling silence, they went side by side to the stairs and up until they came to the winding side steps that led to the northwest tower. It was too narrow here to walk abreast, and Tyndale took the lead, Devenish following until they reached a certain narrow window, where he paused. He had fought against looking out, but now his Uncle Alastair's sombre voice echoed again in his ears. . . . "I saw a dark-ness flash past the window. I heard this . . . this terrible scream. . . ." He stood immobile, gazing at the narrow aperture. How terrible a thing to have seen what Alastair Tyndale had seen. How frightful to see someone of whom you are fond, plunge—

"Well? Are you coming, or not?"

A look of irritation on his face, Tyndale waited at the next landing. "Insensitive clod!" thought Devenish. "*He* should be plagued by guilt and remorse!" Yet it was very obvious that if Tyndale felt anything at all, it was merely impatience. Cursing under his breath, Devenish resumed his climb. They must, he was sure, have negotiated literally thousands of steps when the stair at last ended before a diminutive landing and a Gothic arched door. Tyndale hesitated briefly, then raised the heavy iron latch and the door creaked open.

They stepped out on to the battlements and into a brisk, clear afternoon with the wind coming straight off the sea and full of the damp, clean smell of it. On their first day here they had found two flags in the basement, one the Union Jack, and the other a banner bearing the arms of the House of Tyndale. Montelongo had decided that these must be flown, and they were now whipping merrily at the flagpole. A line of clouds was building in the northeast; westward, the wind raised little whitecaps on the waves and sent surf crashing against the guarding rocks, and, far off, the islands in the Firth of Clyde were clearly visible.

Postponing the inevitable, Devenish sauntered to the east battlements to scan a fair prospect of rolling hills, lush meadows, and forest land. He breathed deeply of the bracing air and could not wonder that his mother had been so fond of this home of her childhood. Craig stood at the western side between two merlons of the battlements, at the very edge of the embrasure, looking straight down. Devenish thought, "My God! How simple it would be! There's nothing to stay his fall. . . ." He went over and murmured a dry, "You're a trusting soul, I'll give you that!" His cousin neither replied nor moved and, reluctantly, Devenish looked down, also. It seemed terribly far to the jagged rocks. What had been in his father's mind as he fell? Only the ghastly certainty that death awaited him? Or had he thought of the wife and little son he loved? Shrinking, Devenish wondered what he himself would think of at such a moment. And he knew: Yolande.

Tyndale said huskily, "I had so hoped the roof would be faulty. That your father might, perhaps, have stumbled over an uneven or sloping surface. But—see, it is clear, and level." He drove one fist against the parapet and cried, "I still cannot credit it! I *cannot!* He may have been wild and reckless; resentful, perhaps. Obsessed with his conviction that the castle is haunted. But—he adored your mother. He would never have sent the man she loved to so cruel a death, knowing it might very well kill his twin also!"

"You surprise me," said Devenish, with a curl of the lip. "I had come to think you cared not a button for the whole ugly business."

His despairing gaze still fixed on the beach, Craig muttered, "Dolt." He drew a hand across his eyes, then, regaining his control, said, "Now—tell me what has you up in the boughs. I've seen no trace of 'em. Have you?"

Devenish stared his astonishment. "Trace of who?"

"Whoever else is dwelling in the castle. Good God, Dev, you surely have realized we're not alone here?"

"Not . . . *alone?* You—you mean you also have felt—"

"That we are watched? Oh, yes."

"But—but you s-said you had seen nothing!"

"I said I had seen no ghosts. Which I have not." Peering at his cousin's astounded face, he asked keenly, "Lord, is that it? Have you been subjected to more—er—jousts with the Unseen?"

Devenish fixed him with a defiant glare. "Several!"

"The deuce! Tell me!"

So Devenish told him and, because he was extremely angry, spared no details but did not embellish with dramatics, biting out his words in such terse fashion that the fearsomeness of the episodes he described became very vivid to his listener. "Well," he finished, "do not deny yourself, Major Tyndale, sir! Tell me what I already know; that you do not believe a word of it!"

Instead, watching him with wide, shocked eyes, Tyndale breathed, "By Jupiter! And you faced that all alone . . . ! What a total clunch! Why in the *devil* did you not tell me?"

"Because," snarled Devenish, "I knew what a fine laugh you would have at my expense, and how you would delight in telling me I ate too much rich food for dinner, or some such fustian. As you did to Monty on that first night!"

"Gudgeon! Had you only swallowed that ridiculous pride and told me all this sooner! I had my suspicions, but—"

"You had your suspicions, did you? And kept them to *yourself!*" His eyes fairly sparking, Devenish raged on, "While I endured hell's own misery. One word from you—one hint that it was all contrived would have spared me! But—no! Because you have no sensibilities yourself, you just sat back and watched. Gloating! Dammitall! I should . . ."

He had paced nearer, thrusting his flushed face under his cousin's nose, and stepping back instinctively, Craig teetered on the brink, and made a grab for the edge of the parapet. "*Will* you control that insufferable temper of yours? We must take no chances up here!"

Devenish paled at the reminder and all but leapt back. "Then let us go inside at once so I can punch your smug head!"

Tyndale moved away from the sheer drop behind him and caught his cousin's arm. "Don't be such a fool! Can you seriously judge me so base as to serve you so vile a turn? I thought *someone* had been racking up in the castle, but I fancied them vagrants merely, or homeless soldiery. Nothing more. This sheds a new light on it."

"Vagrants, indeed! And where did you think these poor starving soldiers hid themselves so that we never saw them—or their belongings? You have inspected every inch of your ancestral home!"

"Why, in the secret rooms and passages, of course. I thought you had guessed that when you quizzed me about pacing off and measuring all the rooms."

"Secret . . . rooms . . .?" breathed Devenish, his eyes

kindling. "By thunder, but you're right! I recall Uncle Alastair once telling me that the old place is fairly riddled with them. But—what did your sketches and measurements prove?"

"That there is a wide discrepancy between interior and exterior dimensions. When we were locked out in the rain and prowling about trying to find a way in, I paced off the exterior measurements, and—"

The elation that had begun to dawn in Devenish's face vanished. "Then—you knew *very* early in the game! When *exactly,* Major Tyndale, sir?"

Tyndale stifled exasperation. "The first time we went inside I noticed that although there was dust everywhere, one end of the dining table was free of it. I surmised that the table had been in use. No, Dev! Hear me out! I really thought they were demobilized soldiers, and I suspect you have little use for the military. Some of the poor devils have had such a bitter time since the war ended. It seems every man's hand is against them, so I thought—"

"You thought I would have them hanged for trespassing!" snarled Devenish.

Tyndale reddened and his eyes fell. "I—don't know . . . but they seemed to be causing no trouble. I thought they would either leave, or show themselves and we—I—could offer them work. I even said as much once, when I was alone in the book room." He shrugged, embarrassed. "Perhaps no one was listening."

"Likely not! They were all too busy 'haunting' me!"

"Well, dammit, I did not know of any of it! I knew you were a trifle shaken that first night, but it seemed perfectly understandable—in the circumstances. When you said no more of it, I thought you had adjusted, and—"

"Adjusted! My God! To what? Bedlam?"

"No, really, Dev. You seemed calm most of the time, so I—"

"Thunderation, man! I came near to losing my mind!"

Tyndale hung his head, looking and feeling like a chastened schoolboy. "What an unobservant fool I am." He looked up with his crooked, apologetic grin. "I never even suspected what was going on right under my nose. Poor Dev. A harrowing week you have had!"

Touched, Devenish cleared his throat and grunted, "Gad, there's no call to be so damned patronizing. I'm near as old as you, you know!"

Scanning him, Tyndale thought, "Not really. You are just

a boy; a likeable, warm-hearted, but rather too impulsive boy." And aloud he said, "Oh, but I was born a greybeard."

"I'll agree with you on that point." Devenish chuckled and went on, "So tell me, O Ancient Sage, what is it all about, think you?"

Tyndale knit his brows for a moment. "I had thought," he answered carefully, "it was a relatively minor problem. It is not, very obviously. That portrait business took not only scheming, but either the talent to create such an atrocity, or the funds to commission it done. It could, I suppose, prove an excellent means of frightening away curious children or occasional vagrants, but . . ."

"I wonder," Devenish mused. "By daylight, only those who have seen the original painting, or who remember my mother would be really scared by it. Strangers might merely fancy it an excessive ugly painting—of which there are many, God knows. And I rather doubt many people would wander to so lonely a spot after dark, so as to get the full effect." He frowned. "How the deuce did they manage it, d'you suppose? How could they have switched 'em so fast?"

"A hidden panel, perhaps."

"What—in a rock wall?"

Tyndale argued, "Well, perhaps it isn't rock. Perhaps there is a wooden section, carven and painted to resemble rock, that can be slid aside—lots of priest's holes have steps leading from a chimney, you know. Someone could have opened the panel while you slept, substituted the changed portrait, and then contrived to wake you. The night you said you tripped over something in the dark, obstacles could easily have been moved into unexpected spots just in case you did have the gumption to charge before they had a chance to switch portraits."

Gratified by this small compliment, Devenish nodded. "It fits, all right."

They began to pace slowly towards the door to the stairs, each deep in thought. "It was planned from the start," muttered Tyndale, "with one end in view. I was to be scared off. So terrified that I decided to live anywhere but here."

"If they wanted to scare *you*," Devenish protested indignantly, "why am *I* the one to have been victimized? The picture was in the room intended for *me!*"

"Not necessarily. Perhaps I was meant to choose that room.

"Hmmn. Perhaps . . . No! The voices, coz! They called

'*Alain!*' and begged I 'avenge' them." And recalling the anguish he had suffered because of that trickery, he fumed, "Those miserable blasted vermin!"

"True," Tyndale acknowledged. "Unless they planned to thoroughly panic you, so that you would leave. And then—go to work on me. They certainly have succeeded in frightening the local people away."

"And Montelongo. . . . But—why? Regardless of *how* they went about it, why go to so much trouble? All this skulduggery, when there ain't nothing hereabouts save for hills and cows and sheep and such."

"And . . . the sea," murmured Tyndale.

Devenish caught his breath. "Jove!" he breathed, awed. "You have it! The sea! Free Traders! Of course, but—no, surely this is the wrong coast?"

"Sometimes the longest way is the quickest. And the safest. I believe there is at least one large cellar here I have been unable to find. If it has been stocked by smugglers, only think how perfect this is for them. They could sail from France, around Land's End, up through the Irish Sea, slip through the channel, and land here any night there's moon enough, secure in the knowledge that no one would be the wiser."

Devenish eyed him askance. "It may not seem far to someone who's done as much travelling as you, old boy, but it seems a devilish roundabout way to me!"

"It is a bit of a haul, I grant you. But—only think, they could offload into wagons with perfect safety, for no locals would dare venture near the castle by night, and be well on their way before dawn. Why, they could likely even hire Pickford's in Kilmarnock, or Glasgow perhaps, and have their smuggled goods shipped to London, free as air. 'Twould be worth the long journey, I'd say. And unless I'm fair and far off, there is an entrance to the castle somewhere down among the cliffs. A cave, perhaps!" His eyes bright with triumph, he exclaimed, "That *has* to be the answer! No wonder they're so desperate to drive us away, Dev! They've the ideal hideaway and do not mean to give it up!"

Devenish swung the door open and, lowering his voice, murmured, "If you *are* right, we're likely to find ourselves nose to nose with some very irate gents! At any moment!"

"Yes," Craig acknowledged with his slow smile. "In which case, I should not have been so irked with Monty today. He was convinced we were going to wake some

198

morning with our throats cut. Advised me, just as he was riding out, that he meant to report our uninvited guests to the Constable at Kilmarnock. He means to bring reinforcements this evening!''

"Good old Monty!" said Devenish blithely. "By George! And to think I fancied this would be a dull journey! With a little bit of luck, my bonnie Colonial, we shall land ourselves a jolly good scrap before your reinforcements arrive!''

Even as one part of his mind marvelled at his cousin's transformation from a brooding man of mercurial temper to a cheerful, high-couraged youth, Tyndale still pondered the one detail that plagued him. He had the uneasy feeling that the substitute portrait did not fit into his solution of their puzzle.

*   *   *

The wind was brisk this morning, hurrying the clouds across the pale blue sky, and setting the heather to whipping about beneath the hooves of the horses. Their habits fluttering, the two ladies urged their mounts up the hill beside the pass road, from the top of which eminence Castle Tyndale could be seen, a distant, darkly powerful thrust against the encompassing slate of the sea. The eyes of both riders were fixed upon the fortress, and in green eyes and brown was longing and a measure of hopelessness.

Heaving a deep sigh, the smaller of the pair murmured, "Whatever will I do if he don't never come back?"

Yolande pushed her own dreary reflections aside and, forcing a smile, said reassuringly, "Of course he will come back. And very soon."

By mutual accord they stopped the horses. "I'd like him to see me new have-it," said Josie.

"I know you would, dear." The child looked quite lady-like in her pink velvet, a demure little bonnet tied over her dark curls. Watching her, Yolande pointed out gently, "But the word is 'habit,' Josie."

"It is? I thought a habit was something you did when you shouldn't ought to have."

"Yes. But it is also a riding dress. And you look very pretty in yours. Mr. Devenish will be pleased."

"I hope so." Josie sighed again.

Yolande suggested bracingly, "Only think of the future. We shall all drive back to England together. Will you not like that?"

"Not Mr. Craig. He cannot go. Not if you marriages Mr. Dev." Josie turned to look up at this beautiful vision beside her and ask hopefully, "I don't 'spect as you would sooner marriage with Mr. Craig, would you?"

Yolande's heart gave a terrifying jolt, and she stared at the child speechlessly.

Alarm came into the small, pointed face. "You ain't never going to have a bad turn, is you, Miss Yolande?" cried Josie. "Old Ruby used to have 'em, and stagger about carrying on something drefful 'bout her poor old eyes and limbs. But Benjo said it was the gin, and I ain't never seed you swig blue ruin. Your face is awful red, though, so p'raps—"

With a shaken laugh, Yolande denied an addiction to blue ruin. "What—whatever," she asked, "would cause you to think I might wish to marry Mr. Tyndale?"

A third sigh was torn from the child. "I didn't really think it. I knowed there wasn't much hope. What lady would want Mr. Craig when Mr. Dev is there? Only I knows how bad Mr. Craig wants *you*, and—"

Her breathing becoming highly erratic, Yolande intervened, "Good—gracious, what an imagination! I—I thank you, dear Josie, but—there are lots of ladies much prettier than I for—for Mr. Craig to—er, choose."

"Are there? I never see one." A gleam coming into her dark eyes, Josie asked thoughtfully, "Is there one up here? Like—in Drumdownie, p'raps? I like Mr. Craig. He's kind, and he has scrumptious eyes." She thought for a moment, then said sadly, "It'd be *so* much easier if you would just marriage Mr. Craig, ma'am." And with a rather pathetic desperation, she enquired, "Are you *quite* sure as you wants Mr. Dev?"

"Are you *quite* sure as you wants Mr. Dev . . .?" For an aching moment, Yolande saw a strong, lean, rather pale face, with steadfast grey eyes and a wide, humorous mouth. Her own eyes dimmed. Wracked by anguish, she thought, "Dear God! Is there never to be an end to it?" And afraid her misery might be seen and understood by the discerning small woman beside her, she spurred her horse forward. "Come dear, I'll race you back to the house!"

Josie gazed remorsefully after the graceful retreating figure. She'd really gone and done it now. She'd made Miss Yolande cross, and Miss Yolande was good and gentle, and had promised to help, just in case Mr. Dev didn't take her to live with him. Starting her pony and following the chestnut mare, Josie could not wonder that Miss Yolande had not bothered to answer such a silly question. No lady could resist Mr. Dev, with his beautiful face and happy nature. Just to think of the smile that could so suddenly warm his blue eyes was enough to give her goose bumps, and she was only a little girl. As from a very great distance came the echo of a soft voice, "*Aide-toi, le ciel t'aidera.*" Her small chin set. It was possible. If she helped herself, heaven might indeed help her! She touched one heel to her pony's sleek side and began to weave plans. Lost in her own introspection, Yolande did not notice how quiet the little girl had become, and two subdued ladies made their way back to Steep Drummond.

When they arrived they found the grooms all agog because young Mr. MacInnes had come to show off the paces of his fine new hunter. Yolande went at once to join the small crowd gathered in the meadow, but Josie stayed to watch as the mare and the pony were unsaddled, rubbed down, and turned out to graze. She declined the offer of Mr. Laing, the head groom, for a piggyback ride to the meadow, saying that she wanted to play with Molly-My-Lass's foal for a little while, and watched as the genial man hurried off to join his colleagues in the meadow. They would be busied there for a good half hour, she knew. Ample time, surely, for her to get to Castle Tyndale and dear Mr. Dev. How she was to plead her case did not concern her. Time enough for that when she faced her god. She went over to Molly-My-Lass, and the Clydesdale nuzzled her affectionately. Molly wouldn't mind helping, though it was unfortunate, Josie admitted, that she did not herself possess the Rat Paws, as did dear Mr. Dev. Nonetheless, it was the work of a few seconds only, to climb up the first few rungs of the fence and hop onto that broad back. A kick of heels, a tug at the thick mane, and they were off, Molly-My-Lass perfectly willing to get some moderate exercise.

Josie wasn't too sure just how to get to Castle Tyndale (having only been there once), but she could smell the sea, and once they were safely out of sight of the house, turned confidently in what she imagined to be a lane leading westward.

Half an hour later, she was a rather frightened little girl harbouring the uneasy suspicion that she was a wee bit lost. The sun was starting to be blotted out by clouds, and she wished she had brought the new cloak Miss Yolande had given her. She looked about worriedly. Scotland was nice, and the hills was bigger than in England. The trouble was, there wasn't never many folks about, and not many houses nor signposts, neither. How a body was to know which way

201

to go was hard to tell. If the sun would start to go down she would know where was the west, but the sun, uncooperative, was high in the sky. Her heart gave a jump when she heard a cantering horse, and she guided Molly-My-Lass into some tall shrubs by the lane, fearing the grooms from Steep Drummond were after her. She was vastly relieved to see Major Craig's Indian man riding up. She almost called out to him, but then realized he would be just as liable to return her to Steep Drummond as would the General's grooms, and so sat quietly while he went on past. She watched him, admiring the easy grace with which he rode, almost as if he was one with the sleek bay mare. He was headed for the castle, that was sure.

Josie coaxed Molly-My-Lass into a trot and followed, careful to stay out of sight and earshot.

*   *   *

In all his life Montelongo had never seen such a climate as that which bedevilled the occupants of the British Isles. Nor had he imagined that so small an island could manage to be so perplexing. He had been quite sure of his route when he left the castle this morning. Now, not only was he lost, but he would wager a paint pony that the last knock-in-the-cradle who had assured him it was only three miles at the outside from the Kilmarnock road, "give or take a half-mile" was more lost than he! That had been at least five miles back, and he still had not come to the promised large signpost and the turn he was to take. To add to his indignation, the bright weather that had blessed his departure had given way to heavy clouds, so that he could not now judge the position of the sun.

Thus he was pleased to observe two mounted gentlemen a short distance ahead. They were riding at a walk and turned to him amiably as he approached, evincing neither surprise nor curiosity by reason of his unorthodox appearance.

"Hello there," called the taller of the pair, a well set up individual wearing a frieze coat. "You'll be Major Tyndale's man, eh?"

Montelongo nodded.

"Heard of you. I'm in the service of Mr. Walter Donald," vouchsafed the stranger. "Name of Wood. This here gent is Mr. Barnham."

Montelongo acknowledged the introduction and asked, in his terse fashion, if they could direct him to Kilmarnock.

They could. They were, in fact, going that way themselves and would be glad to set him on the right road if he wouldn't mind waiting a minute while they stopped at Mr. Wood's house. This detail having been agreed to, they rode along all three, the two Englishmen chatting slanderously about their employers, and Montelongo listening with no small amusement.

Mr. Wood's cottage was located across a field, some way from the lane and so isolated that there was not another house in sight. Messrs. Barnham and Montelongo waited before the battered picket fence while Mr. Wood went later. He reappeared after a few minutes to say that his wife was off somewhere, and if the gentlemen would care to dismount and step inside, he could offer them a spot of ale to wash the dust away before they resumed their journey.

It was the first time the Iroquois had met with such instant hospitality in a strange land, and he willingly accompanied his new friends into the cottage.

Ten minutes later, the shabby parlour swimming dizzily before his eyes, he lowered his head to the table and with a heavy sigh sank into sleep.

Mr. Wood bent over him, seized his shoulder and shook him, at first gently, then roughly. He lifted his eyes to smile with gratification at Mr. Barnham. "Well, that's done!" he observed. "Now we'll truss him up all neat and tidy. Just in case."

"But I thought," demurred Mr. Barnham, "that we wasn't to leave no signs of force."

"No more we won't. We'll loose him come dawn. But mark them shoulders, me lad. This here savage has probably got muscles what you and me never dreamt of! There ain't no telling how long he'll sleep, for one thing I didn't dare do was to give him too much. I ain't taking no chances he'll wake up whilst you and me is having a nice convivial chat as you might say!" Mr. Barnham applauding this decision, they proceeded to bind their unwitting victim. "Very tidy," said Mr. Barnham. "If he does start to wake up early, what you going to do?"

"Leave his knife close to hand. It'll take him some time to get it and get loose, 'cause he won't be thinking clear—spite of all them muscles. Either way, we'll be least in sight and he can go strolling off, free as air, back to the castle, tripping through the daisies in the dawn. Just like Mr. Shotten wants." He laughed. "By which time," he added, "he'll be what you might call a Johnny-come-lately!"

"You mean a Monty-come-morning!" leered Mr. Barnham.

"Aye. Morning. Spelt *m-o-u-r-n-i-n-g*," said Mr. Wood.

This clever play on words so titillated them that they repaired to the kitchen and found a bottle of much stronger content than ale, with which they decided to celebrate their success.

They went back to the parlour, settled down, and enjoyed the bottle together, while Montelongo slept.

Chapter Thirteen

Unwilling to provide the smugglers with any cause for suspicion, the cousins agreed that they would proceed in their usual manner while awaiting Montelongo's return with the "reinforcements." They spent most of the afternoon, therefore, in thoroughly inspecting the stables and barn, returning to the castle in a chilly dusk with a long list of necessary repairs.

The fact that Montelongo had not as yet come back was worrying Tyndale. Devenish, however, reasoned that the Constable at Kilmarnock might have felt it advisable to refer the matter to a higher authority, or might at this very moment be positioning his men about the castle. "Suppose they do come," Devenish whispered as they walked across the stableyard. "What in the deuce are we to show them? We don't know how to find either Free Traders or contraband! The Constable will laugh at us!"

"I don't think he will take action yet, but if he does, we will at least be enabled to make a proper search of the basements. That's where the hidden rooms are, I'm sure of it. And even if we are laughed at, someone in authority will have been warned of what's going on here. Just—in case."

Those last three last words caused Devenish considerable disquiet as he walked along the hall towards his bedchamber. It had not occurred to him that the smugglers might really be willing to commit murder. If they did decide to cut up stiff and were able to put a period to him and Tyndale, it would be a proper bumble broth, for everyone would merely think the feud had been fought over again. He was dismayed and, as he opened the door, called down a blessing on the head of the absent Montelongo. It was a jolly good thing that—

He checked, his hand still on the doorknob, his eyes glued to the opposite wall. The portrait was macabre once more and, even knowing that the cruel distortion of his mother's loveliness was a ruse, goosebumps rose on his flesh. He drew a hissing breath, then sprinted along the corridor to his cousin's room. "Craig!" he gasped, plunging in without ceremony. "The portrait!"

Tyndale was in his shirt sleeves, in the act of pouring water into his washbowl. He looked up, startled, as Devenish flung the door open, and at once set down the water pitcher and ran with him to the adjoining room. The sight of the portrait checked his hurried progress. He paused in the open doorway, gazing at it. "Lord!" he breathed. "Small wonder it so distressed you!" And he wandered closer, drawn by that monstrous image.

"At least you've seen it!" said Devenish. "This time we were quick enough."

"And there wasn't no need," sneered a crude London voice. " 'Cause it's all done, coves. All over with!"

The cousins spun about as the door slammed shut. Four men leaned against the wall, watching them with various degrees of amusement. The one who had spoken was a large, powerful individual, dressed without elegance in a brown riding coat, breeches, and topboots. He was whistling in a soft, hissing monotone, as ostlers whistle when currying a horse, and his small, hard eyes were fixed on Devenish in leering mockery.

"Shotten . . . !" breathed Devenish. "So—*Sanguinet* is behind this?"

Shotten laughed. "Monsewer's a vindictive man,'e is."

Glancing at his cousin, Tyndale said, "Your French—er, acquaintance in Dinan? Aha! So this is a vendetta. Whatever did you do to so upset the gentleman?"

"Yer kinsman was so foolish, sir," volunteered Shotten, "so downright stupid as ter kick Claude Sanguinet in the jaw and then throw him in a nasty wet pond! Monsewer,'e hadn't never bin treated like that afore. And 'e didn't take to it!"

Devenish made a swift appraisal of the others. One was lean and leathery, his narrow face holding an expression of sneering malevolence. The other two were as burly as Shotten, and both held horse pistols. This, he thought, his pulses beginning to race with excitement, would be a close-run thing. . . .

With unruffled calm, Tyndale drawled, "If you expect us

to believe that Monsieur Sanguinet has expended all this time and effort on a simple matter of revenge—''

"You mistake that, sir," said Shotten, with that infuriatingly oily deference. "Fact is, we don't give beans fer what you believe. And just look at me, fergettin' me manners! That there thin little cove as ye see aholding up the wall—that's Fritch. The chap with all the pretty curls"—he gestured to a man who was quite bald—"his monicker is Jethro—he's a very gentle, friendly type o'cove."

The "friendly type" uttered a roar of mirth at this witticism, displaying a few crooked teeth. The younger, sandy-haired man next to him stood away from the wall and interrupted harshly, "You talk too much, Shotten. They can live without knowing of my name!"

"Ar," giggled Fritch. "But not fer long, Walter, me bucko!"

The cousins exchanged swift glances. "A fine set of rum touches you cry friends with!" protested Tyndale. He turned from Devenish's irrepressible grin to Shotten's beady-eyed antagonism. "When shall we meet your master?"

"You know what, Major War Hero?" said Shotten, strolling forward. "I don't like yer face, nor yer way o' talkin', nor nothing else about yer. Ain't no man is *my* master! No man! Clear?"

"The words." Tyndale shrugged. "But they are of doubtful veracity."

Shotten's little eyes narrowed, and the pistol in his hand swung upwards a trifle. "And wot might that jawbreaker mean?"

The sandy-haired man laughed. "He means as you be lying, Shotten. Which you is. Sanguinet's *your* master just as much as what he's *ours*."

"Keep yer dirty fat mouth in yer pocket!" Shotten snarled murderously.

"Never mind about Walter," Fritch advised in his nasal, whining voice. "He's a bit upset like."

"*You'll* be upset if we make a hog wallow of this," snapped Walter, his pale eyes glinting. "It could mean the nubbing cheat for the lot on us!"

"You would do well to heed him," Devenish corroborated. "Else you will most certainly end up swinging on Tyburn."

"Well, don't worry about it, me dear old friend," said Shotten with a broad grin. " 'Cause you won't be invited ter watch us kick!"

206

Devenish clicked his tongue. "Pity. I would so enjoy it."

"I think it all a Canterbury tale from start to finish," Tyndale interposed hurriedly, misliking the way Shotten advanced on his indomitable cousin. "You were using my castle long before we chanced up here, and for something more profitable than pure vengeance, I'll wager."

Shotten halted abruptly. Fritch looked shaken. Jethro and Walter exchanged scared glances, and the bald man wiped off the top of his head with a grimy sleeve. "If the soldier come at that much," he muttered uneasily, "maybe he told that old devil up at Steep Drummond."

"And maybe that 'old devil' is bringing up his men this very minute," taunted Devenish. "My military cousin is full of tricks, I warn you. You had best scamper whilst yet you may."

"Shut him up, Shotten!" whined Fritch, his cunning eyes darting about. "As well snuff him now as later."

"Wot?" exclaimed Shotten, much shocked. "Rush me dear old friend off quick and easy? Oh, no, my cove. I want Mr. Devenish ter be give plenty o' time ter think of it . . . afore he follers his poor dad orf the roof."

Something very cold clamped around Devenish's heart.

Tyndale, his fists clenching, said, "I see. You mean to keep the legend alive by a repeat performance. So it was Sanguinet who spread the news of the original tragedy. Had he planned this from the start?"

" 'Course not," jeered Shotten. "We didn't know nothing about *you*, Major, sir. Monsieur didn't even know as the owner o' this ruin was related ter our old friend Mr. Devenish. But—well, strike a light, guv, you can't 'ardly blame him. I mean—arter all, it was fair made to order, eh?" He sighed and shook his head dolefully. "Wot a shame as you went and bubbled it. We was so hoping ter surprise yer."

"I doubt you will surprise anyone," Tyndale said contemptuously. "If I am believed to have pushed my cousin off the battlements, how shall you explain my own demise?"

"Simple, sir. Mr. Devenish will be found with a pistol still clutched in his cold meat hand. He shot you, Canada, just afore he went over!" He laughed his triumph and added, "Tidy, ain't it?"

Devenish swore under his breath and took a step forward. The pistols were raised at once, and Tyndale put a restraining hand on his arm. "You must all be deeply devoted to Monsieur Sanguinet," he said dryly, "to be willing to commit two murders for him."

Walter scowled. Fritch said with exaggerated innocence, "But *we* ain't goin' ter murder no one, Major, sir. You two loving cousins been a'fighting and a'quarrelling halfway 'cross England. And only fancy—just s'arternoon you was almost coming ter blows, right in front o' Mr. Respectability Hennessey. Most shocked, he was. *Most* shocked!" He folded his hands piously, his eyes mocking, while his friends hooted their mirth.

Tyndale threw his cousin a wry look. "We properly set the scene for them."

"You are, like the flash coves say, all consideration," Fritch agreed.

Leering, Shotten added with relish, "And ternight when it's nice and dark so no gawking yokels can't see what's goin' on, we'll 'ave the final act. And arter that, me fine coves, there ain't none o' these country blubberheads what'll set foot within a mile o' yer cozy castle. Not a one, gents. Not a blessed one."

Devenish looked grimly from one face to the next. They were savagely inflexible. Even Walter, who seemed to have sufficient sensitivity to know nervousness, if not conscience, looked merciless.

Tyndale glanced to the windows. Already it was dusk. Within an hour, it would be full dark. "Monty," he thought, "please do bring your reinforcements. And soon!"

*   *   *

At about the same time that Mr. Hennessey was delivering the supplies to Castle Tyndale, Josie, concealed by an overgrown hedge, was waiting for Montelongo and his friends to come out of the cottage. She had been quite dismayed by their meeting, but had followed them, believing it to have been a chance encounter, and that the Indian would soon resume his journey back to the castle. After a while, when he still did not come out, she dismounted, tied Molly-My-Lass's halter to a branch and began to wander up and down. She really should not stay away from Steep Drummond much longer. Molly's foal would be needing to be fed, and the family had probably noticed by now that both the mare and herself were missing. Dismay seized her as the thought came that because she was a gypsy they might fancy she'd stolen the valuable animal. She glanced apprehensively at the cottage. It must be at least an hour since the men went inside. Goodness knows how long it would take to get to the castle, and then Mr. Dev would probably make her go back to Steep Drummond and everyone would be in a proper pucker. She'd likely be walloped and sent to bed without supper. Well, she would simply have to go and ask Mr. Monty the way. Sighing and reluctant, she crossed the weedy lawn and knocked on the front door.

A roar of laughter was the only response, but it was sufficient to send her scuttling around the corner of the house, for she had seen men when they were shot in the neck, and she knew from bitter experience that they were best given a wide berth. If they went on drinking much longer, she could not hope for any help from Mr. Monty. She waited undecidedly, and, full of nervous fears, wandered around to the back of the house. The laughter was louder here, and the voices more clear, but the conversation, such as it was, puzzled her.

"Lor'!" howled a man's voice. "How I'd love to've seen them throw the Frog in the pool! Wonder he didn't drown of hisself!"

"Frogs don't—don't drown, friend," advised another voice. "They just gives a sorta hop . . . and out they come!"

This sent them into guffaws again, though why a frog being tossed into a pool should be amusing was more than the child could fathom.

"I'll tell you one thing," said the first man. "I'm g-glad as bedamned *I* didn't do it! The Frenchy will hold that grudge as long as Devenish lives!"

"Then he ain't got long to hold it, has he, my cove?"

Another roar of laughter, but Josie didn't think it funny at all. Whatever did they mean? Mr. Dev was a young man. He wasn't going to die for years and years! Especially now there wasn't any wars what killed all the nice soldiers. She worried at it while the rough talk went on and on, growing ever more raucous, until it dawned on her that through it all, not once had she heard Mr. Monty say anything. She was quite frightened by this time, her fears having nothing to do with whether or not she had been missed at Steep Drummond. A window of the room stood open, the curtains flirting in the rising wind. She thought, "I must not be a coward. I must have a look, for Mr. Dev's sake."

The very thought of serving her god strengthened her. She crept nearer, but the window was too high. Her glance around discovered some bricks piled against one wall and, the fear of detection spurring her on, she trotted back and forth carrying one heavy brick at a time, until three were piled below the casement. They were a bit wobbly, but it was the best she could do. She stepped up, crouching, then slowly straightened.

An involuntary gasp of horror escaped her. Mr. Monty was slumped in a chair. He looked dead, but he was tied hand and foot and one does not tie a dead man, so she supposed he must have been struck on the head. At a table to one side, the two men she had thought to be his friends sat with a half-full wine bottle between them, their flushed faces and another empty bottle on the floor testifying to their state. Even as she gazed, petrified, the taller of the pair glanced to the window, lurched to his feet, and with an oath stumbled towards her. Sick with terror, she tried to run, but her legs had turned to water and would not stir. The slurred voice, just above her, snarled a profanity. She sank against the wall, eyes half closed, waiting in a helpless panic to be seized and dragged into that horrid room. Dimly, she saw a large hand thrusting at her. She felt sick, and the bright afternoon grew dim. A coarse voice snarled, ''Blasted damned wind!'' The window was slammed shut, the lower edge of the frame brushing her curls.

He had not seen her! By some miracle she was still free! She clapped her hands over her mouth to muffle her terrified sobs, and collapsed to the ground, a small, crumpled heap, weeping softly, and whispering fervent prayers of gratitude for her narrow escape.

It was several moments before she was sufficiently recovered to think coherently, but gradually her numbed mind began to function again. What it was all about, she did not know, but those two men were bad. They had tied up poor Mr. Monty, and it looked as if they had hurt him, besides. He might be, as Mrs. Arabella was fond of remarking, a ''heathen savage,'' but he had never done anything savage that she'd seen. His voice on the few occasions he'd spoken to her had been gruff, but kind, and Major Craig thought the world of him. He had very nice eyes, that Major Craig . . . not that he was a patch on Mr. Dev for looks, but eyes were important. And that was another thing: those men had said something about Mr. Dev dying. Soon, they'd said. Perhaps that was why the Indian was tied up. So he couldn't go and help Mr. Dev. Her blood ran cold with the fear that a plot existed to murder the only person who had ever really befriended her. If that was so, she must get away quick, and warn him!

The window was tight closed, the curtains drawn, but if

there was anyone else in the cottage she would be in full view if she ran across the lawn to the mare. Shivering with fear, she tried to be as brave as Mr. Dev would want her to be. Perhaps, even if they saw her, she could climb onto Molly-My-Lass and be away in time. How fast the Clydesdale could run, she had no idea, but an animal so big simply had to be powerful and would likely be a fine goer.

And so, a very young lady gathered up her sadly tested courage and made a wild dart across the open space of the lawn. She reached the hedge and trees that shielded the cottage from the meadow in a flash, and with no enraged shouts following. With a hand over her madly pounding heart, she paused to catch her breath, only to utter a moan of despair. Molly-My-Lass was gone!

* * *

"I cannot understand it!" Yolande exclaimed distractedly. She turned to Mrs. Drummond, who was brushing a disgusted Socrates. It crossed her mind that the General might not care to see the dog standing upon the piano bench while being groomed, but it was a thought that did not linger, her main concentration being upon the missing child.

"*I* understand it *perfectly* well," said Mrs. Drummond, with the condescension of superior wisdom. "The child went to see her friend, is all. She is lonely here, Yolande, and it is but natural for her to want to be with her own kind, and to grieve when forcibly removed from her natural environment. Far be it from me to criticize, but it was wrong of Devenish to abduct the child so thoughtlessly. His besetting sin, alas! I could have told him no good would come of it, but he would not have attended me—or anyone else, for that matter!"

Sorting the wheat from the chaff, Yolande decided that her aunt was very likely in the right of it, at least in so far as Josie's destination was concerned. It was foolish to indulge this frightening sense of something being very wrong. After all, what could happen to a little girl at Steep Drummond? "I'll go down there," she murmured.

Astonished, Mrs. Drummond glanced up. "To the MacFarlane cottage?" she asked, in the tone she might have employed if told the minister had run naked through the village. "Good gracious, why?" There is no call for you to so demean yourself. Besides, I heard the MacFarlane girl has contracted measles. Send one of the footmen."

"Send a footman where?" enquired General Drummond, wandering at that moment into the music room.

211

"Down to the gardener's house," supplied Arabella, casting a wide smile at her father-in-law. "If you can credit it, dear sir, *Yolande* was about to go!"

"Josie has wandered off, Grandpapa," Yolande explained. "I thought I would go and see if she is there. In fact, since Aunt Arabella tells me little Maisie is ill, I've no doubt that is where I shall find her."

"Very likely," he said, rather pleased to discover his granddaughter was speaking to him in a friendly way and that she had not held a grudge because he'd forbidden those two rapscallion cousins to call on her. "I'll go with you."

"Oh, in that case," purred Arabella, "nothing could be more proper."

The General escorted his granddaughter to the door, and turned back to fix his son's widow with a minatory eye. "How glad I am that we hae your approval, ma'am," he said cuttingly. "'Tis an emotion I canna returrrn however; not while yon beastie distributes his fleas over my pianoforte! Be sae good as tae remove the wee currr tae the barrn whar he belongs!"

He ignored Mrs. Drummond's flustered protestations that Socrates would not be caught dead with a nasty flea on him and, ushering Yolande from the room, growled his thanks for providing an excuse to escape that "absurd female! You must, however," he admonished as they started into the gardens, "impress upon little Miss Storm that she should not wander off like this. If the child's to become an abigail, m'dear, she must learn proper behaviour."

But when they reached the gardener's cottage, it was to discover that Josie had not visited that establishment since the day Maisie had been caught at the summer house "tea party."

Her eyes dark shadows against her tired, pale face, Mrs. MacFarlane said, "The wee lassie is nae lost, I hope?"

Losing some of her own colour, Yolande turned a frightened glance to her grandfather. He patted her hand and said bracingly, "Wandered off, merely. I fancy she's lonely here, poor mite."

"I'm sorry for that," Mrs. MacFarlane said. "Wherever can she hae got to? I—" And, as if suddenly becoming aware that she kept her illustrious guests standing on the step, she flushed darkly and stepped back, gesturing for them to enter. "Ye're more than—than welcome tae come inside," she stammered. "Unless ye've nae had the measles."

The General nodded. "We both have, I thank you." He

stepped over the threshold immediately dwarfing the small, immaculate parlour, and, when Yolande had seated herself on the ornate red sofa, followed suit, and enquired as to Maisie's condition.

Mrs. MacFarlane, who had perched on the very edge of a straight-backed cane chair, sighed. "Och, but she's awful bad, puir bairn." Her eyes distressed, she added brokenly, "I never saw her in such a waeful state."

"I am so sorry, ma'am," Yolande sympathized with her customary warm-heartedness. "She's a truly delightful little girl. Can we help? You've had the doctor out, I—"

Mrs. MacFarlane sprang up again and backed away, an expression almost of frenzy on her face. "I dinna wish . . . your aid. . . ." she gasped out. "We none of us—want nothing frae ye!"

From the corner of her eye, Yolande saw the General's whiskers bristle alarmingly. Not glancing at him, she placed a gently restraining hand on his arm. "I quite understand, ma'am," she said. "You likely wish us at Jericho, so we will take ourselves off and ask only that, if you should see Miss Storm, you will send word up to the house."

"Aye." Mrs. MacFarlane's lip trembled. "I will, that. I—I'm sorry, Miss Yolande. It's not— I dinna mean— I'm a mite fashed, y'ken."

"Of course you are. Any mother would be." Yolande stood, her grandfather at once, almost protectively, standing beside her. "Measles is a wretched illness, and we—"

"Aye! If it *be* measles!" And with a sudden resumption of her former hostility, this strange little woman said fiercely, "I pray to the good Lord it is nae something worse. Heaven only knows what may be brought intae the district when we're infested with foreigners and heathens! Ye'll mind that MacFarlane can read, sir? He told me he'd read somewhere that red men are awful subject tae—" Her eyes all but starting from her head, she gripped and wrung her hands and whispered, awfully, "tae—the smallpox!"

"Good God!" the General exploded. "What utter balderdash!"

"Dear ma'am!" cried Yolande, "I beg you will not so distress yourself! If Major Tyndale thought his man to be ill, he would have called in a doctor at once, I do assure you! And certainly you would have been warned if—"

"Oh, aye!" the woman interposed shrilly. "Warned we *should* hae been! Mark my words, miss, that savage and his

213

foreign master will bring death and destruction doon upon us all! If little Miss Storm is missing, *he's* likely responsible! And if my bairn should dee—" She passed a distracted hand across her brow, darted to the door and, swinging it open, regarded her astonished callers more wildly than ever.

Yolande thought, "She is mad, or near it, poor creature!" and as she passed the woman, murmured a compassionate, "God bless you, poor soul!"

Her only answer was the door, slamming behind them.

" 'Pon my soul!" gasped the General, unnerved. "You've more charity than I, m'dear! Perkins told me distinctly this morning he had examined the bairn and she's only a verra mild case of measles! The woman must be fair daft!"

"Listen," said Yolande, pausing as they started down the path.

From behind that closed door came the sound of weeping so intense and so laced with despair that she hesitated, directing an anxious gaze up at her grandfather.

He drew her hand firmly through his arm. "Let her be!" he commanded. "No telling what she might do next! I'll have to speak with MacFarlane, poor devil. His wife is plainly ready for Bedlam! A sad thing for so young a woman."

"Young?" Yolande said uncertainly. "Why, I'd thought . . . that is, she looks to be forty at least, no?"

"She looks it, poor lass. But, no. She's a decade younger, to say the least of it."

"Good heavens! I can scarcely believe— Grandpapa, has she been ill?"

"Not that I'm aware. Fey, perhaps. She was a strange little girl, I mind, full of odd fancies. But she was pretty enough! I recall her at the castle when old Tyndale was alive. A bonnie wee lass she was, but—"

"At the *castle?*" Yolande intervened, breathlessly. "She *lived* there, sir?"

"Aye. With her parents. Her mama was abigail to poor Esme Devenish, and her father a groom or a gardener, or some such." He caught Yolande's arm as she turned back. "Hey! Hey, my lass. You'll nae disturb the woman the noo?"

"But I must! I *must!* She might know something that could be of help to Cr— I mean, to Devenish!"

Watching her, frowning a little, the old gentleman growled, "She doesnae. She was a wee lassie—maybe six or seven at most—when it happened."

214

"Old enough to have some recollection, then," she persisted stubbornly. "I can remember things that happened when I was six—can not you?"

"I've me work cut oot to recall what happened yesterday," he said with a grin and, becoming very English again, added, "You'll do well to let the lady alone now, Yolande. She has her hands full and her poor mind is obviously hovering on the brink. Besides, I'll own I'm becoming a touch concerned for our own missing young lady."

"Oh, my goodness! How could I have forgotten Josie!"

"Hmmmn," said the General. "I wonder, indeed! Come, m'dear. We'll send the grooms out seeking her, can we find any. The place was empty as a drum when I looked in a wee bit ago. The rascals were up to no good, I'll be bound. They'd best be about their business now, or there'll be much explaining to be done!"

When they reached the stables, however, it was to find them far from deserted, grooms and stablehands milling about, and an air of exultation very apparent.

"Here comes the guv'nor!" the head groom proclaimed, as the General and Yolande crossed the yard. "All's bowman, sir! We found her."

"Oh, thank heaven!" gasped Yolande, not until that moment realizing just how worried she had been.

"That saucy rascal!" the General exclaimed. "Good work! Who found her?"

"It was Graham, sir. He was fair beside himself! Thought he should've kept a closer eye on her."

The General nodded. "Commendable. Where was she?"

"Halfway to Tarbolton, by what I gather."

"Tarbolton! The devil you say! What did she want up there?"

The groom shrugged. "Who knows what goes on in their minds, sir? Such as they have!"

"Oh, come now, Laing!" Yolande protested. "Females are not completely blockheaded, you know!"

"I'll not deny that, miss," he allowed with a chuckle. "Though she was blockheaded enough to be frisking about in the stream that runs alongside Mr. Willoughby's east field."

"Good heavens! Whatever possessed her? The wind is quite chill today, and this is no weather for a swim. Oh, I do hope she has not taken a chill."

"Tush, child," the General said reassuringly. "Do I know anything of the matter, she's being thoroughly pampered and

215

cossetted. And after all, we must not forget her background. I doubt she was even slightly remorseful, eh Laing?"

The groom laughed. "Not the slightest, sir."

"A sound night's sleep, snug under her blankets, and she'll be good as new. She should be spanked, but I'll own she's lots of spirit. Strong as a horse, too, don't you agree, Laing?"

Yolande, who had always thought Laing to be a sensible man, began to wonder if she had rated him too high, for at this he gave another shout of laughter, so hearty that the General stared at him in surprise.

"That's a good one, sir! And glad I am that you're not angered. It's a bit of luck it was Graham who came up with her. Eyes like a hawk has Graham, else he'd never have noticed her nose sticking through the branches."

The General's jaw dropped in a most undignified fashion. "Her . . . nose?" he echoed faintly.

"Sticking . . . through the branches . . . ?" gasped Yolande.

"Aye, miss. Chewing them leaves like she'd not ate for a week, Graham said, or—"

Having recovered itself, General Drummond's jaw began to chomp alarmingly. "Are ye gone puir daft, mon?" he exploded. "What a' God's name are ye babbling?"

Yolande asked urgently, "Of whom are you speaking, Laing?"

Paling, the groom faltered, "Why—why, Molly-My-Lass, of course, miss. Wasn't that—"

"Molly . . . My . . . Lass!" The General's lung power made Yolande jump. "Why, you bacon-brained gapeseed! You let my prize mare wander off and stand about in a cold stream all day? Dammitall! That's what I get for allowing a Londoner at my cattle! Of all the—" He glanced, fuming, at Yolande, and closed his lips, his whiskers continuing to vibrate like reeds in a high wind.

Her hopes dashed, Yolande seized her chance and explained, "We were speaking of Miss Josie. She seems to have wandered off, also. Is Molly all right?"

"Quite all right, miss." And with a cautious look at the fiery old gentleman, Laing ventured, "As the General said, we've pampered her and she's warm and—"

"I was not speaking of a *horse*, blast your impudence!" howled Drummond. "If you but had the brains you were born with—"

"Sir!" Yolande cried, tugging at his sleeve urgently. "Sir! We must do as you suggested and send the grooms out to search! It is starting to rain, and if Josie is trying to reach Devenish at the castle, the poor child will still be walking after dark.''

"That curst boy!'' the General raged, quite willing to turn his anger from Laing, who really was an excellent head groom. "He should never have brought the lassie here in the first place. A fine bog we'll be in, does she come to grief! Well, talking pays no toll. Turn oot the men, Laing, and set 'em tae the west road. But—do *you* stay with the mare!''

Laing knuckled his brow respectfully. "I'll set the men out, right enough, sir. But I don't think Miss Josie took the west road. Two of the stablehands rode that way while we were looking for Molly. They went clear to the Pass, and would certainly have seen the little girl.''

"Unless she did not want to be seen,'' argued Yolande. "If she was running away again. She adores Dev, you know, Grandpapa.''

"Lord knows why,'' he grunted. "You're right, though. Saddle up Crusher for me, Laing. Yolande, I'll change my clothes and be off. Never worry, lass. We'll find her.''

"I'm going with you. Please, Grandpapa! I feel responsible. I could not bear to just sit here and wait.''

He frowned, but in the end, of course, was won over, and they hurried to the house together. Ten minutes later, having changed into her habit in record time, Yolande hurried downstairs, train over one arm, a dashing hat set upon her curls, and riding whip and gloves in her hand.

Her aunts walked into the Great Hall as she descended, and Mrs. Fraser said with one of her rare smiles, "What a bonnie green that is! You look very fetching, Yolande. May one ask whither ye're bound at this hour?''

"I wish I knew, ma'am. Grandpapa has asked Laing to send all the men out to look for Josie. She's wandered off somewhere, the tiresome child.''

Snatching up Socrates and thus foiling his attempt to nip her sister-in-law's ankle, Mrs. Drummond murmured that he was a very naughty doggie today, then expostulated, "You never mean to ride *with* them? Yolande, your wits are gone begging! You must let the gentlemen handle such things!''

"I would, did I not feel so wretchedly responsible. I might have known she would try to find Devenish.''

"Aye.'' Mrs. Fraser nodded. "The poor wee mite idolizes the lad.'' She looked at her niece enigmatically. "Children and dogs. He canna be all bad.''

"Bad!" flared Yolande, her cheeks flushing. "Dev is a very fine young man! He is not at all bad!"

"Well, you love him, of course. Your pardon, dear, I keep forgetting. I had in fact meant to ask you for the date you've selected."

The voice was mild, but Yolande's eyes fell before her aunt's steady gaze and, concentrating on adjusting her gloves, she answered, "We have not quite decided on the exact date, but mean to set it and make the formal announcement as soon as Dev returns." She looked up and said gratefully, "Oh, there you are, Grandpapa. Have the men started yet?"

"They wait for us to join them. Never fret so, girl! We'll likely find her long before she reaches the castle." His whiskers twitched. "I hope we do, for I've nae wish tae encounter that Canadian mushroom!"

Aware that her Aunt Caroline's covertly amused gaze was upon her, Yolande did not utter the indignant retort that trembled on her tongue, saying instead that she did not see how Josie could possibly have reached the castle by this time, even had she left at ten o'clock.

Mrs. Drummond caressed Socrates fondly, and murmured, "Well, she did not. It was well after noon, as I recall."

With his hand on the doorknob, the General stiffened, glared at the panelled door, assumed a smile that might well have caused the paint to blister, and turned to his daughter-in-law. "You *saw* the child leave, Arabella?"

"I suppose that is what she was doing. At the time, I merely thought she was going for a little ride."

"How grand in ye tae inform us of it the noo," said Mrs. Fraser ironically.

"Ride—ye said?" Sir Andrew snapped. "Upon what, ma'am?"

"That great big animal. Jolly Nelly—or whatever it is called."

"Molly-My-Lass?" said Yolande. "Oh, Aunt! If only you had told us!"

"But, I *am* telling you, my love! And I cannot think why you should go to the castle, for she never meant to go there, unless perhaps she experienced some difficulty in guiding that monster, which I own she did not seem to, as the horse moved off in quite a docile fashion."

His brows beetling, the General snarled, "Which *way* did the wee girl go?"

"I am striving to tell you that, sir. It was *not* in the

direction of Castle Tyndale, for to reach there one would have to take the estate road to the west, I do believe, and—Sir Andrew! Are you feeling quite the thing? Your face is alarmingly red, and—"

"Fer losh sakes, woman!" cried Mrs. Fraser. "Put it in tae simple English if ye please! If Josie Storm dinna take the western road, which way *did* she go?"

"She took the north road, my dear Caroline. As if she meant to go north, do you see? Though *why*, or whom she meant to visit, is more than I could say!"

"Och-unnnh!" snorted Drummond. "At last the gem is extrrrracted! Come lassie, we must come up with the wee girl before dusk!"

With Yolande hurrying beside him, he stalked to the hall and the stableyard, from whence he could soon be heard roaring orders to Mr. Laing.

"Good gracious," murmured Mrs. Drummond, nervously. "How you ever stand it here, Caroline, is quite beyond me! My father-in-law's temperament would drive me distracted!"

" 'Tis a mutual emotion," Mrs. Fraser informed her dourly.

Arabella smiled. It was nice, thought she, that for once they were in accord.

Chapter Fourteen

*T*he small store room in the second basement was musty, icy cold, and pitch-black. From the moment they had been thrust down the short flight of steps and the great door slammed and barred upon them, the cousins had explored in frantic search of a way out, or something with which to defend themselves when the door was opened. Neither effort met with success. Now, shivering and defeated, they sat against the wooden door, shoulder to shoulder, in an attempt to keep warm.

"They could at least," Devenish grumbled, "have left us a lantern."

"Probably thought we'd burn the door down," said Tyndale, and the faint note of strain in his cousin's voice having been noted, asked, "That leg bothering you?"

"Just a trifle."

"If you had managed to refrain from advising that nasty little weasel he was a nasty little weasel, he might not have pushed you down the steps."

"But he might. And I am not in the habit of grovelling to such as he."

"Very true, Master High and Mighty. Are you instead in the habit of escaping predicaments such as this? I gather you've had more experience in these matters than I have."

"You refer to my little jaunt with Tristram Leith?" Devenish grinned into the darkness. "What a jolly good adventure that was! I'll say one thing for that rascally Frenchman, it was all conducted on a far more gentlemanly plane than this! We'd interfered with his plans, so he meant to kill us. But there was none of this shutting people up in haunted dungeons and then shoving 'em off the top of a . . . a damned great tower!"

There was a rather heavy silence, the imminence of that horror daunting them both, if only for a moment.

Tyndale said coolly, "I wonder if it's dark yet."

"I suppose it must be. We've been in here at least an hour, wouldn't you say?"

"At least. In which case they're liable to come for us at any minute. Dev, we must *think* of something!"

"Simple. The instant they open the door, we'll toddle out and lay about right and left. Likely they'll not expect it, and we'll grass the lot!"

His optimism proved ill-founded, however. Another long hour crawled by before the door swung open, revealing the pallid features and sandy hair of the man Walter, standing well back, with a large musket aimed unerringly at Tyndale, so that Devenish's well-planned charge was brought up short.

"That's a good lad," sneered Walter.

"You do not dare shoot," said Devenish, his eyes flashing to the grim faces of the three who watched.

"Oh, we wouldn't shoot *you*, sir," Fritch admitted, a sly leer illuminating his narrow features. He nodded to Tyndale. "But if you try anything, *he* gets snuffed. You're going to shoot him anyway, so it could just as well be now."

This information, intended to terrify the helpless victims, was ill-judged. With a shout of triumph, Devenish sprang directly in front of the musket. "Go on, Craig!" he howled.

Tyndale needed no urging. He experienced a brief sense of awe that his cousin should have the pluck to throw himself against that yawning muzzle, then he sailed into action.

220

Simultaneously, Devenish sent a right hurtling at Walter's jaw. His was a slender fist, even when clenched, but his slim grace had deceived men before this. When in Town, he had seen a good deal of the interior of Gentleman Jackson's Boxing Saloon and, while he was not muscular, he was tough and wiry and had proven an apt pupil. Besides that, he was both angered and in the grip of the exhilaration that always seized him when action or danger beckoned. Thus, Mr. Fritch was amazed to see his cohort reel backward to bring up with a crash against the far wall of the corridor. His surprise was brief. Craig had height, reach, and solid power to comple- ment his cousin's steel. An uppercut to the point of Mr. Fritch's very pointed chin sent him first to the tips of his toes, and then diving to join the crumpled Walter. Recovering from their momentary stupefaction, Messrs. Jethro and Shotten now plunged into the fray, and the narrow hall, lighted only by the flickering flames of torches set in iron brackets, was suddenly very busy indeed. Craig was jolted to his knees when Shotten rammed a large fist under his ribs. Spinning triumphantly from his encounter with Walter, Devenish was too late to block the left that Jethro smashed at him. Dazed and half blind, he struck out instinctively and, howling, his nose streaming crimson, Jethro staggered, colliding with Shotten, who had also turned his attention to Devenish. Reprieved for an instant, Devenish fought away dizziness and scooped up the fallen musket. The quarters were too close to fire it without hitting Tyndale, so he swung it instead, and Jethro went down. Tyndale, who had struggled to his feet, tapped Shotten on the shoulder and, as the bully whirled to attack, drove home a jab that dropped him like a sack of oats.

"Hah!" panted Devenish, bruised but exuberant.

"Come on!" cried the more practical Tyndale.

They ran for a door at the far end of that long, descending corridor. The door burst open. A bearded man appeared; a voice shouted, *"Ils se sont échappés! Alors! Alors!"*

"Whoops!" Swinging sharply about, Devenish panted, "Retreat, coz! No—*ahead* of me! Hurry! They don't want a bullet in *me!*"

Thus protected, they safely reached the stairs leading to the kitchen quarters. Many feet pounded behind them. Never had Tyndale mounted stairs with such desperate haste. But there must, he knew, be a rearguard action, and as they reached the landing and sprinted for the Great Hall, he gasped, "Dev. You run like hell when you—get outside. I'll . . . hold the doors!"

"Noble," Tyndale acknowledged breathlessly. "But pointless. If either one of us . . . stays . . . he will be killed and—and the survivor accused of his murder! It's—all or nothing, coz!"

It appeared perilously likely to be nothing, for as they rounded the corner and headed across the Great Hall, voices could be heard on the drivepath, and one, ominously close, howled, "Something's wrong inside. Hurry!"

Tyndale swore.

"The back!" gasped Devenish, and once more they wheeled about.

They were too late. Already, their pursuers were between them and the rear corridor. A pistol in Shotten's eager hand was pointing at Tyndale. The explosion was shattering, but he missed his shot and the ball thudded into the wall.

"Upstairs!" Tyndale shouted, leading the way in a mad dash for the main stairs.

Fritch howled, "We've got 'em! There's no way out, and they're goin' where we want 'em, lads!"

"Blast him! He's . . . right!" Tyndale panted as they toiled upward.

"We'll set fire . . . to . . . the blasted pile!" Devenish clutched his leg painfully. "That'll attract half the . . . countryside."

They reached the first floor balcony ahead of their pursuers. It was, thought Devenish, too close, besides which, his blasted leg was becoming too much of a nuisance for him to climb any further. Belatedly, he realized he still clutched the musket. "You—go on, coz! I'll hold 'em while—you build . . . a bonfire." Not waiting for consent, he swung around, musket levelled. "Platoon . . . halt!" he shouted. "Guided tour . . . stops here!"

Behind him, Tyndale hesitated, but the fierce gallop had halted before the wide mouth of the musket that waved gently to and fro. "Go *on*, dash it all!" urged Devenish.

Tyndale plunged into the nearest bedchamber, which chanced to be the one his cousin had occupied, and began dragging chairs, tables, draperies, into a pile before the windows. Inspired, he wrenched down the ghoulish portrait, propped it against the pile, and smashed the still burning oil lamp at it.

A gout of fire exploded. Tyndale leapt back. The flames licked upward, reaching hungrily for the draperies. They caught, and in a trice the windows were edged with fire.

222

Smoke began to billow out, and Tyndale, coughing, ran back to his cousin, still at bay on the balcony.

"He done it, damn him!" howled an enraged voice. "He's fired the blasted place. If it reaches the stores . . . !"

Strong faces blanched. Murderous glares faded into unease. The rear rank began to edge downwards. "Shoot! You perishin' fools—*shoot!*" raved Shotten, brandishing his empty pistol.

The front door burst open. A new arrival ran in, shouting, "There's a damn great bunch of riders coming!"

"Hurrah!" Devenish exulted.

The smugglers hesitated, exchanging scared glances. A thunder of hooves could be heard outside. Simultaneously, a great billow of smoke gushed onto the landing. It was the *coup de grâce*. As one man, the group on the stairs broke and ran. From the corner of his eye Tyndale saw Shotten wrest a pistol from the newcomer and turn—aiming. With a cry of warning, he leapt to push his cousin out of the line of fire. The pistol shot cracked deafeningly, even above the tumult. Tyndale staggered and clutched his shoulder. Devenish steadied himself and fired, his shot sounding as an echo to the first, the twin retorts almost simultaneous, and Shotten gave a howl, grabbed his arm and reeled away, assisted by a comrade.

Tyndale swayed, missed his footing, and fell, tumbling limply down the precipitous stairs even as the front door was flung wide.

General Drummond, Yolande behind him, rushed in. They halted, and stood as though rooted to the spot. Yolande gave a small, shrill scream. With an appalled groan, Devenish started to hurry to his cousin, but Yolande was before him. She flew to sink down beside Tyndale's sprawled form, another despairing cry escaping her as she saw the blood that stained his shirt. Tearing his cravat aside, her distraught gaze flashed up to Devenish and the still-smoking pistol in his hand. "Murderous savage!" she sobbed, in fierce accusation. "*Had* you to try to kill him, then? Would *nothing* satisfy your vengeance, your insane jealousy, but his death?" And bending to investigate the wound high on Tyndale's shoulder, she pleaded brokenly, "My darling, my darling! Oh, my dearest beloved—do not die! Please, *please*, do not die!"

Two steps above her, Devenish halted and groped blindly for the banister rail. For years to come that scene would haunt him: Craig, sprawled and silent, Yolande weeping over him; the General standing as one dazed, while the grooms and stablehands from Steep Drummond crowded noisily in behind

223

him to gaze in awed condemnation at the dramatic tableaux before them.

"It is not true," he thought numbly. "It *cannot* be true! She is *mine*. We are betrothed. She does not love Craig. She *must not* love Craig!" But Yolande's tears, her tender efforts to help the wounded man, and above all else the bitter, accusing words that rang in his brain, left no room for doubt. She *did* love Craig. That terrible knowledge seared like a sword through him. Her love was forever lost. The Colonial bastard had stolen her away, and in so doing had taken every hope for the future, and all meaning in life. . . .

Craig struggled feebly and came to one elbow. His eyes were full of pain, and he must have struck his head in falling, for blood was streaking down his face, but he held back Yolande's ministering hand, his gaze fixed on his cousin. "Dev," he gasped faintly, "Dev—I tried . . . not to love her, but . . . but I—I did not— I would . . . not . . ." And he slumped down again, Yolande supporting his fall so that his head sank into her lap. Her tears fell like bright diamonds onto his unresponsive face. She lifted her head to glare up at Devenish and demand through clenched teeth, "Are you satisfied now? Oh—may God forgive you! I never shall!"

The General moved forward, breaking the spell that had held them all still for what seemed like a long time, yet had actually been only seconds. "Good God, man!" he breathed. "Have you entirely lost your wits? I'd not thought to find something like this when the child said there was trouble here!"

A door, distantly slammed, brought his head swinging around, and jolted Devenish from his personal misery. "The smugglers!" he cried.

Montelongo staggered into the hall, saw Tyndale, and ran to him weavingly.

The General brightened. If there were smugglers about, this tragedy might not be so black as he had at first surmised. Smoke was boiling out of one of the upper rooms. "Some of you men," he roared, "get upstairs and put that fire out! Todd and Blake—stay with Miss Yolande. The rest of you, come with me!"

"This way!" shouted Devenish. He sprinted to the kitchen hall and the basement stairs and with whoops of excitement, the General and his men followed. At top speed, they clattered down the stairs and raced along the hall. The door to the store room in which the cousins had been imprisoned was still open. The rear door stood wide, but as Devenish ran through it, he slowed. A large cupboard just beyond the door jutted crazily into the corridor, revealing a small aperture in the wall behind it, and a glimpse of deep-cut steps leading downwards.

Holding up a flaming torch that he'd snatched from its bracket, the General muttered, "Have a care, lad. They may be waiting!"

Devenish smiled without mirth. Much he cared! He stepped over the low wainscot and onto the first step. The darkness was intense, the light of the torch penetrating a very few feet ahead, but the steps wound steadily down. They were slippery and treacherous, but he went on with reckless haste, and as he went the smell of the sea came ever more clearly to his nostrils. Had not Tyndale once made some remark about the possibility of an entrance to the castle through a cave? His heart began to hammer with anticipation.

The steps curved around a wall, and suddenly they were in an enormous chamber, one side of which was formed by the living rock of the cliff-face. Torches still burned in wall brackets, but of Sanguinet's minions the only sign was the open door at the far side of the room, a door of solid stone, so formed as to be invisible from without once it was securely closed.

Coming up with Devenish at the foot of the steps, Drummond exclaimed, "By God, but this is a fine haul! There's a deal more here than brandy and perfumes and the like!"

And indeed, there were innumerable boxes, bales, and barrels of every shape, row upon row of them, stored very neatly by their various sizes.

"No wonder there were so many of them," muttered Devenish.

"D'ye see any of the rogues? Be damned if I do!"

They quickened their steps, but when they had run across that great storage room and passed through the open door, they encountered a misty, deserted cove, with only the fast-diminishing sails of a yawl to vouch for the hurried flight of the Free Traders.

Devenish cursed bitterly. "They're safely away! And I've not one witness to attest to the fact that I did not shoot my wretched cousin!"

"Tyndale will attest to it," said the General. "The wound did not look to be serious. Not much more than a deep score across the base of his throat. D'you know which one shot him?"

225

"Yes," Devenish said reluctantly, "The leader of that unsavoury crew was a lout named Shotten. He fired at me. Tyndale ran to push me clear, and so took the ball himself."

"By Jove!" exclaimed the General, eyes kindling. "That was well—"

"Sir!" called one of the grooms, his voice ringing with excitement. "Come and have a look here!"

They went back inside. Several of the crates had been broken open, and the grooms were busily unloading bottles of rum and cognac from one large barrel. "Let that stuff alone, men!" Drummond ordered crisply. "The Excise people will want to find it undisturbed." His eyes fell on a bottle of '71 port. He amended hurriedly, "Or relatively so," and grinning into Devenish's stern face, murmured, "Finders keepers—eh?"

Devenish shrugged and wandered to a clear area of the room. It had very obviously been occupied recently. There were scratches and grooves in the rocky floor indicating that heavy objects had been dragged across it, and from the disposition of dust and straw it appeared that many large crates must have been removed. "I'd give a good deal," he muttered, "to know what was stored here. . . ."

The General nodded briskly. "Likely a cargo bound for London markets. And more likely, there's many a gentleman will be the better of a case or two of duty-free brandy before another week's out. Oh, well—this haul alone must be worth a fortune. There may be a reward, m'boy. You're liable to become famous. But you cannot stay here alone. You must come and rack up at Steep Drummond for a while."

With bleak control, Devenish thanked him. "I will impose on you sir, only until I can be assured of my cousin's condition. Then, I must get home."

The General slanted a compassionate glance at him. "Of course," he agreed understandingly. "Only natural you'd want to go."

* * *

Yolande closed the bedchamber door softly and trod her weary way down the hall. Reaching up to push back an errant strand of hair, she stopped, her heart contracting. Devenish had been sitting beside an ornately carven old chest, but came to his feet when he saw her, and waited, his face pale and expressionless. She reached out to him tentatively.

He did not take her proffered hands, saying in a voice she did not know at all, "How is he?"

She blinked, allowing her hands to lower again. "Not very

226

good, I'm afraid. The gunshot wound is slight, but—but it seems he struck his head when he fell. He keeps going off into unconsciousness, and the doctor . . . just—'' Her voice scratched a little. "He does not really know . . ."

He had not expected this and, shocked, stepped a pace closer, peering at her in the dim light of the one lamp that was lit and asking, "He must have come around, surely?"

"He spoke twice. You are quite exonerated, Dev." Tears blinding her, she said pleadingly, "Oh, Dev . . . dear Dev. I am—so sorry. I wish—how I wish I had not said it!"

He did not answer, and she dashed her tears away, impatient because she was so very tired and distraught and could not seem to see him clearly. He had moved over to the window and stood looking into the night, his back very straight, his hands loosely clasped behind him. Humbly, she begged, "Can you please tell me what has been happening? I heard people coming and going all night long, I think."

"Oh, yes. There has been a very great fuss. Your grandfather sent riders to Kilmarnock, and the Constable came and Sir Hugh somebody-or-other called out the militia, who are guarding the castle until the powers-that-be arrive. And—'' The clasped hands gripped tighter. His head tilted upwards as though he was bracing himself. He asked hoarsely, "Do you— Yolande, do you mean to wed him?"

She bit her lip, her heart aching for him. But said firmly, "Yes. If he lives, I will marry him."

"If he lives!" He spun around. "There's no question of that—is there?"

"I . . . I don't know. He has been unconscious for hours now." Her lip trembled and she said with unknowing pathos, "I am—very frightened."

How strange that the sight of her grief still had such power to move him. How strange that, even now, he loved her, worshipped her, wanted so desperately to make her his wife. And yet somehow, he heard himself saying, "He saved my life again, you know. The bullet that struck him down would likely have caught me in the head, had he not pushed me aside. I . . . I suppose you must resent that fact."

With a muffled whimper, she shrank, turning from him, her face buried in her hands. "Do not . . . oh, please, Dev. Do not hate me!"

"Hate you!" He stepped closer to seize her shoulders, pull her against him, and press desperate kisses on the cool silk of her hair. "I adore you! I always have—you know it. Yolande—

227

for the love of God—*think!* What are you doing? We have been promised all our lives! Do you really—''

''I know!'' She wrenched free and faced him. ''I feel sick and ashamed. But I cannot change my heart. I have broken my promise to you. But—but at least our betrothal was never made public. You will not have to suffer that humiliation.''

''It is no less binding because it wasn't published! You gave me your word!'' And knowing he could choose no worse time to plead his cause, driven by desperation he plunged on. ''You said you would name the day when I came back from the castle.''

Her eyes fell. She wrung her hands and admitted miserably, ''I did. Oh, I know how I have hurt you. I—I cannot tell you . . . how I wish I might not.''

''*I* can tell *you!*'' Again, he took her by the arms, gazing into her strained upturned face, and demanding, ''Admit to yourself that he is not for you. Could you adapt to his way of life? Could you give up everything you have ever known? Home, family, friends, even your country. Admit you will break the hearts of all who love you! Can you do it? Yolande—*can* you? And not care?'' She was weeping openly now, but he shook her a little and rasped, ''*Think,* love! Stop and think what you are doing!''

''Dev . . . oh, heaven, how . . . how frightful it is . . . ! How can I make you understand? I love my family . . . my friends—my country. But . . . I love Craig more. I—I would follow him . . . to the ends of the earth.''

He flinched as if she had struck him. A groan was torn from him, and he again turned from her. Sobbing, she took his arm and leaned her cheek against it. And despite himself, his hand went out to caress her bowed head. Despite the aching anguish within him, he soothed, ''Never weep, my—my dear one. What a—a dolt I am. Just as . . . clumsy as ever, you see.''

''No . . . you are not at all . . .''

''I should not have spoken. You are too upset to think clearly. I do apologize. But, Yolande—'' he looked down at her, forcing a smile. ''It will pass. You'll see. It is just an infatuation.''

She stiffened and drew away. Her sobs eased as she stood there, gazing at him in silence. Then she said with a quiet resolve that terrified him, ''No, Dev. It is not infatuation. I know now that from the first moment I met him, I have loved

Craig. And that I always will love him. The only thing ever to come between us will be—death.''

His face convulsed. With typical abruptness, his mood changed and he looked so maddened that for the first time in her life, Yolande was afraid of him. Fists clenching, eyes narrowed and blazing with passion, he snarled, "Then, I pray to God he *dies!*" And strode rapidly away, leaving her to gaze after him, her eyes wide with shock and an emotion that would have further enraged him—pity.

*   *   *

The days that followed were busy ones for all concerned, which was perhaps as well. The authorities from Glasgow arrived and were soon superseded by the authorities from Edinburgh. Writers from several newspapers and periodicals descended upon Steep Drummond and infuriated the General by conducting understanding and sympathetic interviews, then writing articles that grossly misrepresented the facts. Devenish said nothing of Sanguinet's part in the matter, nor would he until he had reported to the Horse Guards. But the newspapermen promoted the smugglers to "Bonapartists"; Drummond and his men had galloped to the rescue of his "headstrong young nephews," arriving in the nick of time, and driving off the ruffians by means of a pitched battle during which half of the castle had been burned to the ground. The ultimate offence was a piece by one writer describing Drummond as "a peaceable little old gentleman," which so infuriated the General he all but foamed at the mouth. Devenish was questioned interminably, praised lavishly, and then depicted in the newspapers as having sadly mismanaged the affair. It was, it appeared, very obvious that had the authorities been "properly notified," the criminals could have been seized and brought to justice. Instead of which, thanks to Devenish's ineptitude, not only had they escaped but war hero Major Craig Tyndale now lay at death's door.

Devenish read this with fuming resentment and joined the General in calling down maledictions upon all newspaper writers. Even Mrs. Drummond was offended. "It is not," she sniffed, as they sat in the drawing room after dinner one evening, "as if Devenish did not do all that he was capable of doing. They surely must realize he is *not* a big strong fellow. And he certainly did not *mean* Major Tyndale Winters to be hurt." She turned curious eyes upon the seething Devenish and murmured, "Now, did you, Alain?"

"I must own, ma'am," he answered with a brittle smile, "that I'd not had the wit to consider it."

Arabella blinked at him, uncertainly. Mrs. Fraser uttered a faint snort and took up her embroidery. General Drummond fixing Devenish with a stern eye, said, "I understand you'd a letter from Alastair Tyndale today. Does he mean to come up here, may I ask?"

"He did not say so, sir. I had written to tell him of what transpired, of course, and of Craig's condition. He asks that I remain until— Well, one way or the other. If this goes on much longer, I shall take myself to the Gold Florin in the village. Lord knows you have been more than kind to allow me to stay here, under the circumstances."

"The circumstances," the General said with deliberate emphasis and a darkling look, "have changed. You have redeemed yourself. In my eyes, at least." He noted Devenish's faint, cynical smile, and frowned. "The lass is properly in the boughs now, and little wonder. She is grateful to Tyndale, and is besides a good girl who would bend every effort to help *anyone* in so wretched a condition."

Mrs. Fraser did not look up from her embroidery, but her scornful, "Hoot toot!" was quite audible.

Devenish said politely, "Thank you, sir. But I think that is not all there is to it."

"It had best be! Your cousin has shown himself a right gallant gentleman. What's gone before cannot be changed, nonetheless, and I'll not give my approval to my grand-daughter's marrying into such a house. No more, I doubt, will her parents."

"She is of age, sir."

"Aye, she is that. But if you think she would wed over the objections of her family, *I* do not. And besides—whatever else, Tyndale is a gentleman. He'd neither propose marriage to a lady he well knows is already promised, nor allow her to go against the wishes of her family. Give her time, lad. She'll come to her senses!"

For the next five days and nights, however, Yolande rarely emerged from the sickroom. Her grandfather had installed competent nurses to care for the injured man, and the devoted Montelongo seldom left him, so that her help was not needed, but she dreaded lest Craig regain consciousness and did not find her at his bedside. Often, during those weary days, she would think his awakening imminent, for he would begin to toss about and mumble, and sometimes he tried to get up,

230

shouting incoherently. Always, hers was the only hand that could quiet him. But always, he sank back into the depths without having recognized her.

The nurses who shared her vigil were kind and capable, but uncommunicative. The doctor talked to her gravely of Tyndale's splendid constitution, but of the often bewildering effects of concussion, and the fact that only last year Craig had almost died of wounds received at the Battle of Waterloo. " 'Twould be a shock tae any man's system, ma'am," he observed, nodding his white head ponderously. "We must gie the body time tae recover!"

But it seemed to Yolande that her love was not recovering. Each day, he appeared to her anxious eyes to become more gaunt and thin. The periods of activity were fewer, and on several terrible occasions she feared he had ceased to breathe. When she begged the doctor to do *something* to help him, he patted her shoulder and said kindly, "Ye gie me more credit than I deserve, lassie. Better you should broach the subject tae the good Lord. And be willing tae abide by His decision."

Those ominous words sent a shiver down Yolande's spine. She sank to her knees beside the bed and prayed as she had never prayed before. The nurse, coming silently into the room following a quiet consultation with the doctor, saw that sad little scene, and her heart was wrung. She went quickly into the adjoining dressing room where they had set up her trundle bed and offered up a few prayers of her own.

*   *   *

There was a hill on the General's estate from which one could obtain a very fine view of the surrounding countryside and, on a clear day, see all the way to the Isle of Arran. It was a pleasant spot, the thick turf providing a soft blanket underfoot, and several large old trees offering sprawling patches of shade if the sun should prove too warm. Josie and her friend Maisie had sometimes brought their dolls up here, and the hill had served variously as the afterdeck of a great galleon deliciously pursued by bloodthirsty pirates, or as the topmost parapet of some mighty castle from which the two "ladies" had watched their knightly lords set forth to battle oppression and tyranny, with an occasional dragon thrown in for good measure.

To this peaceful retreat on a warm afternoon some eight days after the confrontation at Castle Tyndale came Alain Devenish, head down bent and heart as heavy as his dragging steps. He strolled to the tree that was closest to the western side of the hill and settled himself down with his back propped against the trunk. The valley between this hill and the one whereon stood Steep Drummond stretched out lush and green below him, smoke wound lazily into the air from two chimneys of the great house, and, far off, the sea, incredibly blue under the azure bowl of the heavens, stretched into a misty distance.

The young man's brooding gaze saw none of this beauty, but saw instead a slim girl on her knees in the vast hall of Castle Tyndale, her great eyes, hate-filled, flashing up at him. . . . Down in the meadow, a small disgruntled creature named Socrates came upon a placid milk cow and hurled himself into battle, barking shrilly. The sound travelled all the way to the hilltop on the warm air, but Devenish heard only a beloved voice railing at him as it never had railed before. ''Murderous savage . . . May God forgive you! I never shall!'' And he thought with longing that was a pain, ''Yolande . . . Yolande . . .'' Her face, fondly smiling now, was before his eyes, wherefore he closed them and leaned his head back.

Perversely, it was Tyndale he saw then. Tyndale, standing astride him during the fight with Akim and Benjo; laughing when he was staggered by a blow, and fighting on dauntlessly; Tyndale, looking so confoundedly magnificent in his Scots regalia, with that uncertain grin on his face. Tyndale, shouting a warning and leaping forward to push him clear, thus taking the ball that had been meant for him . . . Somewhere at the back of his bedevilled brain a soft voice whispered, ''Greater love hath no man . . .'' He swore and bowed his head into his hands, and though he would fiercely have denied it, his grief was not entirely for his lost love, but some was for the man he had come to like and admire; and who had betrayed him.

For a long time he remained thus, trying to form some plan for the future; trying to envision a future in which there was no sparkle of laughing green eyes, no soft, teasing, musical little voice, no warmth of hearth and home—and children. . . . But gradually he sensed that he was not alone and, looking up, found a small figure kneeling beside him. When the wistful dark eyes encountered his own, the child said nothing, but thrust a small, rather wilted bouquet of tiny daisies at him. Touched, and faintly smiling, he took it, and she sighed, murmuring regretfully, ''I got nothing else to give you.''

''This is just right,'' he said. ''Thank you.'' And, with an attempt at lightness, ''But it is not my birthday, you know.''

"I picked 'em for you 'cause you was hurting so bad. I'd have bringed hundreds of roses and great big dailies, if I could. Or I'd have made him better for you. I asked God to make him better, so p'raps He will." A small grubby hand was placed comfortingly on Devenish's immaculate sleeve. "Don't you never grieve so. If God needs him in Heaven, you shouldn't ought to argify about it."

He looked away from her earnest face, flushing slightly. "I expect you are right." Her eyes seemed so piercingly intent. There was no telling what might be going on in her funny little head. Hurriedly, he asked, "What have you been up to these past few days? I fear I've neglected you. Have you been playing with your friend?"

"No. Her mum wouldn't let us. Don't you remember?"

"Oh, of course. Maisie, wasn't it? And she has the measles."

"She's better. But Mrs. MacFarlane's poorly. I thought she was cocking up her toes, 'cause they asked the vicar to come and see her—only they call him a minster. Next day when I went to take her a rose, she was up, and she was lots better. I was s'prised. That minster must be God's bosom bow to make her well so quick. P'raps we should get him to come and make Major Craig better."

"Perhaps," he gritted. "Was Mrs. MacFarlane cross because you went to her house?"

"No. I thought she would be, but she wasn't. She was nice, even when she talked so funny."

"Funny?"

"Mmmm. She asked me how Miss Yolande was, and I said I hadn't hardly seen her, because she's been so busy nursing of Major Craig. And she started to look all weepy and said something about how good Miss Yolande is, and now her heart is breaking 'cause her love is dying under her very eyes. I told her she'd got it all wrong, 'cause *you* are—" She faltered to a stop, Devenish's suddenly bleak expression causing her own eyes to become very big indeed. "Oh . . . my!" she gasped. And without warning she threw her frail arms around his neck, hugging him so hard he all but choked. "Never look so, dear soul! Oh, my poor, dear soul!" she said with a sob. "I'll take care of ye. Ah—never look so!"

Succeeding in freeing himself from her stranglehold, Devenish regarded her wonderingly. "What are these?" he smiled, removing a glittering drop from her cheek. "Tears? For me? No need, m'dear. I'm fine as fivepence, I do assure you!"

233

His grin was as bright and cheerful as ever, but she was undeceived. She buried her cheek against his cravat and hugged as much of him as she could reach. "How *could* she?" she gulped. "Oh, how *could* she like him best—when she could have *you?*"

Devenish's grin took on a set look. But, after all, there was no need to dissemble with the child. "Tell you the truth," he said wryly, "I've wondered as much myself. But—no accounting for tastes." Once more, he gently disentangled himself and, looking down at her woebegone face, said, "And there really is no cause for all these high flights and tragic airs, milady elf. I wasn't thoroughly set on getting leg-shackled. This is probably—probably better for everyone."

Having been deprived of throat and cravat, Josie hugged his arm and, looking worshipfully up into his face, said with a sigh, "You say that, but I know how your poor insides really feel. Anyone else, they'd be waiting for Major Craig to get up, so they could shoot a hole right through his breadbasket. But not you! He's lucky you love him, else—"

"*Love* him?" exclaimed Devenish, revolted. "I cannot *abide* the fellow!"

She gave a rather watery giggle. "I know. And you'll say you don't give a button if he saved your life, or 'cause his dad and your dad was such fine friends. You both pretend you don't like each other. But you fights together, and you keeps together. You didn't run off and leave him alone at that horrid castle, however creepy it is. And I think he's very lucky that you . . . cannot 'bide him. Poor Mr. Dev! You want her for your lady wife, but you're so good you'll probably wish her happy—even if she's hacked your poor heart to little pieces!"

Shattered, Devenish scrambled hurriedly to his feet. He strode to the brink of the hill and stood staring across the valley to that other hill and the great house wherein was a quiet bedchamber and a lovely lady—waiting. And he thought in stark misery, "Perhaps when my dear cousin wakes up—if he wakes up—I *shall* shoot a hole through his breadbasket."

Chapter Fifteen

Yolande came swiftly down the stairs and hurried to the small parlour into which her unexpected guest had been shown. "Mrs. MacFarlane!" she said, walking forward, hand outstretched. "I heard you had been unwell. I am so glad you came to me. Is there some way in which I may help you?"

The emaciated little woman sprang up to take her hand shyly and drop a curtsy. Her own fingers trembled as she said in short nervous gasps, "Ye—ye have always been sae . . . sae verra good tae me. I come tae find oot—how the poor gentleman goes on."

"How kind. Will you not sit here beside me? There, now we can be comfortable. Major Craig remains the same. There is—no change, I'm afraid." For an instant a look of desolation crossed that beauteous face. Then Yolande bit her lip, raised her chin a little and, putting aside her own sorrow, asked, "How is your little girl?"

"Och, sae much better, miss. She'd like fine for Miss Josie tae come and see her, if it's nae forward tae ask it."

"But of course it is not." Yolande searched her face; it seemed calmer. "Maisie is—quite better?" she asked, wondering at this new demeanour.

"Aye. Thank you. But if ye fear Miss Josie might catch it, we could wait a wee while."

"No, no. I expect Josie was exposed when they played together at all events. She might already have had measles. I only wondered . . . you seem less, er—"

"Troubled, Miss? Well, I am. I've come tae—" She drew a deep breath. Almost, thought Yolande, as though she were nerving herself for some tremendous task. "I'd not thought tae ever do this," Mrs. MacFarlane said, gripping her bony hands. "Likely I'd nae be doing it the noo, but—ye've been sae good. And even with your man lying there, ye came doon, thinking I had need of ye. I felt fair horrid, and I could nae—" She broke off with a gasp, her frightened gaze darting to the open doorway.

235

Yolande glanced around. Devenish stood there. His fair curls were disarrayed, and he looked out of breath as though he had come in haste, but in his eyes was an expression she had never thought to see there again, and that brought hope to brighten her heavy heart a little. So it was that for one of the very few times in her life, Yolande Drummond was so discourteous as to completely forget a visitor. She stood, saying eagerly, "Dev . . . ? Oh, Dev—have you forgiven me, then?"

"No," he replied tenderly, reaching out to her. "For the only one who needs forgiveness is this hot-tempered idiot."

With a glad little sob, she flew to take his hands and then allow herself to be enveloped in a hug.

Devenish closed his eyes for an instant, savouring to the full that bitter-sweet embrace. "Lord," he said, his voice low and husky with emotion, "what an ill-grained clod I am! The most important challenge of my life, and I was so unsportsmanlike as to lose without grace—without honesty; having the unspeakable arrogance to suppose that merely because I so love you, it must follow that—"

She put up one soft hand to silence his words, then said very gently, "I do love you, Dev. I always have. That is what made it so very hard. But—it wasn't in . . . in just that very special way, do you see?"

The same cruel lance was piercing him, but he managed a smile. "I do—now. And if I cannot have you for—my wife, I . . . I hope I may still have you for my friend."

She blinked tears away. "Always, Dev. Dear Dev. Always."

"It's as well you agreed," he said shakily. "Else I might not have told you." Her lovely brows arched enquiringly. How he longed to kiss them. . . . Instead, he took his handkerchief and carefully dried her tears. "There is a curst great clod of a Colonial upstairs," he imparted, "of whom I have, unhappily, become quite fond. That starched Amazon of a nurse tells me that—he is calling for you."

Yolande uttered a gasp and, paling, put a trembling hand to her throat. She searched his face and as he nodded, she sped to the door. Watching her, Devenish's fond smile faded into a wistful sadness. He had to replace the smile very quickly when Yolande paused and spun about, but she had seen that changed expression and suffered her own pang. "Dev," she said timidly. "Will you—come? I'm . . . afraid. . . ."

He went at once to her side. "Silly chit," he said.

They entered the room together. Montelongo stood beside the bed, beaming. Craig's eyes turned to them eagerly, but

236

saw only Yolande. With a glad little cry she went to take the hand he raised and clasp it between both her own. For a few moments, neither spoke a word, but looking from one rapturous face to the other, besides grief and yearning, Devenish experienced a sense of awe.

"Oh, my dear," breathed Yolande at length. "You have come back to me at last. How are you?"

"I feel . . . splendid," he said, faint but radiant. "Only—a touch pulled. What a clunch to have gone off like that, yesterday."

Devenish chuckled, and his cousin's eyes flashed to him. "It wasn't yesterday, gudgeon. It was eight days since. And if you doubt me, feel your chin!"

Tyndale's hand wavered upward. He touched the thick beard and gasped a disbelieving, *"Eight . . . days . . . ?"*

"Slugabed," said Devenish, and thought, "Lord, but he looks a rail!"

Briefly, bewilderment held sway, then remorse rushed in on Tyndale. He started up. "Dev! Yolande—what she said in the castle—I mean— There was nothing ever— She didn't mean . . ." The words trailed off, and he gave a helpless gesture.

Devenish said with a wry smile, "Do you tell me I have so nobly stepped aside for no cause? If you do not want the lady . . ."

"Want her . . . ?" Tyndale gazed at Yolande with total adoration. "There are no words. But—" Again, his hollow eyes turned to Devenish. He said with sober intensity, "I swear to you—I have done nothing—said nothing, to betray you, Devenish. Nor to bring dishonour upon her."

" 'I could not love thee dear so much, loved I not honour more . . .'?" Devenish quoted softly. He walked to the bed and looked squarely at Tyndale. "You are in that bed, cousin, because you took something meant for me. It was bravely done, and I thank you."

Tyndale's thin cheek flushed. "It was not done with any thought to claim as reward your every happiness!"

Devenish kept his eyes from Yolande and said lightly, "You rate the lady high."

"I do indeed. And so do you."

"Dear," Yolande inserted in her most gentle voice, "I think you are talking too much. We must not allow you to tire yourself so soon."

The term of endearment caused his hand to tighten on hers.

"No, really, I feel perfectly fit. And have so many questions, but—"

"Aha!" cried the General, marching briskly into the room. "So our sleeper has come out from hibernation at last! Jove, but it's good to see you with your eyes open, m'boy!" He shook Tyndale's hand cautiously. "You did very well oot at your castle, but I surmise Devenish has told you what happened."

Devenish said, "I've not had time to—"

"Is he awake, then?" Mrs. Drummond bustled in, followed by her sister-in-law. "Oh, my!" She fumbled for her handkerchief. "What a blessing that you did not die after all, Tyndale. We all thought you would, you know. But—"

"But we're powerful glad tae see ye didnae!" said Mrs. Fraser, adding with an irked glance at Arabella, "Of all the bird-witted things tae remark!"

"Never mind, dear," purred Mrs. Drummond. "We do not expect you to be brilliant, after all. Oh!" She blinked rapidly. "Is it not affecting? See how they gaze into each other's eyes . . ."

The General, having already noted this blissful gaze, scowled, "Pairhaps I should warn ye, Tyndale—"

"Not now, Sir Andrew!" Mrs. Fraser inserted with a warning frown.

Devenish said hurriedly, "The smugglers got clean away, Craig, but—"

"But we found a damn—a dashed great stockpile o' contraband hidden in a cellar," the General put in, his eyes sparkling with excitement at that memory.

"And you should have seen all the newspaper reporters . . ." said Mrs. Drummond.

They all began to talk at once, so that poor Tyndale was quite bewildered and struggled to comprehend Montelongo's kidnapping, the dramatic arrival of the rescue party, and the fact that not once was Sanguinet's name mentioned. Watching him narrowly, the Iroquois abruptly strode forward and pronounced, "You tired. Me show door to these people."

The General uttered a snort of indignation, and Devenish laughed, but Yolande was relieved. "Perfectly right," she agreed. "You must rest, Craig. We will have plenty of time to explain everything."

"Just one more thing, I beg of you," he pleaded, smiling at her in a way that warmed the hearts of most of those gathered in the bedchamber. "Monty, how did you escape your two new friends?"

"Little squaw, sir. She peep in through window." Montelongo forgot his customary pose in the recollection of that moment, and said with enthusiasm. "It was very brave. She was shaking with fear, but she managed to find a way into the cottage and used the kitchen knife to cut me free while those two rogues snored!"

"Goodness me!" gasped Mrs. Drummond, staring at him in astonishment. "Whenever did you learn to speak English so well?"

The Iroquois folded his arms across his chest and assumed a characteristic stance. "Monty talk good," he declared woodenly.

"We were searching for the child," said the General, impatient with this digression, "and came upon the wee lass trying to help your man, who was in a sorry plight, I do assure you. He could scarce speak at all, and the child told us there was trouble at Castle Tyndale, so we turned aboot and galloped hell-for-leather to investigate!"

"And arrived in time to see me murder you," said Devenish.

Yolande flinched a little.

Tyndale gasped, "Good God! They never thought—"

Mrs. Drummond emitted a trill of laughter. "Well, we know better now. Though one could scarcely blame poor Alain had he indeed done so dreadful a thing. . . ." And she glanced coyly from the flushed Yolande to Tyndale's enigmatic face.

"Dinna talk such fustian!" the General barked. "Say rather, all's well that ends well. Yon smugglers are routed; Tyndale here can live in his castle in peace and be assured of the good will of his neighbours. Or most of 'em, at least. And Yolande and Devenish can—"

"Grandpapa!" Yolande interpolated desperately. "This is not the time or place to speak of these things."

"Aye, the lass is right. Tyndale, we'll leave ye tae your slumbers. Come everyone. Oot! Oot! Devenish, ye're welcome tae stay here wi' us for as long as suits, but I fancy ye'll be wishful tae escort your lady back tae London Toon, eh?"

Devenish smiled rather bleakly; Yolande blushed and looked distressed, and Tyndale lay in helpless silence, watching them all leave. Having ushered everyone from the room, the General turned back at the last minute. He said nothing, but the warning contained in his grim stare was very obvious. Alain

239

Devenish might be so unselfish as to step aside, but the barriers between Tyndale and his love were as insurmountable as ever.

Outside, the westering sun laid soft shadows upon the scythed lawns. The air was warm and the summer house loomed cool, quiet, and inviting. Approaching that charming structure, Mrs. MacFarlane glanced around. There was no sign of anyone. She went timidly up the steps, remembering the last time she had been in this little house, and how kind Miss Drummond had been to her Maisie. "Puir wee lassie," she thought, "she'll nae have the man o' her heart, I doot." But she had tried. It had taken days and days to gather sufficient courage to go up to the great house as she'd done today. She *had* tried! She directed a small, silent prayer at the cloudless heavens, apologizing for her inability to have completed her task. Leaving the summer house she began to walk across the lawns. The smell of the freshly cut grass wafted about her. The golden afternoon was like a benediction. It could only be viewed as an omen; she had been spared. With a small sigh of relief, she hurried back to her cottage.

* * *

At the edge of the Atlantic Ocean, off the northwest coast of Scotland, lie the islands called the Hebrides, and among them, remote and often uncharted, one small cluster is known as the Darrochs. The first three, bleak, inhospitable, and uninhabited, form a rough circle about the fourth. This, the largest, enjoys a milder climate than its fellows, being protected to an extent by a high range of hills on the eastern side, which cut off the freezing winds. Despite this redeeming feature, it falls far short of being a beauty spot, and no one was more surprised than the impoverished owner when, in 1812, all four islands were purchased by a Greek company, the president of which allegedly intended to make the big island—Tordarroch—his home.

For a while, all was as before; the gulls continued to shout and circle indisturbed among the rocks and along the shore; the breakers pounded an incessant assault upon the impregnable cliffs to the east, north, and south, and on its high hill, the ancient structure called Tor Keep squatted mouldering under the chill skies, as it had done for centuries.

Early in 1813, however, a ship put in and anchored in the western cove of Tordarroch; many men landed, and much cargo was unloaded. When the ship sailed away, most of the men remained. A week later, another ship put in, and the next day was followed by yet another. Suddenly, Tordarroch became a beehive of activity: the debris-strewn beach was cleared; the little bay was deepened and new docks were constructed; several buildings appeared; Tor Keep swarmed with workmen; new roads were built, and the face of the island changed in other ways as tall shrubs and trees that were able to withstand the harsh climate replaced the rough broom and bracken and stunted pines. The trees grew rapidly. Within two years they had formed a screen that completed the work of the eastern hills in shielding Tordarroch from any chance sailing vessel with a prying spyglass. The workmen completed their tasks, but did not depart. Instead, they moved onto first one, then another of the three outer islands, and started to labour all over again.

It was to Tordarroch, however, that most shipping travelled, and it was to the much improved harbour that a fishing boat sailed one afternoon in early summer of 1816, and despatched a dinghy to the dock. A gentleman disembarked from the dinghy, entered a dog cart, was duly conveyed into the courtyard of Tor Keep, and thence to a magnificent chamber, part-library, part-study, where the powdered lackey bowed low and requested that Monsieur Garvey should be *"à l'aise, s'il vous plaît."*

Mr. James Garvey did not obey this behest, but instead strolled about, gazing in awe from the massive hearth whereon a great fire licked up the chimney, to richly panelled walls, to elaborate plastered ceilings. Thick carpets deadened his footsteps, *objets d'art* delighted his eyes, the warm air was faintly scented, and he'd have been not in the least surprised had a trio of minstrels put in an appearance and serenaded him. When the door opened, however, it disclosed a comparatively plebeian figure clad without ostentation in a maroon jacket of peerless cut, pearl-grey unmentionables, and an off-white waistcoat embellished with embroidered maroon clocks.

"Claude!" Mr. Garvey smiled, advancing to take the hand that was languidly extended. "What miracles you have wrought here! I might have known! In five years or less you will boast another such showplace as your chateau in Dinan."

"I never boast," Monsieur Sanguinet murmured in French. "And you are inaccurate. The gardens of Dinan required the better part of my father's lifetime to bring to perfection. In five years I will have no need of this place. Besides which, my so dear James . . ." He wandered to seat himself in a fine

241

Chippendale chair beside the glowing hearth. "Flattery does not prevail with me. You waste your efforts."

He interlaced the fingers of his hands and looked up benignly. To any casual observer he would appear as mild as any rural clergyman. But deep in his light brown eyes burned an echo of the fire's glow that was yet not of the fire.

Garvey's nerves tightened. "You are displeased." He shrugged, turning away and taking up a position against the edge of a superb walnut desk. "I did my best. The crates you wanted removed were gone long before your men bungled matters with Devenish."

"How clever of you to remind me that they were 'my men.' " Sanguinet demurred with a silken smile. "They really are not, you know. They are my brawn, rather. And it is because I know their brains are small and ineffectual that I required Shotten to take his orders from—you."

Garvey folded his arms and said sulkily, "It should have gone off perfectly. We had the portrait ready and used it to good effect, I assure you. Shotten said Devenish turned fairly green when first he saw it, and the pivoting panel in the wall worked perfectly. His cousin all but laughed when he was told of the matter. Devenish said no more, but Shotten reported his nerves were ready to snap, and the dislike between the cousins deepening hourly."

"So that you were sure our plans would come to full fruition, and they would kill one another."

Garvey grinned. "How choice that would have been!"

"Poetic justice," said Sanguinet broodingly. "My dear brother Parnell died for this cause. By rights—I should be in deep mourning at this very moment. . . ." He stared into the fire and was silent.

From all that Garvey had heard, Parnell Sanguinet had died while attempting a brutal murder that had little to do with Claude's ambitious plans. If Claude was capable of affection, thought Garvey, that affection had been given to his brother Parnell—as depraved a sadist as ever lived. Yet even his sudden death had neither swerved Claude from his self-appointed task nor caused him to go into blacks. "He is without mercy," thought Garvey. "Without warmth, or kindness, or feelings!" But when the sombre gaze turned to him, he said apologetically, "It was very close, you know. They were so often at each other's throats the world would have believed Tyndale took vengeance. A lovely plan . . ."

242

He sighed. "Who could guess that lunatic would do so crazy a thing as to toss himself at the wrong end of a musket?"

"I could," purred Sanguinet. "And you should. He is of a type, Garvey. The British public schools mould the type and inculcate into it a worship of valour and chivalry, and a fear of one thing—fear itself." He waved a finger at his companion, and went on, "Your own Wellington knew it. He said, 'The Battle of Waterloo was won on the playing fields of Eton.' Honour, my James. Integrity. Sportsmanship. Had your country one single brain in its collective head it would take that remark and spread those values through *all* its young men. Expensive? Pah! How expensive is a war? I tell you this— you call it lunacy—but could I inspire my men with such lunacy, I should rule the world!" Garvey stared at him, his incredulity so obvious that Sanguinet was irked, and re- marked in his gentle fashion, "I cannot think, my dear, how *you* came to avoid such—ah, contamination. . . ."

Garvey flushed and in an effort to turn aside the attack, said, "You will likely rule the world soon or late, at all events."

"Not, James, if one of these—*only one!*—is discovered in the store room at Castle Tyndale." He held up a round lead ball of about three-quarters of an inch diameter. "Tristram Leith, or Redmond, or my very dear friend General Smollet— any of them would only have to see such as this, and know Shotten was there, and—they would know *everything*, James!" He leaned forward, half whispering, "They would *know!*"

Garvey said irritably, "Nothing was left, I tell you! Only the brandy we sacrificed as a red herring. Besides, if they found something they'd likely think we were gun runners, is all."

"No! Damn you! I tell you, *Leith* would know! Harry Redmond would be quick to suspect. And through either of those thorns in my flesh, the Horse Guards would know! Our friend Devenish is the catalyst. He must be silenced. See to it!"

The glare in those strange eyes had flared, and Garvey quailed inwardly. He loathed Alain Devenish and would have been delighted to see him die as slowly and painfully as possible, provided that someone else was responsible. Not that he shrank from murder, but he had plans of his own to bring to fruition, and any public scandal would ruin these. He dare not mention this, however, and avoided Sanguinet's keen scrutiny, muttering, "Nothing would please me more. But I doubt it is necessary, and the least fuss would be our best protection, no?"

Sanguinet continued to regard him for a long moment. Then he settled back in his chair, the flame faded from his eyes, and in a faintly contemptuous tone he enquired, "Why is it not necessary, *mon ami?*"

"Devenish is mad for Yolande Drummond. I have learned she's chosen Tyndale and that Devenish is a broken man. If Tyndale dies, all his energies will go to winning back his light o' love. If the Colonial lives, I fancy he will slink back to England like a whipped cur, with his tail 'twixt his legs. Either way, he will present no further threat to us."

Sanguinet uttered a soft laugh. "You are a philosopher, James. This comes from your own vast experience with *affaires de cœur*, eh?" The sly gleam in his eyes brought a deeper flush to Garvey's countenance, and Sanguinet laughed again. "Perhaps you are right. We will see. Devenish must be watched closely, and destroyed does he make one false move! I have been twice thwarted and now must find another distribution point. Annoying. And it will delay me. I had thought to strike this year. Now—it must be next. Who ever would have dreamed the Canadian would survive Waterloo, much less come to claim our castle! Fate can be so wayward!" he sighed. "I doubt we will ever again find an end for Devenish that would have been so well accepted as our lovely ploy in Castle Tyndale. And how well it would have served us. . . . Such a great pity. . . ."

For a while there was silence, each man busied with his own thoughts.

Sanguinet glanced up at length. "It could have been worse. And—what is it you English say? Better luck the next time? Let us drink to that, my dear James."

They did.

*　　*　　*

The following Saturday afternoon was sultry, with clouds piling up over the sea and a warm fitful breeze occasionally stirring the banner atop Steep Drummond. The great house was quiet: Mrs. Drummond was laid down upon her bed, softly snoring, with Socrates at her feet, loudly snoring; Mrs. Fraser had gone into the village to supervise the flower arrangements for tomorrow's church service; and in the kitchen, Montelongo was comparing bread recipes with the General's chef. In a certain small study, three people were involved in an intense discussion, the outcome of which would most logically spell defeat and despair for two, and a hollow victory for the third. And because of that same discussion,

Alain Devenish was as far away as possible, riding through the hills with a very small person at his side.

These two also had plans to discuss, and Devenish, having just been dealt what he was later to describe "a leveller," turned in the saddle to demand, "What the deuce d'you mean— 'thank you, no'? Lord, child, do you not know the future you would have as the General's ward? The old gentleman has taken a great liking to you. He's vastly well breeched and can offer you the best in life. You'll have a splendid education, and when the time comes, be presented, I shouldn't wonder! You'll have a Season in London, and—and everything any chit could wish for! And you say—'thank you, no'? You're wits to let is what it is!"

She peered at him anxiously. "You bean't angry with Josie?"

"No, but—" He straightened and muttered, "I should have more sense. You are too young to understand what's best, so—dash it all—I must make your decisions."

Staring straight ahead between her mount's ears, Josie rode on. She was not a sullen child, but Devenish had come to know that mulish set to her small mouth and, covertly watching her, he waited in amused anticipation for the next move.

"I don't know why he wants me," she said, judicially. "I bean't pretty, Mr. Dev. I don't think I ever will be. Not a Beauty, anyway."

"No," he agreed. "But there are more important things."

She stifled the hurt and said stoutly, "Yes. And I don't give a button for being one. Nor would you, if you stopped to think of it."

"Me?" he exclaimed, startled. "But I've no wish to be a Beauty, elf!"

She giggled. "*Me*, I mean, silly! I might not grow up to be pretty like—" She checked, seeing a muscle ripple in his jaw, and went on quickly, "I mean, I c'n *do* things, Mr. Dev. And in a year or a bit, I'll be all growed and you can—"

"Jo . . . *sie* . . . !" he uttered trenchantly.

"You can turn off your housekeeper," she went on, twinkling at him. " 'Cause I'll be able to keep house for you and sew on your buttons and cook, and—"

"And scrub the floors and wash the windows and do the laundry, I suppose? Devil take it! Can I not make you understand that the General offers you the life of a Lady of Quality? I remember you once said that you wanted to be just like—like Miss Yolande. This is your chance."

245

She said rather wistfully, "If I *was* like her, would you like me then?"

Devenish's heart twisted. If she were like Yolande . . . Poor little plain, ignorant, lowly born child, how could she ever begin to be like the exquisite lady he had lost . . . ? But the poignant note to her voice had not escaped him, and therefore he shifted in the saddle and, drawing his mount to a halt, appraised her critically. It was not an unpleasant face. It simply had no one feature that was noteworthy. The eyes were bright and alert but neither large nor of exceptional hue; the dark curls showed a regrettable tendency to frizz, the chin was too pointed, and the nose, although straight, lacked distinction. And yet, despite the many hardships she had endured in her short life, her mouth seemed always to tremble on the brink of a smile, and whenever he spoke, her eyes would fly to him with a look of eager expectancy. He thought, "She is like a cheerful little bird, waiting confidently for the crumbs of happiness she knows will come," and realized he had become fond of her.

He said with a smile, "I like you just as you are, but I've nothing to offer you, little one. You cannot live in a house with two bachelors, it wouldn't be right."

"But—but couldn't you ward me, like the General was going to?" she asked desperately. "I want to stay with *you*, Mr. Dev."

"You think you do now, but the time will come when you'll thank me for making you stay here. I've scarce a feather to fly with, but General Drummond's an extreme wealthy gentleman."

"I don't give a button!" she declared fiercely. " 'Sides, you're getting older all the time. I heered you tell the Major that you'll come into your 'heritance soon. So then we could go to your other house to live, and I wouldn't have to live with two bach'lors."

"No. With one. Infinitely worse!"

"No, oh no!" She reached out, tears glistening on her lashes. "If you don't take Josie, who will take care of you? You don't like that other house of yours. You'll go there and be lonely and sad inside, 'cause of—her."

Astounded, Devenish gasped, "How do you know I don't like Devencourt?"

She dashed tears away with an impatient hand. " 'Cause I know your looks," she said, sniffing. "And you get such a funny one when you talk about it."

He was silent. It was true, he still had the same feeling of being trapped whenever he thought of living in the old place. When he had planned to take Yolande there as his bride it had been so different; the house had been often in his thoughts, then, and he'd known a sense of contentment, envisioning their life together, and the improvements they would make. With Yolande at his side, he could have been perfectly happy. Now . . . "I will not be going to Devencourt," he said slowly. "I shall stay with my Uncle Alastair, until—" Cold drops struck his face. "Heigh-ho! Rain again! Come along, Milady Elf! I'll race you back to the house!"

*　　*　　*

"Sir," Tyndale said earnestly, leaning forward in his chair, I will most gladly lay my financial expectations before you. I think you will find them not contemptible."

General Drummond was miserable, but this remark diverted him. "You've the castle, I'll admit, and some very fine land about it. But I had supposed that to be the sum of your fortune."

"I doubt you were the only one to do so," Tyndale said, adding with a wry smile, "It does not seem to have occurred to anyone that my mother may have been an heiress."

The General blinked. "It didnae occur tae me! Is that the case? Have ye a respectable competence, perhaps?"

"No, sir. I rather think I'd have to name it a—a considerable fortune."

Yolande gave a gasp and stared at her love in astonishment.

Tyndale turned to take up the slender hand resting on the arm of her chair. "I'd not intended to deceive you, my dearest girl. You did not seem to care, one way or the other. And I thought my chances to be nil, so said nothing."

"And did not press your suit, because you are so honourable a gentleman," she murmured.

He was silent, mesmerized by the look of adoration in her beautiful eyes, and they gazed at one another through a breathless moment.

The General gave an irritated snort. "Oh, do stop your fondling! How can I discuss business matters with you looking at each other like a couple of moonlings? This is a perfect example of why the ladies are usually excluded frae such conferences." He cast a darkling glance at his granddaughter's radiance. "As they should hae been this time, too!"

"Yes, and I know just what would have happened had I

247

not insisted upon coming," she asserted with rare defiance. "You would have convinced Craig of his unworthiness—"

"I need no convincing of that," murmured Tyndale, pressing the hand he still held.

"—for my sake," Yolande went on, a dimple appearing briefly beside her pretty mouth. "And he would have agreed that it would be inhuman to tear me from family, friends, and country—"

"Very true. But I've no intention of so doing," he interjected, again.

"Also for my sake," she continued resolutely. "And the upshot of it all would have been that—for my sake—he would have walked out of my life. Only, *for my sake*, I cannot let that happen."

"I apprehend," the old gentleman said gravely, "that the Major is a splendid young fellow. I've had word from a friend at Whitehall concerning his military record, and I'd be a clod not to be impressed. Now, it would seem he is eminently qualified from a more practical aspect to seek your hand. Besides which—" a faint smile warmed his troubled eyes—"any fool can see you care for each other."

Yolande's fingers gripped very tightly about Craig's lean hand. Two young hearts thundered as they waited tensely for the decision.

"Accidents do happen," said the General with slow deliberation. "I had one myself was almost fatal. I was just a lad, and shot an arrow into a rustling bush. Nigh killed my favourite cousin. . . . Never have been able to touch a bow and arrow since. But—had I the slightest proof that Stuart Devenish died as the result of such an accident, however foolish, I'd withdraw my objections in a trice, and do all I might to convince my son and his lady to accept you, Tyndale. But . . . dammitall! I'll be honest, even though my words will be unwelcome to you both. It is my belief that Jonas, with his wild temper and intolerance, did just as he stood accused of doing. That he deliberately pushed his unwanted brother-in-law to his death. And to have my beloved granddaughter sneered at and derided because she had wed the son of a murderer . . . ! No! Tyndale, I've no wish to distress you. But—*that* is what I cannot countenance. I wish—I really wish that I could offer you hope, but . . ." One powerful hand was raised in a helpless gesture, then fell back onto the mahogany desk again.

Tyndale's head had lowered. It was no more than he had

expected. And one could not blame the old fellow: He was doing his utmost to protect his beloved granddaughter. Lord knows, the decision was one he himself would likely have made, under the circumstances. But . . . how could he bear to part with her, knowing that she loved him, and loving her so much that life had taken on so new and glorious a glow of happiness?

"No!" cried Yolande, jumping up. "This is so wrong! Grandpapa, you must see that Craig has done *nothing!* Oh, do not, I beg of you—do not drive me to run away with him!"

Craig, who had stood also, said gently, "That you will never do, my beautiful lady. I'll wed you with honour, or not at all."

General Drummond grunted his approval of these sentiments. Yolande, however, watched Craig with frantic eyes, and said a shaken, "Not even if you know I will never marry anyone else?"

He took her hand and kissed it and, holding it in both of his, said softly. "I came to Ayrshire with two aims in view. One was to find my inheritance. The other was to clear my father's name. I've found my inheritance, but I've scarcely begun an enquiry into what really happened out at the castle four and twenty years since. Have faith in me, dear heart. I'll prove it was an accident—I know it!"

Her heart sank. She said miserably, "And what if it is not possible to prove it?"

"Then I shall be so crude as to go to your papa over your grandfather's protest, lay my claim before him, and beg his understanding."

He smiled at her confidently, but her answering smile was wan, for she sensed that his hopes for a happy resolution to their problems were as forlorn as her own.

The General said kindly, "Never despair, Yolande. We'll all throw our efforts into discovering the truth of matters. Between us—" He paused as a knock sounded.

The door swung open, and Devenish entered to say cheerfully, "Only look at who we found coming up the drive!"

Colonel Alastair Tyndale strode briskly into the room, shook hands with Drummond, bestowed a kiss upon Yolande's cheek, looked with obvious shock at Craig, and exclaimed, "Good God! Dev wrote you was better, but you look in very queer stirrups still, poor fellow. The effect of this beastly climate, I suppose."

"There speaks a fugitive from London's clammy fogs!" Drummond retaliated, laughing. "Devenish, be so good as to pour your uncle a glass of Madeira. You'll stay with us, of course, Alastair, and very welcome. But what brings you up here? We'd understood you didnae plan a trip."

"No more did I." The Colonel raised his glass to the assembled company and sipped the wine appreciatively. "Three things brought me. The first, naturally, was to see for myself how Craig goes on. Secondly, I received a rather strange letter from a lady who lives on your estate, Andy. And, thirdly"—he reddened and said with boyish shyness—"and to me most importantly, to announce my forthcoming marriage."

Sir Andrew, in the act of sampling his wine, spluttered and choked. Devenish, who had put down the decanter, fumbled with the stopper, caught it, juggled it frantically, but dropped it, fortunately onto the carpet. Yolande clapped her hands and cried a joyous, "Oh, how lovely! To Lady Grenfell, sir?"

"Thank *you*, at least, my dear," he said, his eyes glinting with amusement at these reactions.

"At *your* age . . . ?" wheezed the General.

Devenish, utterly incredulous, gasped, "The Silver Widow? B-but—she's the most sought after lady in Town!"

"And the best catch, I heard!" Craig grinned broadly. "Congratulations, sir!"

"Thank you, Craig. Have I quite bowled you out, Dev?"

"What? Oh—er, no, of course not, sir. I only thought— That is to say, I *didn't* think— Well, what I mean to say is—at your time of life, who would guess you'd do such a thing?"

"Devenish!" said Yolande indignantly. "Uncle Alastair is in the prime of his life! And is, besides, a very handsome gentleman. Lady Grenfell has been setting out lures for him this age!"

Colonel Tyndale laughed. "Oh, no! You put me to the blush. I count myself a very lucky man."

"Well, so you should, by Jove!" said the General heartily, coming around the desk to shake his hand again and pound him on the back. "A beautiful lady, The Grenfell. I'll own my eyes have strayed in that direction a time or two since poor Stephen got himself killed, although I know she is too young for me, despite that pretty silver hair of hers."

Recovering himself, Devenish hastened to also offer congratulations but, shaking the hand of this man who had been his family for so long, chided, "What a sly dog you are, sir! I

250

do think you might have let me know you was contemplating becoming a Benedick. I was never so taken in."

"To tell you the truth, Dev, I should probably have delayed my announcement until after you and Yolande are wed. But now that is . . . imminent . . ." He was struck to silence by the sudden bleakness in his nephew's eyes and, glancing quickly at Yolande, saw her face flushed and distressed.

"The lady won't have me, sir," Devenish imparted with a forced grin. "Prefers a dashed Colonial bumpkin, if you can credit it."

It was the Colonel's turn to be bowled out. His gaze flying to Craig's grave features, he gasped, "Does she—by God!" And then, ruefully, "Gad, but I properly wedged both feet into my mouth!"

"Not at all," said Devenish, filling a sudden awkward silence. "But, it's as well I'd intended to remove to Devencourt before the summer's out."

The Colonel frowned. "No need for that, Dev. There's more than enough room at Aspenhill for all of us."

Do you seriously expect me to live bodkin between two newlyweds?" Appalled by such a prospect, Devenish made a swift decision. "I've a lady of my own now. You've not met my—my ward, sir."

Colonel Tyndale's jaw dropped. Then he uttered a hearty laugh. "Young varmint! You really had me for a moment. Lord, if there was ever a here-and-therian less qualified to take on an adopted daughter!"

"How I am maligned!" mourned Devenish. "I assure you, sir, Josie don't share your opinion of me. Does she, Craig?"

"Viewing you with the trusting eyes of childhood," said Craig with his slow grin, "I'd say she has endowed you with halo and wings."

"Oh, Dev!" cried Yolande with delight. "Do you really mean to make her your ward? She will be in heaven!"

"The devil!" exploded Sir Andrew. "She's mine, you rogue! I've already spoke for her!"

"Yes, but I've stolen her away, sir."

"You mean . . . it really *is* true?" the Colonel stammered. "But—"

From the door no one had heard open, Enderby announced, "Mrs. MacFarlane!" and absented himself before his indignant employer could request that the gardener's wife be denied at this particular moment.

Yolande went at once to welcome the little woman, exclaiming, "Good heavens! I completely abandoned you when you came last week! I do pray you will forgive me such disgraceful conduct."

The hand she took was like ice and violently trembling. Mrs. MacFarlane's sharp eyes darted about the room, finding curiosity in some faces, amusement in others, and annoyance in the eyes of the General. She mumbled a response to Yolande and nodded to Alastair Tyndale. "I seed you come, sir, and I reckoned I'd best do it the noo, before I—I lose my . . . courage. It's—" she drew herself up, gripped her hands tightly, and finished—"it's right ye should all be here."

Yolande's heart began to race. She said, "Do sit down, ma'am, and tell us whatever troubles you."

Mrs. MacFarlane allowed herself to be settled into a comfortable chair, but when Yolande made to draw back, she tightened her hold on the girl's hand and said huskily, "It's yourself has brought me to this pass, Miss Yolande. Your gentle ways and kind words, even in your own sorrows, were an endless barb in my immortal soul! The Good Book says 'there is no peace unto the wicked' and so it is. So I've come here." Tears began to glitter in her eyes. She bit her lip and finished threadily, "I didnae think I'd find the courage tae come again. . . . I only hope I can—can go through wi' it!"

Intent now, the General returned to the chair behind his desk. Alastair Tyndale sat on the leather sofa, Craig stood behind Yolande's chair, and Devenish settled his shoulders against the bookcase.

"I expect," Mrs. MacFarlane began nervously, "I expect ye all ken I lived at Castle Tyndale when I was a wee bairn."

Devenish tensed, pushed himself away from the bookcase, and the smile vanished from his eyes, to be replaced by a keen stare. Yolande reached up, and Craig at once took her hand in a strong, brief clasp.

Pleating and unpleating a fold of her dress with trembling fingers, Mrs. MacFarlane quavered, "I should've told . . . years syne . . . what happened that day, b-but—"

"By thunder!" the General ground out, leaning both hands on the desk top as he bent forward. "You *saw* it? Now, why in the name of— Why did ye not come *forward*? Why did your *parrents* nae speak?"

His tone of voice and fierce mien caused the little woman to become even more nervous. She shrank and pressed both hands to her lips, a stifled moan escaping her.

Colonel Tyndale said, *sotto voce*, "Easy, Andrew. Easy."

Craig and Devenish exchanged glances of flashing excitement.

Yolande stood, and clinging to Craig's arm, whispered, "Oh, my dear—I have prayed for this, but . . . I am so afraid!"

He patted her hand and drew her closer.

"We are more than grateful to you, Mrs. MacFarlane," said Colonel Tyndale kindly. "But—can you tell us why nothing has been said in all this while?"

She blinked at him. "Me mum and dad didnae dare speak, sir. They was terrified they'd be turned off. And besides, we're only simple folk. It—it don't always do tae—tae tell truth to the Quality." Her drawn face twisting with emotion, she wailed wretchedly, "Oh, if ye but knew how I longed tae speak oot! All these years I've knowed the truth! I've knowed the murderer!"

Craig was jolted as though he had been struck. *"Murderer?"* he echoed, his hopes crashing.

"Whatever ye've tae tell us," said Sir Andrew, his own heart sinking, "ye'll be fairly dealt with here, ma'am. As well ye know."

She closed her eyes for an instant, then began almost inaudibly. "I was only six, then. I minded my ma verra well, usually. But—I'd a toy. Me brother Ian had carved it out fer me, and—and it was me most favourite, but Ma didnae like tae see me always playing with it, and bade me tae put it by and tend tae me chores and schooling. She was teaching me tae read and write." She sat with head bowed, her eyes fixed on the hands that wrung and wrung in her lap. "I hid it, though," she said chokingly. "I daren't leave it aboot or it would've been taken and burnt, so—so I hid it, and every afternoon when Ma was busy with her sewing of Miss Esme's pretty things, I'd go and—and take oot me toy. And play with it. Oh!" She gave a wail and clutched her head in near frenzy. " 'Twas wicked! I ken that well!"

"Poor soul," said Yolande, touched by such anguish. "As if anyone could condemn so natural a thing. You were scarcely more than a babe, and likely had very few toys. Was it a doll your brother made for you?"

For a moment the unhappy woman seemed too lost in remorse to hear the gentle words. Then she looked up at the girl's sympathetic face and answered, "No, miss. But it was my only real toy. Och, but I thought it the finest Diabolino ever . . ."

Baffled, Craig murmured, "Finest—what?"

253

"Diabolino," rasped the General, more than a little impatient with all this talk of toys. "A wooden ball on a string that is swung up so as to fall into a cup."

"I was playing that day," Mrs. MacFarlane muttered, her wide gaze very obviously looking back into the past that so terrified her. "I heered someone coming. I was awful scared, for me ma had always told me I was *never* tae go up to the battlements. So I ran so fast as ever I could, and hid on t'other side of the tower. Only . . . I dropped me toy."

Again, she paused, and now the room was so still that the soughing of the wind outside sounded like the voice of a hurricane. They waited, breathlessly, for no one dared to ask that Mrs. MacFarlane resume her tale lest her obviously teetering intellect should be pushed too far and completely give way.

"Stuart Devenish, it was," she said in a half whisper. "And he walked over tae stand where he always did, looking oot tae sea. I remember praying he'd soon go inside, but he didnae. And then—then Mr. Tyndale come. He was running almost, and I could tell he was cross again. Mr. Devenish turned round and said, 'Hello, Jonas' in his nice, friendly way, but Mr. Tyndale started ranting and cursing. And all this time I was sae afeared they'd see my toy, for it was close by them."

Under his breath the General snorted, "The devil fly away with the toy!" He asked, "Can you recall ma'am, what the two men were discussing? I suppose 'tis a lot to expect of a lady who was only six at the time."

"I can remember," she said, her stare still fixed and vacant, "as if it was yesterday."

"Can you, by God!" breathed Devenish, moving to stand beside his uncle.

"Miss Esme—Mrs. Devenish, I should say," muttered Mrs. MacFarlane, "was increasing, ye'll mind. Her brother wanted her back in London Town. 'She dinna look right, Stuart,' he said. 'I be afeared fer her! If ye'll nae go, let me take her back with me.' Mr. Devenish said he couldnae allow it, for 'twould be a weary way fer her tae travel. He was verra quiet and calm, and the quieter he was, the angrier Mr. Tyndale got. I was sure as they were going tae start fighting, and so was Mr. Devenish, fer he said, 'Jonas—mon, ye dinna understand! I canna take her back! I *canna!*' Mr. Tyndale shouted, '*Will* not, ye mean!' and he took hold of Mr. Devenish's arm and said, 'Ye *want* her tae die, sae ye can get

254

your hands on her fortune!' Mr. Devenish told him he was a fool, and then he said in a funny sort of voice, 'If she must die, it will be here, where she's been so happy.' I remember it was all quiet then, and they stood there, staring at each other. And Mr. Tyndale asked what was meant by that, and Mr. Devenish says, near weepinglike, 'I'm going tae lose her, Jonas. The doctor says she canna survive this birthing.' "

She stopped speaking, and there was a long, hushed pause. Then, she went on slowly, "Mr. Tyndale wouldnae heed him at first. He kept ranting it was all none but lies, and Mr. Devenish kept saying it was truth, and he looked so sad and sounded so—sort of lost, that I reckon poor Mr. Tyndale had tae face it at the last. He put his head in his hands and began tae weep. Mr. Devenish tried to comfort him, but he was fair crazy with grief. He shouted, 'If ye knowed she would die, why did you get her with child?' And he marched smack up tae Mr. Devenish, like he meant tae throttle the life frae him. Mr. Devenish said he *hadn't* knowed until a few days syne, fer the doctor hadnae told him of it. But Jonas Tyndale wouldnae listen. He screamed oot that Mr. Devenish was nae better than a murderer. That he'd murdered Miss Esme. Lor', but I was scared! He was throwing his arms aboot and raving sae wild. Mr. Devenish grabbed him and said sharp-like, 'Have a care, mon! Ye're tae close tae the edge!' Mr. Tyndale pulled free and then—he hit Mr. Devenish. Not hardlike. More as if he didnae want tae be held. But . . . but Mr. Devenish jumped back and then . . . and then . . ." She cowered, bending over and rocking to and fro in a paroxysm of grief.

Through that hushed silence, Tyndale said, "And then my uncle stepped on your toy. Is that it, ma'am?"

Devenish gave a gasp of horrified comprehension. The General whispered, "My God! Oh, my God!"

Mrs. MacFarlane looked up and gulped, "Aye, sir. Oh, how terrible it were tae see him fly back like that! And . . . and tae think I done it! *I* murdered your poor papa, Mr. Devenish! A eye fer an eye, says the Good Book. And . . . and here I be, sir, I owned up . . . at last. . . ."

Chapter Sixteen

Sprawling comfortably on the bed in his nephew's spacious bedchamber, Colonel Alastair Tyndale watched Devenish bestow gratuities on the abigail who had cared for Josie during their stay at Steep Drummond, pinch her blushing cheek, and escort her to the door as though she were a duchess. "The boy has changed," he thought. "A month since, he'd have demanded a kiss!" And, as Devenish closed the door and turned to take up his hat and gloves, he said, "I apprehend that you're eager to be on your way, Dev. But—will you please spare me a minute before you go?"

"Of course I will, sir," said Devenish, regarding him fondly. "Are you quite sure you won't ride with us? Lord knows there's room in the coach, and nothing would please me more. Or Josie."

"Thank you, my boy. But I'm promised to help Craig plan the refurbishing of the castle. Still—since you mentioned the child, it is of her that I wish to speak."

He hesitated, and Devenish, limping to pull up a chair, straddle it and watch him over the back, was fairly sure of what was going to be said. He was correct.

Cautiously feeling his way, the Colonel said, "I've no wish to discourage you, for it's a fine thing you plan. But— you really have no notion of what may lie behind her, you know. Blood will out. In a few years you may regret your kindness."

"Forgive me, but I cannot agree, sir. You'd not believe how Josie has blossomed since I found her. And I've a notion there's good blood in her. She may, I think, be of French parentage, for she sometimes will speak the language, and with a flawless accent."

The Colonel's brows went up. "Will she, indeed? I take it you have questioned her in the matter."

"Oh, yes. But to no avail. She remembers only that she was stolen, and—" He frowned. "And—brutality."

"Poor mite! Small wonder she worships you."

Devenish grinned. "All the ladies worship me," he quipped. And thought, "Save only the one *I* worship. . . ."

The Colonel knew him well and thus knew how deep was the wound he had suffered. He kept silent for a moment, dreading to add to that hurt, and at last, tracing the design of the eiderdown with one well-manicured finger, asked softly, "Have you told her you mean to make her your ward?"

"Er—no. Not yet, sir. I—er, I thought I would break the news on our way back to Devencourt." He stared rather blankly at his uncle's muscular hand. The truth was that he still had not really decided to adopt Josie. At the back of his mind was the thought that he'd see if he could land a position on the staff on an ambassador. His blasted leg would keep him out of the military, but he'd as soon leave England for a while. He might even go out to India, as Justin Strand had done; which reminded him that he must drop in on Justin and see if a date had been set for his wedding. Everyone seemed to be getting leg-shackled these days . . . lucky dogs. . . .

"If you do tell her," murmured Colonel Tyndale shrewdly, "and later change your mind, I think it would break her heart."

Devenish started and, glancing up, found those keen blue eyes fixed on him as piercingly as they had done when as a small boy he'd quailed before the Colonel's desk. He wondered resentfully if the guv'nor really could read his mind, and, aware he was flushing, said, "Whatever I do, sir, you may believe she will be well taken care of."

"I was not speaking of material things. I do not mean to prose at you, but—this is a very serious undertaking, and a potentially lengthy one. You mean to take upon yourself the responsibility for another living being. Another soul, Dev, to be shaped and moulded and—provided for, through many years to come. If you are to do it well, it will entail self-lessness, compassion, and—love. A large order. Are you—quite sure . . . ?"

Rage, swift and white-hot, tightened Devenish's lips. He had been judged yet again, and found irresponsible! He stood and, taking up his many-caped drab coat, shrugged into it and said with a taut smile, "Well, I collect I'd best say the rest of my goodbyes."

Shocked by this unfamiliar hauteur, the Colonel came to his feet also. He had been very distinctly warned off; a door closed in his face as it never had before. "I'll not detain you longer," he said politely. But his love was deep, so that with his hand on the doorknob, he swallowed his pride and turned about. "Dev, lad, I am so sorry. I only meant— Don't be too hasty in your plans! This—infatuation of Yolande's . . ."

Devenish flinched. "It is no infatuation, sir. Have you not seen them together? It is . . . as though they were—one being."

His heart aching, the Colonel gripped the younger man's shoulder. "If only there was *something* I could do! I know how—how deeply you have loved her all your life. It must be . . ." And he stopped, the words eluding him.

Devenish lifted a hand almost absently to cover the one that rested on his shoulder. "If I thought," he muttered, "that I would have the least chance of winning her, I would call Craig out and . . ." He was silent for a moment, then raised his brooding gaze, saw the helpless sympathy in his uncle's eyes, and smiled wryly. "But, do you know, sir? Of late I've begun to wonder . . ."

"What, Dev?"

"Only that . . . I have loved her, as you said, all my life. But—when I see her with Craig, I think . . . perhaps, there are degrees of loving, and—and theirs is something . . . almost holy. That I will not ever be granted."

The Colonel had the same thought about the relationship he shared with his own lady, and so it was that his affection for this valiant young man, and his comprehension of the grief that he knew must be intense, overmastered him. He spun around and strode rapidly to the window, to stand staring blindly into the sunny morning.

A quick uneven step. A strong arm, tight about his shoulders. And his nephew's voice, husky with emotion, said, "Now, God love you for that sympathy. You always were true blue. The best and kindest uncle who ever took in a lonely scamp, and was curst seldom thanked for it! But—" Devenish turned the Colonel to face him, and smiling rather uncertainly into those blurred eyes, said, "You know—sir, I have always felt . . . I have always, er . . ."

Tyndale gripped his elbow. "Yes," he said huskily. "I know."

*   *   *

"You were not going to leave without saying goodbye, I hope?"

Craig! Devenish thought, "Damn!" but turned, and said lightly, "Lord, no. I just came down to see if Monty has assembled the luggage. My elf seems to have acquired a prodigious amount of paraphernalia since we come.''

"Yes. Dev, I—''

"Don't, Craig!'' Despite himself, Devenish's voice was harsh. "You saved my life, and you're a damned good fellow. If I had to—to lose her, I could not wish . . . it to be to a better man.''

Craig swore furiously at him. "What a perfectly wretched thing to say! You might at least have knocked me down.''

Devenish laughed. But the worst, he knew, was yet to come.

*   *   *

Yolande's eyes were red, but she put out her hand like the thoroughbred she was, and said composedly, "Ride safely, my dear. And take care of your little lady.''

He took her hand, stared down at it, so sweetly resting in his own, and released it hurriedly. Looking up, he saw that she was blinking rather fast and, reaching back into the many happy years he had so stupidly taken for granted, feigned indignation. "Now, dash it all, Yolande. If you're going to turn into a watering pot . . .''

She laughed shakily. "Odious creature! You always did treat me as if I were a tiresome little sister.''

"Is that what drove me to the ropes?'' The words were out before he could stop them. He saw her mouth twist and said a swift, "I shall have to be more careful. And I shall expect a very special invitation to the—ceremony.''

"You shall have it—of course. And . . . Josie shall be a flower girl, if she would—like . . .'' Her voice broke. "Oh . . . Dev . . .''

She was in his arms, weeping. He held her very tight, hoarding these priceless seconds. "Yolande . . .'' he whispered. And, fighting for control, said, "No tears, if you please. I seem to—bring you very often to tears, of late.''

"I love you, Dev,'' she sniffed. "I wish I did not love you—quite so much.'' And she pulled away, looked up at him for an instant, the tears bright on her cheeks, then leaned to kiss him.

"You will . . . find your happiness . . . my very dear,'' she managed, and fled.

*   *   *

Josie had been granted her wish to ride Molly-My-Lass to the edge of the Drummond estates; beside her, Devenish rode his beloved Miss Farthing, and the carriage followed with a

259

groom behind, to lead the Clydesdale back to Steep Drummond. Montelongo had ridden ahead to arrange rooms for them in New Galloway, so that they were now quite alone, and Josie thought she had never been so happy.

"Oh," she sighed, looking with glad eyes at clear heaven, lush meadows, and contentedly grazing cows. "Oh, ain't it a 'licious morning?"

"What?" muttered Devenish. "Oh—er, yes. Delicious."

"I doesn't see," she persisted, "how everything in the whole world couldn't be anything but filled with happy on a day like today."

"You cannot be filled with *happy*, my elf," he protested. "Frightful grammar."

"Yes, Mr. Dev." She slanted a mischievous glance up at him. "Just the same—I is."

He smiled, his heart like lead.

" 'Course," said Josie thoughtfully. "You ain't. Not just at this minute, p'raps. But afore you knows it—*voilà!* you will be."

As always, her use of French intrigued him so that for a moment he forgot his misery. "How so? What I mean to say is, I *am* happy. As a cursed lark, in fact."

"No." She shook her small head so that the curls bounced beneath the bonnet of primose straw that Yolande had bought her.

"Nonsense. After all, we're going to Devencourt, my, er, home, and—"

"And you hates Devencourt."

He stared at her. "Josie—are you *quite* sure you're only eleven?"

"I be very old sometimes," she said, matter-of-factly. "All ladies is. And I be a lady—or, I will be, when you—" She broke off, looking guilty.

"When I—what?"

"I'm not s'posed to know."

He thought, "Oh, God!" "But," he said rather stiffly, "you, ah—*do* know?"

"Yes. Oh, yes!" She all but jumped up and down in the saddle, her small face radiating joy. "And you won't be sorry, Mr. Dev. Not never! I'll be the bestest daughter what ever you had! I'll take care of you and be perlite and learn to talk pretty like—her. I know I won't ever *be* pretty like—her, but you won't have to go to that great crawly place and be sad all alone."

Torn between dismay and laughter, he asked, "Who told you?"

"Oh, the servants knew." She said airily, "You cannot keep nothin' from the servants, you know. Aunty Caroline says."

He blinked. "*Aunty . . . Caroline?*"

"She told me to call her that. I was frighted of her at first, but she's a dear. Monty says she talks too much." She giggled.

They rode in silence for a while, then he said carefully, "I hope poor General Drummond may not be utterly cast down because I took you away from him."

She thought about that. "I 'spect he was. But some folks gets to dance on a bubble, and some gets to be casted down. Like me and you."

There should be an answer to that, he thought dully. But he could not seem to find one. They were at the brow of the hill. In another minute Steep Drummond would be out of side. It was as well. He did not want to see it. Never again. But somehow he was drawing his horse to a halt, motioning the carriage and groom to move ahead, and turning aside to guide his mare to the brow of the hill and the shade of a great tree where he had sat once before. His mount began to crop at the rich grass, and Devenish, quite forgetting the child beside him, leant forward in the saddle and gazed across the lush green valley to Steep Drummond. Was she at one of the windows that twinkled in the morning sunlight, looking out, trying to see him? Was she—out of the affection she bore him—grieving to see him go? Yolande . . . my own, my love . . . Yolande. . . .

A small sound roused him from this hopeless yearning. He glanced around and straightened in dismay. Josie's head was bowed. Even as he watched, something bright and glittering splashed down upon Molly-My-Lass's broad shoulder. He reined closer. "Child . . . ? Josie? Do not! Whatever is it? Please—do not cry!"

"I can't . . . help it," she sobbed, raising a woebegone countenance. "I cannot bear it when your eyes gets . . . so awful sad. Like you was all full of tears inside. I—I *wants* to make you happy. I *wants* so for you to not—not give a button for her. But—I cannot help! I cannot *help* you. And, oh, Mr. Dev—Josie *loves* ye so!"

Who could not be touched? A heart of stone must have melted before that youthful anguish. And however cracked it

261

might be at present, the heart of Alain Devenish had never resembled stone. He reached out, Josie leaned to him, and in a trice she was sitting across his saddle bow, sobbing gustily into his cravat and clinging to him with her skinny little arms.

"Milady Elf," he said, stroking her soft curls, for her bonnet had fallen back during the change of mounts. "Hush, now. If you keep weeping, you will make me even more full of tears."

She at once wiped fiercely at her flowing eyes. Devenish groped for and offered his handkerchief. Josie dragged it across her face, blew her nose stridently, and tucked the handkerchief into the front of his jacket. It was quite soggy, but he gave no sign of his inner dubiety. "That's better." He smiled. "Now"—he slapped the reins against the neck of the mare and started her towards the waiting carriage, Molly-My-Lass following amiably—"am I to understand then, that you are willing to be a dutiful and obedient daughter, brightening my declining years, and caring for me in my dotage?"

Josie gave a watery giggle.

"I see." He fought against looking back as they started down the hill. "In that case, we shall have to arrive at an understanding, my elf."

She peeped at him, uncertainly.

"I will have no more popping off at the least little whim to consort with drunken rogues," he adjured.

Josie chortled.

"To say nothing," he went on, "of going about putting bears into the toolsheds of respectable farmers."

She snuggled against him. "Oh, Mr. Dev," she sighed, blissfully aware that Steep Drummond was now safely out of sight. "What a complete hand you are."

"That is *precisely* the sort of remark you must not repeat!" he groaned. "Now—pay heed to your papa, child, if you please. . . ."

On they went, Devenish speaking with grave earnestness, and the child's piping laugh threading through his remarks like quicksilver. Now, whether it was because of the infectious happiness in that youthful laughter, or because, in seeking to lead Josie from sorrow, Devenish briefly forgot his own woes, who shall say? Certain it is that the sharpness of his anguish eased a trifle, and despair's dark shadow began to lift from his heart. After a while, he restored the child to her own saddle. They resumed their journey then, travelling side by side through the brilliant morning, towards England, and home, and whatever the future had in store for them in that bright promise that is called—tomorrow.

Epilogue

Major Craig Tyndale ushered his lady up the deep steps of the castle. "We've done very little as yet," he said with a trace of anxiety. "I hope you'll not be disappointed, Yolande."

"No, but how could I be? This is to be my home. I've been so anxious to see it ever since you and Uncle Alastair began the work."

"And I have longed to bring you these whole ten days. It was very kind of your papa to let you come."

"And even kinder of him to travel up here. But, now that we are officially betrothed, it is not very shocking for me to be here alone with you—is it?"

He smiled down into her face, so enchantingly framed by the pink ruffles of the dainty bonnet she wore. "A little, perhaps, but Laing is with us, after all."

He threw open the heavy door, revealing the majestic sweep of the Great Hall, gleaming with fresh paint, brightened by rich carpets, and mellowed by the careful placement of fine furniture. Watching his love with no little anxiety, he said, "It is rather isolated, I daresay, but we'll only spend the summer here, you know. I thought we would purchase a house in Town for the Season, if you should care to. And you will wish to spend time with your parents of course."

"And you will want to take me to see your home in Canada—no?"

"You would not object?" he asked eagerly. "It would be a long, tiresome journey, but I thought perhaps, if we should be—er, that is—when we have set up our—our nursery, perhaps you might be willing to go."

"Foolish, foolish man." Yolande looked up at him, her eyes soft with love. "I can see that you have done beautifully with Castle Tyndale, and I shall enjoy being here with you.

Or in Town—with you. Or on the high seas—with you. Oh, Craig—my very dearest love . . . do you not yet know? My happiness lies not in *where* we are—only that we are . . . together."

Mr. Laing, checking the chestnut mare's harness, shook his head bodingly. "Did you see that, Heather?" he enquired. "Picked her up in his arms and carried her across the threshold like they was already wed! Shocking! These young people today have no least notion of how to go on!"

He was quite mistaken. Standing in the Great Hall, a slender girl clasped against him, her arms about his neck, and his lips pressed crushingly to hers, Major Craig Winters Tyndale knew exactly how to go on.

About the Author

PATRICIA VERYAN was born in London, England, and moved to the United States after the Second World War. She now lives in Riverside, California. Ms. Veryan is the recipient of the first Barbara Cartland Silver Cup for Idealizing Romance.

From Fawcett Books

Historical Romance at its Best...

Regency Romances